M.R. Mackenzie was born and li  at Glasgow University and has a Studies.

In addition to writing, he works as a Blu-ray/DVD producer and has overseen releases of films by a number of acclaimed directors, among them Dario Argento, Joe Dante, Hideo Nakata and Jacques Tourneur. Writing as Michael Mackenzie, he has contributed chapters to books on cult cinema and regularly provides video essays and liner notes for new releases of celebrated films. He used to work in a library, before leaving to spend more time with books.

In 2019, his first novel, *In the Silence*, was shortlisted for the Bloody Scotland Scottish Crime Debut of the Year and longlisted for the McIlvanney Prize. His third novel, *The Library Murders*, was featured in Crime Time's Best of the Year 2020 list.

Praise for M.R. Mackenzie

'Brings a fresh new voice to the field of Tartan Noir.'
JAMES OSWALD

'Writes with precision and passion.' CARO RAMSAY

'Splendidly written stuff.' BARRY FORSHAW, *CRIME TIME*

'An immersive slow burn of a tale, peppered with disquieting fire-crackers of revelation.' MORGAN CRY

'Mackenzie has come up with something that defies easy definition and is truly original.'
PAUL BURKE, *NB MAGAZINE*

'Up there with the best contemporary authors working today.'
DAVID B. LYONS

Also by M.R. Mackenzie

The Anna Scavolini series
In the Silence
Cruel Summer
The Shadow Men
Women Who Kill

Other novels
The Library Murders
Bury Your Secrets

Box sets
The Anna Scavolini Mysteries – Volume One

M.R. MACKENZIE

THE LIBRARY MURDERS

MAD**HOUSE**

Cover design by
Tim Barber / Dissect Designs

Typeset in 11pt Minion Pro

First published in 2020 by Mad House
This edition published in 2022

ISBN: 978-1-9160948-1-9

Text version 1.0a

www.mrmackenzieauthor.com
facebook.com/MRMackenzieAuthor
@landofwhimsy

For my library colleagues from times past, who were nothing at all like the staff of North Kelvin District Libraries.

It is easy to dodge our responsibilities, but we cannot dodge the consequences of dodging our responsibilities.

Josiah Stamp

The incident at Thornhill Library on Monday the first of March took just eighteen seconds to play out in its entirety.

The effects were felt for considerably longer.

PART ONE

1

Sixty-three minutes before

They say a life's trajectory can change in an instant, transformed beyond all recognition purely by virtue of being in the right place at the right time. Or more often than not, the *wrong* place at the wrong time.

The place was an unfamiliar sofa. The time had just gone 8.30 a.m. And for Alyssa Clark, waking up with the hangover from hell and breath to match, both were, beyond a shadow of a doubt, all sorts of wrong.

Swallowing a wave of nausea, she manoeuvred into an upright position and set her Wayfarers in place on the bridge of her nose, bringing her surroundings into as much focus as she was going to get given her present condition. Once the room had – for the most part – stopped spinning, she forced herself onto her feet and staggered to the door, sidestepping the slumbering form of Jenny Nicholson, prostrate on the floor and snoring contentedly. In the bathroom, she gulped down a glass of water and tried to recollect the precise order of events which had led to her waking up on someone else's couch with half the alcohol reserve in Glasgow in her bloodstream. They'd met up at Sleazy's on Sauchiehall Street just after nine, she recalled – her, Jenny, Gobby and Spud – and spent the next several hours drinking the place dry and hollering at each other over the deafening roar of music, before stumbling out into the street in the wee hours and making their way, by a meandering and circuitous route, back to Spud's flat in Cowcaddens for videogames and more drinking. Somewhere between three and four in the morning, they'd finally succumbed to the inevitable after Jenny, who'd spent much of the night alternating between trying to seduce the perennially unobservant Gobby and declaring that she was almost certainly dying of alcohol poisoning, had lain down on the floor and failed to get back up – which had seemed as good a sign as any to the rest of them that it was time to call it a night.

Alyssa squinted at the grubby mirror and stuck her tongue out at her reflection. She concluded she looked almost as bad as she felt. Almost, but not quite. Her makeup, still in place and only suffering from minimal smudging, hid the worst effects of last night's frivolities, the bleariness in her eyes masked by the tinted lenses of her Wayfarers. And she had an infallible plan for a full and speedy recovery: catch the next bus back to Laurieston, hop straight into bed, spend the rest of the day catching up on some much-needed shut-eye and be fresh as a daisy for starting her new job tomorrow.

As she stood there, trying to work up the enthusiasm to actually put one foot in front of the other and make a move, her eyes strayed to the calendar on the wall. For a moment, the significance of what she was seeing failed to register. Then, with a pin-sharp clarity that belied her booze-marinated brain, she saw it. *Monday the first of March.* It was tomorrow *today*.

'HOLY SHITBALLS!'

She was out of the flat in seconds, crashing out into the grey morning with her jacket trailing from one arm. She cast around wildly, blinking as the harsh daylight seared her poor, delicate eyeballs. Traffic roared past in both directions, the busy Cowcaddens Road already at full capacity despite the ungodly hour. Across the road, she spotted a number three bus idling at the stop. After a moment, a break in the traffic materialised, but by the time she made it to the other side, the bus had already pulled away from the kerb. There then followed an ungainly dash up the pavement behind it until it came to a halt at a set of lights where, after much hammering on the door, the driver finally took pity on her and let her in. She shoved what she was sure was far too much money into his hand, snatched her ticket from the dispenser, staggered up the gangway and collapsed into the back row seat, breathless and sweaty and with a nagging sense that, sooner or later, she was going to spew.

It's OK, she told herself. You can still make it. And even if you *are* late, so what? It's an entry-level job in a public library, not fricking NASA.

Twenty-two minutes before

At just after 9.10 a.m. – or to be precise, ten minutes after her shift was due to start – the bus finally came to a juddering halt on Chancery Street. She hurried down the gangway, flashing a perfunctory smile at the young man who stepped aside to let her pass. Alighting on the pavement, she clocked the library fifty yards up ahead, then realised there was no way she was going to be able to face an entire day on the trot without first getting some form of both hydration and pain relief.

Five minutes later, she emerged from the newsagent across the road, armed with a bottle of Irn Bru and a pack of Paracetamol Plus.

'Spare some change, wee pet?' said the homeless guy with the matted beard and stained cagoule sitting cross-legged outside the shop, as she paused to pop a couple of pills.

'Gave it all to the bus driver, sorry,' she said absentmindedly, and slugged back a mouthful of fizz. 'And I'm not your wee pet.'

He held up both hands in a gesture of truce. 'My mistake. Go in peace to love and serve the Lord.'

She crossed the road, playing cat-and-mouse with the traffic, and found herself gazing up at one of those grand old Carnegie buildings, so consecrated in the minds of the city's decision-makers that any attempt to bring them even vaguely into the twenty-first century with such radical notions as disabled access and properly functioning central heating were immediately met with howls of outrage and can't-be-dones. The words 'THORNHILL PUBLIC LIBRARY' were engraved on the stone arch above the doorway. On the door itself was a laminated sign declaring that, owing to repeated abuse of staff goodwill, the public toilet was for service users only and that access was contingent on production of a valid library card. Alyssa hoped no one around here ever got the runs.

Stepping inside, she found herself in a low-ceilinged foyer, the marble flooring scuffed and stained by the passage of countless feet. 'GLASGOW *LOVES* READING' proclaimed a tall banner near the door, its bold assertion illustrated by a picture of a group of people, all improbably photogenic and infinitely more multi-coloured than the average Scottish family, smiling at one another as they enjoyed their suspiciously pristine books – which, much like the people themselves, looked fresh off the assembly line. Even the baby was beaming, clutching a board-book while its doting parents looked on approvingly. Alyssa strongly suspected it was a stock photo and that the family wasn't actually Scottish at all . . . or, for that matter, a family.

Crossing the foyer, she headed through another door into the main library – a roomy affair with a faintly damp smell. Straight ahead was a work area encircled by a wooden countertop, behind which three people were gathered. One – a tall, rake-thin man in

his forties with a quiff and a feeble-looking excuse for a beard – was holding court while his two companions, both women, listened with weary disinterest. Beyond the desk, a wrought-iron spiral staircase in the middle of the room created a natural central well around which the bookshelves were arranged like spokes on a wheel. Dust-motes danced in light rays filtering down from a glass dome some thirty feet up, giving the place a vaguely ecclesiastical atmosphere. Alyssa counted perhaps half a dozen customers browsing the shelves, most of them decidedly on the elderly side. Not exactly heaving.

She came to a halt at the desk while the quiff-haired guy continued to pontificate.

'I'm telling yous,' he declared, voice raised several orders of magnitude beyond what was necessary for such an intimate gathering, 'we shouldnae let 'em divide us like this. If we adopted a united front, they'd not have a leg to stand on.'

'Oh, hark at him!' declared one of the two women – barrel-chested, in her late fifties, sporting granny glasses and puckered lips. 'United front, is it? He'll be having us all stand up shouting "I'm Spartacus!" next.'

The other woman, a good twenty-five years younger, her blonde hair in bunches, tittered into her coffee cup and said nothing, but that didn't stop Quiff Hair shooting her an acrid look.

'Dunno what's supposed to be so funny,' he snapped. 'This is a serious matter. There's principles at stake here.'

'You're right, Jason, you're right,' said Blondie, doing an impressive job of sounding utterly sincere even as her face simultaneously betrayed her true feelings. 'It's a matter of life and death. And you *know* that, all things being equal, I'd be first in line to take this particular bullet for you. But unless you're willing to take over Tiny Tots for me, I'm afraid my presence here is fairly essential.'

'Oh no.' Jason shook his head firmly. 'No way. If they think I'm gonnae get down on my knees to sing "Old McDonald had a farm" with the babbies, they've got another thing coming.'

'And I'm sure the babies and their mums are profoundly grateful for your strong and principled stance.'

Just then, Granny Glasses caught sight of Alyssa over Jason's shoulder. She instantly stiffened and cleared her throat. Jason swung around to face her, eyes narrowing suspiciously. She got the distinct impression he wasn't thrilled to discover he had an audience.

'If it's a computer you're after, just away through and log yourself on,' he said, nodding to a door off to the left. 'There's hunners of empty machines. We don't need to see your card.'

'Huh?' Alyssa was momentarily thrown. 'No, no, I don't need a computer. I'm Alyssa Clark. New library assistant?' she added hopefully.

Jason gave her a look that might best be described as scepticism laced with contempt, then glanced over at his two companions. 'Never knew we were getting fresh meat. Either of yous hear anything about this?'

Blondie shrugged, while Granny Glasses laughed. 'And why, pray tell, would they tell me anything? Me, a humble slave to the machine? I just do as I'm telt. They say "jump", I say "how high?" They tell me to clean the public loos, I set off with a smile and a skip in my step.'

Jason turned to Alyssa again, his expression only marginally less hostile than before. 'Sure you're meant to be here? Wouldnae be the first time so-called management got their wires crossed.'

Alyssa was about to respond when a fourth person materialised alongside her, a stack of books tucked under one arm. 'What's the trouble?' he inquired, pleasantly enough.

He was in his late twenties, Alyssa reckoned. Short and overweight, he reminded her of one of the Seven Dwarfs, minus the beard and pickaxe.

'Reckons she's meant to be working here,' said Jason, jerking a thumb in Alyssa's direction.

'I don't *reckon*,' said Alyssa. She'd reached the limits of her patience with people talking about her as if she wasn't there. 'I *am* supposed to be working here. I was told to report here at nine for my induction.'

'You get that in writing?'

'No – they told me over the phone. I didn't—'

Jason raised a chiding finger. 'Always get everything in writing from that lot. If there's a paper trail, they cannae pull the wool over your eyes and make out you signed up to something you never did.'

'Should we get Denise on the blower?' suggested the tubby guy. 'She ought to be able to straighten this out.'

Alyssa perked up, recognising the name. 'Denise? As in Denise Forsyth? She's supposed to do my—'

'Can't contact a VMO about a work matter while they're on annual leave,' said Granny Glasses adamantly. 'Them's the rules.'

Jason rubbed the underside of his chin with a long finger. 'Four of us plus new girl here puts us over capacity, and I'm buggered if I'm getting sent on relief just cos HR couldnae handle a piss-up in a brewery.' He glanced briefly in Alyssa's direction. 'Nae offence, darling.'

'None taken,' said Alyssa, not sure she particularly liked being referred to either as 'new girl' or 'darling' – though she supposed both were a step up from 'fresh meat'.

'Yeah, but she won't be counted as staff,' pointed out Blondie. 'New hires are meant to shadow for the first fortnight. So we're technically still only four bodies.'

Granny Glasses shook her head. 'Not true. Safe operating levels guidelines are purely about how many bodies you have in the building, not how many of those bodies are fully qualified. Check the Business Processes folder if you don't believe me.'

As an uneasy silence descended, the tubby guy turned to Alyssa with the first genuine smile she'd received since arriving. 'Well, never mind. You're here now. Might as well muck in. C'mon, I'll give you the grand tour.'

Not trusting herself to say anything – and not convinced anyone would listen if she did – Alyssa allowed herself to be led away, following him as he set off at a surprisingly brisk pace for one so short and stocky.

'Welcome to Thornhill Library,' he said, doing a passable imitation of a flight attendant running through the emergency landing procedure. 'There's not a whole lot to it, but I'd consider it a dereliction of duty if I didn't subject you to the full carnival of delights. What did you say your name was, again?'

'Alyssa.'

'Pleased to meet you, Alyssa. I'm Davy. Is that "Alyssa" with a "Y" or an "I"? You'll have to excuse Jason, by the way. He's our union rep. Takes his role dead seriously.'

'I can tell.'

His strident, overly cheerful tones would have been tough to endure at the best of times. In her present state, they were about as pleasurable as having her teeth pulled with rusty pliers.

'And his sparring partner with the oh-so-stylish bifocals is Eva. Nearly three decades' service and still as upbeat and positive as the day she started. We also have the lovely Laura with us today. Anything to do with entertaining the kiddies, she's your girl. Ask nicely and she'll also stretch to birthday parties, christenings and baby showers.'

Davy turned to face Alyssa, arms spread wide, which only added to his impression of a flight attendant. 'Now, to your right and to your left are the children's library and the reading room respectively. Not that much reading goes on in there these days. Nowadays it's your de facto internet café, which makes up the bulk of our footfall.

Word to the wise: do not, under any circumstances, be tempted to set foot in there. Step through that door and you'll be in there all day helping folk download boarding passes and supermarket vouchers.'

Alyssa wondered how it was possible, in this day and age, for a human being to function without basic IT skills.

'Up there,' continued Davy, pointing up the spiral staircase as they wound their way past it, 'are all the non-fiction and reference books. 'Not to be tackled if you suffer from vertigo. You don't suffer from vertigo, do you? The office is up there too, where our boss, the Mistress of Pain, spends her time plotting our demise and lord knows what else. When she's not off living it up in sunny Barbados, that is.'

They'd reached the back of the library now and were facing a door labelled 'STAFF ONLY'. Alyssa, who'd long since concluded that Davy was someone who did a lot of talking and next to no listening, abandoned any thought of interjecting as he rabbited on about the staff toilets, the kitchen and the ins and outs of the milk rota, wondering when he was going to finally shut up and give the pneumatic drill inside her skull a rest.

'And here we have the break room,' he went on, ushering her into a low-ceilinged room with a table, an assortment of mis-matched chairs and, at the far end, a row of metal lockers. 'Your stuff should be safe enough in here, but we'll get you a locker just as soon as. Shame we didn't have advance notice of your coming or we'd've had everything all set up.'

'What about this one?' Alyssa pointed to the locker at the end of the row. Its door, emblazoned with a dog-eared 'SCOTTISH SUR-VIVALISTS SOCIETY' sticker, lay slightly ajar.

Davy eyed it dubiously. 'Probably best if we leave that one be for now.' A shadow seemed to fall on his face. 'Then, as quickly as it had come, it passed and his expression brightened. 'Hey, nice ink-work.'

'Oh . . . right. Thanks.'

She rubbed her bare arms self-consciously, aware that the baggy T-shirt she had on showed off her sleeve tattoos – just some of the many pieces of body art, of varying designs and levels of quality, that festooned her person – in all their glory. She wasn't sure how her new employers felt about tattoos and had planned on keeping hers covered, at least until she'd settled into the job and it would be harder for them to get rid of her on a whim. But then, she hadn't reckoned with rucking up to her first shift in last night's clothes.

'Always fancied getting one myself. Nothing too in-your-face – just something small and tasteful, somewhere nobody can see it except me.'

'So why don't you?'

Davy made a sheepish face. 'Scared of needles.' A moment elapsed, then his brain appeared to shift gears again. 'Love the accent, by the way. Which part of the States you from?'

'I'm not,' said Alyssa flatly.

'Oh. I thought—'

'You thought wrong. I'm from Canada.'

'Well, which part of Canada are you from, then?' he said impatiently, as if the distinction was of no importance.

'You won't have heard of it.'

'I might've.'

'My dude, trust me – you won't.'

Davy thought about it for a moment, then shrugged. 'Fair enough. Odds are I'll winkle it out of you one way or another before long. I'm persistent that way. Now then, what's it to be? Officially, there's a whole heap of boring paperwork you're supposed to go through before I let you loose on the poor unsuspecting public, but I always say it's better to just get stuck in and get your hands dirty. There's nothing in those dusty old tomes you won't pick up a gazillion times faster learning by doing. What say you?'

The idea of sitting in some secluded corner working her way

14

through a stack of instruction manuals didn't sound to Alyssa like the worst thing in the world. At least, if she was left to her own devices, she could get through her hangover without having to suffer Davy's incessant running commentary. But then, she wasn't sure she trusted herself to keep her eyes open without serious stimulation. Odds were she'd be passed out on the floor long before the clock struck ten.

In any event, Davy, taking her silence as acquiescence, made the decision for her. 'Knew we'd be on the same page. No time like the present, then!'

Eleven minutes before

They got back to find Jason and Eva still at each other's throats. Laura was nowhere to be seen, and a small queue had begun to develop at the counter, which clearly neither Jason nor Eva had any intention of seeing to anytime soon.

'It's the boiled frog phenomenon,' Jason was saying. 'We should've put our feet down years back when it first started, refused all they extra responsibilities and they'd've had no choice but to go back to the drawing board. 'Stead, everyone's just got used to it and now, when you even so much as *mention* industrial action, their eyes just glaze over.'

'Can't *imagine* why that could be,' said Davy. He flashed Alyssa a conspiratorial wink. 'Mark me, he'll still be banging on about this by lunchtime.' Slipping behind the counter, he turned to face the elderly woman at the front of the queue. 'Morning, Mrs Mackie. Find everything you were looking for . . . ?'

Alyssa stepped behind the counter and plonked herself on a vacant stool, seemingly forgotten by all and sundry. She'd always imagined libraries as oases of calm: sacred, peaceful places where time stood still and the denizens consisted of obsessive book-worms, the elderly and people who hadn't yet discovered Google. This one appeared to be a hotbed of insanity that served as a homing beacon to society's most profoundly dysfunctional – and that was just the staff.

As Alyssa sat there, acutely conscious that her clothes reeked of cigarette smoke, booze and her own sweat, Laura emerged from the reading room off to the left, a rolled-up floor-mat over her shoulder, and stormed over to the desk with a face like thunder.

'Just so you know,' she announced, 'that creep's in again, *and* he's on a computer.'

Her assembled colleagues exchanged sighs and exclamations of exasperation.

'I thought you changed his pin-code,' said Jason, looking accusingly at Davy.

Davy turned to face him as Mrs Mackie departed, her books successfully checked out. 'Aye, well, someone obviously changed it back.'

'You can't change a service user's pin-code without their permission,' said Eva. 'Says so in the Business Processes folder.'

'It'll be they pricks at Tollcross Library,' said Jason, ignoring her – something, Alyssa was coming to realise, he was extremely good at. 'Bloody free-for-all there, so it is. They let the punters away with murder. Don't want to pay your late fees? Fine, we'll wipe 'em. Barred from libraries for a year? It's OK, we'll set you up with a brand new card . . . '

'What's this guy supposed to have done that's so bad, anyway?' Alyssa asked.

Four pairs of eyes instantly turned to face her, and she was once again left with the impression that she'd said something she shouldn't.

'Who did you say you were again?' said Jason.

Sigh. 'Alyssa. Alyssa Clark.'

'And you're sure you're supposed to be here?'

'Positive,' she said. Though she was starting to wonder.

'Porn,' said Laura flatly. 'He spends all day looking at porn. And it's, like, a *public* computer? In any sane organisation, he'd've been out on his ear before he knew what hit him.'

'Ah.' Jason raised a finger. 'But you forget, this *isn't* a sane organisation. This is North Kelvin District Libraries. We provide a vital service to this fair city and must have reasonable grounds to deny it to any of its citizens.'

'He was caught looking at smut in a place used by families and children. I'd call that reasonable grounds.'

'Hey, I don't make up the rules. Dinnae shoot the messenger.'

'Yeah, well, I doubt the mums coming to Tiny Tots would be too happy to learn there was a *pervert* in the building.'

Davy piped up, 'Denise said, if he came in again, we weren't to antagonise him. We're to contact Head Office and let *them* deal with it.'

Laura, ignoring him, continued to stare Jason down with a steely gaze. 'Well, if he's still here when the little ones start to arrive, I'm cancelling the entire session.' There was an unspoken *and THEN you'll be sorry* buried in there somewhere.

'Ah, for Christ's sake,' muttered Jason. Then, brushing past Alyssa like she wasn't even there, he commandeered the nearest computer and began tapping at the keys.

Davy turned to Eva. 'Gonnae give North Hanover Street a bell? Tell 'em we've got a developing situation.'

'Why me?' Eva retorted, adopting an arms-folded, standoffish pose. 'It was me who spoke to 'em last time. Me who got an earful off of bloody Nikki Wyatt for not using my initiative.'

'Yes, but you always manage to sweet-talk her so beautifully. It's a joy to behold.'

Eva was momentarily tongue-tied and, to Alyssa's eyes, seemed to be on the verge of blushing. Eventually, muttering a rather flustered 'Well all right then', she made her way over to the phone, lifted the receiver and began to dial.

Jason, meanwhile, looked up from his computer screen with a sly, satisfied smile. 'Here we go. Meltdown in five, four, three, two . . . '

As if on cue, a large man in his mid-forties came storming out of the reading room and made a beeline for the desk, fists clenched by his sides. He had pock-marked skin and tufts of badly cut hair sticking out from under a navy-blue beanie hat emblazoned with a Scotland flag. He stomped up to the desk and stood there, breathing loudly through flared nostrils. Laura, still standing on the same side of the counter as him, edged away from him, eyeing him the way one normally would shit on a shoe.

'My–my–my computer's broke,' he announced.

Jason gazed at him laconically. 'That seems highly improbable.'

'It went off and–and now it won't let me back on. I tell you, it's broke.'

'Mr Ramage, were you, by any chance, looking at things you weren't supposed to again?'

'No!' Ramage's face, including the tips of his very prominent ears, flushed scarlet. Alyssa half-expected steam to rise from his head.

'You sure about that?'

'I–I–I wasn't. You–you–you trying to make out that I'm some sort of a, that I'm a liar?'

'No one's trying to make out anything, Mr Ramage. But if you think we can't see what you're looking at just cos you sit at the back of the room, you're sorely mistaken. We'll get someone from Head Office to deal with your enquiry just as soon as. In the meantime, may I suggest perusing the contents of one of our many fine books?'

He pointed toward the rows of shelves to the back of the library. 'Preferably over there and downwind of the desk.'

Ramage eyed each of the assembled staff in turn, his eyes coming to rest on Alyssa. She swiftly wiped anything approaching a smile from her face.

'You . . . you . . . bastards!' he spluttered, his voice rising to a crescendo. 'Stuck-up, evil, spiteful *bastards!*'

Davy stepped forward with his hands raised in a plea for calm. 'Now, now, Mr Ramage, there's no need for language like that. As my colleague said, we're on the phone to Head Office as we speak. If you'll just be patient a bit longer—'

Ramage jabbed a trembling finger at Davy, extending his entire arm across the desk so that the tip came close to touching his nose. 'Just wait. A reckoning's coming. One of these days, yous'll bite off more than yous can chew. Then yous'll be s–s–sorry.'

Davy, for his part, did an admirable job of not appearing fazed by either the threat or the invasion of his personal space. 'Like I said, the matter's being dealt with. I'm sure this can all be resolved perfectly amicably.'

Ramage made what Alyssa initially assumed was merely a noise of disgust at the back of his throat. Her illusions were swiftly shattered as a gob of phlegm landed a few inches from her elbow on the countertop. She leapt off the stool and backed off to the other side of the work area.

Ramage pointed at each of the assembled staff, leaving Alyssa till last. 'J–j–just wait,' he repeated, then turned on his heel and stormed out.

An uneasy silence lingered in the wake of his departure. The various customers, who'd stopped to watch the unfolding encounter, continued to stare apprehensively in the direction of the desk. Then, almost as one, they returned to browsing the shelves, a low murmur of conversation once again rising.

Laura was first to speak. 'What an *arse*! Well, that's it. They'll have to bar him now. You can't go around making threats against people and not expect to face the consequences.'

'Ah, it was never a threat,' said Jason. 'The man's all mooth and nae troosers. He's just raging cos he got caught with his pants down.'

'Well, I'm glad *you* can be so blasé about it, but if you ask me, someone should be calling the police right this minute.'

Jason made a sweeping gesture with his hand. 'You go right ahead – just as soon as madam gets off the blower to our lords and masters.'

Eva, who still had the phone clamped between ear and shoulder, made an obscene-looking gesture before turning her back on him.

With the drama having subsided, staff and punters alike started to go about their business once more. Davy began to gather up the books lying on the returns trolley at the foot of the desk. Jason produced a packet of digestive biscuits from under the counter and proceeded to cram one into his mouth whole. Eva, still waiting for someone to deal with her enquiry, began to hum the tune to 'Take This Job and Shove It'.

At that moment, there was a sound of footsteps on the marble floor in the foyer. The hinges on the door to the main library squeaked as it swung open. Laura glanced in the direction of the new arrival, then gave a squeak of horror and dropped her floor-mat. Alyssa turned to see what the fuss was about.

A man stood facing the desk. He was dressed all in black. A balaclava covered most of his face, leaving only his eyes visible through a narrow slit. In his right hand, he held a black plastic handgun.

For the next few seconds, time seemed to stand still. No one moved or spoke. A few stray crumbs fell from Jason's mouth. At the other end of the phone line, a woman's voice could be faintly heard, asking Eva if she was still there.

Alyssa felt a nervous laugh bubbling up in her diaphragm. It got as far as her mouth before the man raised the gun and opened fire.

The first blast exploded into Jason's face, spraying an arc of blood and biscuit into the air.

The second hit Laura in the chest. She dropped like a sack of potatoes.

The third took out Eva, the bullet entering the centre of her forehead. She was still holding the phone when she went down.

The fourth hit Davy in the back as he made a run for it. He crumpled to the floor and lay still.

The shooter turned to Alyssa. Their eyes met, the distance between them less than an arm's length. For a moment, they just stared at one another. Alyssa could hear her own heart beating a totem against her ribcage. She felt something warm and wet running down the inside of her leggings.

'Please,' she said. 'I'm only new.'

The man raised his gun and pulled the trigger.

2

Three minutes after

Detective Chief Inspector Claire Metcalfe glanced at the phone nestled in the docking station on the dashboard of her VW Golf and swore under her breath. Google Maps had told her this was the most efficient route to Strathkelvin Police's city centre headquarters – which, under normal circumstances, it would have been. Today, however, a spot of unscheduled gas mains repair had turned the A814 into something resembling one of those endless lorry parks at ferry ports. So much for making it to the Chief Super's morning briefing at ten. There'd be hell to pay when her absence was noted, as it undoubtedly would be.

As she sat there, drumming her fingers against the wheel, the police radio below her phone crackled into life. The voice of the on-duty dispatch drowned out the audiobook on the CD player:

'Attention all units. Multiple reports of shots fired inside Thornhill Public Library, over.'

For a moment, Metcalfe wondered if she'd heard correctly. She replayed the dispatch's words in her head, decided she had and snatched up the receiver. 'This is DCI Metcalfe, Major Investigations Team. Sorry, but I distinctly heard you say shots fired in a public library. Can you confirm, over?'

'Affirmative, ma'am. Thornhill Public Library on Chancery

Street. We've had three calls now. Most recent claims to have been in the building when the shooting started, over.'

'Is the incident still ongoing? Any indication as to whether it's a single shooter or multiple, over?'

'Not clear, ma'am, but the most recent caller says there are casualties, over.'

'Who's been assigned incident commander, over?'

'No one at present, but ARVs are en route, over.'

Metcalfe crunched the logistics. Chancery Street was close. Serendipitously close. The odds of there being another officer of her rank in such close proximity were slim to non-existent.

'Put me down as IC,' she said. 'I'll be there in five minutes.'

She replaced the receiver, flicked on her siren and emergency lights and did a hard turn onto the grass verge. With her tyres kicking up great clods of earth, she reversed past the queue of vehicles until she came to the turn-off for Chancery Street. Ignoring the barrage of horns that greeted her, she backed down the turn-off, one set of wheels on the verge, the other on the road, spun the car one hundred and eighty degrees and set off like the clappers.

In the time it took Metcalfe to reach the library, a flurry of updates came through, including one report from a squad car which had arrived at the scene ahead of her. The two officers in attendance reported that all appeared quiet inside the library, with no further shots fired, but had remained at a safe distance and made no attempt to enter the building – for which Metcalfe, who had long held the belief that heroes were people who got themselves and occasionally others killed, was profoundly thankful.

She parked next to Cash Converters and continued for the remaining hundred yards or so on foot, conscious all the while that the street was positively milling with people – local shopkeepers and residents, alerted either by the sounds of gunfire or the ensuing hullaballoo and determined not to miss anything.

'Police officer!' she shouted, holding her warrant card aloft as she continued up the street. 'Please go back indoors and await further instruction. I repeat, go back indoors!'

One man, a burly apron-clad giant leaning on the doorframe of a barber's shop, made some pithy comment about the Gestapo before reluctantly retreating indoors in the face of Metcalfe's razor-sharp glare. Most of the assembled throng did likewise, though a few more foolhardy souls remained in the street. Metcalfe figured that, if the combined forces of her warrant card and the prospect of being mowed down by a stray bullet weren't enough to make them shift, nothing would. So she left them to it and covered the rest of the ground in double-quick time, ducking behind the squad car where the two uniforms were sheltering, just feet from the library.

'DCI Metcalfe?' enquired one, who looked to be in the process of shitting bricks.

'The same,' she said. 'What can you tell me?'

In the three and a half minutes it took for the armed response unit to arrive, the two officers gave Metcalfe a surprisingly coherent rundown of the order of events, as far as they were currently understood. At around 9.35 a.m., passersby on Chancery Street had heard a series of loud pops coming from within the library. Moments later, a figure in dark clothes was observed emerging from the building at considerable speed. According to eyewitnesses, he – and the current hypothesis was that he *was* a 'he', having been universally described as such – ran along Chancery Street in a westerly direction before turning off onto Edgehill Drive. Less than a minute later, several more people began to emerge from the library, many in a state of considerable distress. They were reckoned to number six or seven, though an exact figure could not be determined, for amid the panic and confusion, all but three had fled the scene. These three had been instructed to take cover inside the newsagent across the street – a commendable bit of quick thinking by the two officers to ensure that they too didn't simply scatter to the four winds. Several others, it had subsequently emerged, had escaped via the fire exit onto nearby Alderbrook Street. These were believed to be computer users from the adjoining reading room, where the fire exit was located. Again, their precise number could not be ascertained. Metcalfe hoped the computer logs would prove more enlightening.

Those that had remained behind had been consistent about what had occurred. At some point after nine-thirty but before nine-thirty-five, a figure in a black coat and balaclava had entered the main library, produced a handgun and begun to shoot the employees gathered at the issue desk. There had been five members of staff and five shots fired – all of them direct hits. One of the three who had remained at the scene, a retired security guard, described it as 'a fucking bloodbath'. The gunman had then pocketed his weapon and fled the building. The security guard, having confirmed the coast was clear, had marshalled his fellow customers into making a swift and orderly exit, remaining behind to ensure the building was empty and that there were no signs of life from the bodies at the desk. Though, as he had rather tersely informed the officers when asked whether, in his opinion, all five victims were dead, 'I wasnae sticking around to go looking for a bloody pulse.'

It took a veritable eternity for the armed officers to certify the building as safe to enter, during which time several more squad cars arrived, alongside a trio of ambulances, whose crews were instructed to wait behind the hastily erected cordon amid much grousing and griping. When the cordon was finally lifted, Metcalfe accompanied the paramedics into the building, though she only went as far as the foyer, concluding that her presence was neither required nor would it be gratefully received. As she waited for them to do what was necessary, she clocked a security camera mounted in the corner of the ceiling overlooking the entrance doors. With any luck, the footage it had captured would provide some pointers as to the shooter's identity.

In the meantime, she set about updating the Chief Super, whose increasingly insistent messages were steadily clogging up her answerphone. She was in the process of filling her in on the latest developments when a shout went up from inside the library proper.

'We've got a live one here!'

Metcalfe spun around, almost dropping her phone. With bated breath she waited, ignoring the Chief Super's demands to know what was happening, until the doors swung open and two paramedics emerged, escorting a heavily tattooed woman in her midtwenties between them like a condemned prisoner. Long black hair framed a chalk-white face sporting a pair of rectangular glasses perched at a crooked angle on her nose, the left lens exhibiting a spider's web pattern of cracks. Blood streamed down the left side of her face from a wound to her temple in spite of a hastily taped-on compress, while the dark patch on the crotch area of her leggings indicated that, at some point during the ordeal, she'd lost control of her bladder. For a few brief seconds Metcalfe and the girl's eyes met from opposite sides of the hallway, before the moment abruptly passed and the girl was ushered out by her two minders.

Metcalfe headed over to the door to the main library and peered through the narrow glass window. She could make out the issue desk, the gleaming bald head of one of the paramedics visible as he knelt behind it. At first, Metcalfe could see no evidence of the carnage that had supposedly taken place there. It took her a moment to notice the limp, lifeless hand protruding from behind the desk, lying in a pool of congealed blood.

As Metcalfe drank in the grisly spectacle, too transfixed to look away, she remembered the phone in her hand and once again became aware of the Chief Super's tinny, distorted voice, demanding an explanation for her silence. Forcing herself to wrest her eyes away, Metcalfe turned her back on the door and held the phone to her ear.

'Hello? Yes, ma'am, still here . . . '

By the time Metcalfe emerged from the building, the ranks of the uniforms at the scene had been bolstered by a number of her colleagues from CID – as well as a plethora of rubberneckers who, having got wind that something dramatic was happening, had come along to get a glimpse of the action. She also spotted a handful of vans parked beyond the cordon, bearing the insignias of the local and national news networks, and an alarming number of people rushing to and fro armed with cameras, microphones and other broadcasting equipment.

As she stood on the library steps, surveying the scene unfolding before her, she spotted the familiar figure of Detective Sergeant Renshaw standing in the middle of the road like a lost child, wearing the perpetually pained expression that was his hallmark. She made her way down the steps and strode across to him.

'Sergeant! Fancy running into you here! Contemplating life's great mysteries?'

Renshaw snapped to attention, all but saluting her. 'Ma'am. Sorry. Just . . . well, I mean, bloody hell.'

Under the circumstances, she supposed Renshaw could be forgiven for a momentary lapse in concentration, provided it was indeed momentary. But she knew she couldn't afford to carry anyone on this venture. It was going to be all hands to the pump, and time was of the essence.

'Right,' she said, 'I want the eyewitnesses holed up in the news-agent over the road interviewed ASAP. I want their recollections while they're still fresh in their minds, and before they've had time to compare notes. Can you see to that?'

Renshaw whipped out his notebook and began to write. 'Got it.'

'Also, I spotted a security camera in the foyer. Get onto the council or whoever's responsible for these things and have them hand over this morning's footage.'

Renshaw continued to scribble in his notebook, nodding vigorously.

'And I want the particulars of the library staff on duty today: names, next of kin, anyone they may or may not have pissed off recently. And find out everything you can about the girl who survived. About twenty-five, yea-high, dark hair and glasses, tattoos up the wazoo. Got all that?'

Renshaw scribbled some more, his pen virtually a blur as he struggled to keep up with Metcalfe's list of demands. 'Yes, ma'am. Got it.'

'Good. Bell me with any updates.' She was already off, striding up the road towards her car.

'Right-o. Er . . . where are you off to, ma'am?'

'To see the Chief Super. She's requested an urgent briefing . . . in person.'

Gillian Langley was not the worst boss in the world to have, though she had an annoying tendency to demand certainty where none could reasonably be expected. 'We're keeping an open mind' was not a phrase you uttered in her presence if you knew what was good for you. She favoured decisive action and wholesale commitment to a single, airtight hypothesis. Which, given that for the time being they had the square root of bugger all to work with, meant Metcalfe didn't particularly relish this encounter.

'How long have you been with us here in MIT, Claire?'

Wrong-footed by this opening gambit, Metcalfe hesitated before responding. 'Er . . . just over a year, ma'am.'

'And before that you were attached to the Human Trafficking and Modern Slavery taskforce.'

'That's correct.' Wondering where this was heading.

'During which you spearheaded a two-year operation to dismantle a network of traffickers operating in our own fair city of Glasgow' – Langley fingered a dossier lying in front of her on her desk – 'resulting in a string of arrests of high-ranking people-smugglers and brothel-keepers – and securing your promotion to DCI.'

'And a commendation from the Cabinet Secretary for Justice,' Metcalfe couldn't help adding.

'Hmm, yes.' Langley seemed less than impressed by that particular detail. 'I'm just off the phone from him, actually. Both he and the First Minister are following this morning's events closely and expect to be kept firmly abreast of all developments.'

'That's understandable, given the circumstances.'

'Quite. He wanted to know who was heading up the investigation. I explained that an SIO had yet to be appointed.'

So this is it, Metcalfe thought. I've been called in here to be told I'm getting the boot. Shunted aside in favour of one of the ACC's golden boys – someone with a track record in schmoozing the nation's media with PR-friendly soundbites.

'Since news broke, the matter has been the subject of much debate between myself and the rest of senior management,' Langley continued. 'A number of voices expressed a belief that the job should go to someone with experience dealing with firearms offences, and mass shootings in particular. As you'll appreciate, such people are fairly thin on the ground in this part of the world, though a handful of names were put forward.' She took a clearly rehearsed pause for dramatic effect. 'Be that as it may, on this occasion I felt it best to trust to aptitude rather than to experience.

For that reason, my recommendation is that you remain in overall command of the investigation.'

Metcalfe opened her mouth to speak, but didn't get anywhere.

'I want to make it clear that this decision had nothing to do with any past history between yourself and the Justice Secretary. Your name didn't come up in our discussions; nor did he make any recommendation as to who to appoint. I do, of course, value the minister's judgement in all matters of operational policy, but this unit's independence is jealously guarded. We can't be seen to have government bureaucrats interfering with our ability to do our jobs.'

'Perish the thought.'

'I'm saying all this so you can rest assured that your appointment is based entirely on your own merits. You've a strong record when it comes to getting results, even if they don't lie in this particular field. Plus, you do have certain advantages over the old-timers. Politically neutral; untainted by any of the scandals that have plagued the Strathkelvin force in recent years.'

'I do my best to keep my nose clean, ma'am.'

Langley's eyes narrowed, this brief attempt at levity clearly not having gone down well. 'I'm putting my neck on the line here, Claire. I trust that I won't have cause to regret it.'

This time, Metcalfe determined that the best course of action was for her to say nothing. Best to let the vote of confidence – and the implied threat – pass without comment.

'So.' Langley folded her hands on the desk. 'What's your working hypothesis?'

Ah, yes, the infamous working hypothesis of which the Chief Super was so fond.

'Well,' Metcalfe chose her words carefully, 'I of course want to avoid jumping to any conclusions without a full picture of what happened, but if the initial eyewitness accounts are accurate, we know two things about the shooter. One, he was a crack shot, so we're most likely looking for someone with extensive firearms experience. Two, despite the place being chock full of customers, he only shot at the staff. It therefore seems reasonable to assume he was deliberately targeting library employees. For that reason, my immediate priority – besides tracing the missing witnesses – is to interview everyone on the staffing rota to establish whether they're aware of anyone with reason to hold a grudge against either an individual employee or the staff collectively.'

Langley nodded her approval. Metcalfe allowed herself to relax slightly. So far, so good.

'There *is* one major consideration we haven't discussed,' the Chief Super said after a moment, 'and that's whether we treat this as a terrorist incident.'

Metcalfe swallowed, the 'T' word settling in her stomach like a lead weight. She saw what would come next with Ultra High Definition clarity. If a terrorist incident was declared, public hysteria would go through the roof and reprisals against the usual targets would begin as surely as night followed day. All of which would lead to further hysteria, and the allocation of already thinly spread resources to quell any unrest.

'For the time being,' she said, once more selecting her words carefully, 'I feel it would be better to treat this as a common-or-garden murder case. We've no evidence to suggest the attack was ideologically motivated, and until that picture changes I see no sense in frightening the horses.'

'Mm.' Langley nodded her approval. 'Plus, this being declared a terrorist incident would almost certainly lead to ceding at least partial authority to Counter Terrorism Command. And the last thing anyone wants is a gaggle of know-nothing toffs from down south coming stomping up here in their jackboots and telling us what to do.' She winced, realising her faux pas as the words left her mouth. 'No offence intended, of course.'

Metcalfe gave a thin smile. 'That's all right, ma'am. I've always thought of myself as more of an "up north" girl.'

Langley appeared relieved. 'That's right. Leeds, wasn't it?'

'Rochdale.'

Langley's expression indicated that she considered the distinction to be of little relevance. 'All right, then. We'll treat it as straightforward homicide for now. But bear in mind, that position will be harder to sustain the more time passes without establishing a motive and a suspect.'

'Duly noted, ma'am. And I appreciate being given this opportunity.' Metcalfe began to edge pre-emptively towards the door. 'If there's nothing else, I'd like to get back out there and see if I can't knock some heads together.'

Langley nodded. 'Needless to say, I'll expect detailed progress reports on my desk by close of play each day.'

'Of course,' said Metcalfe, reflecting, as she turned to go, that 'close of play' was a phrase which, in this line of work, held little meaning to all but the most senior of managers.

'Oh, and Claire?'

Metcalfe stopped in her tracks and turned to face Langley. 'Ma'am?'

'Allow me to once again stress that rather a lot of very important people are expecting a speedy and decisive result. Don't let them down.'

Metcalfe nodded her assent and, not trusting herself to say anything more, turned and slipped out, shutting the door to Langley's office behind her.

Stepping out onto the pavement, Metcalfe rang Renshaw on his mobile.

'Ma'am?' The DS sounded breathless and flustered.

'Good news, Sergeant. They've given me the keys to the kingdom.'

'Sorry?'

'I've been appointed SIO, and you're my lady-in-waiting. What have you got for me?'

She pictured Renshaw with his phone clamped between shoulder and ear as he rifled through his notebook. 'Not a whole lot, I'm afraid. I rang the libraries' central office on North Hanover Street and got put through to the Director of Library Services – one Nikki Wyatt. She was, needless to say, anxious to let us know how eager she was to assist with our enquiries. I asked about accessing the footage from the security cameras.'

'And?'

'It's . . . not great news. She told me security cameras were recently installed in several buildings operated by North Kelvin District Council following complaints by staff about intimidating behaviour from members of the public, but that only the worst hotspots got the real thing. Thornhill was officially designated a moderate-risk venue, so the ones there are non-operational replicas.'

Metcalfe bit back a curse. Something told her that, somewhere on the upper floors of North Hanover Street, several highly paid individuals were now deeply regretting this decision. 'What about the computer logs? Any luck with those?'

She heard Renshaw exhaling heavily. 'Marginally more. I managed to establish that records do exist, but the same Nikki Wyatt gave me a whole lot of guff about data protection and insisted she could only countenance authorising their release if the proper application was made in writing. Same deal with the register of employees.'

'For Christ's sake! What goes through these people's heads? You'd think . . . '

She stopped herself before she said something she'd regret. An in-person visit to this Nikki Wyatt was clearly going to be in order, with or without a written application.

'What about further down the chain of command? I'm assuming there's someone who handles the day-to-day operations at the library. A foreman or a supervisor or whatever.'

'That would be the VMO.'

'The *what*?'

'That was my reaction too. Stands for Venue Management Operative. One Denise Forsythe. Forty-two years of age; in the post five years and counting.'

'Well, have we set about arranging a chat with her, then? Maybe she'll be more forthcoming.'

'That's the thing, ma'am. She flew out to Barbados on Saturday night for a two-week holiday.'

Metcalfe once again had to bite back the urge to swear with abandon. 'You're killing me here, Renshaw. Please tell me you've got *something* for me.'

'Well . . . ' There was a note of something approaching pride in Renshaw's voice. 'I haven't had a whole lot of luck tracking down the absentee eyewitnesses, but I *did* manage to identify the girl with the tattoos.'

'Let's hear it.'

'Name's Alyssa Marie Clark. Canadian national, twenty-four years of age. Came over here on an ancestry visa back in 2013. Doesn't seem to have done much of any note since then – a bunch of low-level part-time jobs, most of them lasting a few months at most. Oh, and get this – today was her first day working at Thornhill Library.'

Metcalfe let out a low whistle. 'Talk about your bad luck.'

But even as she spoke, a thought occurred to her. *Was* it just luck, or was there more to this seeming coincidence?

'Well then, Sergeant,' she said, 'it seems you and I will be paying a visit to this Alyssa Clark at the earliest possible opportunity.'

'There's one other thing,' said Renshaw, 'and you're going to want to prepare yourself for this . . . '

3

Two days after

Alyssa was drowning, swimming against the tide in an endless sea of black nothingness, desperately trying to reach a surface that she couldn't even be sure existed. Her lungs burned, her limbs ached, and it seemed to her that the more she thrashed around, the further she sank, pulled down by a powerful, invisible current. Every so often it would relinquish its hold long enough for her to feel like she was winning, only to resurge and drag her back down into the inky depths.

She had no idea how long she'd been underwater. Time had ceased to hold any meaning. All she knew was that she had to keep swimming, no matter how tired she was, no matter how pointless it seemed.

Because if it caught her, the nameless, shapeless horror that lurked in the impenetrable darkness below would devour her whole.

She came to with a start, jolting upright with her breath caught in the pit of her chest. She looked around, confused and disoriented, only to realise she was on the sofa in the living room of her flat in Laurieston. As her breathing slowed and her heart rate returned to something approaching a normal rhythm, the familiar sounds of traffic reached her ears from the street outside.

She must have nodded off again. She'd been doing a lot of that over the last couple of days, and couldn't recall a time in her life when she'd ever felt so exhausted – though whether it was because of the trauma of what had happened, or the drugs the doctors had given her, or a combination of the two, was anyone's guess. They'd kept her in hospital overnight – standard practice with head injuries, they'd said – before discharging her – rather reluctantly, she thought – the following morning, just under twenty-four hours after The Event, armed with a goody-bag full of painkillers and anti-anxiety meds, the latter of which she had no intention of touching. She was already more out of it than she felt comfortable being, and that was *without* dosing herself up on mood suppressors.

The bullet, they'd told her, had grazed the side of her temple. A few millimetres further to the right and it would have been a whole other story. They'd debrided and sutured the wound, shaving a significant portion of the side of her head in the process – something she wasn't remotely happy about. For good measure, they'd also taped on an excessively large bandage which interfered with her vision and left her convinced, whenever she caught sight of herself in the mirror, that she looked like she'd just undergone a lobotomy. Which, given how utterly zombified she felt, didn't seem entirely inappropriate. She was still wearing her broken Wayfarers, despite them no longer sitting straight on her nose and the cracks on the left lens making it nigh-on impossible to see anything out of that eye with any clarity. She knew she was going to have to take herself to the opticians and get new ones ordered up, but she wasn't ready to face the prospect of leaving the flat yet. At least, if she closed her left eye, she could still see reasonably well. Maybe she should go the whole hog and get herself a pirate's patch.

A series of loud, sharp bangs made her leap to attention. She sat there, barely breathing, heart hammering in her ribcage, every muscle stretched taut.

A couple more bangs followed, and she realised they weren't gunfire. Someone was knocking on her front door.

'Alyssa Clark?' A woman's voice. 'Ms Clark, are you in there?'

Still she didn't move.

'Ms Clark, can you open up, please? It's the police.'

Alyssa slid off the sofa and headed down the corridor, bare feet padding on the hardwood flooring. Placing the security chain in its slot, she opened the door a couple of inches and peered out. Standing in the stairwell outside were two figures – a woman in her early forties, and a slightly younger man standing just behind her. Both wore cheap-looking charcoal suits, their sombre expressions making her briefly wonder if they were here to read her the last rites.

'DCI Metcalfe, Major Investigations Team,' said the woman, holding open a wallet to show a warrant card. She gestured to her accomplice. 'This is DS Renshaw. Would you mind letting us in?'

She sounded like a fellow out-of-towner. English, though that was as specific as Alyssa was able to get. It was a never-ending source of fascination to her that such a small island was home to such a diverse array of accents. She had dark hair scraped back into a bun, a pinched face and a thin little mouth that curled upwards at one side. Alyssa wondered whether she was self-conscious about it at all.

She hesitated for a moment, then took the door off its chain and opened it wide. The two detectives crossed the threshold without waiting to be invited, the man – Renshaw, was it? – giving Alyssa a brief nod but otherwise keeping his eyes downcast. Alyssa followed them through to the living room and lingered in the doorway, watching them as they eyed up their surroundings, silently appraising the dirty plates and food containers piled up on the coffee table, the crumpled duvet on the sofa, the general shabbiness of the whole place. She sensed them judging her for it and felt about six inches tall.

'We tried to see you at the hospital,' Metcalfe said, turning to face her, 'but we were told you weren't up to receiving visitors.'

There was something approaching an accusatory note in that statement, Alyssa thought, as if she herself was to blame for this state of affairs. She felt like saying something cutting and sarcastic but, standing there in her broken glasses and 'Gamers Do It All Night' PJs, she doubted she had the necessary gravitas to pull it off.

'I've been here since yesterday morning,' she said, indicating that it wasn't *her* fault it had taken them till now to catch up with her.

Metcalfe dipped her head slightly in acknowledgement. 'Unfortunately, we're a small team with finite resources. When we learned you were indisposed, we chose for the time being to focus our attentions elsewhere.' She paused. 'Are you alone right now? No friends or family here with you?' She looked around as if she expected to find someone lurking in a corner somewhere.

'It's just me,' said Alyssa, more than a little defensively.

Her employers, in their infinite wisdom, had taken it upon themselves to contact her parents – without either her knowledge or permission, naturally – to inform them that their daughter had been involved in a life-and-death situation. She'd found this out shortly after being discharged from hospital, when her mother had rung her in a blind panic, alternating between floods of tears and remonstrations about how this showed she'd been right all along to object to Alyssa upping sticks and flying halfway round the world where *anything* might happen to her. She'd been all set to hop on the next plane out of rural Saskatchewan to come and be with her poor, fragile daughter in her hour of need – the prospect of which had been almost enough to make Alyssa wish the bullet *had* been a few millimetres further to the right. She'd tried insisting she was fine – claiming it was all a misunderstanding, that her bosses had got the wrong end of the stick and she hadn't even been there when it'd all kicked off – but to no avail. So she'd reverted to her tried and tested method for getting her mom off her back: being a belligerent little shit. She'd goaded her something rotten, calling her 'Diane' and doing that California valley girl thing she knew drove her nuts, adding inflections to the ends of her sentences, turning flat statements into questions. 'I don't *want* you here,' she'd finally snapped when her mom still refused to take the hint. It had done the trick, and the call had ended the way they always did – with her mom in a sulk and Alyssa feeling guilty for even existing.

'And how are you feeling now?' Metcalfe interrupted her thoughts. 'Up to answering some of our questions?'

Alyssa leant on the doorframe, as if expecting it to lend her moral support. 'Do I need a lawyer?'

'Do *you* think you need a lawyer?' said Metcalfe enigmatically, then gave an unexpected smile. She had an intriguingly asymmetrical face, one eye slightly more open than the other, one side of her mouth turning up while the other turned down. 'No, I don't think you need one, but that's your prerogative, and if you prefer . . . '

Alyssa sighed. 'No, it's OK.' Stepping past the two detectives, she plonked herself on the sofa and stared up at them, arms spread across the backrest in her best come-at-me pose. 'Ask away.'

They asked a whole bunch of questions that to her seemed trivial and unrelated to the small matter of being shot. How long she'd been in Scotland, what sort of a visa she was here on, what she did before working in the library, and so on. It occurred to her that if they were any sort of detectives at all, they must know all this information already, and she wondered whether they were testing her to make sure she was on the level – like when you take a lie detector test and they start by asking your favourite flavour of ice cream so they've got a baseline to refer back to once they start asking where you hid the body. Metcalfe did all the talking, perched on the armchair facing the sofa, leaning forward with her hands folded between her knees, with the taciturn DS Renshaw standing behind her, taking notes in a small pocketbook and saying nothing. Metcalfe's manner was brisk and business-like, which suited Alyssa fine. The last thing she wanted was more handholding. Nor, however, was Metcalfe completely heartless, and her occasional sympathetic lip curls came across as genuine.

Gradually, she steered the conversation to the morning of The Event, asking Alyssa about her route to work, what form of transportation she'd used, whether she'd seen anyone acting suspiciously – either outside or inside the library. Alyssa said no, not that she could recall. She didn't want to admit that her memory of that time was decidedly hazy, the individual fragments all jumbled up in the wrong order. She tried to picture her colleagues – where they were, what they were doing. Two of them had been arguing about something – Jason and Laura, she thought, or was it Jason and Eva? About some library procedure one of them didn't agree with. And then there was the guy who'd been kicked off the computers for some transgression, the nature of which she couldn't remember.

'Porn?' suggested Metcalfe.

'That's right. How did you . . . ?'

Metcalfe arched a knowing eyebrow. 'When is it anything else? Can you remember his name?'

Ram-something. Ramsgate? Rammstein? That didn't sound right. Alyssa shrugged. 'Sorry.'

'That's all right. If it comes back to you, you can always get in touch. And what happened when he was kicked off the computers? Was there a confrontation?'

Alyssa racked her brains, trying to visualise the scene. 'Kinda. He came up to the desk and mouthed off a bit, said there was going to be a reckoning and the staff were gonna be sorry. But then he left, and I don't think . . . ' She trailed off.

'Don't think what?' said Metcalfe.

Alyssa gave a small, sheepish laugh, though she wasn't sure what was supposed to be so funny. 'I mean, I don't think it could have been *him*. Not unless he was dumb enough to announce his plans to commit mass murder in front of witnesses, *and* was organised enough to have a disguise and a gun conveniently stashed somewhere nearby for him to pick up and come back with just a few minutes later. And one kinda rules out the other, doesn't it?'

Metcalfe gave no indication as to whether it did or not. 'Let's talk about the shooter. When were you first aware of his presence?'

Alyssa's throat tightened. She'd been doing her best to avoid thinking about The Event itself, high-tailing it in the opposite direction whenever she found her mind wandering back to the library. Now, though, they were going to make her relive it, the bastards. She swallowed, forcing the saliva down like it was glue.

'I heard footsteps in the foyer. One of the staff – Laura, I think – gasped or squealed or something. I turned to see what was happening, and he was just standing there on the other side of the desk.'

'How was he dressed?'

'Black ski-mask. Black gloves. Black coat.'

'What sort of coat?'

'A duffle coat, I think. You know, with toggles. Thick, heavy, reached down almost to his knees. But I . . . I don't . . . '

'What about his physique? Was he tall, short, fat, thin . . . ?'

'Average height, I guess. Five foot eight, five foot nine? That's normal, right?'

Again, Metcalfe neither confirmed nor denied this. Behind her, Renshaw's pen was scratching away furiously.

'But I can't tell you about his build. He could've been anything under that coat. I mean, not a great big fatty or anything, obviously, but . . . '

'What about ethnicity?'

'Well, I mean, he was covered up from head to toe, just his eyes visible . . . but I'm pretty sure he was white.'

'And did you happen to notice what colour his eyes were?'

Alyssa thought about it. 'Grey, I think. Or maybe blue. Or brown. I don't . . . ' She shrugged helplessly.

'So,' Metcalfe steepled her hands together, 'you heard footsteps entering the library, your colleague reacted verbally, you turned, and there he was, standing at the desk. What then?'

BANG. Jason's face explodes.

Alyssa clenched her eyes shut.

BANG. Laura goes down with a bullet in her chest.

BANG. A hole appears in Eva's forehead.

BANG. Davy takes one in the back.

'And then . . . and then he shot them. One by one. Bang-bang-bang-bang, just like that.'

And now they're dead. All of them. All dead, except me.

The knowledge filled Alyssa with such bottomless despair that she could have wept there and then, and only the limited remnants of self-respect that she clung to prevented her from doing so.

Metcalfe nodded sombrely. 'And then he shot you.'

'And then he shot me.'

Something in her voice must have hinted at her anxiety, for Metcalfe reached across the expanse of the coffee table and squeezed her hand. 'It's OK. Take your time.'

'I'm all right,' Alyssa insisted, jerking her hand away. 'It's just . . . it's just something that happened, y'know? No point getting sentimental about it.'

Metcalfe looked rather sceptical, but she didn't pause for more than a second or two before resuming her questions.

'And did he at any point say anything?'

Alyssa shook her head. 'I said "Don't hurt me, I'm new", something like that. But he never said a word. He just looked at me, then pointed the gun at me and—'

BANG. A sudden, intense pressure to her temple, like someone had just cuffed her hard, knocking the wind clean out of her. Adrenaline coursing through her veins. A thousand electric shocks exploding throughout her skull.

'And . . . and just as he shot me, I ducked.'

Metcalfe frowned. 'Ducked? That was lucky.'

Lucky. Alyssa felt the blood rising in her cheeks. Throughout her twenty-four-hour stay in hospital, she'd heard that word more times than she could count. She hadn't felt it then, and she didn't feel it now. Luck would have been starting work a day or a week or several months later, or in a different library, or not in a library at all. As it was, she was convinced the only thing that had saved her had been her own quick thinking. Luck didn't come into it.

'And after he shot you, while you were lying there on the floor, did you see or hear anything?'

She was back there now, lying in a heap behind the desk with her head resting on the backs of Jason's – or was it Eva's? – legs, eyes clenched shut, trying her damnedest not to shake or cry or breathe or do anything to draw attention to the fact that she was still alive, all the time conscious of the blood running from the side of her head into her eye socket.

She shook her head. 'Sorry. I . . . I think maybe I blacked out for a bit. Next thing I knew, someone had their fingers on the side of my neck, and then there was a whole lot of shouting, and then someone was shining a torch in my eyes and asking me if I knew where I was.'

'And there's absolutely nothing else you can tell us about the gunman? A distinctive smell, maybe, or something about his overall demeanour, or . . . '

Alyssa shut her eyes, forcing herself to rewind to those last agonising seconds before the shooter pulled the trigger, willing a concrete image to form.

She shook her head. 'No, nothing. He was just kinda . . . *ordinary*, y'know? I mean, apart from the ski-mask and the gun and everything. Like, he didn't have a limp or a lazy eye or smell of garlic or anything.'

Metcalfe reached into her handbag – a clapped-out, rather tasteless beige affair – and handed over a print-out. It showed a police mugshot of a gaunt-faced man with short black hair in a buzz-cut and a slack-jawed expression that made him look surprised to be there, wherever 'there' was. He stared back at the camera with sunken, haunted eyes. Alyssa took one look at him and thought *junkie.* She put him in his late twenties, but he looked so ravaged by the effects of whatever he was on that it was hard to be sure.

'Recognise him?'

Alyssa shook her head. 'Don't think so, sorry. Who is he?'

'Just a person of interest.'

'A suspect, you mean?'

Metcalfe pursed her lips disapprovingly. 'He's one of several people we're actively investigating.'

And yet you haven't shown me photos of any of the others.

Metcalfe got to her feet, shouldering her handbag. Renshaw closed his pocketbook and slipped it inside his suit jacket.

'Well, thank you for answering our questions,' said Metcalfe, smoothing down the creases in her slacks. 'It can't be easy, reliving what happened.'

Alyssa stared up at her. 'So that's it?'

'For now. If we have further questions, we'll be in touch.' She took a business card out of her bag and handed it to Alyssa. 'My number. If anything else comes back to you – anything at all, no matter how unimportant it might seem – you can reach me there.'

Alyssa took the card and tossed it on the table without looking at it.

'I'm serious,' said Metcalfe. 'Any time, day or night. We don't have office hours in our line of work.'

Out of obligation, Alyssa saw the two detectives out.

'So what's next for Glasgow's finest?' she said, opening the door for them. 'D'you get to go home and put your feet up, or have you got more honest citizens to harass?'

She meant it as a joke, but it just came out sounding smarmy and impertinent, like an obnoxious kid fishing for street cred. She winced internally as her words hung in the air like a ripe fart.

Metcalfe smiled thinly. 'No rest for the wicked, I'm afraid. We might fit in a spot of skull-bashing later, but right now we're heading to the Southern General to see if your colleague's up to speaking to us.'

She said it so matter-of-factly it took Alyssa a moment to actually process what she'd heard.

'Hospital? Colleague?' The words came spilling out of her mouth like verbal vomit, her brain stubbornly refusing to process what she was hearing.

'The other survivor. Davy Grogan.' Metcalfe looked at Alyssa like she was touched.

'I . . . I thought they all died.' *I saw them. I SAW them all getting shot.*

'So did everyone, it seems – us included. Turns out, though, that he's very much alive – and I'm sure he'd be thrilled to see you.'

4

Six days after

Alyssa stepped out of the elevator and onto the floor of one of the many recovery wards at the Southern General. Her hands, hanging limp by her sides, felt heavy and oversized, like cumbersome, unwanted appendages that served no earthly function. She wished she had something to do with them. She tried putting them in her pockets, but that felt too nonchalant, like she was making light of the situation or whatever. She should have brought fruit or a bunch of flowers or something – you know, the things normal people do when they're sick-visiting.

She wiped her clammy palms on the backs of her jeans and approached the enquiry desk, where a young nurse in blue scrubs was writing up notes with a ballpoint pen. She looked up, her expression instantly melting into one of saccharine pity.

'Oh my, what's happened to *you*?' she exclaimed, oozing sympathetic condescension.

Alyssa automatically lifted her hand to tuck her hair behind her ear, only for her fingers to brush against the dressing taped to the side of her head. She'd been doing that a lot lately.

'I'm here to see someone,' she said stiffly.

'I'm afraid you're in the wrong part of the hospital, then.

46

Outpatients is back down thataway.' The nurse pointed her pen over Alyssa's shoulder.

'What? No, I'm not here for myself. I've come to visit another patient. Davy Grogan? I was told he was here?'

'Oh. *Oh!*' The nurse looked like she wasn't sure whether to be relieved or disappointed. 'Sorry, I thought . . . I mean . . . ' She waved her hand as if trying to flap away all the awkwardness. 'He'll be so happy to see a friendly face,' she added, with the sort of wholesome, infantilising smile that made Alyssa want to punch her teeth out.

'If you could just point me in the right direction . . . '

In the end the nurse insisted on escorting her personally, all the while chirping about what an absolute tragedy it was what happened, how you wouldn't believe something like that could ever happen *here*, not in Glasgow, oh my, no. America, yes, but then, they were all gun crazy over there. And then she caught herself and apologised profusely, saying she hadn't meant any offence. Alyssa, not wanting to get drawn into anything approaching a conversation with this irritating little ray of sunshine, chose not to correct her.

They came to a door near the end of the corridor. The nurse stopped and turned to face Alyssa. 'Before we go in, you kinda need to prepare yourself. It's . . . pretty full-on.'

It sounded like one of those disclaimers they always put on before horror movies or films with lots of humping. *Caution: viewer discretion advised.* How bad could it possibly be?

She soon found out. The nurse swung the door open and Alyssa stepped over the threshold to find herself in a brightly lit room dominated by a large hydraulic bed. There, dwarfed by a dizzying array of bleeping machines and pulsing monitors, was Davy. He looked like death warmed up, with a greyish complexion and oxygen tubes protruding from his nostrils. His eyes were closed, his head lolling slightly to one side, and, from the rise and fall of his not inconsiderable bulk beneath the blanket, he looked to be sound asleep. By his side sat a squat, middle-aged woman, hands clasped in her lap, eyes fixed on him. She didn't seem to have noticed they had visitors – or, perhaps more likely, deemed it an irrelevance.

'I'll leave you to it,' said the nurse, then reversed out and shut the door behind her with a soft click.

Alyssa remained where she was, feeling distinctly like she was intruding on some deeply private moment. She was giving serious consideration to beating a hasty retreat when the woman by the bed lifted her head and smiled.

'Oh, hello. You must be Davy's friend.'

She had a wholesome sort of face, her smile warm and welcoming in spite of the obvious strain she was under. The resemblance was unmissable: she must be Davy's mother.

'No. I mean, sort of. I mean, we work together. Worked together. Briefly.'

'I'm Sharon.' The woman got to her feet, extended a hand across the bed. Alyssa leaned forward, shook it limply. 'And you'll be Alyssa.'

'How did you . . . ?'

'Davy's spoken about you.'

'He . . . he has?' The revelation took her by surprise. She couldn't imagine what she could possibly have said or done during the brief time they'd spent together to have made such a lasting impression on him. 'Why?' she added, a touch apprehensively. 'What's he said?'

Sharon made a rueful face. 'To be honest, he's not been making a whole lot of sense. He's been pretty out of it. The stuff they've got him on is fairly heavy-duty.'

Alyssa chanced another look at Davy. She was once again struck by how deathly pale he was, and by the sheer quantity of machines to which he was hooked up. She wondered if they were all just there to tell the doctors he was still alive, or if any of them were actively assisting in this state of affairs.

Sharon smiled sympathetically. 'It's a lot to take in, I know. It was touch and go for a while. They reckon he's going to be OK, but . . . ' She trailed off, seemingly reluctant to follow that train of thought to wherever it led, then cleared her throat. 'Would you like to sit with him for a bit? I could do with stretching my legs, but I didn't like to leave him.'

Alyssa opened her mouth to object, but Sharon was already moving towards the door, giving her shoulder a grateful squeeze as she passed. 'Won't be long,' she whispered, before slipping out.

As the door shut behind her, Alyssa's eyes drifted over to Davy again. The thought of sitting vigil by his sickbed held about as much appeal as getting her teeth drilled, but she couldn't bring herself to just slink away. So she took herself over to the bed, eyeing the various accoutrements piled on every available surface – from the cliché-defying bag of grapes and 'get well' cards to an oversized teddy with a bandage round its head. Davy certainly didn't lack for fans.

As her gaze came to rest on him once more, he opened a solitary eye. 'She gone?'

She could scarcely have been more surprised if he'd risen from the grave right in front of her.

With no answer forthcoming, Davy opened his other eye. 'Thank the Lord. I thought she'd never leave.'

Alyssa, unable to contain herself any longer, exploded with a barrage of half-formed questions. 'But what . . . ? How did you . . . ? *When* did you . . . ?'

'About a half-hour after they evacuated *you*, it would seem,' said Davy, parsing the intent behind her spluttered outburst with remarkable deftness for someone in his condition. 'I figured you and the others were goners, so there wasn't much point my sticking around out of solidarity. I wasn't writing off the possibility of our friendly neighbourhood killer coming back to finish the job, so I guessed I needed to at least *try* to get myself to safety. Managed to drag myself as far as the second row of shelves before I gave up the ghost. Must've gave the poor officer who found me quite the fright, tripping over me between the Romances and the Spoken Words.'

He gave a feeble little chuckle, as if this was some fond memory which kept him warm on long winter nights. Alyssa didn't join in. Even if she lived to be a hundred, she doubted she'd ever feel able to make light of what had happened that day.

'But why did no one *tell* me? It was that policewoman, Metcalfe, who let slip. Said she was off to interview you, like it was common knowledge.'

'Well, you know how it is. Probably the usual blend of red tape and good old-fashioned incompetence. I doubt anyone *deliberately* kept you in the dark. So riddle me this,' he went on, as Alyssa slipped into the empty chair by the bed, 'how comes it's taken you till now to come and see me? Metcalfe and her boyfriend spoke to me on Wednesday. It's Sunday now. Anyone'd think you'd been avoiding me.'

'Well, I . . . I mean, I've been recovering myself,' muttered Alyssa, aware of how feeble it sounded. 'And I didn't . . . well, I wasn't sure if you were up to having visitors.'

Davy shrugged nonchalantly. 'Hey, it's cool. You're a busy gal, got your own life to lead. Good thing I'm not the jealous type, mind.'

'Yeah, terrific. So you knew all along I'd pulled through, then?'

Davy adopted a conspiratorial whisper. 'Don't mean to alarm you, but there's a lovely picture doing the rounds of you being whisked out of the building by a pair of strapping young men in uniform. Mm-hmm,' he nodded, as Alyssa stared at him in a mix-ture of amazement and horror, 'you heard right. You made the front page of the *Tribune*. And the *Chronicle*, and the *Morning News*, and every other two-bit gutter rag in the land. They blanked out your face but, um, kinda obvious from the tats who it was. Some local gawker with a cameraphone is laughing all the way to the bank as we speak.'

Alyssa rolled her eyes. 'I should demand royalties.'

Davy grinned. 'You should. You'd be able to retire early on the proceeds. And hey – don't sweat it about not coming to see me straight away. I get that you've had other things to deal with. Would've come looking for you myself, only I'm not exactly mobile at the moment.'

Alyssa smiled. She was starting to relax, almost enjoying the easy back-and-forth between the two of them. 'And the others? Laura and Eva and whatsisname aren't suddenly gonna come crawling out of the woodwork, are they?'

Any trace of a smile left Davy's face. 'No, they're all gone,' he said quietly.

An unhappy silence fell. For a while they said nothing, looking anywhere but at each other.

At length, Alyssa broke the impasse. 'So tell me, were the cops as cagey with you as they were with me?'

Davy shook his head, his features compressing into a scowl. 'They've got it all wrong. Barking up the wrong tree entirely. I tried to tell them—'

But before he got any further, footsteps sounded in the corridor. The door swung open and Sharon re-entered the room, the nurse hot on her heels. Davy instantly shut his mouth like a Venus flytrap.

'There now.' Sharon stood at the foot of the bed, beaming obliviously at all and sundry. 'I've had my constitutional, I'm fed and I'm watered.' She smiled at Alyssa and Davy in turn. 'Did the two of you have a nice talk?'

'Yes, Mrs Grogan,' said Alyssa, before she could stop herself. It felt like she was a little girl again, on a playdate with one of the other kids from school.

Davy gave a yawn that, to Alyssa's eyes and ears, was far too theatrical to convince. It had the intended effect, however.

'And now,' said the nurse, stepping forward and giving Alyssa a severe look, 'it's way past time for you to go. Can't have you tiring out our star patient – not after all he's been through. He needs to keep his strength up.'

Feeling more like an errant child than ever, Alyssa relinquished the chair to Sharon and allowed herself to be escorted out by the nurse. As they reached the door, she stole a glance back at the bed and saw Davy miming the words *call me*, thumb and forefinger to his ear.

She didn't, and, as the days gave way to weeks, the impetus to do so grew less and less. She had an uneasy feeling he expected them to be forever bonded by their shared trauma, and with the best will in the world, that wasn't something she was looking for in her life right now. At one point, she rang the ward and asked how he was doing, only to be told – after much humming and hawing about patient confidentiality – that he'd been moved to a specialist unit to continue his recovery. She supposed she could probably have asked for contact details, but that was a step more than she was prepared to take in the name of maintaining what barely amounted to a passing acquaintance. As a result, she never did get to the bottom of what he'd been about to tell her before his mother and the nurse interrupted him, and gradually, one thing and another drove it from her mind.

Metcalfe and her mute assistant came to see her once more just over a week after their initial visit. They asked a series of follow-up questions and clarified a few extant matters, but there wasn't much Alyssa could tell them that she hadn't during her original interview, and they remained as tight-lipped as ever when she asked if they'd made any progress on apprehending the shooter. She also received a visit from a tall, scrawny woman in a power-suit, with long, claw-like nail extensions and the sort of complexion no one got in Scotland without regular visits to a tanning salon. She introduced herself as Nikki Wyatt, the Director of Library Services, and expressed the entire organisation's deep and profound regret that Alyssa had had such a traumatic introduction to her new job. She told Alyssa she was to take all the time she needed and to not even *think* about coming back to work until she was completely ready and that, furthermore, the company was prepared to award her a generous cash settlement – subject, of course, to her signing a waiver agreeing not to pursue damages. She was accompanied by a grey-haired, grey-faced man in a grey suit, carrying a grey briefcase, and whose role in the affair, if it hadn't already been apparent, was now toe-curlingly obvious.

'I must stress,' she said, 'that this is in no way an admission of any culpability on the part of North Kelvin District Libraries. Rather, it's a gesture in recognition of the emotional and physical trauma you endured, and of how highly we value our extended council family.'

It sounded like grade-A horseshit to Alyssa, and, if she'd been in a more robust frame of mind, she'd have told them to take a running jump and then sue them for all they were worth. As it happened, though, she'd had a particularly bad night – plagued by the same nightmares about drowning in that dark, endless sea that had blighted her sleep since The Event – and she hadn't the stomach for a fight. Besides, she hadn't made her mind up yet about what she was going to do about work. The thought of resuming her employment with the libraries seemed like someone's idea of a bad joke, and as such, she was minded to simply cut her losses, take the money they were dangling in front of her and run for the nearest hill. So she signed the multi-page document placed in front of her by the grey man, barely glancing at the wall of dense type, and heaved a sigh of relief when they finally left.

Two weeks after The Event, a memorial service – attended by the great and the good and trailed heavily by the media – was held at Glasgow Cathedral for Eva Baldini, 57, Laura Craddock, 30 and Jason Stockridge, 42. Alyssa was invited, of course, but she put the letter straight in the bin. Churches gave her the heebie-jeebies at the best of times, and she could think of few things more depressing than sitting on a cold pew, listening to a bunch of people giving speeches about the victims and how they'd been cruelly taken before their time. Besides, it would have felt like gate-crashing, somehow. She'd been their colleague for a grand total of fifteen minutes. She hadn't known them, not really, and she wouldn't have known any of the other mourners either. Apart from Davy, of course. She imagined he would have been there front and centre, looking sombre in his black suit and tie. Sombre? No – on second thoughts, she couldn't picture him in anything approaching a funereal frame of mind. He'd be one of those 'don't mourn their passing, celebrate their lives' types, telling humorous anecdotes about his late colleagues; perhaps cracking an inappropriate joke or two to lighten the mood. Another reason to be glad she hadn't gone.

From time to time she wondered what progress the police were making, and at times she was sorely tempted to check her phone or the TV to see what was being said. But she resisted the urge. She knew from experience that once she got started, she'd get sucked in and be unable to resist pouring over all the news and commentary relating to the shootings. Which, she concluded, wouldn't do her the slightest good. For the sake of her sanity, it was better to disconnect from the Matrix for a bit. She knew she'd have to switch her phone on sooner or later, and that when she did, she'd find her email and assorted social media accounts full to brimming with messages from concerned well-wishers, each demanding an individual and personalised response. And she would, in time, reconnect and respond. For now, though, she was content to exist in limbo, detached from it all, making the most of her invalid status – excused, for now at any rate, from participating in the great con known as adulting. She could afford to rest easy. After all, the worst was over.

Wasn't it?

5

Gordo made his way down the slope of Saltcoats Street, eyes glued to the glowing screen of his phone. He grinned to himself as he watched the shaky, handheld footage of a teenager not much older than himself lining up his bike to face the makeshift ramp – consisting of a sheet of plywood balanced on top of an overturned dustbin – in the middle of an otherwise empty road in what looked to be a housing estate. Off-screen, his friends could be heard shouting encouragement to him. 'Go on, Dougie, you can do it' and the like.

'S'all right, lads,' he declared, raising both hands for calm. 'I got this. Nae danger.'

Gordo came to a standstill and, pausing the video with a tap on the screen, turned to look over his shoulder. The street behind him was deserted, the ageing tenement buildings on either side looming dark and foreboding against the bruised night sky. He'd heard something. What, he couldn't say. Whatever it was, it had been all but drowned out by the hooting and hollering on the video. But he was sure he'd heard *something*. He listened intently, trying to screen out the far-off sounds of traffic from the main road. Nothing. He resumed the video and moved on again.

On the screen, the tension was building, the off-screen cheerleaders chanting *Jump! Jump! Jump!* while the star of the show bounced up and down on his seat, psyching himself up for his daredevil stunt. *Jump! Jump! Jump!*

'Jump! Jump! Jump!' Gordo found himself mouthing the words in time with the others, all his attention focused on the jittery, pixelated image on the screen, the noise he'd heard earlier completely forgotten.

Finally, with a sudden movement – which the video, struggling to keep up, rendered as a cluster of giant, blocky pixels – the cyclist shot forward, haring it up the road towards the makeshift ramp, buttocks raised up off the seat, legs pumping up and down like pistons. He reached the ramp in a matter of seconds, shot up it and flew into the air. For a brief moment, it was as if he was suspended in space, soaring high above the ground like a bird. Then, with crushing, brutal reality, the rules of gravity kicked in and he went plummeting back down to earth. He hit the concrete with a vicious crunch which Gordo heard even on the tinny speakers of his phone, and lay still.

Gordo's first instinct – as it so often is when people are presented with a gruesome sight beyond their understanding – was to laugh. He came to a standstill and watched, rapt, as the cyclist's friends tore across the concrete towards him. He saw their pounding legs, viewed at an angle – the cameraman had dropped his phone, abandoning it to join the charge to his downed companion. Gordo watched as they gathered round the cyclist in a nervous semi-circle, hanging back slightly, fearing to get too close. One of them finally plucked up the courage to bend down and shake his shoulder. He didn't move.

'No way, man,' Gordo breathed, shaking his head as the reality of what he'd just witnessed slowly dawned on him. 'That's not right.'

Those were the last words to ever leave his mouth. Even as he pinched the screen, trying to zoom the image in to get a better look at the morbid spectacle, he sensed movement behind him.

The knife sliced across his throat with savage precision, his attacker gone before he even had time to process what had happened, melting into the dark like a shadow. His hands rose to stem the flow of blood, but it was too late. For a few moments, they scrabbled uselessly at the slick skin below the long horizontal slash just above his Adam's apple. Then they went slack and he slumped to his knees. He remained like that for a few seconds, swaying like a reed in a gentle breeze, before toppling sideways.

By the time his cheek touched the concrete it was already too late.

6

For the next couple of weeks, Alyssa didn't leave the flat at all. She mooched around in her PJs, binge-watching empty-headed popcorn movies and cheery, undemanding sitcoms or playing games on Xbox Live Arcade – comfortingly retro titles with bright colours and cheery music. For the time being, there was enough food in the fridge, provided she didn't mind existing on a diet consisting exclusively of Pot Noodles, and she avoided having to go to the launderette by wearing the same clothes for as long as possible. Amazing what you could get away with when you were prepared to tolerate your own stink. Sooner or later, though, she knew she was going to have to bite the bullet and engage with the outside world again.

She got her first taste of human interaction when, early on Saturday afternoon, her friends showed up at her door unannounced. She would have preferred her reintroduction to society to have taken place on her own terms, at a time and place of her choosing, but like it or not, there they were: Spud, Gobby and Jenny, all crammed into the narrow hallway outside her flat, grinning from ear to ear as she opened the door and waltzing in like they owned the place.

'So this is where you've been hiding,' said Spud, flopping down on the sofa and spreading himself across the entire length of it. 'You know what they're calling you? Arachnophobic Alyssa.'

'It's *agora*phobic, ya turnip,' said Jenny, slapping his legs to make him budge up. 'Arachnophobia's fear of spiders.'

'We heard you got shot,' grinned Gobby. 'Like, with a gun. It was in the papers and everything.'

'Like *you* read the papers,' said Spud, rolling his eyes as Jenny gave up trying to get him to shift and simply plonked herself on top of his legs. 'He saw the photos of you on Twitter,' he explained to Alyssa. 'I mean, your face was blurred out, but straight away we were like, "That's Alyssa!"'

'And you waited till now to come and see if I was OK,' said Alyssa, baring her teeth in a parody of a smile. 'That's . . . heart-warming.'

Gobby continued to stare at Alyssa with a relish she found decidedly off-putting. 'So what was it like? Were you dead scared? Did you see your life passing before your eyes?'

Alyssa realised all three of them were staring at her intently in anticipation of an answer. For a couple of seconds there was total silence, punctuated only by faint sounds from the street outside.

'Nah,' she said, with a casual shrug and shake of her head. 'Piece of piss. Played too much *Call of Duty* in my time to be fazed by some dude sticking a peashooter in my face.'

Again, there was a period of awkward silence as the trio processed what they'd just heard. Then Spud burst out laughing, followed by the other two. Then Alyssa, concluding that it was best to go with the flow, joined in as well, and the four of them spent a great deal of time in hysterics over something that really wasn't funny. Like, at *all*. But her glibness had done the trick. It had broken the ice and reset the dynamic between them to its default state, jettisoning any awkwardness or need for the others to tread on eggshells around her. Not that Spud, Jenny and particularly Gobby had ever been known for their tact. But it was undeniably nice to spend some time in the company of people who didn't feel the need to treat her like a victim or tiptoe around the facts of what had happened to her. They all wanted to see the wound and to touch it – as if, by doing so, the power to deflect speeding bullets would be magically transferred to them.

'You should get a buzzcut all over,' said Jenny, stroking the shaved part of Alyssa's head, where a layer of stubble had now grown. 'Then you'd be like Furiosa from *Mad Max* . . . 'cept, y'know, with both your arms.'

'Yeah, no thanks,' said Alyssa. 'With my big old head, I'd probably end up looking more like Britney Spears in her wackadoodle period.'

'Oh, I nearly forgot,' Spud exclaimed, 'this was lying on your doormat when we got here.'

He took a small red envelope out of his pocket and handed it to Alyssa. There was nothing written on the outside. She tore it open and pulled out a 'get well soon' card – as generic and plain-looking as you'd find in any number of shops. As she opened it, hoping to find some indication as to who'd sent it, a solitary crushed flower slid out and landed on the floor. An iris, starkly white against the dark hardwood surface.

As her heart rate ramped up, the card – its interior as blank as the envelope it had come in – fell from her suddenly limp hand. But she didn't need a 'yours faithfully' to know who it was from. There was only one person in this city who'd have sent her *that* flower.

Ignoring the questioning looks from her friends, she hurried to the door, wrenched it open and leaned out into the hallway. She looked left and right, but there was no sign of anyone. Of course there wasn't. Why would there be? The person who delivered the card would have been and gone long before Spud and the others got here.

Please, she thought, *don't let this be starting again.*

She stood in the doorway, arms wrapped tight around herself, suddenly feeling chilled to the bone. Behind her, she sensed the presence of her three friends, all saying nothing. Stunned into silence, probably. She could hardly blame them. She must have properly put the wind up them with her freakish behaviour.

Steeling herself, she turned to face them with a big, breezy smile. 'So, who's up for some *Super Smash Bros*?'

Bit by bit, Alyssa re-engaged with civilisation. A couple of days later, she caught the bus into town to pick up her new Wayfarers from the optician, followed by a trip to Billy's Tattoo Parlour to add a new design to her already extensive collection of ink: a raised middle finger on her right flank – her way of commemorating her recent near-death experience and cocking a defiant snook at the fate she'd so narrowly avoided. The tattooist, a lanky guy in his twenties with massive plug earrings that brought his earlobes down to his shoulders, kept looking up from his work to stare, awestruck, at the scar on the side of her head.

'Did a *bullet* do that?' he breathed at one point.

She confirmed that this was indeed this case.

'How'd it happen?'

'Accident.'

He nodded sagely. 'Aye, you Americans, yese love yer guns, don't yese?'

She glared daggers at him, and he didn't say another word for the rest of the session.

That same day, she charged her phone for the first time since The Event. When it turned on, she was a little surprised by the lack of concerned OMG-are-you-OK messages waiting in her inbox, and couldn't decide whether she was relieved or disappointed. On balance, she supposed it didn't much matter. She'd probably have ignored them all anyway. Still, it would've been nice to think there were people out there who cared enough to at least dash off a pithy text or email expressing concern about her wellbeing.

Among the few correspondences waiting for her – which weren't automated messages trying to sell her erectile dysfunction tablets or persuade her to set up a standing order to save the dolphins – were a string of voicemails from a velvet-tongued man who introduced himself as Ewan Caulfield, a journalist with the *Glasgow Tribune*. He was *so* sorry to intrude on her at what must be an incredibly difficult time, but did she think she would feel up to giving him a few words for an article he was writing about the Library Murders? Often with a trauma, he said, talking through the experience had a profoundly liberating effect. It would be a chance for her to put forward her side of the story. After all, when a crime was committed, the victim's point of view was all too often forgotten. Over a period of several weeks, the messages had become both more frequent and more belligerent, as his bosses no doubt intensified the squeeze on his nuts for a result. God alone knew how he'd managed to get hold of her number.

And so life went on, with one day blending into the next until she'd completely lost track of any discernible metric of time. Not that it was all fun and games. On the contrary, she slowly but surely came to realise that The Event had changed her in all sorts of unexpected ways – as if the act of the bullet colliding with her head had shaken up her brain, causing it to make connections it hadn't previously. She began to notice that everyday sounds had a power over her that they hadn't previously possessed. Sounds like one of her neighbours slamming a door or raised voices in the stairwell. In all, she counted at least three occasions where she'd heard something and instantly frozen, feet rooted to the spot, breath caught in her throat, the hairs on the back of her neck standing to attention. She hadn't become a gibbering, jelly-limbed wreck or anything like that – but all the same she was glad no one else had been around to witness these brief episodes. She'd even come to dread the way the refuse collectors noisily tossed their bins back onto the pavement once they'd finished emptying them, to the extent that she'd taken to setting her alarm for 6 a.m. so she was up before they arrived, blasting music out of her speakers at full volume to drown them out.

She'd also developed a marked aversion to chance encounters with the building's other inhabitants, and particularly dreaded situations where she found herself crossing paths with someone else in the dank stairwell with its solitary, perpetually malfunctioning light. Without consciously working at it, she'd cut her excursions to the bare minimum, streamlining her weekly visit to the supermarket and trip to the laundrette into a single journey and preparing a detailed shopping list – for which, if it had been anyone else, her former self would have ripped the piss mercilessly – to ensure she didn't end up in a situation where she discovered she'd unexpectedly run out of bog-roll or whatever and have to go out again. Whenever she was about to head out, she would stop at the door and listen to make sure the coast was clear. Only then would she emerge, hurrying down the stairs and out into the sunlight as quickly as possible, holding her breath until she felt the wind on her cheeks. On one occasion she was halfway down when she heard the main door below slamming as another resident entered the building. She instantly fled back upstairs, locked herself in her flat and didn't try again until several hours later, when the sun was sinking low in the sky and she knew she'd have to make a move now if she wanted to find the laundrette still open. She knew these fears were irrational; that the world hadn't suddenly become an inordinately more dangerous place at 9.35 a.m. on Monday the first of March, and that every person she encountered wasn't suddenly a potential rapist or serial killer. But knowing in a purely intellectual sense and *actually* knowing, on a deeper, more visceral level, were two entirely different things. As she'd come to realise, when your brain has become hardwired to anticipate the worst, all the rationalisation and appeals to reason in the world won't make a blind bit of difference.

And then, of course, there were the dreams. Since it had happened, she'd had at least one of them a week. Occasionally, she'd get a few days' respite, but that only meant a particularly nasty, vivid one was overdue. And then she'd get a run of them several nights in a row, each ending with her waking up gasping for breath and dripping with sweat, convinced she was dying. Once, she even managed to wet the bed in the process – something she hadn't done since pre-school, and even though there was no one around to see her, she felt so humiliated as she gathered up her sodden sheets that the whole affair might as well have been simulcast on every major TV network worldwide.

On a more positive note, there hadn't been any more creepy deliveries since the card and the iris the day Spud and the others had dropped by, and the more time that passed, the more she allowed herself to indulge the idea that that was as far as it was going to go. But it was only wishful thinking – a comforting lie of the sort grown-ups told to children. Deep down, she knew it was only a matter of time before *HE* made his presence felt again.

She would probably have carried on in this vein indefinitely, a virtual hermit existing on a diet of ready meals, *Super Smash Bros* and bad TV, had her present living circumstances not collided with the immovable force of financial reality. One morning, a little over six weeks after The Event, she woke to discover an email in her inbox informing her that her latest Netflix subscription payment had been declined. A visit to her online banking app swiftly shed light on the reason why: there was a grand total of £2.94 sitting in her account.

Going back through the transcript, she discovered that North Kelvin District Libraries had, two weeks ago, paid her first month's salary, amounting to the princely sum of £63.84 – which had been spent almost as soon as it had come in. The money she'd saved from her previous job – and which, until now, she'd been relying on to pay the rent – was long gone too. After a lengthy spell of staring at her screen in stupefied disbelief, she concluded someone in the finance department had simply made an honest mistake and set about calling Human Resources.

'There's no mistake,' said the woman at the other end of the line with a cheerfulness that seemed wholly inappropriate given the unfolding financial crisis. 'You had a seven-hour shift on Monday the first of March, for which you were paid the standard hourly rate for new hires of nine pounds and twelve pence.'

'Dude, what the actual . . . ' With considerable effort, Alyssa resisted the urge to scream obscenities down the phone. 'I've only worked one shift cos I've been off sick – on account of, y'know, getting shot in my actual head!'

'I'm *terribly* sorry,' cooed the woman from HR, 'but our sick pay entitlement only covers employees who've been with us for at least six months. I'm afraid it's council policy.'

By the time Alyssa put the phone down, she was practically shaking with rage. 'Take all the time you need,' Nikki Wyatt had said. Any reasonable person would have interpreted that as meaning *you put your feet up and let us take care of you*. This lot clearly had a thoroughly loose interpretation of the words 'duty of care'. Probably thought they were being generous paying her for the full seven hours instead of stopping the clock the second the bullet connected with her head. And no sign of her generous cash settlement either. She'd asked about it, naturally – only to be told that these things could take a few months to work their way through the system. Multiple forms to be filled out and signed in triplicate, et cetera.

She forced herself to stop pacing, plonked herself down on the sofa and tried to think things through rationally. Deep down, she'd always known the library wasn't going to carry on letting her continue as a lady of leisure on their dime indefinitely, but she'd thought they'd at least give her *something*. At the very least she'd assumed she'd have a bit more time before she actually had to make a decision about her future.

And she did have a decision to make – and a pretty major one at that. The idea of going back to work for the same company that had allowed her to take a bullet to the head would have been funny if it wasn't now staring her square in the face as a very real possibility. She could, she supposed, try to find a new job. But there was no guarantee she would be successful – not within the sort of timeframe the Home Office would consider acceptable for someone whose right to remain was dependent on her ability to support herself 'without recourse to public funds'. It had taken her long enough to secure the library gig, following a slew of rejection letters, and there weren't a whole lot of jobs out there for someone with her lack of qualifications – not ones that would support a roof over her head and still leave her with enough cash in hand to indulge her whims and vices, at any rate.

With a sinking feeling in the pit of her stomach, she realised she had about as much choice in the matter as a condemned man being asked to choose which variety of rope he'd like to be hanged with. She picked up the phone and called HR.

7

Seven weeks after

Alyssa gazed up at the ageing granite building and drew in a deep breath. On some abstract level she recognised the grim humour in her being back here, standing on more or less the same spot as she had on the morning of March the first, minutes before her world changed beyond recognition. She didn't feel much like laughing, though – not even ironically.

There had been a lot of handwringing about where Alyssa was going to be placed on her return to the bosom of the North Kelvin District Council family. Initially, she'd been promised a posting in a branch far away from Thornhill – because of course, the HR lady had said, it would be completely unreasonable to expect Alyssa to go back there after what had happened to her. A couple of days later, however, she'd received another call from the same HR lady, now adopting a contrite and rather sheepish tone. With much umming and erring, she admitted that actually, in spite of what she'd said previously, it might not be possible to move Alyssa to an alternative venue and would she perhaps consider a return to Thornhill? It was entirely her decision, and they wouldn't feel remotely comfortable about insisting. It was just that – well, there were no vacancies elsewhere, and they *were* having an *awful* time finding people willing to work there, even though it was *preposterous* to think something like that could *ever* happen there again. They *could* perhaps transfer her to one of the South Kelvin facilities if she'd feel more comfortable working elsewhere, but that would mean a whole lot of paperwork – different local authority, you see – and there was no guarantee she'd end up in a library as opposed to, say, a gym or a youth centre. Besides, there was a lot to be said for getting things back to normal as quickly as possible . . . Sensing that any suggestion of choice was purely illusory, Alyssa had conceded defeat and agreed to a phased return starting the following Monday at 2 p.m., then promptly hung up and rung the bank to plead with them to extend her overdraft to tide her over till her first paycheque.

'Penny for your thoughts, wee pet.'

She turned to find a scruffy-looking man in a weather-beaten cagoule standing next to her, facing in the opposite direction. He appeared to have just come out of the library and was in the process of rolling a cigarette with nicotine-stained fingers. It took her a moment to recognise him as the homeless guy who'd asked her for change on the morning of The Event.

'I'm sorry, what?'

'You're looking a little shaken, if I may be so bold.'

'And what business is that of yours?' she retorted, automatically on the defensive.

If the man took offence at her tone, he didn't let it show. 'None whatsoever. Word of advice, though: if you're heading in there to use the lavvy, I'd give it a moment if I were you. Just came from there myself. Some inconsiderate git dropped an absolute steamer just before me, the aftertaste of which continues to linger in the back of one's throat.'

'I'll bear that in mind, thanks,' she said, and headed on into the building.

* * *

She'd expected to feel something as she crossed the threshold – a sharp twinge at the site of her head wound, perhaps, or some intangible, leaden sense of doom weighing her down. But there was nothing like that. Just the familiar poster of the non-Scottish non-family non-reading non-books, and what looked suspiciously like faecal matter that had been tramped into the foyer from outside. Canine or human – who could tell? In a way, it was weirdly anticlimactic. She's prepared herself for this being a monumentally challenging experience, but here she was standing in the foyer, mere feet away from where it had all gone down, her heart rate barely above one hundred.

The sight that greeted her when she stepped into the main library was a familiar one too. The trio of faces gathered behind the desk were different, but in every other respect the scene was instantly recognisable. She found herself sizing them up for tell-tale signs of insanity or whatever other personality defect could have persuaded them to accept this posting.

'Hey,' she said, pulling up to the counter, 'I'm—'

'Oh my God,' exclaimed one of the three – a pimply, red-haired lad who looked like shaving was still a relatively novel experience for him. 'You're *her*.'

'Her?'

'*Her*,' he insisted, as if saying it yet again helped clarify things. 'The one who survived! You're, like, a local celebrity around here or something. Shot in the head on your first day on shift. I mean, what were the odds of that?'

'What indeed,' said Alyssa, through clenched teeth.

'Leave the lassie alone, Stevie-boy,' said one of his colleagues – a solidly-built man in his fifties with the air of an old sea-dog. 'Sure if she'd wanted the red carpet rolling out, she'd've rang up in advance. That right, hen?' He turned to Alyssa with a commiserating smile. 'Wouldnae even organise a transfer for you, then? Evil shower a' bastards, so they are.'

'I don't see what all the hoopla's about,' said the third member of the band – a long-legged, distractingly attractive woman in her twenties with a flowing chestnut mane, massive bangles on both wrists and more than a hint of 'spoiled Indian princess' about her. 'It's not like she actually *did* anything.' She curled her lip in Alyssa's direction, in what Alyssa assumed was meant to be a smile. 'I mean, soz to be blunt, darling, but you didn't, did you?'

Alyssa took one look at this overly glammed-up dolly-bird and decided she disliked her immensely, but also that, of the three, she was the one coming closest to speaking a degree of sense, and thus deserving of her grudging respect.

'No, you're right,' she said. 'There wasn't much active participation on my part.'

The old sea-dog tutted. 'You're all heart, Bindi.'

Bindi gave a simpering smile. 'And you're a sap, Pat.' She glanced briefly in Alyssa's direction. 'Well, now she's here, someone should alert the Mistress of Pain.'

'That's what we call the boss,' Pat explained to Alyssa in an overly loud whisper, 'though not within her earshot, course.' He turned to Bindi. 'Any reason why that someone can't be your good self?'

Bindi made a simpering face. 'Love to, but I pulled a hamstring at pilates last week. Doctor says I'm to avoid stairs.'

'I can go,' Stevie said brightly, raising a hand like a kinder-gartener asking to be excused to go to the bathroom.

'You stay right where you are, sonny,' said Pat, moving to block Stevie's path. 'If the climb's too steep for her, she knows there's a perfectly good phone she can dial right there.'

'I would, but I've just had these done.' Bindi raised both her hands in front of her face, showing off a full set of alarmingly long extensions, the sight of which made Alyssa's own stubby, *au naturel* nails tingle painfully.

With a world-weary roll of his eyes, Pat took himself over to the phone, tapped out an extension and put the receiver to his ear. 'Madame,' he said, in silken tones, 'your two o'clock is here.' He put the phone down and turned to Alyssa. 'She'll be down in a minute.'

'You worked with Davy, then,' said Bindi, looking in Alyssa's direction while at the same time not quite *looking* at her.

'That's right, uh-huh.' *For all of fifteen minutes.*

'You should sign his card, then.'

Without further explanation, Bindi produced an oversized 'get well' card from under the desk and held it out in Alyssa's direction. Alyssa took it from her reluctantly.

'He's not come back to work, then?'

'Still off sick, poor mite.' Pat made a sympathetic face. 'Thought this'd cheer him up. We're having a whip-round too if ye feel like contributing. Nae pressure, mind. Only if ye want to.'

As she opened the card and skimmed the multiple messages of support covering virtually every free scrap of space, many of them lengthy and all of them effusive in their commiseration, Alyssa couldn't help but feel a tad cynical. Here she was back at work, while Davy, it seemed, was still milking the sick pay she'd been so cruelly denied. She grabbed a pen, scribbled 'Get well soon' in one of the few free bits of white space, and signed it 'A'.

Stevie, meanwhile, was still gawping at her with wide-eyed awe. 'I can't believe I'm talking to someone who literally got shot – like, for *real*. Is it true you faced him down while everyone else hit the deck?'

Actually, no, dumbass. I watched everyone else get blown away in front of me. He just happened to save me for last.

'So have you any idea who did it?' Stevie went on, seemingly incapable of taking the hint. 'We all had to go in and speak to the police one at a time. Weren't even allowed to take a union rep in with us.'

Bindi tutted. 'Shocking. And you without your appropriate adult. Can't imagine how you coped.'

'Aye, it's true,' Pat agreed, ignoring Bindi. 'Here – grab a pew. Nae sense standing on ceremony.'

He drew a stool out from under the counter. Alyssa, more out of politeness than because she actually wanted to, joined them behind the desk and plonked herself down, feeling a little like an exhibit – or a schoolchild in the dunce's seat.

'I reckon it was a random nutter, personally,' Pat went on, speaking in the authoritative tone of one who's seen it all. 'A crime as senseless as that, there's no point looking for rhyme or reason in it. Odds are the fella who *did* it doesn't even know why he did it. And that's assuming he even knows he did it.'

Bindi sniffed disdainfully. '*Please.* Whoever heard of a random nutter just waking up one morning and deciding to shoot up a library? A million to one it's one of our regulars. Someone who had their account locked or got short-changed by the photocopier or whatever.' She pirouetted to face Alyssa, actually making eye contact with her this time. 'You need to watch the types that come in here. They're an unsavoury lot – all criminals and soap-dodgers.' She half-glanced in the direction of a middle-aged woman who'd just shown up at the counter with an armful of books. 'Not you, darling, you're all right,' she said absentmindedly, before turning back to Alyssa again. 'Seriously, might want to avoid wearing your good clothes while you're working here. You never know whose bodily fluids you might be mopping up.'

Alyssa took one look at Bindi's sequined top and designer leggings and wondered what her good clothes must look like if these weren't them, then concluded that she of the pulled hamstring and freshly done nails probably had a ready-made set of reasons to excuse herself from any task involving bodily fluids.

'Well, if you ask *me*,' said Stevie, though no one had, 'I reckon it's some sort of a turf war.'

Pat gave a weary, paternalistic sigh and shook his head. 'Now, now, Stevie-boy, we've been through this before . . . '

'No, hear me out,' said Stevie in a petulant tone. He took to the centre of the work area, drawing himself up straight and puffing out his chest like he was gearing himself up to give a presentation to the rest of the class. 'The Craigslee Fleeto and the Thornhill Mental Posse have been at each other's throats since time began. We used to have terrible trouble with them. They'd come in here on a Thursday night, noising each other up right here in the library. One time Monica Ivanova went to break up a punch-up between a couple of them and got herself a black eye for her trouble.'

'Aye, but we're talking about a few weans getting intae scraps cos some'dy in one gang called one of the other lot a poofter,' said Pat. 'We're no exactly talking armed warfare here. Doubt any one of the wee scrotes ever handled a gun that didnae shoot water.'

'Well, it's a free country and I'm entitled to my opinion,' said Stevie, folding his arms sulkily.

'So we've heard from boy genius here,' said Bindi, somehow managing to sound even more contemptuous than before. 'Who do *you* think did it?'

Alyssa suddenly realised that all three of her new colleagues were staring at her intently, clearly anticipating a considered answer. Her throat suddenly felt dry, her tongue thick in her mouth.

'I quite honestly don't care,' she muttered.

There was silence for a moment, then Pat clapped his hands together, beaming approvingly. 'Quite right. Nae sense sweating the small stuff. What's done is done. *Que será, será.*'

Alyssa was spared any further awkwardness by the sound of footsteps clanging down the central staircase. A diminutive woman in her early forties with short, peroxide-blonde hair came into view, making up for her height disadvantage by affecting the gait and bearing of a seven-foot bodybuilder.

'Alyssa, *hi*,' she exclaimed, stepping behind the counter and laying a hand on each of Alyssa's forearms, even as Alyssa rose from the stool to meet her. 'So you made it. I'm so glad. I trust this lot have been treating you all right? Hopefully they've not been filling your head with all sorts of rubbish.' She gave the others a look that was more pantomime than truly reproachful.

'I can promise you, hand on heart, we've all of us been paragons of tact,' said Pat grandly.

The blonde woman scoffed. 'A likely story.' She turned to Alyssa. 'Come on – let's get the boring stuff out of the way and then you can start earning your crust. Follow me.'

Alyssa set off towards the stairs after her.

'I'm Denise Forsythe, by the way. I'm in charge of this madhouse . . . well, as in charge as I'm permitted to be. I'm what you'd call your classic middle manager – too far up the pecking order to qualify as one of the gang, too low down to make any *real* decisions. Mind how you go, by the way – the climb's pretty steep. We call it the crow's nest, on account of . . . well, you get the picture.'

As she followed Denise up the narrow spiral staircase, Alyssa glanced back and caught sight of Pat miming cracking a whip and grinning broadly.

'You're probably wondering,' Denise continued, the climb rendering her a trifle breathless, 'how it can be that this place is still standing after what happened. Believe me, it's a question I've asked myself countless times. I know there *were* discussions behind closed doors about demolishing it and starting from scratch at another site, but they never came to anything. They'd never have got permission to tear down a listed building, so it was either let it lie empty or put it to use. And besides, the council's too cash-strapped to fork out for a brand-new library when there's a perfectly good one standing right here.'

They reached the top floor. Denise ushered Alyssa into the

cluttered office, every available surface piled high with paperwork, books and old coffee mugs. 'Have a seat. I've got a whole lot of Health & Safety bumf which I'm obliged to get you to read before you can be declared fit to be unleashed on the public . . . but I've been here since the ass-crack of dawn this morning and I've got a nice bottle of Shiraz with my name on it waiting at home, so howsabout I just give you the gist and you can put your John Hancock on it?'

Alyssa couldn't help but feel a little thrown. *This* was the Mistress of Pain? She'd been anticipating some sort of dragon woman, tossing out diktats like they were candy and bawling out her staff at the smallest infraction. Instead she seemed kinda . . . nice?

'Sounds good to me.'

'By the way,' said Denise, 'I'm so sorry I wasn't around to welcome you on your first day.'

No you're not, Alyssa thought, *cos if you had been, chances are you'd have got a bullet in the brain.* But she managed to keep her mouth clamped firmly shut. No sense getting off on the wrong foot.

'On a semi-related note, I'm obliged to make you aware that North Kelvin District Libraries offers a comprehensive counselling service to any staff who've experienced stress or emotional trauma in the workplace.' Denise gave Alyssa a meaningful look. 'I'm not just saying that. We have a partnership with a top-notch firm, and I've only heard good things.'

Alyssa nodded unenthusiastically. 'Duly noted.'

'I'm serious. If you need to talk to someone about . . . well . . . '

Alyssa shook her head. 'Look, that sort of touchy-feely crap might work for some people, but it's not for me.' She shrugged – she hoped disarmingly. 'I'm here, aren't I? Give me a job and I'll do it. But don't expect me to bare my soul. Ask me no questions and I'll tell you no lies.'

Denise looked pensive for a moment, then gave a gruff nod, evidently considering the matter settled. 'Right.' She plonked a thick booklet on the desk. 'Have a quick skim through that and we'll call it even Stevens. Oh,' she added, as Alyssa flicked to the next page, 'and I'm going to put you down to go on an emergency first aid course just as soon as.'

That sounded a bit like shutting the stable door after the horse had bolted. 'You mean so if there's another shooting, I can tend the wounded with bandages and sticking-plaster?'

Denise looked at her for a long, hard moment. 'No,' she said, her tone now decidedly chilly. 'It's something we send all our staff on.'

'Oh. Right. Gotcha.' *Nice one, Alyssa. Way to put your foot in it.*

Denise stood there for a moment, lips pursed, then drew up a chair of her own and sat down facing her. 'I need you to understand that what happened in here back in March shook us all up badly. We lost three valued and much-loved colleagues. You only knew them for a few minutes, but the rest of us had worked with them for years. Decades, in some cases. So, while I'm all for a spot of gallows humour in the workplace to get us through a tough shift, there's a time and a place for it, and right now is the living embodiment of "too soon".'

Alyssa said nothing. She felt like pointing out that she was the only person in the room who'd actually *been* shot. That the last thing she needed was a lecture about how awful it had been. That, as someone who'd dragged herself back to work today, to the very place where she'd almost carked it, now was *precisely* the time and place for a spot of gallows humour.

'Do we understand one another?' said Denise.

Alyssa nodded, sullen eyes cast downwards.

'Good.' Denise's tone, and her whole demeanour, instantly lightened. 'Now shake a leg and get those forms signed so I can be reunited with that bottle of Shiraz.'

8

Ten weeks after

'So what you want tae do,' said Pat, leaning over Alyssa's shoulder and pressing a greasy finger to the computer screen, 'is tab down tae Commit Record and hit Control-Alt-F11. Got that?'

'I think so,' said Alyssa.

'All right. But just mind it's definitely Control-Alt-F11 you're pressing. Cos if you press Control-*Shift*-F11, 'stead of saving, it'll wipe the whole book clean off the system.'

Alyssa nodded slowly. 'But if I accidentally delete it, surely I can just re-add it.'

Pat gave a patient, world-weary shake of his head. 'See, here's the thing. When a book gets added tae the system, it gets assigned an item number that's always on file, even if the book gets deleted. Each book has its own unique code, and if you try tae add it again . . . EHHHHH!' He did a passable impression of a machine making an angry error noise. 'System says, "No can do. That number's already been used".'

Alyssa frowned, trying hard to make sense of this nonsensical slice of information. 'So I can delete the book but I can't add it again? Explain to me how that makes any kind of sense.'

Pat shrugged airily. 'Don't have tae, hen. I'm no the mug who programmed it. Point is, if your finger should slip and you nuke the only surviving copy of the complete works of the Marquis de Sade, it'll no be me having tae get on the blower tae Cataloguing Services and ask 'em nicely tae add it back in for you.'

Alyssa bit back the urge to make some comment on the shoddiness of the software's design. Over the last two and a half weeks, she'd come to learn that such observations rarely got you anywhere in this organisation. Indeed, getting to grips with the library's various operating practices had proved surprisingly tricky, thanks in no small part to a bunch of bizarre and convoluted rules and procedures which made absolutely no sense but to which everyone was expected to adhere because 'that's the way it's always been'. She'd quickly learned that suggesting simpler alternatives fell, at best, on deaf ears, and were more likely to earn her a disapproving head-shake and a quiet 'best not make trouble, hen'.

Behind her, Marli Perrow – an overly exuberant first-year university student who worked in the library a few hours a week, and whose tendency to dress like a dirty old man's idea of a schoolgirl made her a frequent recipient of inappropriate comments – exclaimed 'Ah, away and get yourself a girlfriend, ya creep!' and slammed down the phone like it was radioactive.

Pat gave a sympathetic grimace. 'Was it the heavy breathing again?'

Marli gave an exaggerated shudder. 'Not even breathing. Just dead silence – which, if you ask me, is *way* freakier.'

'Number withheld, I take it?'

'Naturally. That's the third this week. Should we be getting the police in, d'you think?'

'Ach, no worth the hassle. Sure they've got more important things tae worry about than some wee saddo who gets his jollies making creepy calls.'

Alyssa, pretending to be engrossed in the cataloguing task on the screen in front of her, listened to the entire exchange without saying anything. She couldn't explain it on any rational level, but somehow she just knew those calls were intended for her, and who was responsible for them. So far, she'd never taken one of them, but she knew it was only a matter of time. There were only so many excuses you could come up with for not answering a ringing phone when you were the nearest to it, and hers were all wearing pretty thin. Perhaps she should take a leaf out of Bindi's book and get freakishly long nail extensions.

At that moment, the door to the foyer swung open. Alyssa looked up in anticipation of her first customer of what had been an eerily quiet morning. She watched as a scrawny man in a tracksuit came hurrying in, a rucksack hanging from one shoulder. In every possible respect, he was the very definition of shifty: hands jammed into his pockets, walking fast, glancing furtively over his shoulder. It occurred to Alyssa that he looked vaguely familiar, though she couldn't place where she'd seen him before. She and the others watched as the man clocked their presence, then hurried on past them, heading for the bookshelves at the back of the room.

Marli groaned and shut her eyes. 'That's all we need!'

'Who is he?' asked Alyssa.

'Paul McGuigan,' said Pat quietly, in a tone that conveyed beyond a shadow of a doubt how he felt about the name's owner. 'Local petty crook and all-round ne'er-do-well. We've had all sorts of bother off him – nicking DVDs, vandalising cooncil property, shooting up in the lavvies. He's been barred a bunch of times, but it never does a bit of good.'

'If he's so much of a nuisance why don't you just bar him for good?' said Alyssa, watching McGuigan as he picked a book off a carousel and began to flick through it without actually looking at it, his eyes constantly flicking this way and that.

'Because that would amount to a complete withdrawal of service, which would be reckoned to have an unacceptably adverse effect on his access to the knowledge and cultural enrichment we provide.'

'Looks to me like he's having an adverse effect on his cultural enrichment all by himself,' said Marli, as McGuigan paused to polish a blackened tooth with a grubby finger.

As she spoke, the door swung open again. They turned as two more men came striding in. They could easily have been twins – dressed identically in black polo neck sweaters, both muscular and shaven-headed, like a couple of bouncers on day release. Or a couple of enforcers for a mob boss. To Alyssa, they looked about the least likely people to ever frequent a library – though, as she was quickly learning, it took all sorts. Catching sight of them, McGuigan instantly dropped the book he was holding and disappeared behind a stack of shelves.

While one of the baldie men headed further into the library, sticking close to the wall like a hunter stalking his prey, the other approached the desk. 'All right?' he nodded to Pat, clearly judging him, whether by virtue of age or some other indeterminable sign, to be in charge. 'How's it going?'

'Aye, cannae complain,' said Pat, matching the man's gruff tone and eyeing him cautiously.

The man rested both elbows on the counter, positioning himself so that those behind it didn't have a clear view of the rest of the library. It looked deliberate, and Alyssa got the distinct impression he was keeping them preoccupied while his partner in crime did whatever it was he was here to do.

'Been busy, aye?'

Pat gave a slight shrug. 'Just as you see it.'

Out of the corner of her eye, Alyssa caught sight of McGuigan's head rising up from behind a bookshelf like a periscope. Catching sight of the baldie guy at the desk, he immediately ducked out of sight.

The man turned his attention to Alyssa and Marli, both standing a little behind Pat. 'All right, girls? What's the gossip?'

Alyssa gave no response, while Marli merely shrugged.

'Ah, come on. Yous must have *something* juicy yous can share. Betcha see all sorts in here.' He was making the sort of sustained eye contact that was both deeply uncomfortable and hard to break.

'Well,' said Alyssa, emboldened by her growing irritation at his insolence, 'we see our fair share of time-wasters, that's for sure.'

The man chuckled drily at the back of his throat – more a cough than an actual laugh – and wagged a knowing finger in Alyssa's direction. 'Ah, that's good, that is.' He turned his attention to Marli, evidently judging her to be more pliable. 'How's about you, sweetness? You like working in a library? Is it a good job to have?'

'Why?' said Alyssa, before Marli could respond. 'Your career as a Right Said Fred tribute band not working out for you?'

The man smiled thinly, then turned away, laughing softly to himself. It made Alyssa feel like she was the butt of some joke she wasn't party to, and she didn't like it one bit. It was only as he continued to stand there, leaning one elbow on the counter as he gazed out across the library floor, that she noticed the flesh-coloured wire snaking up his neck and into his ear.

'There something we can help ye with?' said Pat. 'A particular book ye're after, or—'

At that moment there was a shout from behind the bookshelves – more akin to a bird squawking than the sort of noise a human would make – followed by what sounded suspiciously like someone being slammed against a shelf and the accompanying sound of several books hitting the ground. As the man who'd been chatting them up at the desk moved forward, a hand slipping into his pocket, there was an anguished yell. A second later, Paul McGuigan came shooting out from behind the shelves as if someone had fired a rocket up his ass. He ran pell-mell towards the exit, losing his footing on the linoleum flooring and only narrowly managing to right himself. As the man from the desk advanced to block his path, he swerved sideways, heading for the door leading off to the junior library. Not looking where he was going, he collided with a carousel of CDs. Both he and it went crashing to the floor, cases flying open and discs spilling everywhere. Before McGuigan, lying spread-eagled on the floor, could get up, the man was on top of him, firmly planting a foot in the small of his back.

'Don't tempt me, sunshine,' he growled.

As McGuigan went limp and lay whimpering on the ground, the other baldie man emerged from behind the bookshelves, holding up a bleeding hand. 'Wee prick *bit* me! Can you believe it?'

At the desk, Alyssa, Marli and Pat could only stare slack-jawed at the scene playing out in front of them. Overhead, there was a clatter of boots on metal as Denise came hurrying down the staircase. She came to a halt a few steps from the bottom and took in the sight of McGuigan lying on the floor with his captor's foot on his back.

'Just what the hell's going on here?' she demanded.

'CID,' said the man, producing a warrant card from his pocket and holding it aloft. 'Nothing to concern yourself with, miss.'

'This is *my* library,' snapped Denise, alighting on the ground floor, her hair seeming even spikier than usual. 'I'll be the judge of that.'

The CID man ignored her. 'Grab that, will you?' he said to his colleague, nodding in the direction of McGuigan's rucksack – which, amid the fracas, had come free of his shoulder and landed a few feet away.

His colleague headed over to it, still flapping his injured hand. With the good one, he picked it up and shot a look in McGuigan's direction. 'Don't mind if I have a little look-see, do you?'

Without waiting for any input from McGuigan, he unzipped the bag and tipped it upside down. A few items fell out – crumpled bus tickets, a half-eaten Mars bar – but they were as nothing compared to the large, heavy object that landed on the lino with a thunk.

Alyssa suddenly felt faint. Sensing that her legs were in danger of giving way under her, she slid onto a nearby stool, clutching the side of the countertop to steady herself.

The CID man bent down and looped the end of a biro through the trigger guard of the black plastic handgun, lifting it without touching it. He held it at arm's length, examining it like an admiring connoisseur.

'Well, well, well,' mused his colleague, his boot still on McGuigan's back. 'Care to explain yourself, sunshine?'

'It's no mine!' bleated McGuigan, his hollow features contorted into a Munch-like gawp. 'I'm just lookin' after it for a mate!'

'Glock 17 nine millimetre,' said the one holding the gun. 'The same model, as per the ballistics reports, used in the attack that took place in this very building on March first.'

'Quite the coincidence, that,' said his colleague, casting a baleful eye downwards at McGuigan. 'Don't you agree?'

'I told ye, I'm holdin' ontae it for a mate!' McGuigan wailed.

'And I'm Idris Elba's better-looking older brother. Paul Joseph McGuigan, I am detaining you under Section Fourteen of the Criminal Procedure (Scotland) Act 1995, on the grounds that I suspect you of having committed an offence punishable by imprisonment, namely the murders of Eva Baldini, Laura Craddock and Jason Stockridge – and the attempted murders of David Grogan and Alyssa Clark. Do you understand?'

'Naw, naw, *naw*!' wailed McGuigan, bashing his head against the lino with each 'naw'.

'You will be detained to enable further investigations to be carried out regarding the offence. You are not obliged to say anything, but anything you do say will be noted and may be used in evidence. Do you understand *that*?'

The long, anguished howl McGuigan emitted was evidently deemed sufficient grounds for assuming the affirmative, for, without another word, the plain-clothes detective cuffed his hands behind his back and hauled him upright, while his colleague sealed the gun inside a see-through plastic bag he'd produced from his back pocket. The door to the foyer, meanwhile, swung open once again – this time heralding the arrival of four more burly plain-clothes men, who headed over to receive McGuigan.

'Stick him in the van,' said the bald officer. 'We'll take him to HQ and get him booked in as soon as.'

As McGuigan was marched away, Denise made her way over to the officer, fists bunched by her sides.

'You said you're in charge here?' he enquired.

'That's right,' said Denise, clearly putting a great amount of energy into holding it together. 'Would you care to give me an explanation as to what precisely I just witnessed?'

'DI Hanlon,' said the officer, again showing her his warrant card. 'We've had an eye on Mr McGuigan for some time. Reports from a number of witnesses gave us reason to suspect his involvement in the murders of March first, but we preferred not to make a move without more solid intelligence. His return to the crime scene, in possession of a weapon similar – if not identical – to the one used to commit said murders, would appear to indicate that our suspicions were well-justified.'

'Am I to understand,' said Denise, her voice like frozen steel, 'that you allowed a man you suspected of murder to wander the streets unchecked – to come into my library, in the full knowledge that he might well have been planning another attack?'

Hanlon shrugged. 'Nothing happened, did it? And we were on his tail every step of the way. It's not like you were ever in any danger.'

His words could hardly have been less reassuring if he'd tried.

Alyssa, still perched on the stool, felt light-headed and nauseous, as if someone had just punched her hard in the stomach. She thought she might be about to pass out and wondered if she should get herself closer to ground level just in case. Out of the corner of her eye, she glimpsed Pat surreptitiously making the sign of the cross.

'Oh my God,' Marli breathed, addressing no one in particular. 'The stories I'm going to have to tell the grandkids.'

As she spoke, Alyssa caught the briefest glimpse, through the narrow window in the door, of DCI Metcalfe sweeping out of the foyer, hot on the heels of the other officers and their prisoner of war. It was only then that, in an unexpected flash of clear-headedness, she finally realised why she'd recognised McGuigan.

He was the strung-out junkie-looking suspect whose mugshot Metcalfe had shown her during her visit to her flat back in March.

9

Jamie staggered into the foyer of the high-rise, pausing to flick the light-switch by the entrance. Nothing happened. He tried it again. Same. The entire stairwell remained shrouded in darkness. Fucksake. Power must be out again. Pain in the arse, but he wasn't surprised. Somecunt must've tripped the wrong switch or forgotten to pay the bill. Or something. He didn't know how it worked. All he knew was it was happening more and more, and it was about time someone got their head kicked in over it.

He whipped out his phone, switched on the torch and, using it to light his way, headed over to the nearby lift and pressed the button. Again, nothing. Power must be out throughout the entire building.

Fucksaking under his breath, he took to the stairs. It was a tough climb at the best of times – fourteen floors in all – and it would have been fair to say that he *really* wasn't at his best tonight. Unsteady on his legs and severely dehydrated on account of all the bevvying him and his pals had been doing, it turned out to be too much for him to accomplish all in one go, and he had to content himself with making a couple of pit stops along the way, leaning against the wall while he got his breath back, waiting for his surroundings to stop spinning.

About halfway up he stopped in his tracks, ears pricking to attention. Even in his booze-addled state, he was in no doubt as to what he'd just heard: the scrape of someone's shoe on one of the concrete steps a couple of floors down. He stood there, not moving, listening hard, but heard nothing else. Clutching the handrail to steady himself, he leaned over the bannister, shining his phone into the stairwell. He swung it in an uneven circle, picking out the contours of the stairs, but found no signs of life.

As he stood there, straining bleary eyes in an attempt to see into the shadowy recesses out of range of his phone, the torch suddenly gave out, plunging him into darkness.

'Ach, shite . . . '

He fumbled with his phone, trying to turn it on again. The screen briefly showed a blinking red battery symbol, then went black.

'Fer fuck's *sake* . . . '

Reaching into the pocket of his Tommy Hilfiger parka, he felt the reassuring contours of his cigarette lighter. He got it out, flicked the wheel. It didn't catch. He tried again. And again. On the fourth attempt, it finally caught, illuminating his immediate surroundings with its pale, flickering flame. Its reach was nothing like as good as his phone's torch, but it would have to do. Holding it at arm's length and moving slowly to avoid any sudden movement snuffing it out, he resumed his ascent.

By the time he finally reached the fourteenth floor, he was breathless and lashing with sweat, but the flame remained triumphantly alive. Reaching the door to his flat, he fumbled with his keys, making as little noise as possible, lest his stepdad wake up and give him a leathering for interrupting his beauty sleep. He pushed the key towards the lock, missed it and instead connected with the doorframe, gouging a chip of wood out of it in the process. He swore to himself again. There'd be hell to pay in the morning.

Then his lighter went out.

'Shit!'

In the process, the keys fell out of his hand, landing with a clang on the stone floor. Dropping to a crouch, he felt around, patting the ground gingerly. Feeling nothing, he expanded his search in ever-widening semi-circles, all the while flicking the switch of his lighter in his other hand, his frustration growing by the second as it stubbornly refused to catch. He had his back to the door now, still down on his hunkers, patting away at the ground like a blind man.

At last, his hand touched on something hard and cool. At the same instant, the flame finally caught, illuminating the long, black-clad legs of a figure standing directly in front of him, mere inches away. Jamie opened his mouth, a 'what the fuck?' on the tip of his tongue.

The words never reached his lips. The figure shot out an arm, jerking upwards, plunging a knife into his jaw, the blade slipping into the soft flesh between his neck and his mandible.

His eyes widened in surprise. He dropped both his lighter and keys and sank to the floor, clutching his neck, trying in vain to stem the blood oozing between his fingers like a leaking hose. He landed on his side, his head connecting with the cold concrete. A couple of feet in front of him, his lighter lay on the ground, the flame flickering feebly but still emitting enough light for him to see his assailant fleeing down the stairs. As the flame finally gave up the ghost, he lay there in the pitch darkness, listening as the clattering footsteps reached the ground floor and the communal door slammed shut. Then, silence.

None of the building's other inhabitants came out to see what had caused the disturbance – not even Jamie's mum and stepdad, who slept on through the night and didn't discover their son's body until 9.15 the following morning.

10

Four months after

'Nah,' said Bindi, lowering her coffee mug and gazing up disapprovingly at the banner hanging from the twin pillars on either side of the desk, 'it's still squeegee. Needs shifting up a bit at your end, Pat.'

'Aye, well,' Pat huffed from halfway up a decidedly rickety-looking ladder, 'if you're gonnae be so pernickety about it, you're more than welcome to take my place.'

'Can't.' Bindi gave a shrug which looked considerably more smug than apologetic. 'I haven't been on stepladder training. Besides, you need me down here to give direction.'

'That what they're calling it these days?' Pat growled, while Stevie, at the top of a matching ladder on the other side, merely assumed a pained expression, as if he wished nothing more than for this to be over.

'What's all this?'

Alyssa, arriving a few minutes before the start of her 1–8 shift, stopped to gaze up at the banner, reading the words 'WELCOME BACK DAVY' printed across it in a succession of garish colours, accompanied by drawings of beaming suns, rainbows and other assorted symbols of joy and happiness.

'You can read, can't you?' said Bindi. 'Our Davy's making his grand return to the bosom of the council family.' She sighed and shook her head. 'No, it's *still* not straight. Why don't you go and get a tape measure? I'm pretty sure there's one in the cleaner's cupboard.'

'And I suppose you'll be swapping places wi' me to hold this in position while I'm off rooting around amongst the mops and buckets?' Pat shot back.

They never did get to hear what Bindi thought of that particular suggestion, for at that moment Denise came bustling down the stairs, hurriedly buttoning the cuff of her shirt.

'Is everything ready?' she demanded. 'He'll be here any minute.'

She was turned out more smartly than usual, having forgone her usual less formal attire for a dark trouser suit and pale blue button shirt. Alyssa was pretty sure she'd even had her hair done.

'Funny,' Alyssa remarked to Bindi, as Denise scurried over to one of the display shelves to do some last-minute straightening of the books, 'I don't remember anyone showering me with all this attention when I came back to work.'

'Why,' said Bindi, 'would you have *wanted* bunting and a cake?'

'Oh *God*, no,' said Alyssa immediately, wondering if it was possible to feel both jealous and relieved at the same time. 'All this fuss just for spending a few months on the sick? Talk about cringe-tastic.'

'Thought as much. Besides, Davy's funny and adorable whereas you're just a weird-ass American with tattoos.'

As Alyssa stood there, reduced to open-mouthed silence by this blunt assessment of her place in the library pecking order, the sound of a vehicle coming to a stop outside reached her ears. A moment later, Marli came scurrying in from the foyer in a state of considerable excitement.

'He's here!' she cried. 'They just pulled up.'

Denise immediately abandoned the display she'd been tinkering with and hurried over to the desk, heels clacking on the linoleum, positioning herself facing the door like an official waiting to receive a visiting dignitary. 'Right! Places, everyone! Leave that, you two.'

She snapped her fingers in the direction of Pat and Stevie, who dutifully descended their respective stepladders, leaving the banner hanging slightly off angle. Alyssa, who wished she'd turned down the offer of a shift this afternoon and thus avoided this whole palaver, melted away into the background behind the others. All six of them stared at the door with bated breath, listening to the sound of approaching footsteps, accompanied by a curious squeaking sound. Then the door swung open and a woman entered, pushing a loaded wheelchair.

At first Alyssa thought there had been some great misunderstanding – that they'd got themselves all worked up over a false alarm and that the pair who'd just come through the door were nothing more than some poor unsuspecting customers, no doubt wondering what they'd done to warrant such an extravagant welcome. Then she took a proper look at the woman's face and recognised her as Sharon Grogan, Davy's mother. Her eyes strayed down to the figure in the wheelchair and it was all she could do to stop herself gasping out loud in surprise.

'Welcome back, Davy!' exclaimed Denise, to much whooping and applause from the rest of the team, sans Alyssa.

'Oh my!' said Davy, clapping a hand to each cheek in a manner that looked decidedly rehearsed. 'If I'd known I was going to get this nice a reception, I'd have got myself shot way sooner.'

As Denise stepped forward to kiss him on the cheek, Alyssa struggled to process the emotions she was experiencing. Surprise, yes, and bafflement, but strongest and most unreasonably of all – *anger*. Anger that no one had thought to tell her, and at herself for having been so utterly convinced Davy was just milking the council's sick pay policy while she, who'd gone through exactly the same ordeal as he had, was back at work busting her hump.

'Did you know he was like this?' she asked Marli, who was standing closest to her, a great big smile plastered across her features.

'Of course.' Marli turned to her, oblivious. 'Everyone knew. They say he'll never walk again, the poor soul, but you wouldn't think it to look at him.'

Alyssa, watching as Davy performed a couple of wheelies to adoring coos of delight from Denise and Bindi, said nothing. If what Marli said was true, then, on the face of it, Davy *was* coping remarkably well. In fact, she couldn't help but feel more than a little irritated by how at ease he seemed about his newfound circumstances. Here she was, having to contend with nightmares and panic attacks while he, despite his physical setback, still seemed to be the same annoyingly upbeat Davy as ever, all the while being fussed over by his adoring audience.

'I'll be back to pick him up at eight sharp,' Sharon said, once the levels of excitement had been dialled down from manic to merely exuberant. 'See he doesn't work himself too hard now. I know what my boy's like.'

'*Mu*-um,' Davy sighed, like one of those children whose parents are forever publicly embarrassing them.

'Don't you worry – we'll take good care of him,' said Denise, beaming down at him. 'It's to be light duties only till he's back into the swing of things. And he'll not want for cups or tea and jam donuts either. Believe me, nothing's too much for our Davy.'

Alyssa, judging now to be the optimal time to make her escape, slipped away unnoticed.

She managed, for the most part, to keep out of Davy's way for the rest of the afternoon. It wasn't too difficult. He was still very much the man of the hour and had no shortage of people – both colleagues and the public – lavishing him with attention, telling him how well he was looking and what a credit he was to himself. Word of his return had evidently got around, and the phone was ringing off the hook most of the afternoon with colleagues from other branches phoning up to have words with him. Alyssa took herself upstairs and busied herself with organising the reference section. It was a job she normally hated, but right now she was more than glad of an excuse to disappear for a few hours. The lack of an elevator meant there was no danger of her running into Davy up there.

Come five o'clock, however, avoiding the counter was no longer an option. Denise, Pat, Marli and Bindi were all off home, leaving only Alyssa, Davy and Stevie to hold the fort. So she slunk back downstairs and pretended to be transfixed by some crucial task on one of the computers while Denise, coat slung over her arm, clucked around, asking Davy over and over if he was sure he had everything he needed and insisting they were to ring her at home if there were any problems – an invitation, Alyssa noted, that hadn't been extended to *her* on her first night back.

'Oh!' Marli – who, along with Pat, was still hanging around near the desk, seemingly reluctant to abandon Davy – suddenly exclaimed. 'We should all go out for drinks on Friday night. Celebrate Davy's return in style.'

'Fab idea, hen,' said Pat. 'It's been ages since we had a proper knees-up. What say ye, gaffer? You in?'

'A night on the bevvy with your scintillating company?' said Denise. 'Just try and stop me.'

'Hey, I'm up for it,' said Davy. 'Long as I can get these wheels through the door of the Anchorage.'

'Sounds like nearly a full house, then,' said Marli, grinning. 'I'll text the others, get the word out.'

'What about you, wee hen?' Pat turned to Alyssa. 'You coming?'

'Friday?' Alyssa was so unprepared for the question she had no time to formulate an excuse. 'I, um, well, I . . . '

'Aw, come on!' Marli cried. 'Library nights out are *so* much fun! We do pub quizzes, bingo . . . maybe even a spot of the singing if it's karaoke night.'

Pat clapped an arm round Alyssa's shoulders – an act which necessitated considerable effort on her part to stop herself from flinching. 'Aye, you're one of us now. 'Bout time we initiated you properly.'

'Come on, Alyssa.' Denise smiled encouragingly. 'You're as much a part of this team as any of us.'

'I . . . ' With multiple pairs of expectant eyes boring into her, Alyssa found her brain turning to fudge, a convincing excuse stubbornly refusing to form. 'Well, it's just,' she eventually muttered, 'I think I've got something on.'

'Hey.' Davy spoke for the first time since Alyssa's inclusion in the outing had first been mooted. 'If she's not comfortable coming out with us, there's nothing to be gained by forcing her.'

The others continued to eyeball Alyssa, clearly still far from satisfied.

'It's not that I'm not comfortable,' she said, a little tersely. 'I told you, I've just got something on.'

'Well,' said Denise, with a strained but understanding smile, 'it *was* awfully short notice. Never mind – there's always next time.'

'Aye, that's right.' Pat nodded approvingly. 'We'll get ye sooner or later, hen. Ye cannae escape the karaoke machine forever.'

As the others made noises of agreement, Alyssa made a mental note to come up with some proper excuses so she'd have a ready-made supply of them in future. It wasn't so much that the prospect of a night of socialising and silly games with her work colleagues sounded insufferable – though it absolutely did. It was that she was still smarting from her colleagues having kept Davy's condition from her, and that their odes to her being 'part of the team' rang decidedly hollow as a result.

Denise fussed around for a while longer, making sure the drawers were fully stocked with fresh date labels and registration forms and getting Davy to confirm once more that he had everything he needed, before finally calling it quits. As she, Marli and Pat headed off and the door swung to behind them, a pall of silence descended on the library, and the *really* excruciating phase of the shift began.

For the first half-hour or so, Davy didn't say a word to Alyssa. In fact, he seemed to be behaving as if she wasn't even there. Instead, he chatted away to Stevie about matters of little consequence, and to the slow but steady trickle of customers coming through the door – most of them teenagers and the elderly; the former there for the public PCs, the latter to stock up on the vast quantities of books that Alyssa flatly refused to believe it was humanly possible for them to read in the time they took to return them. For lengthy stretches, though, the place was all but deserted, and the silences grew increasingly longer and more awkward.

During her first couple of weeks back at work, Alyssa had asked various colleagues whether it was normally this quiet. The consensus was that, following The Event, the public were justifiably wary of giving the place their custom, and as a result the library had become increasingly reliant on a coterie of die-hards, or 'high volume service users' as they were officially designated – the ones who'd plough through a blizzard to get their daily reading fix. People like old Mrs Reynolds, who took out mountains of travel guides but never actually seemed to go on holiday; or Mrs Sood, who came in once a week to grab a fresh handful of books from the Hindi section without ever bothering to read the blurbs or even glance at the garish covers; or Mrs Ambrose, who always insisted on talking the ear off anyone foolish enough to make eye contact with her. These encounters always lasted an age and went round and round in circles, and she was perfectly capable of having the same conversation several days running. Still, she invariably brought them cakes, biscuits or baked goods of one variety or another, so the consensus was that it was, on balance, worth it to endure a bit of earache from her every once in a while. She often showed up with her grandson in tow – a clean-cut man in his late twenties with neatly parted hair and a suit that always looked like it could do with a good iron. Watching him trailing around after his grandmother, wheeling her trolley dolly for her and patiently telling her 'No, Nana, you had that one last week' when she alighted on a book she'd already read, Alyssa couldn't help feeling a sense of disdain laced with pity. Whatever had become of his balls – or his self-respect?

As the evening wore on, the little hand on the wall clock slowly inching its way towards the hallowed eight, Stevie – who was chronically incapable of either sitting still or keeping his mouth shut for more than thirty seconds at a time – alternated between wittering about whatever inane thought had most recently entered his head and getting up to go wandering around the building, only to return a minute later to declare that 'nothing needs doing'. He was off on yet another of his manoeuvres when Davy, having completed a handful of administrative tasks which he'd claimed as his responsibility and his alone, closed the folder he'd been working from with a snap and, with an unnerving sense of purpose, manoeuvred his chair round to face Alyssa.

'So – you don't call, you don't write. What's a boy to think?'

Instantly on the defensive, Alyssa bit back a scoff. 'Could say the same of you.'

Davy affected a mock-hurt look. 'Case you hadn't noticed, I've been a bit preoccupied, what with spinal rehabilitation and getting kitted out with my new wheels. What's your excuse?'

She didn't have one, so she said nothing. This, more than anything, was the reason she'd spent the entire afternoon avoiding him.

'So anyway, how's you?'

She shrugged. 'All right, I guess.'

'You're looking well, anyway.'

'Thanks. Uh, you're . . . ' She stopped herself, not sure how best to phrase it, before eventually settling on, 'You seem much the same as ever.'

'Apart from the obvious.'

'Apart from that, yeah.' She hesitated for a moment, then decided to just come out and say what was on her mind. 'I didn't realise you were . . . I mean, I thought you were just shot in the back.'

'Yeah, well, back, spine, full range of movement – they all sorta go together, don't they? Bullet got lodged in the T2 vertebra. There was talk of them removing it, but in the end they decided it'd do more harm than good to go poking around in there.'

'And is there nothing they can do?'

'Apart from give me a bunch of appointments with a nice lady who tells me it's important to understand that it's all right to feel sad? Not a sausage.' He shrugged amiably. 'Hey – could've been a whole lot worse. Couple of inches further up and I'd be sucking my meals through a straw.'

She felt like grabbing him by the lapels, shaking him, telling him to stop being so infuriatingly reasonable. He should be angry, or depressed, or . . . or *something*.

'So,' he ran a casual finger along the edge of the counter in a manner that looked way too deliberate to be natural, 'you must be pretty relieved, knowing the cops've got someone banged up for the murders.'

She got the distinct impression he was fishing – trying, for reasons she couldn't fathom, to probe her on the matter without letting on.

'I'm glad he's not still wandering the streets, free to shoot up another bunch of innocents any time he feels like it,' she said, a tad stiffly.

'Even though he says he didn't do it.'

She scoffed. 'Yeah, right. He *would* say that, wouldn't he?'

Davy leaned back in his chair, regarding her with an expression that verged on contemptuous, as if she'd just said something monumentally stupid. 'So you reckon they've got him bang to rights.'

'I *reckon*,' she said, feeling her hackles rising, 'the smart thing for him to do now is admit responsibility and save us taxpayers having to foot the bill for a pointless, drawn-out trial.'

'And you're absolutely convinced he's guilty.' Again the same contemptuous look and tone.

'I was here the day they grabbed him. Saw the gun they fished out of his rucksack. Looked pretty guilty from where I was standing.'

'Yeah, well,' Davy muttered – more to himself than her, it seemed, 'looks aren't everything, you know.'

She folded her arms. 'And just what's that supposed to mean?'

For a moment, Davy appeared on the verge of letting the matter drop. Then, seemingly changing his mind, he nodded towards one of the desk computers.

'Gimme a shove thataway.'

She took the handles of his wheelchair and pushed him over to the PC, then watched as he called up the web browser and tapped out an address. As a wall of text filled the screen, he turned to her.

'Have a butcher's at that.'

Alyssa moved alongside him and began to read. It was an article about The Event. Well, a blog post, to be more specific – written in a breathless, overly excited style by someone who clearly wasn't a big fan of full stops, commas or paragraph breaks. She skim-read, eyes dancing from one line to the next. There was a vast amount of information to take in, with the author jumping from one half-baked theory to another so often that it amounted to sensory overload, but she was able to get the gist. The author believed Paul McGuigan had been stitched up by a cabal of sinister forces seeking to pervert the course of justice – a conclusion he or she had reached by putting two and two together and coming up with fifty-three.

'Wow, Infowars eat your heart out.'

Davy snatched the mouse from her and minimised the blog, clearly regretting having shared it with her.

'You don't actually believe that crap, do you? You know it's probably just some bored kid with an overactive imagination typing one-handed from his mom's basement.'

Davy's eyes flared in defiance. 'I happen to think he makes some very salient points. There's a lot about this case that doesn't add up.'

'You know they've got these people called detectives to figure out that sort of thing?'

'That a fact?' Davy sounded unimpressed.

'Uh-huh. I hear they even get paid for it.'

'Yeah, well, I happen to think they've not been earning their money's worth so far.'

Alyssa was about to press the matter further when Stevie reappeared, back from his latest sweep of the building. 'Nothing needs doing,' he announced, for the fourteenth time that night.

Neither Alyssa nor Davy said anything. Stevie looked from one to the other and back again, wide-eyed and gormless as ever as he tried to work out what had caused such a chilly atmosphere to develop in his absence.

This time it was Alyssa who broke the silence. 'So, Stevie,' she said brightly, 'this how you always envisaged spending your life?'

The evening dragged on and, though Davy eventually regained much of his usual conviviality, Alyssa continued to sense a degree of resentment from him, even if he wasn't actually *saying* anything to that effect. Eventually, eight o'clock arrived. They shooed out the last remaining stragglers from the reading room and did one final sweep of the building to make sure there was no one hiding in the many nooks and crannies – 'Happens more than you'd think,' said Davy. Stevie loped off to catch his train while Alyssa and Davy hung back. His mum was picking him up, and Alyssa – reticent to leave a guy in a wheelchair parked on a street corner at night, even though it was summer now and still light – reluctantly said she'd wait with him.

As Davy checked his phone for the umpteenth time, Alyssa's curiosity finally got the better of her. 'So,' she said, 'Paul McGuigan. You're totally convinced he didn't do it.'

Davy made a sound at the back of his throat that sounded vaguely like a scoff, but when Alyssa gave him a sharp look, he hastily turned it into a cough.

'Come on, then.' She parked herself directly in front of him, forcing him to give her his undivided attention. 'Let's hear why you're so sure Alex Jones's slightly nuttier cousin is right and everyone else is wrong.'

'Well, for a start, it's not just Alex Jones's nuttier cousin. There's plenty other folk who think the official account doesn't add up.'

'And do any of them happen to be remotely credible? Come on – something must've happened to send you down the conspiracy bullshit rabbit-hole.'

For several seconds, Davy said nothing. He just sat, eyes in his lap, looking surly. 'I just think it's all gone a bit too fast,' he said eventually.

'Well, sure. They had a crazy killer running round with a gun. I dunno about you, but I'm actually kinda glad they grabbed the guy as quickly as possible.'

Davy jerked his head up, eyes flashing like some wild animal scenting its prey. 'Yes. Exactly that. "As quickly as possible." Hold on.'

He tapped away at his phone for a few moments, then found what he was looking for and offered it to Alyssa. She took it reluctantly. It showed the online edition of a newspaper article – one of the lower-end tabloids, judging by the fact every sentence got a paragraph of its own. 'FORMBY: "WE'LL GET OUR MAN"' was the giant, boldface headline. Accompanying it was a photo of a stern-looking man with a white goatee and almond-shaped glasses. It was one of those government publicity shots, neatly furled saltire visible behind him.

'See him?' said Davy. 'That's Kip Formby, the Justice Secretary. This was published just two days before they arrested Paul McGuigan. Says he told the police that if they didn't get a result pronto, heads were going to roll. Demotions, firings, redeployments. A total clear-out from top to bottom.' He looked at Alyssa imploringly, exasperated that she wasn't seeing what was so obvious to him. 'Don't you get it? They were under pressure to get their man – any man. So they pinned it on the first schmuck who happened to look shifty.'

Alyssa scrolled through the article. '"Sources say". In other words, no one's actually willing to go to bat for any of this.'

Davy sighed and snatched his phone back. 'OK, fine, so this article's full of shit, whatever. Believe what you like. Just take it from me, if you'd ever met the guy, you'd know he couldn't have done it.'

'Know him well, did you?'

'Well enough.' He caught her dubious look and sighed. 'Look, he's a cocky wee gobshite, but he's all talk and no action. Always quick with the temper tantrums and the threats, but when push came to shove, he never actually acted on any of them, and anyone who says otherwise is lying.'

'Awfully sure of yourself, aren't you? I bet you anything people said that about Lee Harvey Oswald as well. Or Oscar Pistorius, or any other celebrity killer you care to mention. You never know what a person's really capable of till they actually do it.'

'Quite apart from anything, he's way too much of a fuck-up to plan something like this and pull it off.'

'Oh, come on. You can read the papers as well as I can. He's been in and out of jail since he was a teenager.'

'Yes, but for stupid, trivial things. Nicking car stereos, getting into scraps with other smackheads – and usually getting his backside handed to him. That's a world away from gunning down a bunch of defenceless worker bees.'

Alyssa said nothing. She hated to admit it, but he sounded almost halfway convincing – though whether she was responding to the genuine thrust of his argument or simply the fact he was going at it with all the fervour of an evangelical street preacher was anyone's guess.

'Plus,' said Davy, in a tone that suggested this was him pulling out his trump card, 'there's been other murders since.'

'Really? When? Who?'

'Couple of young guys. One back in April, the other only a week or so past.'

Davy fiddled with his phone again, tapping away at the screen before handing it to Alyssa. Again, same deal – a tabloid newspaper article, all sensationalist scaremongering and one-syllable words, accompanied by the headline 'GANG WAR IN CRAIGSLEE? ANOTHER LOCAL TEEN KILLED IN COLD BLOOD'. She skimmed the article to get the gist.

'Yeah, but these guys were stabbed,' she said, handing the phone back to Davy.

'So?'

'So I don't know if you were aware, but the man who blew three of our colleagues away and put you in that thing used a nine-mil

Glock. It's quite the stretch to connect a couple of juvies getting knifed to that.'

'Yeah, but they were both killed in Craigslee. That's like a stone's throw from here. You're trying to tell me that's not a coincidence?'

'Right, and I suppose no one's ever been killed in Craigslee before, it being such an oasis of law and order.'

Davy scoffed and shook his head in exasperation. 'You know, I'd never have taken you for one of *them*.'

'Them?'

'Folk who swallow the party line hook, line and sinker; who believe everything the men in suits tell them. I had you down as a freethinker. Turns out you're just another sheep.'

'I'm not!' Alyssa bristled at the implication. 'Believe me, I'm as freethinking as they come. But there's a big difference between not believing everything the powers that be tell you and chugging down a bunch of crap dreamt up by some cellar dweller just cos it's what you want to believe. And you, my dude, are clutching at straws.'

An uncomfortable silence descended. Davy simply glowered up at her, as if he regarded her refusal to buy wholesale into his claims as a personal affront.

The silence was broken by a large people carrier pulling up to the kerb next to them. The driver's window wound down and Sharon leaned out.

'I am *so* sorry! You wouldn't *believe* the traffic. Nightmare! Have you had long to wait?'

Davy assured her they hadn't, even though it was now twenty past eight, and his mother could presumably tell the time as well as anyone. She got out of the car and waddled round to the pavement, where she and Alyssa, between them, managed to get Davy and his chair into the back of the vehicle.

'Which way are you headed?' Sharon asked, turning to Alyssa once they were done. 'Can we give you a ride somewhere?'

Alyssa shook her head. 'It's OK. My bus'll be any minute.'

'Are you sure? It's no trouble . . . '

'Honestly, don't worry about it. You'd only be going out of your way.'

It took several more rejections before Sharon finally took the hint and bade her goodnight. Alyssa hurried across the road to the bus stop where, from under the canopy of the shelter, she watched as the people carrier joined the westerly flow of traffic. As its tail-lights disappeared into the distance, she thought about Davy's comments about McGuigan. It scarcely seemed credible and, to be honest, it reflected pretty poorly on his critical faculties that he'd bought wholesale into the fevered ramblings of a handful of beetle-browed bloggers. She supposed, if she wanted to be charitable, she could chalk it up to him having had too much time on his hands while he was recuperating. When you had nothing to do except stare at the ceiling all day, it was all too easy to get sucked into a spiral of speculation and conspiracy. Really, he was more to be pitied than scorned.

It's nothing to do with you, she told herself. *You don't need to know. You don't care.*

As she sat there, hands tapping out a rhythm on her thighs while she waited for her bus, her eyes alighted on a figure standing on the pavement about a hundred yards up the other side of the road, on the corner with Edgehill Drive. A man – about average height, with close-cropped, sandy-coloured hair, his narrow face framed by a pair of wide-rimmed glasses.

A man she'd hoped she'd never see again.

Even as she drew in a sharp intake of breath, a huge double-decker lorry sailed past, blocking her view of him. By the time it was finally gone and her view of the other side of the street clear once again, the corner where he'd previously been standing was empty.

She rose to her feet, straining to catch a glimpse of him, but there was no sign of him. Slowly, she sank back onto the bench, her mind riddled with fresh anxieties. Had he really been standing there? Or had her subconscious been playing tricks on her, causing her to see the very thing that, above all else, had been playing on her mind for weeks now – ever since the 'get well' card and the iris? She wasn't sure which possibility troubled her more – that she was going mad or that it really *was* happening.

At last, her bus hove into view. She got to her feet and signalled to it, boarding quickly and hurrying up the gangway to the back row. There, she plugged in her headphones, cranked up the volume as loud as it would go and forced herself to forget all about Davy and McGuigan and conspiracy bloggers and sinister figures on street corners.

11

In the dead of night, Alyssa came to with a start. She was sure it had been a dream that had woken her, though whether it had been *the* dream was another matter entirely. All she knew was that her heart was racing and she was drenched with sweat, her T-shirt sticking to her like clingfilm. She hauled herself upright and sat there in the dark, motionless, listening to the sounds of silence in her flat.

Only it *wasn't* silence. Not total silence, at any rate. It took a minute for her to become aware of it, but once she heard it, there was no mistaking it: a soft, regular scratching, like tiny claws on a hard surface.

Reaching for her Wayfarers from the nightstand, she slipped out of bed and crept down the hallway, following the noise to her front door. Holding her breath, she put an ear to it and listened. It was the sound of metal on metal, of someone trying and failing to fit a key into the lock.

She shrank back from the door as if she'd been scalded and stood there, staring at it in blind panic, not knowing what to do. Keep quiet and hope whoever it was would eventually give up and leave? Shout 'who's there?' and confirm both that there was someone in the flat and that that someone was a scrawny slip of a girl without a hope in hell of holding her own against a determined intruder?

She was on the verge of hightailing it to the bathroom, locking herself in and calling the cops when she heard the sound of a door being opened on the next floor up. The scratching stopped instantly. A few seconds of silence elapsed. Then, she heard another sound: feet tramping down the corridor and down the stairs. Not running, but certainly walking briskly enough to suggest that wherever this person was going, they were going there in a hurry. Alyssa listened as the feet continued down to the ground floor. The communal door opened and slammed shut. A few seconds later, the door on the floor above her also shut, and silence descended once more.

Her legs, which until now had just about been keeping her upright, finally gave way. She sank to the floor, landing heavily on her knees. As soon as she was able to haul herself upright again, she fled back to bed, dived under the covers and remained there for the rest of the night, listening for the smallest hint of the intruder coming back.

The following morning she readied herself for work, slathering on a ton of makeup to hide her lack of sleep. Prior to exiting the flat, she paused to listen at the door, making sure the coast was clear, before hurrying down the stairs and out into the street. Already, though, last night's events felt somehow less vivid and sinister in the warm light of day. She was probably making a whole lot of fuss over nothing. More likely than not, her nocturnal visitor had merely been some drunken lush who'd staggered home after a few too many beers or whatever and got the wrong door. That's if it had even happened at all. A part of her wondered if the noises she'd heard, and the ensuing business at the door, couldn't simply have been part of the same dream and that she hadn't, in fact, woken up at all. It was possible, she supposed. She *had* been having awfully vivid dreams ever since The Event.

Or so she told herself.

She yawned through the first couple of hours of the morning

shift, for once profoundly grateful for just how quiet it was. Her colleagues worked around her, not commenting on her zombie-like demeanour or the strung-out appearance all the Kohl in the world hadn't managed to hide. Perhaps they genuinely hadn't noticed. Or maybe they had and were simply making the usual allowances.

She was processing some newly delivered stock at the counter when a man she didn't recognise came striding in. To say his was an unusual look would have been putting it mildly. He was in his early forties, with a muscular build, a wild unkempt beard and long reddish-brown hair scraped back into a man-bun. He walked like he owned the place, chin up, chest out, fists clenched as his arms pumped back and forth, army-style. He was wearing just cargo bottoms and a T-shirt – no jacket or even a sweater, despite it being an atypically chilly mid-July morning, even by Glasgow standards. Behind him hurried a smaller and much more out-of-shape man, balding and clutching a stack of loose pages under his arm. Alyssa watched as they headed through the library and let themselves into the staff area, before turning to Stevie, who was staring after them, even more wide-eyed and slack-jawed than usual.

'Who was *that*?'

'That's Tony Barbarossa,' said Stevie in a hushed whisper.

'Who?'

'Tony *Barbarossa*,' Stevie repeated, in a tone that somehow conveyed both fear and awe. 'He used to work here before you came. He got the sack for—'

He suddenly fell silent, shutting his mouth with an audible snap and busying himself with rearranging a bundle of forms that were already in perfect order.

'Got the sack for what?' Alyssa insisted. Then she turned and saw what had caused Stevie's silence.

Into the library strode a trio of suits, headed by Nikki Wyatt, wearing stiletto heels and a too-short-for-those-legs pencil skirt.

One look at them was enough to know that these were Very Important People, at least in their own heads. Nikki came to a halt at the counter and regarded Alyssa and Stevie with barely disguised suspicion.

'Good morning,' she said crisply. 'Have Mr Barbarossa and his representative arrived?'

'Uh . . . yes, Mrs Wyatt,' Stevie stammered, the tips of his ears glowing a majestic pink. 'Just a moment ago.'

'We'll be conducting our business in the break room, and I'd be grateful if you'd pass on the word to your colleagues that we are not to be disturbed.'

'But . . . but my lunch break,' Stevie protested, eyes widening with alarm. 'I need to take it before Marli heads off at one or I won't—'

Nikki scoffed irritably. 'Oh, I don't have time for this! I'm sure you can find it within yourself to hold on till we're done. Tell Denise we've arrived and ask her to meet us through there.'

As a chastened Stevie picked up the phone and dialled the extension for the upstairs office, Nikki turned to Alyssa. 'I'd like a word when we're finished. I have a proposition to put to you.'

'Can't wait.'

Nikki either didn't pick up on the sarcasm or chose to ignore it. Instead she turned and, entourage in tow, swept past the desk, heading in the same direction as Tony Barbarossa and his companion.

As soon as they'd gone, Alyssa turned once more to Stevie. 'Come on, then. What were you going to tell me? You said he got fired?'

Stevie put down the phone and nodded, eyes like saucers. 'He got in a fight with one of the punters.' His voice was a hushed whisper, as if he was afraid Nikki would hear and come charging back out to give him hell.

'You mean like an argument?'

'*No* – I mean an actual fight. I'm talking rolling around on the floor, fists flying, knees to the balls, the works. He'd've took the poor sod's head off if the rest of the staff hadn't pulled him off.'

'You saw this?'

Stevie shook his head. 'I never, but Davy was on that day and he seen the whole thing.'

It scarcely sounded credible, and yet one look at Stevie assured Alyssa that he was fully convinced of what he was telling her. More to the point, one look at Tony Barbarossa had been enough to convince *her* that he was probably more than capable of what was being described.

'What was it all about?'

Stevie shrugged. 'Dunno, but it never took much to set Tony Barbarossa off. He's proper mental. Like, he'd fly off the handle if you looked at him the wrong way, and every now and then he'd threaten to lamp someone just for something they said. There were other incidents too. He'd had a buncha written warnings. This was just the straw that broke the camel's back.'

This had something of an air of mythologising about it, Alyssa instinctively felt. She wondered what the real story was, and whether Stevie had actually witnessed any of these incidents first-hand or was just passing on – or embellishing – gossip from the water-cooler. Given Davy's predilections for conspiracy bullshit, the fact he was the source of this information rendered it doubly suspect.

She was about to ask Stevie to elaborate when she heard footsteps on the stairs. Seeing Denise making her way down, she busied herself with the new stock.

'Like I say,' said Stevie, his voice low but nonetheless emphatic. 'Proper. Mental.'

Barbarossa and the managers remained cloistered in the break room for the better part of an hour and a half. By the time they were done, Marli had been and gone, and Stevie's stomach was audibly rumbling. Barbarossa emerged first with a self-satisfied swagger, his union rep trotting obediently behind him. As they neared the desk Stevie shrank away, but Alyssa held her ground, staring back at Barbarossa defiantly as he eyeballed her with a who-the-fuck-are-*you*? expression.

As he strode out, door swinging behind him, Nikki, Denise and the others emerged. There was a sag to their shoulders, with Nikki and especially Denise looking thoroughly deflated. The two women approached the desk, leaving the entourage to catch flies with their tongues.

'Right, Alyssa, let's have that chat now,' said Nikki, as if it had been at Alyssa's instigation rather than hers.

Giving the bemused-looking Stevie an equally bemused shrug, Alyssa followed Nikki and Denise over to a secluded corner of the library.

'Is Davy not with us today, then?' Nikki inquired, addressing no one in particular.

'Phased return,' Denise explained.

'A pity. I'd have liked to have spoken to them both about this together.'

'Spoken to us about what?' Alyssa demanded, her last vestiges of patience having finally run out.

Nikki pirouetted to face her, fingers laced together in front of her, already in full-on sales pitch mode. '*Well* . . . as you may already be aware, each year North Kelvin District Council holds a prize-giving ceremony to recognise outstanding contributions to the service by members of our extended council family. In light of recent events, myself and the rest of the senior management team have decided to nominate both you and Davy for a special merit award.' She paused for effect. All that was missing was a dramatic drumroll. 'And I'm delighted to tell you that both nominations have been accepted by the awards committee.'

Alyssa stared at her for several seconds. 'What – so I get a gold star for not ducking fast enough?'

Nikki laughed awkwardly. 'There's no need to be *quite* so cynical. You've shown incredible fortitude and an exceptional commitment to the service through your eagerness to return to work.'

Yeah, because you weren't fricking paying me, Alyssa thought. She was amazed Nikki could actually bring herself to stand there and come out with this crap without even a twinge of embarrassment.

'And do I get any say in this?'

'It was a joint decision, made by the entire senior management team,' said Nikki, as if that was all that mattered.

'It's an evening's free entertainment,' said Denise, piping up for the first time. 'It's all good fun. Plus you get a slap-up meal and as much booze as you like.'

She didn't sound especially convinced. Browbeaten into toeing the party line, Alyssa suspected.

She turned to face Nikki again, all set to tell her, in the nicest possible terms, up which particular orifice she could ram her prize-giving, but something stopped her. Perhaps she was feeling a twinge of residual guilt over having already turned down an invitation to a library social gathering without a credible excuse – or perhaps it was because she knew Denise would inevitably bear the brunt of Nikki's wrath if she, one of her underlings, made things difficult.

Just say yes. You can always find an excuse to back out later.

She gave a tight smile. 'Fine. I can't wait.'

Nikki beamed a ninety-thousand-kilowatt grin, all horsy gums and veneers. 'Excellent. It's a week on Sunday at the Excelsior. I'll email you the details. And, um . . . ' She cast a baleful eye at Alyssa's scoop neck T-shirt, and the view it afforded of the winged skull tattooed on her upper torso. 'You might want to avoid anything too low-cut. We want to set the right sort of tone.'

Alyssa instantly made a mental note that, if she did end up going, it would be in her sluttiest outfit.

'Well,' said Nikki, filling the void of silence when it became clear Alyssa wasn't going to, 'I wish I could stay and chat longer, but I've got a meeting with the strategic resilience committee at four. You'll have my email by the end of the day.'

And with that, she was gone, stiletto heels click-clacking on the floor, the rest of her posse hurrying after her as she swept out in an uncanny impersonation of a tornado, complete with the carnage left in its wake.

As the door swung shut, Denise turned to Alyssa, shoulders already arching in a helpless shrug.

'It's all right,' Alyssa said, forestalling whatever apology was coming. 'You don't need to say anything.'

'I *said* she should run it by you before going ahead and organising this,' said Denise, voice crackling with angry vehemence. 'I knew you wouldn't like the sound of it. But they don't think about things like that. They forget we're people with minds of our own.'

'It's fine,' said Alyssa wearily. 'Look, I'll do this prize-giving thingy – walk up on stage and collect my medal or whatever.' She gave a slight smile. 'Just don't expect me to look like I'm enjoying myself.'

Denise returned the smile. She looked tired and exasperated, and Alyssa couldn't help but wonder just what had gone down during the meeting with Tony Barbarossa.

'Look, your shift's nearly over,' said Denise. 'Why don't you get your things and slink off? I'll cover the counter till Bindi gets in.'

Alyssa stepped out of the library and stalked off down to the street. As she walked, a taxi – one of those big four-wheel-drive affairs –

pulled alongside her, slowing to match her pace. She gave it the briefest of glances and kept walking.

The rear window wound down. 'Oi,' said a voice from inside.

She turned to see Davy sitting in the back.

'Oi yourself. What d'you want?'

'We're going on a pilgrimage. Get in.'

'You do what you like. I'm going home.'

She kept walking. The cab kept pace with her.

'You know,' she said, when it continued to show no sign of leaving her in peace, 'where I come from, this sort of behaviour is classed as harassment.'

'Come on,' said Davy. 'You're making us both look ridiculous.'

With a roll of her eyes, Alyssa ground to a halt. The taxi came to a standstill too. She looked at Davy. He looked at her. Gave an expectant little shrug.

She sighed. Convinced she was making a colossal mistake, she hauled open the sliding door and clambered in. As she plonked herself in the seat next to Davy's wheelchair, the driver pulled back out into the traffic stream.

'So are you going to tell me where we're going, or am I going to have to beat it out of you?'

'Violence will not be necessary, I assure you. I sense, my fellow conspirator, that there is a certain – shall we say reticence? – on your part to concede the notion that the individual currently awaiting trial for the events of the first of March might not be the criminal mastermind he's been made out to be.'

'Damn straight there is. And I'm not your fellow conspirator.'

'Not yet, anyway. I'm taking you to hear the truth straight from the horse's mouth.'

Alyssa looked at him in astonishment. 'We're going to see Paul McGuigan?'

'The very same.'

'How in blue blazes did you manage to wrangle that?'

'Oh, I can be very persuasive when I have to. Plus, I have it on good authority that he has an incurable craving for mint creams.' He opened his jacket, revealing a family-sized bag crammed into the inner pocket. 'I inferred I'd be willing to smuggle in some contraband in exchange for an audience with his nibs.'

Alyssa shook her head. 'You're really not going to let this go, are you?'

'You mean turn a blind eye to a major miscarriage of justice? What do you take me for?'

Alyssa didn't trust herself to answer that.

'So are you in? Or have you got something better lined up for your afternoon than a sightseeing trip to Scotland's maximum-security prison?' He stuck out his bottom lip, affecting a pout. 'Come on – humour a poor old cripple.'

Alyssa sighed. 'Fine. If it'll shut you up . . . '

'Smashing.' He cupped his hand to his mouth. 'Onwards, driver!'

12

Barlinnie Prison was located on the eastern limits of Glasgow, about a half-hour drive from Thornhill. With a capacity for approximately one thousand inmates but an actual population severely in excess of that, it was Scotland's largest penitentiary, home to prisoners from all over the country, including both those on remand and those convicted of the most serious offences on the statute book. Renowned as a hard place for hard men, its notoriety extended far beyond its native land, and Alyssa's stomach did a little hop-skip as they neared the prison, its twin flags – the saltire and the emblem of the Scottish Prison Service – fluttering lightly in the breeze.

Mind you, it wasn't at all what she'd been expecting. She'd imagined an imposing-looking building encircled by a high wall topped with barbed wire, possibly with a watchtower or two, each patrolled by a sniper-rifle-toting guard on the lookout for anyone making a break for freedom. What she got, instead, was a modern-looking brick building with a glass-fronted entrance, more akin to a leisure complex than how she imagined a maximum-security prison would look. As if that wasn't bizarre enough, it was built right in the heart of a residential area, with rows of houses just a stone's throw away, their gardens separated from the prison grounds by nothing but a low fence that wouldn't keep out a determined toddler, let alone a runaway felon. She wondered how the occupants felt about living so close to a place that was frequently mentioned in the same breath as Alcatraz and the Maze.

She would, of course, subsequently learn that what she'd seen was merely the visitors' entrance, designed to project a PR-friendly image of the penal system. The main prison – a sprawling, five-wing eyesore originally built in the late nineteenth century – was tucked away at the back, surrounded by a high concrete wall with, naturally, a crown of barbed wire. For the time being, though, she and the driver assisted Davy out of the taxi, and the pair of them headed up the wheelchair-friendly ramp and into the lobby, Alyssa pushing.

'They're talking about closing it down,' Davy said, as they queued at the front desk, identification at the ready. 'Replacing it with a bunch of smaller prisons and turning it into a tourist attraction.'

'A fun day out for all the family,' remarked Alyssa, wondering what would possess anyone to go wandering around a prison, decommissioned or otherwise, for kicks.

They presented themselves and their ID at the desk before progressing through security. They were asked to turn out their pockets and part company with any valuables, before a couple of big bald-headed prison officers treated them to what was quaintly described as a pat-down but, to Alyssa, more closely resembled a full-on groping session. The officers regarded the bag of mint creams Davy had brought with some suspicion, but ultimately agreed McGuigan was unlikely to either OD on them or barter them as currency. There then followed much hilarity – at least, the officers seemed to think it was funny – as the bullet lodged in Davy's spine repeatedly set off the metal detector they had to pass through. Eventually, though, the rigmarole was over and done with, and they were directed through to a wide, low-ceilinged visiting room furnished with multiple chairs and tables, several already occupied by people who, judging by their apparent ease with their environment, had done this before. They chatted easily to one another, greeting old friends with cheery waves and howyas. One or two were even laughing and joking with the guards. Alyssa shot an ominous glance at Davy as they parked themselves at their allotted table and settled in to wait for the inmates to be let through.

Paul McGuigan looked even more gaunt and strung-out than the last time Alyssa had seen him. The red prison-issue sweatshirt looked massive on him, his eyes so dark-rimmed and hollowed-out it was like looking at a skull. He sat down, greeting Alyssa and Davy with a brief, disinterested nod, as if their presence was merely incidental, then slumped forward on the table, chin resting on folded arms, waiting for this interruption to his daily routine to be over.

'And a good afternoon to you too,' said Davy.

McGuigan grunted and shrugged. 'Nothin' too good about it fae where I'm sittin'.'

'Well, I've got something here that might cheer you up.' Davy produced the bag of mint creams and pushed it across the table toward him. 'There ya go, pal. Fill yer boots.'

McGuigan instantly became more engaged. He sat up straighter, eyes lighting up and mouth broadening into a rictus grin that showed off a sparse set of badly decaying teeth. Alyssa couldn't help but think that plying him with candy probably wasn't in his best interests.

For a while, no one spoke as McGuigan's attention was focused entirely on his present. He ripped open the bag, tore the wrapping paper off a mint and stuffed it into his mouth. Before he'd even finished chewing, he was already unwrapping another, ready to cram it in as soon as there was room. And another, and another. Alyssa shot Davy a look that was part-disgusted and part-amused, but Davy paid her no attention. His eyes were on McGuigan, watching as he ate with the efficiency and determination of a man carrying out a military exercise.

Gradually, the munching noises subsided. When the bag was almost empty, Davy broke the silence.

'You keeping OK? Not getting any hassle off of anyone?'

'They've got me in solitary,' McGuigan mumbled, between mouthfuls. 'Say it's for my own safety. Banged up wi' the paedos and rapists – like I've got anything in common with *them*.' He shrugged philosophically. 'But aye, least I get my own cell. And naebody's given me grief so far. Havnae been made tae play "pick up the soap" yet.'

Alyssa wondered whether he was putting on a brave face or if he genuinely didn't understand the trouble he was in. His manner reminded her of a schoolboy who'd been caught clowning around by the teacher but, despite the heavy punishment meted out to him, still couldn't resist mugging to his classmates, hoping they'd be impressed.

'You're managing to keep out of mischief, then,' said Davy. 'That's good. And what about the, uh, the . . . '

McGuigan looked at him blankly for a moment, then smiled. 'Aw, ye mean the smack? Well, it's no somethin' they dish out at the commissary.' He gave a nervous little snicker. 'Got me on a methadone scrip soon as I arrived. S'no exactly prime cut H, but at least it helps take the edge off. Lookit.' He held his hands out, palms down.

Davy nodded, impressed. 'Solid as a rock.'

'Been free o' the shakes almost a month now. Can even write my own name.' He shrugged. 'So hey – upside tae everythin'.'

Alyssa had been watching the pair of them with considerable interest. Their interaction seemed relaxed and unforced, even bordering on companionable. McGuigan clearly regarded Davy as one of the good guys – someone who was in his corner. She certainly couldn't envisage the likes of Bindi or the dearly departed Jason showing him this level of kindness. She wondered if this was Davy's first visit, and if they were the first visitors he'd had.

Davy gestured to Alyssa. 'You ever seen her before now?'

McGuigan glanced briefly at Alyssa and shook his head. 'Never seen her in my life.'

'That's a bare-faced lie for a start,' said Alyssa. 'I was on shift the day you were arrested.'

McGuigan shrugged belligerently. 'And? Nae offence, but I kinda had other things on my mind at the time.'

She supposed it was just possible he'd been so distracted he'd managed to walk straight past the desk without clocking her. Even so, it wasn't an experience she was used to. With her tattoos, she tended to stand out in a crowd, and most people who'd seen her once didn't forget her.

'S'pose *you* think it was me who done it and all?' McGuigan said, interrupting her thoughts.

'That depends. Did you?'

McGuigan looked up at her long enough to smirk. 'Well, I'd hardly say "aye" if I had, would I?' A little trickle of minty drool ran down his jaw from the corner of his mouth.

'He's got you there,' said Davy.

'Kinda the problem, in't it? I say I didnae dae it, and they're all like, "Well, if he did dae it, he *would* say that, wouldn't he?" So do I keep sayin' I'm innocent? Or do I just keep schtum and wait 'n' see what happens? Let 'em dae their worst and hope the mud disnae stick?'

'What's your defence lawyer say?' said Davy.

McGuigan toyed absently with a discarded wrapper. 'My lady solicitor tells me, if I plead guilty, they'll let me out sooner.'

'It'd still mean a lengthy stretch inside. It's not like they're going to let you out in a couple of years for good behaviour.'

McGuigan pulled a face. 'Well, hey. S'no exactly like my prospects on the outside were peaches 'n' cream.'

Davy's face was like stone. 'So that's it, then? You're not even going to put up a fight? You're just going to give up and let yourself get sent down for the rest of your life for something you didn't do?'

'Just cool your jets a minute,' said Alyssa, holding up a hand. 'Why don't we hear him out 'stead of you riding him like a prize showjumper? Maybe he's telling us he *did* do it.'

Davy looked at McGuigan long and hard. 'Is that what you're saying?'

McGuigan sighed despairingly and slumped on the table, resuming the position he'd adopted when he'd first come out. 'Ach, look, what's it matter? Everyone's already decided I'm guilty as sin anyway, so what's the use tryin' tae convince 'em I'm not? Naeb'dy's ever cut me a break in my life. S'no as if they're gonnae start now.'

Davy said nothing. He looked glum and dejected. In the vacuum created by his silence, Alyssa took up the baton.

'If you want us to believe you're innocent,' she said, 'how d'you explain the gun in your rucksack?'

McGuigan let out an exasperated groan. 'I *told* 'em, I was hangin' ontae it for a pal. I never fired it in my life. Never fired *any* gun. But soon as I heard about the shootings, I knew exactly what everyone was gonnae think.' He lifted his head and looked plaintively at his two visitors, eyes huge and wild with desperation, the pupils pinpricks. 'Aye, I had a gun like the one that mad bastard used, and aye, I got caught with it fair and square, but *I didnae dae it.*'

Alyssa hated to admit it, but on the face of it he sounded genuine. She could only conclude he was either telling the truth or a very gifted actor – and she had a hard time believing the guilelessness was all an act.

McGuigan turned to Davy. 'You think I could look you in the eye if it was me who put you in that chair? You think I'd've agreed tae see you? I never had a problem wi' you, man. You never gave me any hassle, no like some of they other pricks. You always done right by me. And you' – he turned to Alyssa – 'I never even *seen* you before. What in the name of blue *fuck* d'ye think I'd get out of puttin' a bullet in you?'

If Davy was moved by this heartfelt outburst, he didn't let it show. 'So who's this pal who gave you the gun, then?' he said sternly. 'Must be someone really special if you're willing to go to jail on his account.'

McGuigan lowered his eyes. 'Cannae tell ye.'

'Why not? From where I'm sitting, he's not much of a pal if he's willing to let you rot in here while he gets to skip around, free as a bird.'

McGuigan said nothing.

'If the boot was on the other foot, d'you think he'd be sitting here refusing to give you up? Cos see, whoever he is, I reckon he'd've sold you out for a song the moment they collared him.' He banged the flat of his hand on the table, trying unsuccessfully to make McGuigan look at him. 'Come on – you tell the cops who he is and we can get this whole thing cleared up by teatime.'

That sounded wildly optimistic to Alyssa, but she refrained from saying anything.

'You know you're not doing yourself any favours, don't you? Look, if you're worried about him finding out it was you who squealed—'

'It's no *that*!' exclaimed McGuigan, so loudly that several of the other inmates and their visitors ceased their conversations and turned in his direction. A nearby guard took a step toward them. Alyssa gave him a little wave to indicate everything was all right.

McGuigan groaned in exasperation, grasping at the air as he struggled to find the words to explain himself. 'It's no about bein' afraid. If I was that bothered about savin' my own skin, I'd've grassed him up weeks ago and got put in witness protection or whatever.'

'Well, what is it about, then?'

McGuigan met Davy's gaze without blinking. 'Honour.'

Davy stared at him in disbelief. '*Scuse* me?'

'It's about giein' yer word tae someone and then no goin' back on it. It's about no landin' yer mates in the shit just tae make yer own life easier.'

Alyssa couldn't help herself: she let out an involuntary, disgusted snort.

McGuigan rounded on her with an ugly smirk. 'You don't get it – I can tell. Mibby you'd stab yer pals in the back at the drop of a hat. Or mibby ye havnae *got* any pals.' He turned to face Davy again, with an air of finality. 'But it is what it is. Ye can ask till ye're blue in the face; it won't dae ye any good. I'm no stool-pigeon.'

Davy met his gaze, unblinking, disappointment and disapproval writ large in his stony expression.

McGuigan, having said his piece, seemed to visibly deflate, slumping even lower and burying his head in his folded arms. It was abundantly clear to Alyssa that they'd get no more out of him.

Davy, it seemed, shared her assessment. He sighed and shook his head. 'Have it your way.'

As he and Alyssa prepared to leave, McGuigan lifted his head and gazed up at them, his eyes dead and devoid of hope. He looked small and incredibly forlorn, sitting there on his lonesome in his oversized sweatshirt.

'I dunno if you could get a message tae my mum?' he said to Davy. 'I figured she'd've come tae see me by now, but she'll no take my calls.'

Davy hesitated, then reached over and patted McGuigan's shoulder. 'I'll see what I can do, pal,' he said gruffly, then turned his chair around and made for the exit.

Alyssa paused at the door to look back at McGuigan. He'd retreated into his own world again and was rummaging inside the bag, on the hunt for any mint creams he might have missed.

They headed back the way they'd come without a word, collecting their things from the lockers in which they'd been stowed. As they emerged into the sunlight, Davy broke the silence.

'Well?'

'Well, what?'

'What did you make of him?'

'I think he's a sad, pathetic little man who's in way over his head.'

'Agreed on all counts. But that's not what I meant.'

'What, then?'

'D'you still think he did it?'

Alyssa thought long and hard before responding. 'The honest answer is I don't know.'

Davy rolled his eyes in exasperation. 'You know the longer you spend sitting on that fence, the more the chance you have of getting piles?'

She turned to him with a scowl. 'Hey, I agreed to come and see the little creep with my own eyes. I never signed a waiver promising to become a true believer.'

'But you admit there's a chance he could be innocent.'

'Of course there's a chance. There's *always* a chance. There's a chance what we think of as life is nothing but a computer sim run by aliens for their own amusement. That's why they have judges and juries and such. Who, incidentally, are way better qualified to figure this stuff out than either you or me. If McGuigan's innocent, he'll get his chance to prove it in court, same as anyone.'

Davy shook his head but said nothing. He slumped low in his chair, shoulders sagging, head bowed. Watching him, Alyssa real-ised just how much their little excursion had taken out of him, both mentally and physically. It stood to reason, she supposed. He'd suffered a major, life-altering injury, and was probably still a long way from a full recovery. Well, as full a recovery as he was ever going to make. She couldn't help feeling sorry for him, in spite of her lingering resentment at him for dragging her on this pointless expedition.

'Come on,' she said. 'Unless we wanna hit rush hour, we'd best make tracks.'

13

The Excelsior was an upmarket hotel in the city centre – the sort of place normally frequented by businessmen on six-figure salaries during overnight stopovers and that charged a small fortune for a night's stay. As Alyssa stood on the pavement, staring up at the glass-fronted façade, she reflected that some people really did have more money than sense, and wondered how the cash-strapped council could justify renting the place out for this glorified circle-jerk. But that wasn't her problem. Tonight she was here on someone else's dime, and she'd made up her mind to treat it as a chance to enjoy a free meal and drink the bar dry.

She presented her ticket to the doorman, who relieved her of her coat and directed her to the function room, where the party was already in full swing, the Top 40 offal on the speaker system assaulting her ears like nails on a chalkboard. Several tables, arranged wedding reception-style throughout the room, were already occupied, while the floor was teeming with people either congregating in little clusters or moving to and fro, wine glasses and beer bottles in their hands. At one end of the room, several trestle tables laden with buffet food were set out. At the other was a podium with a microphone on a stand. Alyssa suppressed a shudder. She just knew this was going to be excruciating.

In the end, she'd decided to forego the super-slutty outfit she'd been contemplating, though she'd still made sure enough of her body art remained visible that no one was going to miss it. Mind you, even if she *had* put on the Party Frock of Shame with its deep scoop neckline and oh-so-short lace trim, she'd hardly have been the most indecently dressed belle at the ball. There was a lot of exposed flesh on display, whether it was the knobbly knees of red-faced, perspiring older men in kilts or the bingo-wings on the middle-aged ladies with their bottle-dyed perms and pointlessly pointy heels that caused them to totter and wobble their way across the varnished floor.

'Over here, Allie Ballie Bee!'

She turned to see Davy seated at a table at the far end of the room with a handful of other guests. Surprised by just how glad she was to see a familiar face, she headed over, picking her way through the throng.

'My favourite illustrated lady!' Davy beamed up at her, a look of dopey, borderline-intoxicated bliss plastered across his features. 'I was just saying we should take bets on whether you'd show.'

'Oh yeah?' said Alyssa, not altogether happy at the thought of Davy discussing her behind her back with a bunch of people she didn't know. 'See you managed to take some time off singlehandedly exposing the deep state.'

A look passed between them, Davy saying nothing but none-theless making it abundantly clear this wasn't a topic for public consumption. She in turn conveyed her displeasure with a silent glower.

'Well, don't stand on ceremony!' cried Davy's nearest neighbour at the table – an older man with an ample gut and a monk's crown. 'Grab a pew! Can I get you something to wet your palate?'

Alyssa slid into an empty chair. 'Sex on the Beach?'

The older guy threw back his head and roared as if this was the funniest thing he'd ever heard. 'Ach, mibby, if this was Malibu and I was thirty years younger. As it is, I'll have to pass.'

Alyssa met his gaze, deadpan. 'Peach schnapps, orange juice, cranberry juice and a spot of *crème de cassis*. Look it up.'

He chuckled again, patting Alyssa on the shoulder with such overfamiliarity that she had to stop herself from grabbing his wrist and snapping it. 'Ah, you're some kid! I'll see what I can muster.'

With considerable effort, he eased himself onto his feet. As he headed off to the bar, Davy turned to Alyssa with a grin, their earlier friction seemingly forgotten.

'Isn't this great? Where else are you going to find such an extra-vagant display of naked cynicism and shameless opportunism? Three hundred and sixty-four days a year they treat us like cogs in a machine. But then, for one day, they get us all together to pretend they actually care about us as individuals, tossing us a few shiny baubles to make us feel valued. And hey – if they can turn a national tragedy into a brand marketing strategy, so much the better.'

'Great' wasn't the word Alyssa would have used, but she was otherwise in agreement, if considerably less amused than he was. 'They sure know how to draw in a crowd.'

Davy shrugged. 'Eh, it's no great mystery. Free booze, free food, a bit of the dancing, plus a chance to catch up with faces we haven't seen for a while. Like Colin, for instance.' He nodded in the direc-tion of the bar, where Alyssa could see the older man trying to explain Sex on the Beach to the bartender. 'You know he showed me the ropes at my first branch back in the day? Pair of us were thick as thieves. I was proper gutted when they split us up. Means the world being able to catch up with him.'

'I'm happy for you,' said Alyssa distractedly. She'd just spotted DCI Metcalfe making her way through the crowd, looking thor-oughly out of place in her charcoal trouser suit. What was *she* doing here? This was, as she understood it, a night for council staff and their opportunistic managers. Where a DCI in charge of a murder investigation fit in was anyone's guess – unless she was in line to pick up an award herself for catching the bad guy.

'Yeah, one big happy family, that's what we are,' Davy continued, oblivious. 'The friendships you make in this job are for life. In't that right, Col?' he said, as Colin returned to the table, carrying a tall glass filled with cloudy liquid and ice, an orange slice on the rim.

'Haven't a clue what you're blethering about, but I'm sure you're right,' said Colin agreeably. He plonked the glass down in front of Alyssa. 'They y'are, my lovely. One Sex on the Beach.'

It looked like a half-respectable effort – and tasted like one too when she sampled it, to the extent that she actually allowed herself to believe this might not turn out to be quite such an excruciating evening after all.

'Here,' Colin turned to Davy in a conspiratorial voice, 'Megan Lowry from payroll tells me Tony Barbarossa's angling to get himself reinstated. Know anything about that?'

Davy's face instantly turned ashen. 'No. What's she been saying?'

'Just that him and his union rep had a sit-down with Nikki Wyatt and the other high heid yins last week. Said he was arguing unfair dismissal – that they didn't follow due process when they gave him his jotters, so he's entitled to reinstatement and back pay.'

'Well, if there's so much as a whisper that he's coming back to Thornhill, I'm putting in for a transfer, and if they don't give me one I'll go off on the sick.'

At that moment, a couple of dolled-up young women, each wearing brightly coloured slip dresses and clutching sequin-encrusted purses, came staggering over, calling Davy's name. They immediately set upon him, wrapping their arms round him in turn, planting kisses all over his face, calling him a poor wee soul and telling him how great it was to see him. Right on cue, Davy immediately slipped back into character, batting away their affectionate cooing in his usual self-effacing manner.

Alyssa turned to Colin. 'What's so bad about this Tony Barbarossa anyway?'

Colin gave her a pained look. 'Oh, he's a nasty, nasty piece of work, love. Made our Davy's life hell. Damn near broke him, so it did, having to work alongside that prick every day, listening to his jibes, putting up with his innuendos. Many's the night he'd call me up in tears over something the bugger had said to him.'

Alyssa turned to look at Davy, regaling the two giggling girls with a no doubt spot-on impression of some mutual acquaintance. She tried to picture him crying down the phone and found the effect profoundly jarring.

'It's not even as if he actually *wants* the job,' Colin went on. 'Always acted like it was beneath him back when he still had it. He's just out to create as much misery as possible for all concerned. I'm telling you: that creep comes anywhere near you, you run a mile.'

Alyssa was about to tell Colin she had no immediate plans to get to know Tony Barbarossa intimately when she heard the clack of heels approaching from behind. She looked over her shoulder as Nikki Wyatt came tottering over and, bending down, squeezed herself into the gap between Alyssa and Colin's chairs. She was wearing a low-cut top, her scraggy tits practically in Alyssa's face, and had slathered on so much makeup that her face looked like it was melting. She had some nerve telling anyone else to dress modestly.

'Are we having a good time, guys and dolls?' she hollered, like a funhouse mirror version of a club rep sent out to gee up the crowd.

Alyssa had to turn her head away. The reek of brandy on the woman's breath was overpowering.

'Alyssa.' Nikki patted her shoulder with such vigour she was practically slapping her. 'So glad you could make it. Our mortality rate might leave something to be desired, but we know how to put on a party . . . AM I RIGHT?' she bellowed, so loudly that several people at adjacent tables turned to look in her direction.

And you've certainly been making the most of what the bar has to offer, Alyssa thought, wondering if Nikki was one of those people who got wasted and photocopied their asses at Christmas parties.

'Oh, by the way' – Nikki lifted Alyssa's glass, slugged back a mouthful, pulled a face and put it back on the table – 'this journo called me the other day. Says he wants to do a piece on you. Y'know, about getting shot and that.'

So, having failed to get her to take the bait with his endless calls, Ewan Caulfield had now resorted to roping her employers into browbeating her into submission. Terrific.

'And what did you say to him?' Alyssa asked.

'I said you'd get back to him.'

Nikki stood there for an awkward moment, swaying a little, clearly awaiting Alyssa's response. Getting none, her face hardened.

'You gonna do it or not?' she slurred.

Alyssa gazed up at her, unblinking, determined not to be pushed into giving an answer, even though she knew it would be an unequivocal 'no'.

'I haven't made up my mind yet,' she said.

Nikki stared at Alyssa for a long moment, then made a sound like she was blowing her nose. 'Yeah, well, don't take too long. Offer's not gonna last forever. You'll be yesterday's news in an eyeblink, toots.'

With that, she turned unsteadily and wobbled away. She collided with a neighbouring table, grabbed hold of it to steady herself, muttered something obscene-sounding to those seated at it, and continued on her way.

'Well,' said Colin, with a wry smile, 'nice to see some things never change.'

* * *

Alyssa excused herself and headed in search of the buffet table. She was feeling peckish and knew she needed something to soak up all the alcohol she was planning on knocking back. Plate in hand, she joined the back of the lengthy queue. Half the room, it seemed, had had the same idea. Both in front and behind her, there was much jollity in the air as people who – like Davy and Colin – presumably hadn't seen one another since last year's knees-up greeted each other and conversed in overly loud voices. She was conscious, as she had been ever since stepping into the room, that an awful lot of people were looking at her. They were trying not to make it too obvious, but she kept catching furtive glances coming her way, invariably accompanied by low murmurs. And she knew exactly what they'd be saying: *That's her – the girl who survived the Library Murders.*

Since her return to work, she'd been slowly but surely coming to grips with her status as a minor celebrity. Everyone in the company, it seemed, knew her story, and each time she encountered someone fresh, it was only a matter of time before the elephant in the room reared its head and she was inundated by all manner of questions about the shooting, ranging from whether it had hurt (it had) to whether her life had flashed before her eyes (it hadn't). And then there were her regular colleagues, whose reactions ran the gamut from wide-eyed awe from Stevie to gruff paternalism from Pat to what seemed like active disdain from Bindi, who Alyssa suspected was nursing a secret jealousy that it hadn't been her. Davy's return had taken much of the heat off her, partly because he was now the cool new flavour of the month and partly, she suspected, because he was a whole lot more receptive to their attentiveness, seeming to revel in his status as a VIP, whereas it took all of Alyssa's self-control not to yell at them to fuck off when they insisted on bringing it up for the umpteenth time. She always got the sense people were miffed by her reluctance to endlessly relive her trauma for their personal gratification.

She checked the time on her phone and sighed. The way things were going, the entire ceremony would be over before she reached the buffet table. She should probably cut her losses and make do without solids. Regardless of how drunk she got, she had a sneaking suspicion there would be plenty others whose indiscretions would eclipse anything she said or did. Nikki Wyatt being chief among them.

She scanned the hall. Everyone seemed to be having a whale of a time. All around her, old friendships were being renewed, the alcohol was flowing freely, and the din of voices was growing more overpowering by the second. Then her eyes fell on someone standing at the far end of the room, leaning against the wall, a glass of what looked depressingly like lemonade in her hand. Metcalfe. She was alone, looking so out of place and lonely that Alyssa was almost tempted to go over and say hi.

Just then, Metcalfe was joined by another person. He was in his late fifties, suited, with white hair and a goatee and small almond-shaped glasses. Alyssa was sure she'd seen him somewhere before, but she couldn't think where. He didn't look like a library manager or council official. It wasn't until he turned to gaze out across the room, giving her a front-on view of his face, that she realised who he was: Kip Formby, the Justice Secretary, last seen by her in a newspaper article on Davy's phone, exerting pressure on the police to make a speedy arrest. What was *he* doing schmoozing with Metcalfe, and why did she look so thoroughly uncomfortable in his presence? As Alyssa watched, Formby's lips moved rapidly as he whispered to Metcalfe, his mouth inches from her ear. She saw the arch of Metcalfe's shoulders, the tightening of her folded arms, her already thin lips becoming virtually invisible as she pursed them into an angry slit.

At that moment, the Shakira or Nelly Furtado or whatever it was on the speaker system cut out abruptly, replaced by the ear-splitting whine of a feedback loop. As the room exclaimed its collective disapproval, Alyssa looked to the stage, where one of the innumerable interchangeable fat old men in kilts was fumbling with the microphone. 'Aaaaahhhhladies and gentlemen,' he purred, his voice booming out of the loudspeakers, 'if yous could make your way to your seats, we'll be getting underway in just a few minutes. That is all.'

He stepped down, and the music and conversation resumed. All around the room, people began to head back toward the tables, still conversing, in no great hurry to take their seats.

Before she did the same, Alyssa looked back in the direction of Metcalfe and Formby, but both had vanished.

The ceremony was as deathly dull and teeth-clenchingly cringeworthy as Alyssa had feared. There were a million and one awards to sit through before they got to Alyssa and Davy's – saving the biggest and best for last, no doubt. Many appeared to be achievements doled out for tenure alone – or, as Alyssa saw it, for people who'd failed to make good their escape before they became part of the furniture. The recipients gamely acted the part, parading on stage to be glad-handed by whichever minor dignitary was presenting their award. They ranged from blubbering middle-aged women from Accounts, expressing teary-eyed gratitude to the company for having briefly taken notice of their existence, to cocksure young men from Sports, who fancied themselves as amateur comedians and mugged for the audience as Mr or Mrs No-Mark Councillor droned on about 'the council family' and 'daring to become the best version of yourself'. Each was handed a little silver envelope, and it occurred to Alyssa that, if there was money inside, maybe she could afford to cut back on all the extra shifts she'd been doing at the library of late.

About an hour and a half into the proceedings, when awards had been doled out for every minor accomplishment under the sun and most of the room was seriously flagging, the big baldie guy serving as MC took to the stage to announce that it was the moment they'd all been waiting for – the crowning highlight of the evening, the presentation of the Special Award for Outstanding Commitment to Public Service. The First Minister, a diminutive woman in a suit-jacket-and-skirt combo, came out amid much fanfare and a few audible boos from the back of the room and launched into a lengthy speech about how she still remembered her first library when she was a child and how, out of all the public services, libraries held a special place in her heart. She and her government, she said, knew all too well what library staff were up against, and thanked them for their commitment, claiming that each and every one of them was valued.

'Give us more money, then!' some wit shouted, to moderate applause and a solitary wolf-whistle.

That caused her to falter, but only momentarily. 'And now, it gives me great pleasure to present this award to two people who, perhaps more than any among us, understand the true meaning of commitment to their profession. Please join me in giving a huge round of applause to this year's recipients for the Special Award for Outstanding Commitment to Public Service – Davy Grogan and Alyssa Clark.'

A spotlight fell on their table and the entire room got to its collective feet to applaud. Together, they crossed the floor – Davy spinning his wheels, Alyssa trudging behind him. When they got to the podium, it quickly became apparent that nobody had considered the logistics of getting someone in a wheelchair up onto an elevated platform, so there was much tutting and consternation from the audience and hasty deliberation between the various head honchos – none of whom, it seemed, was capable of making a decision to save their lives. Eventually, the matter was resolved by two burly men from Leisure Facilities, who volunteered their services and between them lifted Davy, chair and all, onto the stage. The FM shook them both by the hand, gave them their little silver envelopes, then yielded the mic to them to say a few words. Alyssa would rather have committed public seppuku than make a speech to this menagerie, but Davy gamely took up the baton and launched into a rambling, off-the-cuff valedictory that played shamelessly to the gallery while containing just enough genuine sentiment not to seem entirely ungracious.

'Well,' he said, 'if I'd known in advance this was the sort of reception I'd get, I'd've made sure to get shot in the back sooner.'

Alyssa had a vague recollection that he'd used that line before, though she had to admit it was a good one, if not exactly original. As he continued his oratory to much laughter, plus the odd 'awww', her mind began to drift. She gazed out at the sea of faces before her – people she didn't know, and who didn't know her, but who'd nonetheless co-opted her ordeal as part of some shared, collective experience. *We are one people, an attack on one is an attack on us all.*

Her eyes drifted to the back of the room, where she spotted Metcalfe and Formby, standing side by side, watching Davy but clearly not listening to him. They were muttering to one another – well, Formby was doing the muttering while Metcalfe listened, though she did occasionally interject. Her expression was tight and controlled, but her eyes gave the game away. She wasn't happy. Not one bit.

It was as if the height and distance afforded by the podium gave Alyssa clarity. She'd seen that look before – in Denise's eyes the day Nikki Wyatt had ambushed them about the prize-giving. This was someone under duress – backed up against a wall by someone who had the power to shape her career, or to end it, and forced to act in a way that ran contrary to her principles, whatever they might be.

Once again, she heard Davy's words, coming to her as clearly as if he was speaking them now:

Don't you get it? They were under pressure to get their man – any *man.*

She realised the room was applauding, and she was brought back to the here and now like a rubber band snapping. Beside her, the First Minister was applauding too, and shaking her hand again, and then she and Davy were on their way back to their table, Davy once again assisted by the brawny men from Leisure Facilities. Music began to play, and the din of conversation resumed.

As soon as she was back in her seat, she slit open her envelope and tipped it upside down. Two £20 Waterstones vouchers fell into her lap.

Book tokens? They'd given her *book tokens*? This had to be someone's idea of a joke. Was her life, and that of her colleagues, seriously valued so cheaply? But all this was nothing compared to the cover-up she was now convinced was transpiring right before her eyes. Something fishy was afoot, and she was damned if they were going to buy her off with *book tokens*.

She turned to Davy, busy bumping his gums to Colin, and tapped him on the shoulder.

He turned to face her. 'Yes, fellow outstanding employee?'

'I think you're right.'

'What's that?' He cupped a hand to his ear. 'Can barely hear ya.'

She sighed and raised her voice over the din that surrounded them, leaning in to speak directly into his ear.

'I think you're right. I think there's something shady going on.'

PART TWO

14

'The way I see it,' Alyssa said, 'we're looking at three possibilities. One – the shooter was a random madman who decided, apropos of nothing, to head into a library and waste five people at random. Two – it was some kind of armed robbery gone wrong . . . '

' . . . or three,' Davy concluded, 'it was someone with an axe to grind against the staff.'

Alyssa nodded soberly. She was perched on the end of the bed in Davy's bedroom, on the chairlift-accessible upper floor of a rather nice semi-D in Scotstounhill. His mum's place, as she'd realised when, on ringing the bell just after eleven, Sharon had opened the door to her. It had been Davy's suggestion, meeting up here for a council of war before their afternoon shift, and one Alyssa had readily agreed to the previous night – though she now dearly wished she could have spent a couple more hours in bed. She was fighting a raging hangover brought on by what had turned into an epic drinking session at the Excelsior, which had run well into the wee hours – she, Davy and Colin propping up the bar long after most of the other guests had left. At one point, she recalled, Davy and Colin had even duetted a decidedly tuneless rendition of 'Auld Lang Syne'.

'Well,' she said, swallowing the nausea brought on by *that* particular memory, 'if it *was* a random psycho, there's not much point looking for a motive, so we're wasting our time here. And I reckon we can rule out armed robbery, on account of turning up with a gun to rob a till with a ten-pound float being a bit too much like overkill even for someone totally deranged.'

'Which leaves the revenge motive.'

'Precisely. And I think we can agree you've got a way better knowledge of the local clientele than me. So, any names spring to mind?'

Davy stroked his chin. 'Oh, only about a million and a half. You don't work in public libraries for long without pissing off your fair share of punters, mostly for seriously petty reasons. I had one delightful chap threaten to shank me cos we didn't stock the Daniel O'Donnell fan club magazine.'

A few months ago, she'd have assumed he was pulling her leg. Now, she wasn't so sure.

'But if we're talking about the ones who'd be pissed off enough *and* crackers enough to actually commit cold-blooded murder, I could certainly narrow it down a bit.'

'Go on.'

'Well,' Davy began, clearly relishing his role as a purveyor of knowledge, 'a few weeks before it happened, there was a bit of a stooshie when Tiny Tots got cancelled at short notice. Laura called in sick and there was no one else on site to take it cos none of us had had the training. Most of the mums were fine about it. There was a bit of grumping and grousing about wasted journeys and how come we couldn't have warned them in advance – as if Laura should've known ahead of time she was gonna get food poisoning. But there was this one guy – young dad with twins, stress of chasing around after the little demons probably getting on top of him – who absolutely, and I mean *absolutely*, hit the roof. Went stamping all through the library, shouting the odds, saying he was gonna nut whoever was in charge. Denise barricaded herself in the office and wouldn't come out. Guy came back a bit later after he'd calmed down, said he was sorry for losing it, but us lot were all proper shook up over it. Tell ya, it was the only time I ever seen our Jason lost for words.'

'Sounds promising.'

'There's just one problem.'

'What's that?'

'He's about twenty-one stone and four foot ten.'

Great. 'You could've told me that up front and saved us both a bunch of time.'

'Ah, but where would've been the fun in that? If a story's worth telling, it's worth telling properly.'

She ignored that. 'Got anyone else? Anyone credible, I mean. Not to put too fine a point on it, but these are small fry. They might be a bit unhinged, but there's a difference between being a tad eccentric and being capable of . . . you know.'

'Well, I could tell you about the guy who thinks he's the reincarnation of Hermann Göring . . . '

She rolled her eyes. 'Be serious.'

'I *am* being serious. *You* be serious.'

She rose up onto her knees atop the bed, making full use of the height advantage it gave her. 'You want serious? OK, then, how's this for serious – no matter how many weird and wonderful names you pull out of that hat of yours, Paul McGuigan is still the most likely culprit.'

Davy sighed and gazed at the ceiling in despair. 'Not this again! I thought we moved past all that last night.'

Had they? At the time, it had felt like they had. Back then, fresh from the rush of having seen Formby and Metcalfe muttering together, thick as thieves, she'd felt ready to take on the entire system. In the cold light of day, however, she couldn't help but picture herself and Davy as overgrown Harriet the Spy wannabes, solving mysteries and thwarting the bad guys before bedtime.

'Come on, Allie Ballie. Don't be coming over all square on me now. Not now I've finally got you singing from the same hymn sheet.'

Alyssa raised a hand in warning. 'Gonna correct you right there, my dude. You and I are categorically *not* singing from the same hymn sheet. Does it look like there's something shifty going on? Hells, yes. Am I a one hundred percent paid-up member of the tinfoil hat club? Uh-uh. It's for you to prove McGuigan's innocent, not for me to prove he's guilty.'

'That's not how the law works.' Davy's tone was decidedly petulant.

'Yeah, well, I'm not the law. Neither of us are. Which is sort of the point.'

Davy merely folded his arms and stewed.

Relenting somewhat, Alyssa swung her legs over the side of the bed and resumed a sitting position – a move she hoped conveyed a less adversarial stance.

After a moment, Davy stirred. 'What gets me is that, throughout all this, no one's made any effort to track down Gordon Ramage.'

'Who?' The name sounded vaguely familiar, though she wasn't sure why.

'Dodgy-looking guy with bad skin and a stutter? Came roaring up to the desk after Jason kicked him off the PCs? Told us we were all going to get it in the neck and stormed out just before the shooter came in?'

'I remember.'

It was coming back to her – including her sitting in her living room telling Metcalfe all about Ramage's 'warning'.

'Pretty weird, don't you think?' Davy continued. 'Guy tells us we're in line for our own personal day of reckoning minutes before a mass shooting and the folk in charge of the investigation don't even think it's worth tracking him down, finding out what he knows?'

'Oh, come *on*.' Alyssa rolled her eyes. 'He was just mouthing off.

He got pissed cos he got kicked off his computer and Jason insinu-ated that he smelled. That's all. Besides, maybe they did. Maybe Metcalfe went and saw him, the pair of them had a nice old chinwag, and she concluded, like any sane person would, that he was just full of hot air.'

'Nuh-uh.' Davy shook his head firmly. 'She came and spoke to me a buncha times while I was laid up in hospital. I kept trying to talk to her about Ramage, but she didn't want to know. All she wanted was for me to say Paul McGuigan was guilty. Got well pissed off when I wouldn't. Point is, if I was running that investigation, I'd at least want to take a look at the guy who made out he had some sort of advance knowledge something was gonna go down, not bang up some poor schmuck who can barely tie his own shoelaces.'

A poor schmuck who happened to have a gun in his rucksack identical to the one used in the shootings, Alyssa thought, though by this stage she knew there was no point saying it.

'You're not saying you think *he* did it, are you? Because even if he happened to have a gun and a balaclava and an entire change of clothes stashed nearby, the odds of him leaving, getting changed and coming back in the space of what, five minutes, are pretty slim.'

'Of course not,' Davy shot back. 'I'm just saying, I think he *knows* something, and it's high time someone found out what that is.'

Alyssa said nothing. Once again, they'd reached a stalemate, both utterly entrenched in their respective positions.

'How about you?' said Davy suddenly.

Alyssa looked up. 'Me?'

'Yeah. Any psychos lurking in *your* closet? Jilted ex-lover, maybe? Betcha you've broken a few hearts in your time.'

A sudden flash of the figure standing on the corner of Edgehill Drive a couple of Thursdays back entered Alyssa's mind. She quickly shook it off.

'No, nothing like that. Don't be stupid.'

'I'm amazed neither of us thought of it before, actually,' Davy continued, as if she hadn't even spoken. 'We Thornhillers are trucking along just fine before you show up, dealing with the odd spot of aggro now and then, but nothing life-threatening. Then, the day you start work – the *hour*, even – BAM! Every one of us is either on our way to the morgue or intensive care.'

'That doesn't make a lick of sense. Why would someone shoot up a whole bunch of people just to get at me . . . and let me live to tell the tale?'

'Maybe he didn't mean for you to survive. Maybe he botched it. He managed not to kill me too, remember?'

'Then why shoot everyone else before getting round to me? Why not just blow me away and have done with it?'

'Saving the best for last?'

'But why *would* he?' She shook her head – though, as she did, she wondered whether the vociferousness of her denials was because Davy's theory was genuinely unbelievable or simply because she *wanted* it to be. 'If you ask me, it's way more likely I got spared cos his beef was with you lot, not me.'

Davy all but burst out laughing. 'Come *on*. Now you're just reaching. What, you think he took one look at you and was like, "Nope, don't know her, I'll just wound her rather than kill her outright"? You got lucky, that's all.'

There it was again – that inference that her survival had been down to nothing more than dumb luck. It had stung when Metcalfe had suggested it, and it rankled just as much hearing it from Davy. Actually, this was even worse, because he was in effect implying that she was the reason their colleagues were pushing up daisies. That she was *responsible*.

The silence was broken by a knock on the door. Davy's mum entered, carrying a tray laden with biscuits and juice cans.

'Thought you two could probably do with some refreshments right about now.'

It was hard not to notice Davy's exasperated sigh – like a grown-up had come into his secret clubhouse without uttering the correct password. Alyssa, feeling she should show some gratitude on his behalf, got to her feet and stepped forward to take the tray.

'Thanks, Mrs Grogan. It's really thoughtful of you.'

'Don't be silly. It's my pleasure.' She regarded the pair of them with a beatific smile. 'And did the two of you have a nice time last night at your party?'

'It was very nice, yes,' lied Alyssa. 'Thank you.'

'It's so good to see him getting out and about again,' said Sharon, looking past Alyssa's shoulder to Davy, who appeared to be gearing up to strangle someone. 'And to have made a new friend.'

'*Mum*,' said Davy, the tension in his voice so high Alyssa thought his vocal cords were going to snap.

Sharon's smile only broadened. 'All right, all right. I know when I'm not wanted.'

With a quiet chuckle she turned and left, shutting the door behind her. As her footsteps receded down the stairs, Davy groaned and put his head in his hands.

Alyssa set the tray down and shot him a quizzical look. 'What's eating you?'

'Oh, nothing. Just my sainted mother getting *ideas*.'

'What, this?' She nodded to the tray. 'She was just being considerate. A bit of gratitude from her own flesh and blood wouldn't go amiss.'

'You don't get it.' Davy looked up, his expression pained. 'She thinks you're my girlfriend,' he sighed.

Alyssa couldn't help herself. She let out a spontaneous cackle. 'Ha! Dream on, buddy.'

Davy's eyes flared indignantly. 'Hey, believe me – you're about as far from my dreams as it's possible to get.'

'Bindi more to your taste, is she? Hey – I get it. Her personality's about as appealing as gonorrhoea, but I guess when all you're after is some bedtime fapping material, personality doesn't come into it.'

She wasn't sure why she was so put out. It wasn't as if she *wanted* him to be into her. Still, she wasn't used to being given the brush-off quite so blatantly.

Davy sighed again. 'You're still not getting it.'

'Then enlighten me. What's so repulsive about little old me?'

He met her eye, holding it for a long, hard moment. 'I'm gay,' he said simply.

'Oh,' said Alyssa, once she'd recovered from her surprise. 'In that case, you're forgiven.'

In truth, she actually felt something akin to relief. For as long as she could remember, she'd found she related more to guys than to girls, and her close friendships had always invariably been with them, even as a kid. They were more likely to share the same hobbies and interests; the same sense of humour. With the onset of puberty, though, the waters had inevitably grown muddier, and she'd soon found herself having to rebuff the advances of those who mistook friendship for something more – especially growing up in a small town where there wasn't a whole lot of choice on the menu. Davy not being that way inclined simplified matters considerably.

She realised he was giving her the glares. 'Does it make you uncomfortable? You're not one of *them*, are you?'

'Oh, *no!*' she said hastily. 'Total opposite, actually. I love the gays.' And then cringed a little inside.

'How nice. Me, I'm pretty relaxed about the straights. The ones that aren't total dickholes, that is.'

Somewhere, in the depths of her mind, his words triggered a memory from the previous night.

'You mean ones like Tony Barbarossa?'

Davy tensed. 'How d'you mean?'

Alyssa shrugged. 'Heard he made life hard for you. Picked on you.'

'Yeah, well,' Davy muttered, 'there's not many folk he didn't manage to piss off at one point or another.'

She sensed he was trying to shut down this line of conversation, but her mind was churning now. 'Pissed-off ex-employee, feels he was given the boot unfairly – now that's what I'd call a motive. So what's the verdict? He crazy enough to shoot up a room full of his former colleagues?'

Davy pursed his lips, still reluctant to be drawn. 'Well, I'm pretty sure he knows his way around firearms for a start.'

'For real?'

'That's my impression, anyway. He was part of this Looney Tunes "end of the world" outfit – the Scottish Survivalists Society. You know the sort – convinced the next ice age is just round the corner and it's only a matter of time before we're all wearing bearskins and making fires by rubbing sticks together.'

'Think we should check them out? Find out whether they've had any guns go missing lately?'

'I don't think it's that sort of society. It's not like they pay an annual subscription or have a hideout where they store their weapons and get together to practise their secret handshakes. Far as I can tell, they're just a bunch of ultra-macho types who see things like clean water and deboned chicken as a threat to their masculinity.'

Alyssa affected a violent shudder. 'The horror!'

Davy grinned, his mood lightening for the first time since Barbarossa's name had come up. 'I know, right? He was forever going off into the wilds up north on weekends – y'know, bivouacking under the stars, living off the land. He'd come back on Monday with all these grand tales about which Munros he'd conquered and which animals he'd skinned and cooked. They had a Facebook group for a while, but it got shut down cos they kept putting up links to articles on how to make bear-traps and such.'

'Well, if I'm ever looking for someone to show me a wild weekend, I'll know exactly who to hit up.'

'Don't,' said Davy instantly, his earlier ill-temperedness returning in a flash. 'You want to steer well clear of Tony Barbarossa. He's bad news.'

Alyssa thought someone who was bad news was exactly the sort of person they *should* be looking into, but she could see that pressing the matter wasn't going to get her anywhere.

'OK,' she said, 'say I'm prepared to go along with your Gordon Ramage theory—'

Davy's face lightened instantly. 'Now you're talking. See? Knew you'd see the light sooner or later.'

Alyssa held up a hand, cutting him off. 'Let me finish. This is not me "seeing the light" – not by a long shot. I was gonna say, I'll go along with your little wheeze till it hits the skids. But make no mistake, I'm not saying I think he actually knows anything. I'm just saying I'm prepared to look into this until such a time as we've definitively proved your theory to be hooey. Deal?'

Davy hesitated for a moment. Then, evidently concluding that this was as good as he was going to get, he gave a curt nod. 'Deal.'

'Then what's our first move?'

'That's obvious. We find out exactly what he knows about the shootings – from the horse's mouth, if possible.'

'In that case, we need to find out where he lives.'

'Precisely.' Davy grinned, the bit well and truly between his teeth. 'And I know the perfect place to start.'

15

'Are you sure this is where he lives?' said Alyssa, staring up at the ugly, grubby-looking tenement building whose front entrance they were facing.

'This is the address we have on file for him,' said Davy. He angled his phone at her, showing her the entry on the mobile version of the libraries' cataloguing software as proof.

'Well, let's see if he's home, I guess.'

The building's interior was similar to its exterior, with copious amounts of obscene graffiti on the bare concrete walls and a mountain of bulging black plastic bags piled up by the entrance. Alyssa wrinkled her nose. She got that this wasn't the Ritz, but a little pride in one's own living quarters wouldn't go amiss. This was, she concluded, a marginally more productive use of her time than listening to Davy coming up with silly theories about customers gunning people down because Tiny Tots had been cancelled once – but only marginally.

They squeezed into the rickety old wrought-iron elevator and took it up to the second floor. Alyssa rapped sharply on the door to flat number 2/03 – which, according to the system, was Ramage's abode.

No answer. She tried again.

'Mr Ramage?' Davy called. 'Open up! It's that special delivery you ordered.'

151

Alyssa shot him a questioning look.

'What?' he shrugged. 'He might've.'

But special delivery or no, it soon became apparent that no one was coming to the door. They were making their way back to the lift when the door to the adjacent flat opened and a young woman with stringy hair, bags under her eyes and what looked like baby puke on her crumpled T-shirt leaned out.

'Are yous looking for Ramage?' she said with a twenty-a-day rasp.

'That's right,' said Alyssa.

'He's no been round here for ages. Flat's been empty since the beginning of March. Few weeks back, the landlord got fed up waiting on him to pay the rent and had the locks changed.'

'Any idea where he might've gone?' asked Davy.

'Havnae a Scooby. Just upped and left, leaving all this stuff behind. Landlord took anything that looked valuable, binned the rest. There'll be hell to pay if he ever shows his face again.'

'Well,' said Davy, as they emerged into the sunlight, 'I call that mighty suspicious. You don't clear out, leaving all your worldly goods behind, unless you've got a very good reason.'

'Which might have nothing to do with the shootings,' said Alyssa, already way ahead of how his mind worked. 'There's a million and one reasons someone could have for clearing out.'

'Like what?'

She shrugged. 'Debt collectors, maybe? Or perhaps he was behind on his rent. Point is, you can't just assume he's laying low cos, I dunno, he's afraid the killer's gonna come after him or whatever.'

'I know,' said Davy, clearly irked at having the obvious pointed out to him. 'Pretty big coincidence he did his vanishing act right about the time it all kicked off, but.'

They stood – or sat – in silence for some time, entrenched in their respective positions. Eventually, Davy stirred.

'Come on, we'd best make a move. The Mistress of Pain'll have our guts for garters if we're late.'

Denise was waiting for them at the desk.

'Davy, Alyssa, I trust a good night was had by all last night? Smashing. Well, much as I hate to put a dampener on your spirits, I'm afraid I have an urgent task for you both. It's been brought to my attention that, earlier in the year while you had your feet up at the taxpayer's expense, you both missed out on the delight that is stepladder training. I've just had a threateningly worded email informing me that if you haven't both completed the online assessment with at least a seventy percent pass-rate by five o'clock today, heads will roll, namely mine.'

'Is there any actual point my doing it, boss?' said Davy. 'It's not like I'm planning on going up any ladders.'

Denise sighed wearily. 'Unfortunately, whoever designed the assessment forgot to include a "this employee is exempt on account of being wheelchair-bound" checkbox. Go on, humour me.' She nodded in the direction of the reading room. 'The two PCs at the back are free. Just don't take all day.'

'What even *is* stepladder training?' Alyssa whispered to Davy as they headed through to the reading room.

'It's a piece of pish,' said Davy. 'They make us do it every year, and every year it's the exact same questions and the exact same outcome. We all pass, or we keep doing it till we do. Means they've covered their backs, so if you're changing a lightbulb and you fall and break your neck, they can say they gave you adequate training in operating procedures and you can't sue the council for failing to provide a safe working environment.'

'Sounds like a blast.'

Davy chuckled. 'Oh, you don't know the half of it. Just wait till manual handling training comes round again.' He nodded to the two vacant computers. 'Hurry up and get yourself logged in. Don't wanna give the Mistress of Pain an excuse to break out the cat o' nine tails.'

'Why d'you all call her that anyway?' Alyssa asked as they waited for the aged machines to fire up. 'She seems perfectly nice.'

'Oh, she *is* super-nice – believe me. Real salt-of-the-earth type. And she'll always have your back in a dispute with a service user, which is more than can be said for *some*. It's just a little joke we have.'

'Explain?'

Davy hesitated for a moment, then beckoned Alyssa closer. 'OK, about a year ago, me and Eva went up to the office to do some admin work. Denise'd gone home for the day, but she'd left her PC logged in with the browser still open. Course, we just *had* to see what she'd been looking at. Turned out she'd been doing a spot of online shopping.'

'And?'

'Handcuffs,' said Davy solemnly.

Alyssa stared at him in disbelief. 'No *way*.'

'Way. And that's not the half of it. She'd been on this site specialising in BDSM gear – hoods, ball-gags, nipple clamps, the works. Only question we've spent the last year trying to work out is, is she giving or is she receiving?'

Alyssa had a sudden vision of Denise, clear as if she was standing in front of her now, in full-on dominatrix getup, whip in hand.

'Giving,' she said emphatically. 'Definitely giving.'

She didn't know how she was ever going to get that image out of her mind. Glancing at the rows of bowed heads in front of computer screens, she wondered what sort of secret proclivities *they* were indulging. Though, judging by what she'd been able to glean from the brief glances she'd caught of borrowers' browser windows since starting the job, she knew the reality was probably nothing more exciting than the latest Itison vouchers.

She shook her head ruefully. 'I can't believe this lot have nothing better to do on a Monday morning than sit in here Facebooking or playing solitaire. Do none of them have lives?'

'Depends what you class as living. None of them has to do stepladder training, so the way I see it, every single one of them's at an advantage over us.'

Alyssa was only half-listening. As she stared at the spinning circle on the loading screen, a thought struck her. 'Isn't this the computer Ramage got kicked off the morning of the shooting?'

''Tis indeed. Always parked himself at the back so we couldn't see the dodgy shenanigans he was getting up to.'

Alyssa wrinkled her nose in disgust as something thoroughly unpleasant occurred to her. 'He didn't ever . . . you know . . . while he was . . . '

Davy laughed and shook his head. 'Not to the best of my knowledge. Don't worry – you're not sitting in the dried remnants of his unbridled passion. Well, *probably* not, anyway. 'Sides,' he continued, as Alyssa raised one buttock off her chair to check under it, 'I kinda get the impression that wasn't what he was about.'

Alyssa looked at him, incredulous. 'Seriously? What's the point of porn if you're not using it to get off?'

A squeal of high-pitched laughter broke out from behind one of the neighbouring computers. 'Ohmygod, she said "porn"!'

'Oooh, she's for it now!'

A further series of barely stifled giggles followed.

Alyssa got to her feet and stood on tiptoe, trying to identify the culprits. Huddled behind a screen about ten feet away were a pair she'd nicknamed 'the Lovebirds': Craig and Courtney, both sixteen and seemingly joined at the hip. They hung about the library at all hours of the day – often, Alyssa suspected, under the influence of one mind-altering substance or another. She'd never seen one without the other, and on several occasions had stumbled across them in some secluded corner, tongues down each other's throats, and had had to resist the urge to get a bucket of cold water to throw over them. Other times, they came in going at it hammer and tongs, making so much noise she'd have to order them to take it outside. They seemed to alternate between being besotted with one another and wanting to kill each other, often going through both cycles multiple times in a single day. Craig had psoriasis and a pronounced overbite and Courtney was squinty-eyed and riddled with acne, but neither seemed to notice the other's imperfections – and in a way Alyssa almost envied the childlike innocence of their relationship. Now, the pair of them were doing a thoroughly lousy job of pretending to be engrossed in whatever was on their screen, unable to stop themselves from constantly glancing shiftily in Alyssa's direction.

She put her hands on her hips. 'All right, you two, quit dicking around. You think I can't see you?'

Slowly, the Lovebirds got to their feet and stepped out from behind their computer. They stood nudging one another, trying not to laugh or catch each other's eye.

'Shouldn't you two be in school?' said Alyssa.

'In-service day,' said Courtney.

'Free period,' said Craig.

Alyssa rolled her eyes. Not that she much cared. She'd bunked off school a bunch at their age. She could hardly take the moral high ground.

'So, um,' Courtney slowly approached them, Craig close behind her, clutching her hand, 'whatcha doin'?'

'Important library business,' said Davy. 'Go on, piss off or I'll have Denise in here to chuck you out.'

'Aw, you wouldnae,' said Courtney, sticking out her bottom lip.

'Yeah,' said Craig. 'Please – we've nowhere else to go. If you kick us out, we'll only stand on the street corner hasslin' old grannies for smokes.'

Davy hummed and hawed, rubbing his chin. 'Let's do a deal. We'll not report you to Denise if you promise to take yourselves as far away from us as possible, and not make so much as a peep.'

The Lovebirds' faces brightened instantly. 'We'll be as quiet as teeny-tiny little mouses,' said Craig eagerly. 'Yous won't know we're here.'

'It's *mices*, numbnuts!' said Courtney, cuffing Craig round the back of the head. 'See you,' she muttered as they retreated to the other end of the room, 'sometimes your heid's just full of mince.'

Alyssa waited until they were installed behind a fresh computer, out of earshot, then resumed her seat and turned to Davy. 'You were saying . . . '

'Right – Gordon Ramage. Every so often, I'd be in here and I'd happen to catch a glimpse of his screen. Anyway, the stuff he was looking at wasn't strictly speaking porn – though from what I saw, there was plenty bare flesh on display all the same.'

'What *was* he looking at, then?'

'Scottish Skin.'

'Scottish *what*?'

'Scottish Skin. It's a naturist site. You do know what a naturist is, don't you?'

'Course I know what a naturist is,' Alyssa retorted, keeping her voice low in case the Lovebirds were still earwigging. 'My Uncle Andy went through what my folks call "a phase" back in the seventies – not that we talk about *him* anymore. So Ramage went in for the whole "prancing naked through the heather" thing?'

Davy suppressed a shudder. 'Wouldn't really care to speculate. Who knows – maybe he just liked looking at photies of flabby, pasty weirdos in their birthday suits?'

'And it's not blocked by the internet filter?'

'Nope. Keep going on at IT to fix it, but nothing ever gets done. With that lot, I swear it's like talking to a brick—'

'What's the URL?'

'Scottish Skin dot com. *Obviously.* I— Hey!' he exclaimed, as Alyssa commandeered his keyboard. 'Oh right, of course, by all means, look it up on *my* login so *I'm* the one who has to explain my dodgy browser history to Creepy Chris from IT. What are you going on there for anyway?'

'To look for clues, *obviously.*'

'Clues to what?'

'Where he might have gone, for a start. Maybe one of his weird naturist buddies is sheltering him. Come on – you were the one hellbent on tracking him down.' She gave a low whistle as the site loaded. 'Whew! For such a tiny little country, you folks sure don't lack for crazies.'

Scottish Skin was described, in the tagline at the top of the site, as 'a community for open-minded adventure-seekers with a shared love of the naturist lifestyle', its design – if you could call it that – stuck somewhere in the late nineties. Functionally, however, it was like any number of modern social media platforms. You created an account, added people as friends and received access to their profile pages, as well as a continuous feed of status updates from your circle of acquaintances. Its members' main pastimes seemed to be sharing images of themselves in states of undress at various rural locations across the length and breadth of Scotland, and organising meet-ups where presumably they all got together and danced around the maypole or whatever it was people did when they hung out in the buff. Judging by their photos, most of them were of a certain age and predominantly male – though there were a handful of pictures of buff, twentysomething men proudly showing off their meat and two veg, and even a few coquettish, nervous-looking young women, most of them strategically positioning their hands or hair to conceal their unmentionables, peppered among the endless sea of wrinkly old cocks.

'Do a search,' said Davy, his earlier unease having quickly been supplanted by mischievous glee at the prospect of this deep dive into the taboo. 'Put in his name and see what it turns up.'

Alyssa keyed 'GORDON RAMAGE' into the search bar at the top of the screen and hit Enter.

NO RESULTS FOUND.

'Maybe he's just a voyeur rather than an active participant,' said Davy. 'Or maybe . . . I know – try doing a search for members from Glasgow . . . '

Alyssa snorted back a laugh. 'There'll be a few of those on display, for sure.'

Davy shot her a disapproving look, which only served to provoke another fit of the giggles. ' . . . and we'll see if he's using an alias. Bet your bottom dollar most of these folk aren't going by their real names.'

Scottish Skin was divided into several sub-chapters corresponding to Scotland's various regions. The Ayrshire & Arran and Highlands groups were by far the biggest, but the Greater Glasgow one boasted a considerable following as well, with multiple pages of names and headshots in the search results. As Alyssa scrolled through the list, she and Davy skimmed both the names and faces, hoping to spot one they recognised.

'Well, well,' she mused, 'who knew Glasgow was home to so many weird and wonderful characters? Hey – d'you reckon Tony Barbarossa's on here?'

'No I don't,' said Davy, instantly defensive. 'I think he'd see this lot as a bunch of namby-pamby peaceniks who need to man up.'

'I dunno – we know he's big on the whole "at one with nature" thing. Only a hop, skip and a jump from there to ripping off your clothes and cavorting in the glens.'

Davy said nothing. His eyes remained fixed on the screen as face after face scrolled by. Suddenly, he gave a shout. 'Whoa, stop!'

'What is it? Have you seen him?'

'No, but . . . ' Davy leaned in closer, staring at the screen. 'Holy hell, that's Kevin McVeigh from Kelvinbridge Library.'

'It is *not!*' Alyssa all but shrieked.

The name meant nothing to her, but the very notion that someone in the same field of work as her was a closeted – or maybe not so closeted – nudist was too juicy for words. She clicked his profile. Almost immediately, a wall of photos filled the screen, most of which left nothing to the imagination.

'Ha! You're right. "Kevin M. from the West End." Says here he works in the public sector, and— OH MY GOD, WHAT'S *THAT*? Is that a fricking boa constrictor between his legs?'

At the other end of the room, the Lovebirds' heads instantly poked up from behind their screen like a pair of cartoon ostriches.

'Well, well.' Davy regarded the picture in question appreciatively. 'Who'd've thought old Kevino was packing such an impressive specimen?'

Alyssa doubted she'd ever be able to look the over-endowed Kevin in the eye if their paths crossed. She realised Davy was still studying the picture and snapped her fingers under his nose.

'Control yourself, Grogan. Eyes on the prize.'

She continued to scroll down, clicking through a couple more pages before something finally caught her eye.

'There!' She jabbed a finger at the screen.

'"Rambo Ramage",' read Davy. 'Could be. That pic's toaty, but. Zoom in?'

Alyssa clicked the link, taking them to the user profile. The details on display were sparse. His location was given as Glasgow, but it didn't get more specific than that. However, it was clear from the copious array of photos that this was indeed Gordon Ramage, pock-marked skin and badly cut hair and all. Most of the pictures were from the waist up – which was just as well, for Alyssa concluded from the state of his top half that she had no desire to see the rest of him. Many of them were selfies, taken in the bathroom mirror or holding his phone at arm's length, but a few were group shots in rural settings: Ramage and friends up a mountain, Ramage on the shores of Loch Lomond and so on.

'You think they should have to declare this sort of thing when they apply for library membership?' said Alyssa. '"I hereby confirm that I am not now, nor have I ever been, a fully paid-up member of the nudie club".'

'Probably something in the GDPR against that.'

Alyssa kept scrolling through the profile. The continuing deluge of pictures didn't let up. Ramage was clearly an avid photographer, intent on capturing every moment of his life, whether it related to the pursuit of naturism or not, for posterity.

'What's that?' said Davy, pointing suddenly.

'What?'

'Go back up a bit. There.' He gesticulated excitedly. 'That's the third or fourth time that sign's come up.'

The picture in question showed Ramage, mercifully clothed, standing in front of a compact three-storey building with a thatched roof. Alyssa leaned in, squinting at the words written on the sign visible behind his head.

'"The Linview Inn",' she read. '"Bed and breakfast. Hot water. Free wi-fi".' She turned to look at Davy. 'Ever heard of it?'

'No, but Google is your friend.'

A quick search established that there were two Linview Inns in Scotland. One, in the centre of Aberdeen, had a three-and-a-half-star rating on TripAdvisor and was described as 'ideally situated and excellent value'. It was also a grey concrete block that looked nothing like the building in Ramage's photo. The other, located somewhere called Abbotscraig, proved to be the one they were looking for.

'Abbotscraig?' said Alyssa, looking to Davy for guidance. 'Where's that?'

'Village in Perthshire, about eighty miles north of here. Quaint wee place, far removed from civilisation. Popular with tourists and oldies.'

'Popular with our missing friend too. Seems he's been there a bunch of times. And check this out.' She pointed to the text description below the photo of Ramage. '"Me in my happy place, October 2019".'

'Aw,' said Davy, 'bless him.'

Alyssa continued to stare at the picture, rubbing the underside of her chin as the cogs of her brain slowly turned. 'If you had to go into hiding for whatever reason,' she mused aloud, 'where would you go?'

Davy turned to look at her, his face extending into a smile of understanding. 'I'd go to my happy place.'

'And where better to hide out than a quaint little village in the back of beyond?'

As Davy slowly nodded, they both turned to gaze once more at the picture of Ramage and the Linview Inn. It looked almost as if he was waiting for them.

16

'See me,' said Gobby, 'I don't see the point in voting. Never have, never will.'

'I know what you mean, man,' agreed Spud, reaching for a handful of pretzels from the bowl on the coffee table. 'End of the day, you're still gonna get the same old shite whichever name you put your mark next to.'

'God, you're such a cynic,' said Jenny, setting down her gamepad and turning to face him.

'Nah, just calling it how I see it. They all make these grand promises to get themselves elected, but they're all just in it to cream as much dosh as they can off the suckers who put 'em there.'

Alyssa, continuing to mash buttons, tried to tune out her friends' conversation. Her eyes were glued to the zombie survival shooter on the TV screen, though her mind was elsewhere, mulling over what she and Davy had discovered earlier. As a child of the digital age, she was pretty adept at doing two things at once, but three was stretching it, and she was damned if she was going to hang up her controller now – not while she had a kill streak of four hundred and fifty, surpassing her all-time record.

'All of them?' Jenny's tone dipped incredulity. 'You honestly think there's not one single politician out there who's in it for the common good? Take that Mhairi Black, for example. You can't say *she* went into politics just to ride the gravy train.'

'See,' said Spud with a shrug, 'I don't even know who that is.'

'And that,' said Gobby triumphantly, 'is why the likes of me and him shouldn't vote. Like, ever. We'd only end up electing Hitler and Stalin's bastard lovechild without realising.'

Jenny scoffed in disgust and tossed a pretzel at him.

'What do *you* think, Alyssa?' Spud raised his voice in her direction. 'Should we be made to vote?'

'I don't give a crap, personally,' said Alyssa, not looking up from the screen. 'If they wanna put a gun to my head and force me to tick a box, I'll do it, but I'll be fucked if I let them hold me accountable for the consequences.'

Gobby grinned. 'See? *She* gets it.'

'Well,' said Jenny fatalistically, 'I think it's just sad that not one of you has any sense of civic duty.'

Alyssa doubled down her focus on the game. Her fingers danced from one button to another, long hours of practice having committed the moves to muscle memory. She raced up the staircase to her right, picking up the rocket launcher just as it respawned. At the same instant, she heard the long, low groan of one of the walking dead coming up behind her. She spun around instantly, switching to the newly collected weapon, and pulled the trigger.

BANG.

Somehow – her mind being preoccupied, perhaps – she'd misjudged how far she'd turned. Instead of blowing away the approaching zombie, the rocket hit a nearby wall, causing the blast to go off at close range. The entire screen turned red as her character exploded in a sea of flying brains and giblets.

BANG. Jason Stockridge's face explodes in slow motion, the bullet obliterating his features. Blood and biscuit crumbs spray everywhere, like some hideous fountain of death. His body remains upright for a brief moment, the gaping cavity where his face used to be yawning at her like one of those hideous zombie dogs' heads in Resident Evil, *before his knees buckle and he goes down.*

When she became aware of her surroundings once more, she was on her feet, standing in the middle of the living room, the gamepad lying on the floor. In the process, she'd managed to upend the coffee table. There were pretzels and other assorted snacks everywhere, and the carpet was swimming in Diet Coke and cheap cider. On the screen, her character lay dead in a crumpled heap while the game carried on around it, other players to-ing and fro-ing across the screen, blasting away at zombies.

'Oh shit,' Gobby cried, staring at the mess on the floor, 'the new carpet! My mum'll go spare!'

'Alyssa, man, what the fuck?' said Jenny. 'Are you OK?'

Slowly, Alyssa turned to face them. She tried to speak, but nothing came out. She was shaking so violently she could hear the lighting fixtures rattling overhead.

'A cloth!' wailed Gobby. 'Someone get a cloth!'

No one moved. Jenny and Spud were far too transfixed by Alyssa, and Alyssa . . . well, mopping up spillages was the last thing on her mind. She took one shuffling step, then another, reversing towards the door. Then she turned and ran, fleeing the apartment and hurrying down the stairs.

Outside, it was barely dark, the newly switched-on streetlights glowing a dim orange against a dull grey sky. As she stumbled into the street, she collided with a figure who'd been standing at the gates to the apartment block. She caught a flash of sandy hair, saw the glint of those wide-rimmed glasses reflecting the glow of the streetlight and let out a shriek of terror.

'Alyssa, please,' he cried, grabbing her upper arms with both hands, 'I just want to talk to you.'

'Get the fuck away from me!' she screamed, lashing out so violently he released her and stepped back.

She turned tail and ran once more, pelting up the road at full tilt. She didn't stop until some ten minutes later when her lungs ran out of puff and she collapsed, spluttering and gasping and wondering just where the hell she was.

When she got back to her flat, the first thing she did, after locking and bolting her front door, was shut all the curtains and turn on every light in the place. She was shaking uncontrollably, her breath coming out in ragged bursts, and she felt decidedly unsteady on her feet – the way she sometimes got if she hadn't eaten all day. She stared at her reflection in the mirror hanging in the hallway, taking in the sight of herself, eyes wide behind the lenses of her glasses, chalk-white face streaked with tears.

The ringing of her phone, and the sensation of it vibrating in her pocket, caused her to jump a foot in the air. She whipped it out and stared at the screen.

Davy. God, he really picked his moments.

'What?' she snapped.

'Charming! If that's how you're going to be, why don't I just hang up now?'

Yes, why don't you, you insufferable dickweasel? She counted to ten in her head. 'Sorry. You caught me in the middle of something.' She was surprised by how calm and devoid of any tremor her voice was. 'What's up?'

'Just calling to tell you to pack your hiking boots. We're going on a road trip tomorrow.'

'We're *what*?'

'I figured we're not going to find Ramage sitting on our back-sides, so I booked us on a bus to Abbotscraig. Even paid your fare. No need to thank me.'

She couldn't believe what she was hearing. 'Are you *serious*?'

'As a heart attack. Departs eight forty-five sharp from Buchanan Street Station. Don't be late. Oh, and by the way?'

Count to ten, count to ten . . . 'What?'

'Mind and bring a book. It's three hours each way.'

17

Her sleep that night was feverish and plagued by nightmares. As she hurried into the terminus the following morning, Davy, stationed at the sliding doors leading out to the bus rank, gesticulated manically.

'Come on, woman! Shift yer arse! What sort of time d'you call this?'

Not for the first time, she felt a pang of resentment at the fact that, despite having gone through ostensibly the same ordeal as her, he appeared to have walked away from it psychologically unscathed. Well, not *walked* away, but the point still stood.

They boarded the bus, Alyssa installing herself in the front row, while Davy parked himself nearby in the space for buggies and wheelchairs. It soon became apparent that the pair of them were the only passengers under retirement age, as OAP after OAP – predominantly women – clambered aboard, each pausing to present the driver with their over-sixties bus pass, which entitled them to free travel throughout Scotland. The driver, a rotund, jolly-faced man with a pair of sunglasses resting on his forehead, greeted each of them – many by name. Clearly, the trip was a regular occurrence for this menagerie.

'By the way,' said Davy, as Alyssa shrugged off her jacket, 'have you got Find Friends on your phone?'

'Yes . . . ?'

She wasn't sure she should be admitting to this. She didn't give just anyone access to her every movement, and Davy was still someone she put in the category of 'annoying co-worker' rather than 'friend'. And he was being *particularly* annoying today. But before she could figure out how to explain this without prompting an almighty sulk, he'd whipped out his own phone and was pressing it into her hand.

'There we go. Put in your vital statistics and we're all set.'

Reluctantly, she tapped in her number, hit 'SEND' and a moment later was rewarded with a *bling* from her own phone.

'There we go,' said Davy, beaming. 'Now we're BFFs.'

It was hard to shake the sense that he was not only aware of her misgivings but getting a kick out of them into the bargain.

Eventually, some twenty minutes after the scheduled departure time, the last of the stragglers was safely aboard. 'Are yous all sitting comfortably?' the driver called back. 'Seatbelts securely fastened?'

A chorus of 'Yes, driver!' rang out, Davy joining in with as much gusto as the oldies. Only Alyssa kept her lips firmly fastened.

'All righty, then. Next stop, Abbotscraig!'

And then they were off, winding out of the bus rank and joining the northerly flow of traffic up West Nile Street. A hubbub of conversation broke out, accompanied by the scrunching of paper as boiled sweets and Werther's Originals were passed around. The woman in the seat behind Alyssa tapped her on the shoulder and offered her one, which she politely declined.

'I must say,' the old dear said, 'it's nice to have some young blood with us.'

Oh, great. A talker.

If she'd been on her own, Alyssa would just have popped in her earbuds, turned up her music and ignored the woman, but she somehow suspected Davy would take a dim view of that.

Indeed, for much of the initial leg of the journey, Davy and the woman – who introduced herself as Gladys – kept up a cheerful back-and-forth that, mercifully, Alyssa didn't appear to be expected to contribute to. Davy asked her what was taking her to Abbotscraig. Did she go there often? Was she, perhaps, visiting family?

Gladys gave a long, philosophical sigh. 'Well, it gets one out of the house, doesn't it?'

Yes, Davy agreed, as if he knew exactly what she was talking about, and the telly was absolutely dire these days, wasn't it?

'What is it you do, then?' said Gladys. 'I'd have thought a couple of young things like yourselves would be at your work on a weekday morning.'

'We work in a library,' said Davy, and went on to explain all about their shift patterns. 'Thornhill Library on Chancery Street. Know it?'

'How wonderful! My local library is on Auchinleckie Street. Do you know the nice boy with curly hair who works there? He's ever so good to me – always makes sure to keep the newest Lesley Pearse for me. It really is a marvellous service you provide. I don't know what I'd do with myself if it wasn't there.'

Talk strangers to death on buses, probably, thought Alyssa, giving serious thought to leaving Davy and his new best friend to it and moving to the back.

But she didn't, and as they left Glasgow behind, gaining speed on the M8, Gladys seemed to lose interest in her and Davy and struck up a conversation with one of her other neighbours.

'Out of interest,' said Alyssa, 'and I use the term loosely, just what is it you think we're going to find when we get there?'

'Well,' said Davy, with a pleasant shrug, 'in the ideal scenario, we'll find Gordon Ramage hanging out at the nearest watering hole, all neatly parcelled up with a ribbon on top. But if that's too much to ask for, I'll settle for proof of life.'

'Uh-huh? And you do realise the most likely scenario is that we'll get there and find nothing but a one-horse town that hasn't discovered colour television yet?'

'That's what I like about you, Allie Ballie. Always such a positive outlook.'

'Just a realistic one. And stop calling me that.'

'Ah, don't be such a grumpypants. The sun's out, we've got the day off work and this route is home to some of the finest scenery Scotland has to offer. Might as well relax and enjoy the trip.'

'I'll tell you what I'm going to do. I'm going to close my eyes and try to catch up on all the sleep I didn't get last night, and you're going to let me.'

Davy shook his head in an *I'm not mad, just disappointed* sort of way. 'Suit yourself. You don't know what you're missing.'

Ignoring him, she turned in to the window and shut her eyes, using her rolled-up jacket as a pillow.

The dream again, as vivid and terrifying as before, only this time somehow worse. Each time she has it, the ocean seems to become deeper, blacker, more impenetrable. That familiar drowning sensation, of her limbs aching from fighting the current, of her lungs being slowly starved of oxygen, the pain so intense she'd swear it's real.

And then, something else. Something she hasn't experienced before. A hand, reaching up from the depths below, wrapping its fingers around her ankle, holding her in its icy grip, pulling her down into the endless dark . . .

She came to with a start, a hand on her shoulder.

'Don't thump me,' Davy said immediately as she stared up at him, wondering where the hell she was. 'I know you didn't want to be wakened, but you were tossing and turning like a mad thing. I wanted to make sure you were OK.'

'I'm fine,' she said stiffly, hauling herself upright and trying to get her bearings. The wild countryside continued to roll by outside, the steady chatter from the wrinklies suggesting that, however alarming her behaviour had been to Davy, he was the only one who'd noticed.

'Bad dream?' Davy gave a sympathetic grimace. 'I get them too from time to time. Ever since . . . you know.'

'It wasn't a dream,' she said, too quickly and sharply to convince anyone. 'I just . . . woke up suddenly.' She cleared her throat, trying to sound brisk and business-like. 'How far are we?'

'About halfway, I reckon. We've been on the road about an hour and a half.'

Alyssa grunted an acknowledgement and folded her arms about herself, partly because she was feeling unaccountably cold and partly to stop herself from shaking.

'By the way,' said Davy, as she shut her eyes once again, 'who's Emily?'

Her eyes snapped open. 'What did you just say?'

'Emily. You said the name "Emily" a couple of times in your sleep.'

For a long, uncomfortable moment, she didn't respond. She met his gaze defiantly, stalling for time as she tried to dredge up an answer that would explain it all away.

'You're mistaken,' she said eventually. 'You must have misheard.'

She turned away, resting her head against the window once more. But she didn't sleep. She remained wide awake for the rest of the journey, all her senses on red alert, determined not to let her guard down again for even a second.

They trundled into Abbotscraig's town square a little after midday. As Alyssa had predicted, it really was the asshole of civilisation: a tiny, secluded hamlet nestled in a deep glen surrounded by rugged hills. Circling around three hundred and sixty degrees showed you pretty much everything the place had to offer. There was a post office, a grocery store, a tourist shop that sold postcards and trinkets, and a pub whose windows were so cloudy they could have been sacrificing goats or small children in there for all anyone knew.

'Right,' said Alyssa, 'the sooner we get this over and done with, the sooner we'll be on our way. God knows I'm not going to spend all day here pissing in the wind.'

Davy looked thoughtful. '*Can* women piss in the wind? Talk me through how that works.'

Alyssa didn't dignify that with a response. Pushing Davy, she made her way along the main road – which, as it turned out, was Abbotscraig's *only* road. Most of the buildings on either side were residential – detached and semi-detached bungalows with pebble-dash walls and tiny windows to keep the warmth in during the cold winter months. As the houses came to an end, the ground rose in front of them, the road giving way to a rough gravel footpath that wound its way up into the mountains on the town's northern edge. About three hundred yards from the point at which the road ceased and the footpath began, they found the Linview Inn, looking exactly the same as it had in Ramage's photos, down to the sign promising hot water.

Heading up the path, Alyssa shoved open the heavy oak door. The front desk was manned by a solitary figure – a tall, gangly girl of about twenty, pink streaks in her blonde hair and a discrete little ring through her left nostril. Her jaw worked rhythmically, neck tilted downward as she stared intently at her phone, which emitted a continuous stream of tinny bonks and chimes as her fingers mashed the screen. She glanced up briefly as Alyssa struggled to simultaneously hold the door open and get Davy's chair over the threshold before returning to her game.

They approached the desk, Alyssa hanging back to let Davy take the lead. He waited for the girl to acknowledge their presence and, when she didn't, cleared his throat loudly. The girl continued to tap away for a few more seconds, then lowered her phone, lifted her head and stared off into the middle distance, not making eye contact with either of them.

'Welcome to the Linview Inn how may I help you.'

She spoke in a flat monotone, words running together in a continuous stream devoid of any inflection or variation in cadence.

Davy gave his chummiest smile. 'Ah yes, hello. We were looking for some information.'

Wordlessly, the girl reversed to the row of shelves behind her, grabbed a handful of leaflets and slapped them onto the countertop: travel brochures, showcasing the paltry sights and sounds Abbotscraig had to offer.

Davy smiled patiently. 'That wasn't *quite* what we were after. See, it's a touch delicate. Could we perhaps speak to someone in charge?'

The girl looked suddenly alarmed – the first time her expression had changed since they'd come in. 'Is this about the noise we were making the other night? I'm sorry it got a bit out of hand, but I did tell 'em we had to keep it down or the neighbours'd get antsy. I honestly didn't think anyone'd mind.'

Alyssa and Davy shared a puzzled look.

'See, we haven't any guests in at the moment, and Saturday I was on the night watch all by myself, so I figured why not invite some mates rounds, crack open a few cans, put on some tunes, make a night of it?' She scoffed and rolled her eyes. 'I mean, it was hardly a *rave.*'

'What?' Davy sounded baffled. 'No, it's nothing to do with that. We couldn't care less if you decided to hold Abbotscraig's answer to Woodstock in your backyard.'

The girl's features relaxed instantly, reverting to the bored half-scowl Alyssa suspected was her default expression. 'Well then, what d'you want?'

'We're trying to trace a friend of ours,' said Davy. 'Someone who might have passed through here recently. You said you've no guests right now?'

'That's right. Last couple checked out on Friday. Since then it's been deader than a funeral home.' She gave them a look presumably intended to elicit sympathy but which, with her resting bitchface, only made it look like she held them personally responsible.

'Well, like I say, there's a chance our friend might've stayed here recently. If it's not too much trouble, could we see your ledger?'

The girl's expression became even stonier, if that were possible. 'Against company policy.'

'Oh, right.' If Davy felt any disappointment, he hid it well. 'Well, that's fair enough, I suppose. Wouldn't want you to get in trouble with your boss. But maybe if we gave you a description? See, the guy we're after's quite . . . well, distinctive.'

The girl met his gaze insolently. 'I don't care if he's got three eyes and a wooden leg. You're not gonna catch me blabbing about our guests to a pair of total randos. Why don't you try asking your questions at the Swan down the road? Now, unless you're wanting to rent a room . . . '

She folded her arms and turned her back on them – a gesture that would have seemed far more emphatic if she hadn't possessed all the authority of a wet rag. Alyssa and Davy shared a look but didn't move. A moment later, the girl turned and, finding them still there, seemed to visibly deflate.

Davy grimaced, as if it pained him to have to bring this up. 'See, to be perfectly honest, we're a bit worried. Our friend, he disappeared from Glasgow some time ago and we haven't heard hide nor hair from him since. We know he's come out this way in the past and thought maybe he might've decided to hole up here for a bit. He's . . . well, to be frank, he's a bit unstable. Mental problems, y'know? And the thing is, we've reason to believe he didn't take his meds with him, and when he's off them he gets . . . well, it's probably best I don't say.'

Alyssa was impressed. She'd never have guessed Davy could lie so fluently and convincingly.

As the girl tugged at her bottom lip, unsure how to respond, Davy went in for the kill. 'Please – we're at our wits' end. We don't know what he might do to himself.'

'Shit!' the girl muttered to herself, then raised her head to meet Davy's eyes. 'There was a guy staying here till about a week ago,' she said, her sullen tone indicating how much she resented being put in this position. 'He'd been here since, oh, late May, I guess? He was . . . funny. Bad skin. Stuttered a lot. Kept to himself. Took all his meals in his room – hardly came out. Wouldn't let anyone in to clean it either. And he was always behind with his rent, always coming up with excuses. Didn't pay us anything throughout the whole of July. Eventually, my dad . . . he owns the place, see? He had no choice but to turf him out. Went absolutely ballistic when he got his marching orders, so he did. For a minute, I thought he was going to actually deck my old man.'

Her tone was almost nostalgic, and Alyssa suspected that, if a decking had occurred, it would have been the most exciting thing to happen in Abbotscraig since the turn of the millennium.

'But in the end he never,' the girl went on, reverting to her usual tone of bored indifference. 'Just packed his bags and stormed out, saying we were a shithole and he wouldn't be gracing us with his p–p–presence ever again.'

Alyssa and Davy exchanged glances. If the physical description hadn't been enough, the girl's imitation of his speech all but clinched it.

Alyssa took out her phone and tapped the screen, bringing up the photo of Ramage standing outside the inn.

'Was this the man?'

The girl barely glanced at it before shrugging. 'Might be. Dunno. Not exactly great quality, is it?'

Alyssa was about to order her to take a closer look, but she thought better of it. Push her too hard and she'd probably clam up altogether.

Lowering her phone, she tried a different tack. 'And he didn't say where he was going?'

'You kidding? He was a chancer who freeloaded off us till we sussed him and sent him packing. He was lucky my dad didn't call the cops on him. He was hardly gonna leave a *forwarding* address.' She snickered at the very idea.

'And his room – has it been, you know, cleaned, since then?'

The girl shook her head. 'Poked my head in and decided I wasn't going in there without a fricking hazmat suit – no way Jose. Place was an absolute tip and stank to high doh, like he'd not been bothering to wash. There's no excuse for that, right? I mean, we do provide hot water.'

'I know,' said Davy pleasantly. 'It says on the sign outside.'

As the girl looked at Davy, trying to work out whether he was making fun of her, Alyssa cut in. 'I don't suppose you'd let us have a look? Just in case, y'know, he left any clues to where he might've been headed.'

The girl's eyes widened at her brazenness. 'Are you taking the piss?'

'Please,' said Davy. 'We wouldn't ask if we weren't desperate.'

The girl hesitated for a moment, tugging so vigorously at her bottom lip Alyssa was surprised she hadn't drawn blood.

'What's it worth to you?' she said eventually.

Davy craned his neck, looking up at Alyssa expectantly. 'What?'

'Well, I mean, *I* paid for the bus tickets,' he shrugged.

For a moment, she simply stared at him in utter disbelief at his shamelessness. Then, muttering a quiet 'for Chrissakes', she took out her wallet and extracted two twenties she'd withdrawn from a cashpoint the other day. She handed them to Davy, who in turn handed them to the girl, as if they were all playing pass-the-parcel.

The girl pocketed the money immediately, as if she feared they'd change their minds and demand it back. She eyed the two of them severely. 'If word of this gets out to anyone . . . '

'It won't,' said Alyssa.

'My dad's already mad at me on account of the party.'

'We'll be out of here before you know it. Believe me, we don't want to be here any longer than we have to.'

The girl hesitated again. Then, seeming to have made her peace with what she was about to do, she took a ring of keys down from a nail on the wall, raised the hinged flap and emerged from behind the counter. She shot a dubious glance at Davy in his wheelchair.

'Dunno how *he's* gonna get up them stairs.'

'He can stay here and keep a lookout for your old man,' said Alyssa airily. She turned to Davy. 'You don't mind, do you?'

Davy gave such a saccharine smile Alyssa actually felt her teeth tingling.

They headed up to the second floor. At the end of a thickly carpeted corridor, Alyssa waited while the girl identified the right key and unlocked the door in front of them. She pushed it open, then stood well back.

'Aren't you coming in?' Alyssa said.

'Yeah, *right.*'

The smell hit Alyssa the instant she stepped inside: sweaty socks, stale BO and weeks-old take-out all rolled into one. The floor was littered with tinfoil cartons containing congealed sauce. The bedclothes were disarrayed and stained with grime where the occupant had lain.

Burying her nose in her inner elbow, Alyssa advanced and embarked on a root-and-branch search of the room, its various drawers and cupboards. She worked quickly, for fear that either the girl would change her mind and order her out or that she'd collapse from the fumes. Not that she expected to find a smoking gun as to Ramage's present whereabouts. That would be too easy. She was just going through the motions, humouring Davy.

'So um, how d'you know this guy anyway? No offence, but you don't seem like the type who'd hang around with dirty weirdo older men.'

Alyssa glanced up from the drawer she'd been rummaging through to see the girl hanging off the doorframe, still reticent to set foot inside.

'I'm not. I . . . well, Davy knows him better than I do.'

The girl wrinkled her nose. 'Yeah, well, he doesn't seem like the type either.'

'He's nothing if not unpredictable.'

The girl gave a thin smile. It occurred to Alyssa that she and Davy could well be the first people she'd seen all day. She was probably as lonely as sin, stuck behind that desk all day with nothing but *Candy Crush* or whatever for company.

'What's your name?'

'Galatea,' said the girl, as if confessing to a shameful secret.

'I'm Alyssa.'

'That's a nice name. You've got a nice accent too. Kind of exotic, like. You're not from around here, are you?'

'No,' said Alyssa, not sure she much liked being described as exotic, 'but the place I'm from's not a whole lot different to this one.'

'Oh?' Galatea sounded mildly interested. 'What brought you to Scotland?'

'Like I said, the place I'm from's not a whole lot different to this one.'

They looked at one another, and it seemed to Alyssa that something approaching an understanding passed between them, as if they both saw, in the other, a refracted image of themselves – a vision of how they might each have ended up if things had turned out differently.

'You worked here long, Galatea?'

Galatea shrugged. 'Since school.'

'And you like what you do?'

Another shrug. 'It's a job, isn't it? S'not as if I'm spoiled for choice round here.'

'You could always leave.'

'And go where?'

'Anywhere. Stick a pin on a map. Go explore the world.'

Galatea stared at Alyssa, as if she'd just been presented with a choice that she hadn't until now realised existed. Then she seemed visibly to deflate, her eyes clouding over as the brief spark of hope that had been kindled in them went out.

'I like it here,' she said.

'Do you?' said Alyssa, incredulous.

'Yeah.'

There was a tired, resigned tone to Galatea's voice. It was the voice of someone who'd long ago made peace with the knowledge that this was all she would ever amount to. Someone who, at the tender age of twenty and facing another six decades or more on earth, had already accepted her lot in life.

'Fair enough,' said Alyssa. 'Just know the option's there.'

'Right,' said Galatea, unconvinced. She looked around the room and shook her head. 'Don't think you're going to find anything here.'

'Yeah.' Alyssa nodded soberly. 'I think you're right.'

She got to her feet, ready to make tracks.

'Lemme have a look at that picture again,' said Galatea suddenly.

She held out her hand. Alyssa took out her phone and handed it over.

Galatea glanced at the photo of Ramage for barely a second before nodding. 'Yeah. That's him. Dirty greasy weirdo bastard. Not gonna forget *that* face in a hurry.' She shuddered. 'Or the smell.'

Alyssa smiled in agreement and turned to go, thinking Galatea was finished.

'He spoke to me, you know.'

Alyssa stopped in her tracks and turned. 'Huh?'

Galatea nodded – a sharp little chin-tuck, eyes not quite making contact with Alyssa's. 'It was a couple of nights before Dad gave him his marching orders. He came out of his room and took his dinner downstairs like a normal person. Reckon he'd even spruced himself up a bit for the occasion – y'know, brushed his hair and that – though it was hard to tell with him. Afterwards he sat for ages in the bar, drinking on his lonesome. I was on night duty and I . . . well, I might've joined him for a couple of beers. I wouldn't normally,' she added, her voice rising defensively. 'I'm not supposed to drink on the job and, like, hello? Rank, much? But I kinda felt sorry for him. Reckoned he was lonely.'

Alyssa suspected he hadn't been the only one, but she refrained from saying as much.

'He told me a bit about himself – how he'd been in and out of care since he was a little kiddie; how the whole system was rigged to make sure he failed. How he'd come up from Glasgow to get away from it all; how there was folk after him that'd do bad things to him if they caught up with him. And get this.' Galatea moved closer to Alyssa, her eyes lighting up with something that almost passed for genuine excitement. 'There was an old paper lying on the counter. Someone'd left it behind after doing the crossword. And next to the puzzles there was a piece on that shooting down in Glasgow back in March. You hear about that? The one in the library?'

Alyssa nodded, both intrigued as to where this story was going and finding it rather refreshing to be talking to someone who hadn't instantly connected her to The Event.

'Well anyway, guy kinda looks at it, then looks up at me, gives me this proper meaningful stare, and he taps the paper with his finger and says, "See that? I knew that was gonnae happen".'

Alyssa said nothing. She was aware that her heart rate had ratcheted up a notch; that she was waiting, with bated breath, for what came next.

'And I said,' Galatea went on, 'I said, "How d'you mean?" And he hummed and hawed for a bit, then he leaned in close, so I had to try pure hard not to gag, and he said, a few days before it happened, he was on the computers, and this guy next to him was looking up how to get hold of a gun. And then the guy clocked him looking and closed the browser quick as a flash, but not quick enough. And Mr Greasy Weirdo said he winked at him – like, to say, "Your secret's safe with me"? But the guy was proper spooked, and he grabbed his things and got out of there quicker than greased shit. And I said to him, if he knew it was gonna happen, how come he hadn't done anything to stop it? And he just made this face, like' – she screwed up her features into a disgusted scowl – 'and said, "Cos they're a shower of shites and they deserved what they g–g–g–got." And then he finished his drink and went up to his room and that was the last I heard from him till Dad kicked him out.'

Her story finished, Galatea gave a shrug and eyed Alyssa expectantly. 'Well? What d'you think about that?'

Alyssa didn't say anything immediately. Much as she wanted to believe it, the story had more than a whiff of ridiculousness about it. In fact, it reminded her of something that had happened at a birthday party not long after she'd started school. Towards the end of the festivities, it had come to light that one of the birthday girl's presents – a highly prized and very expensive doll, one of those grotesque things with staring eyes and realistic hair – had gone missing. The grown-ups had lined up all the children and asked them one by one if they knew what had happened to it. Everyone had said no, until they got to one girl – a smug little brat well-known for being prize bullshitter – who in the most innocent voice imaginable had declared, 'I saw a hand coming down and taking it.' She had, of course, been duly identified as the culprit and the doll restored to the clutches of its owner. Ramage's account hadn't featured any mysterious disembodied hands, but hardly seemed any less fantastical.

'I dunno,' said Alyssa, finding her voice at last. 'But I reckon I'd better go find my friend before he thinks we've forgotten about him.'

Downstairs, they found Davy looking decidedly fed up. They thanked Galatea for her time, declining her aggressively insistent efforts to entice them to take advantage of the 15% discount on all rooms, and headed back outside.

'Well?' said Davy, as soon as Alyssa had heaved the door shut behind them. 'Did you find anything out? The pair of yous were up there for ages. Must've been quite the bonding session.'

'Oh yeah, best friends forever, me and her.' She filled Davy in, as succinctly as possible, on what Galatea had told her.

'I knew it!' he hissed, struggling to keep his voice down. 'I *knew* he knew something.' Regarding Alyssa with the look of a particularly smug cat who'd just consumed an entire bowl of full fat cream, he said in a singsong voice, 'Who was right?'

'Hey, cool your jets, all right? It's hardly conclusive. OK, so it sounds like he might have known something – that is, assuming he wasn't just mouthing off while he was drunk, trying to impress a pretty girl. It still doesn't get us any closer to finding him, does it? Maybe, if we'd come here a week ago . . . '

'Yeah, well,' Davy shot back, 'a week ago you were still burying your head in the sand and telling me there was nothing untoward going on and Paul McGuigan was guilty as sin.'

'Getting a bit ahead of yourself, aren't you? You are aware that, even if Ramage *did* see the killer researching firearms in a public library – which, by the way, *seriously* dumb move – there's nothing to say it wasn't McGuigan he saw indulging in a spot of Googling.'

'Well,' said Davy stiffly, 'there's only one person who can tell us that for certain.'

'Exactly – and he's flown the coop, which puts us right back where we started. The pair of us could've stayed in our beds this morning and we'd still be just as far forward as we are now.'

Davy said nothing. He sat there in silence for a veritable eternity, gazing out at the view stretching before them. From their vantage point they could see all four corners of the town without even having to turn their heads.

He inhaled a deep, savouring breath. 'Well, all the same, this is nice, don't you think? Dead picturesque. There's just something about sitting here without a care in the universe, watching the world go by.'

Alyssa grimaced. 'Reminds me too much of home.'

Davy turned to look at her. 'And where exactly is home? You never talk about it.'

'There's a reason.'

'Ah, come on. You know everything there is to know about me; I know next to nothing about you. Hardly seems fair, does it?'

Alyssa sighed and perched herself on the low stone wall that bordered the guesthouse's garden. She had no desire to discuss this, but she knew Davy wasn't going to let up.

'Littlehaven, Saskatchewan. Population four hundred and ninety-five. Well, four hundred and ninety-four.'

Davy smiled wryly. 'I'm guessing it's not exactly the most happening place on earth.'

'That's putting it mildly. And coming here, seeing that girl with nothing to look forward to but month after month, year after year of "Welcome to the Linview Inn" . . . ' She suppressed a shudder. 'I tried to talk some sense into her, you know – tried to get her to see that she didn't have to settle for this. But it was like talking to a post. I don't see how you can have a whole world at your fingertips and be willing to settle for . . . this.'

'Perhaps she's scared of things going wrong. There's worse things than being risk-averse. 'Sides, life's a bit more complicated than just packing your bags and jetting off into the wide blue yonder without a second thought. Folk've got commitments. Responsibilities.'

'Fuck responsibility!' Alyssa launched herself onto her feet and faced Davy with shoulders arched in defiance. 'Seriously, fuck it with a giant throbbing dick. What about folks who don't want responsibility? Who never chose it? Who're sick of having expectations foisted upon them, being forced into someone else's idea of who they should be?'

'Well—'

'Expected to stick around in a dead-end town to keep the family business going just cos your folks decided to set up shop in the middle of nowhere? Expected to look after your little brothers or sisters cos you just happened to be born first? It's too much to lay on the shoulders of someone her age, or . . . or . . . or any age. She shouldn't have the rest of her life carved into stone just cos a bunch of grown-ups got there first and decided they were going to define it for her. Cos at the end of the day, when people say you've got responsibilities, it's really just a fancy way of saying "no".'

Davy scratched awkwardly behind his ear, trying to figure out how to respond to this tirade. But Alyssa wasn't finished.

'You really want to know who Emily was?'

Davy raised his shoulders in the beginning of a shrug. 'I mean, I guess—'

'She was my sister, OK? My little sister. And she died. Because of me.'

It hung in the air between them for almost a full minute, neither of them saying a word. A cold wind whipped about them, plastering Alyssa's hair across the lenses of her glasses, but she made no move to brush it away.

'But . . . how?' Davy eventually said.

'You ever heard of Wollaston Lake?'

Davy shook his head.

'It's this big stretch of water in Northern Saskatchewan. Freezes over for more than half the year. My grandparents owned a cabin by the western shore and they let us use it for vacations and such. Anyway, the year I turned twelve and Emily was coming on for five, we went up to spend a couple of weeks there just after Easter. One morning, our folks decided they were going to drive out to the old Wollaston settlement to visit the trading post there. I was at the, uh, contrarian stage.'

She half-expected Davy to utter an incredulous '*Was?*', but he said nothing.

'Yeah, well, I was like: spend hours driving, just to stare at a pile of rubble, then get back in the car and come straight back? No thanks. Said I wanted to stay behind and go off exploring the woods round the cabin. Reckon the Boomers were only too happy to see the back of me for a few hours. And of course, whatever I did, Emily wanted to do too. "I wanna stay with Lyssa", she kept saying. That's what she called me – Lyssa, like she couldn't handle words with more than two syllables or whatever. Anyway, she had, like, this mega-tantrum, and eventually the Boomers gave in. "She'll be fine," my dad said. "She's got her big sister to look out for her."'

'There's this little island about half a mile out from the shore.

You can see it from the cabin. Sometimes in the summer, we'd take my grandpa's boat over for a picnic. That year, there'd been an early thaw and the ice had already melted, and I thought, why not? So I made up sandwiches for me and Emily, got the boat out of the shed and set off. The sun was out, the sky was clear, and Emily was in her absolute element, standing at the prow, shouting out orders, kidding on she was the captain while I was back there with the oars, busting my ass. Not that I was bothered. I was just happy she was happy.

'We were about halfway there when we got into difficulties. The wind started to get up, and I couldn't keep control of the boat. We were getting blown further and further off course. The waters got really choppy. We were getting tossed around all over the shop. Emily was crying and I kept yelling at her to shut up, that it would pass soon, but it didn't do any good. And then, the boat overturned.'

In the silence that followed, she was convinced she actually *heard* Davy swallowing.

'The long and short of it is, I managed to find my way back up to the surface. Emily didn't. I looked for her, but it was so dark down there, and so cold . . . ' She let out a deep breath – one which reverberated through her entire body. 'I managed to get myself back into the boat and paddled to the shore. Of course, they sent out search parties. Boats, divers, helicopters, the works. They mobilised half the province, but they never found her. It was like she never existed.'

She fell silent again, sitting with her head bowed. At length, she looked up and found Davy still watching her intently, his face drawn and pensive. She gave a wan smile.

'So now d'you see why I do everything I can to avoid ending up in anything approaching a position of responsibility? Having people depending on me? I don't ask for much – just a place of my own, warm clothes and enough money to afford rent and the occasional computer game. And to live my life with the least possible impact on the world around me.'

She wanted him to say something. To crack some hideously inappropriate joke to lighten the mood. But he didn't. He just sat there, stunned into uncharacteristic, unsettling silence.

'How about that, then? Betcha it's not every day you meet someone who cheated death twice.'

Her voice sounded thick and husky in her own ears, and she was pretty sure she saw Davy flinch. Far from discharging the tension in the air, all she'd done was make the atmosphere between them even more uncomfortable. She needed to be on the move, doing something. Anything.

'I don't know about you,' she said, 'but I'm starved. Come on – let's see if they've got anything borderline edible in that old man pub we passed on the way up.'

Not waiting for a response, she set off down the path at the brisk march. After a few seconds, she heard the familiar sound of squeaking wheels and crunching gravel. Without looking back, she knew Davy was following her.

'You know,' said Davy, as the bus slowly wound its way out of the valley later that afternoon, 'since today seems to be a day for sharing, I've a confession to make.'

'Oh yeah? What's that?'

'I kinda figured the odds of us finding Ramage just waiting for us when we got here were pretty non-existent.'

Alyssa shot him a crabby look. 'Would've been nice if you'd shared that insight before dragging me out here.'

Davy gave a knowing smile. 'Ah, but see, here's the thing. I figured a day in the country would do us both a power of good. A chance to get out of the city, get a few things off our chests . . . and boy, did we ever.'

It was the first acknowledgement he'd given, direct or otherwise, of her confession about Emily since she'd made it. Until now, they'd spent the last three hours dancing around it, their conversations clipped and monosyllabic.

'In all seriousness,' he said, 'I appreciate you telling me. It explains quite a bit in retrospect.'

'Like why I'm a moody bitch?'

He gave the inklings of a smile. 'Among other things. Seriously though, what you told me? It won't go any further than us, if that's what you want.'

'It is,' she said. 'Thank you.'

A minute or so elapsed, only the gentle hum of the bus's engine filling the silence between them. There wasn't even any chatter from the oldies. The day out seemed to have just about finished them. Indeed, many of them were asleep.

'It's not your fault, by the way.' Davy's voice cut into Alyssa's thoughts. 'What happened – the wind, the boat capsizing and that – you couldn't have predicted it.'

'I know,' she said automatically.

'And your parents – they shouldn't have put you in that position.'

'Ain't that the truth.'

'I'm just saying, you don't have to keep beating yourself up, blaming yourself.' He raised his hands. 'I know, I know – easier said than done. But if you don't try and move on, it'll only end up eating you from the inside.'

They settled into an uneasy silence, Alyssa resting her head on the window, gazing out at the passing scenery. After a while, she became aware of light snoring and realised that Davy, too, was asleep. She herself remained wide awake, wondering if he would have been so quick to absolve her of blame if he knew the whole story of what had happened out on Wollaston Lake.

18

At 2 a.m., the atmosphere inside Metropolis, a basement nightclub located a stone's throw from Central Station, might best have been described as fetid. The air reeked with the twin smells of perspiring flesh and liberally applied deodorant, the dance-floor was too cramped to accommodate the sheer number of people strutting their stuff, the over-cranked speaker system hadn't been designed for the volume levels to which it was being subjected, and the lack of adequate ventilation made everything feel clammy and febrile.

Jackson had noticed the girl within a few minutes of his arrival and hadn't been able to take his eyes off her since. If he could have designed the perfect specimen of womanhood, it would have looked like her. Long-limbed, slender, just shy of six foot, she seemed to positively glow, as if her very skin was radiating light, creating a halo around her – a beacon, beckoning him, calling him. And he'd dutifully obliged. Over the course of the last quarter-hour, he'd been steadily working his way towards her, expertly manoeuvring through the crush of bodies little by little, without making it obvious what he was doing. Didn't want to spook the horses. Now, as the song finished and she made for the bar, he seized his chance. Pushing through the throng, he sauntered over to her and, casually resting an elbow on the countertop, did a carefully choreographed little double take, as if he'd just noticed her for the first time.

'Did I die and go to heaven? Cos I could swear I just saw an angel.'

She glanced at him long enough to register a look of confusion mixed with mild disdain, then turned back to the bartender and resumed giving him her order.

Jackson blinked back disbelief. That line nearly always worked. Perhaps it was too subtle for her. He'd have to try a more direct approach.

'That,' he said to her as she handed over her cash, 'was me paying you a compliment.'

'Uh-huh?' She didn't turn to look at him.

'That's right. I've got this affliction, see? Can't help it. If I see a drop-dead gorgeous girl, I've just gotta say something – and *you* are most certainly drop-dead gorgeous.'

On 'you', he jabbed his index finger at her, aiming for her shoulder, but missed her altogether by several inches, then almost lost his footing and had to grab onto the bar-top to steady himself. The girl watched the entire episode with the air of the distinctly unimpressed.

'Oh,' she said, 'well, thanks . . . I guess.'

'No one ever told you that before?' He shook his head disapprovingly. 'Shocking. Folk are too wishy-washy these days. Too afraid of getting a doing off the PC mob.'

'That right, aye?'

'Me, I call a spade a spade. Some folk might have a problem with that, but that's their lookout.'

'Well, I hope that works out for you,' she said, and turned to go.

'Lemme buy you a drink,' he blurted out. Not the smoothest manoeuvre, perhaps, but desperate times called for desperate measures.

She stopped in her tracks and half-turned to him, raising a

perfectly sculpted eyebrow. 'I've got a drink,' she said, holding the glass of whatever colourful mixer she'd ordered up as evidence.

'I mean a proper drink.'

He took a few steps towards her, even though that meant moving out of reach of the bar. Probably not the wisest move in his current state – but, again, desperate times.

She stared at him for an awkward moment, then gave a quiet, scoffing laugh. 'I don't think so.'

'Whassamatter with you?' He tilted his head, squinting at her, as if regarding her from a different angle might make sense of her irrational behaviour. 'You turn your nose up at a compliment, you turn down the offer of a free drink. You a rug muncher or something?'

The girl just rolled her eyes.

'Pity – s'always the good-looking ones. What a waste.'

Just then, another figure entered Jackson's – rather hazy – field of vision: a guy a good ten years younger and a good forty pounds lighter than him. The new arrival looked first at the girl, then at Jackson, then turned to the girl again.

'This guy bothering you?'

Jackson took an unsteady step towards him. 'Butt out, pal. This here's a private conversation.'

Blanking him completely, the young guy looked questioningly at the girl, who wrinkled her nose slightly and did something with one shoulder. The young guy turned to face Jackson with a strained, condescending smile.

'Look, friend, I think maybe you've had one too many. Time to call it quits for tonight, yeah?'

Jackson glowered at the young man – barely an adult, really – with his tight-fitting skinny jeans and his gelled-up hair, and gave a snarl of disgust.

'Who you talking to, ya fucking ponce?'

The smile faded from the young man's face. He folded his arms, placing himself between Jackson and the girl. 'She's not interested, all right? Now why don't you just beat it?'

With a bellow of rage, Jackson balled up his fist and swung. Unfortunately for him, his aim was no better than before and he staggered sideways. This time, with no bar to save him, he lost his balance completely and landed face-first on the floor. As he rolled onto his back, groaning and prodding his nose to check that it was still where he'd left it, he beheld the unsmiling face of one of Metropolis's bouncers gazing down at him. The square-jawed hulk's expression told Jackson that, for him at least, the party was well and truly over.

Despite being unceremoniously turfed out onto a street teeming with rain, Jackson was in no immediate rush to vacate the area. He paced about for a bit outside the entrance, partly to let off steam and partly as a warning to anyone contemplating giving such a disreputable establishment their patronage. The girl remained at the forefront of his mind, though the shine had definitely come off her. If she thought she could do better with that skinny, hair-gelled Nancy-boy than with him, Jackson Ballantine, God's very own personal gift to the ladies, then good luck to her. She didn't know what she was missing.

As the red mist slowly faded, he found himself with a pressing need to answer the call of nature. Aware that his chances of slipping back into Metropolis undetected were close to non-existent, he instead staggered into the narrow lane beside the building where, stationed in front of a wheelie bin, he unzipped himself, dug out his pecker and set about relieving the pressure on his overstuffed bladder. The resulting stream was both pungent and full, and he couldn't help but feel a sense of pride. Surely only a true giant of a man could produce such an impressive flow?

A noise off to his left, back towards the street, caused him to lose his focus. He turned instinctively, splashing his good shoes in the process. Cursing under his breath, he watched as a quartet of revellers strolled past the mouth of the lane, oblivious to the damage they'd done.

Facing the wall once more, he resumed his ministrations. The stream was as strong as ever and showed no signs of letting up. That was the thing about alcohol: it went right through you, especially if you had nothing to soak it up with. Once again, he marvelled at both the quality and quantity of his output. He'd like to see Nancy-boy try to match *that*.

He wasn't aware of the length of wire being looped round his neck – only of it being pulled tight from behind. He staggered backwards, hands flying to his neck, scrabbling at the flex cutting into his flesh, desperately trying to get his fingers under it. His pecker, continuing to carry out its allotted task hands-free, sprayed an arc in front of him, splashing the bin and the wall beyond it.

He felt the cord digging into his neck, squeezing his airway, crushing the breath from his lungs. He thrashed around violently, trying to land a blow against his assailant – but for the third and final time that night, he failed to make any contact. His eyes watered. He tasted a sourness in his mouth. The burning sensation that had begun in his chest expanded upwards to fill his lungs, his throat, his entire head. His ears were ringing, his vision blurring into swirling shapes and flashes of light.

The last thing he remembered before the end was his assailant's hot breath in his ear.

Then stars.

Then nothing.

19

On Friday morning, Alyssa arrived for work to find Davy in a highly animated mood.

'There you are!' he exclaimed, wheeling himself over to cut her off as she stepped into the main library. 'Heard the news?'

'What news?'

'The *news*.'

She realised then that he was clutching a paper – that morning's edition of the *Daily Chronicle*. He held it aloft, angling the front page towards her. 'SICK STRANGULATION IN CITY CENTRE' was the all-bold, all-caps headline, accompanied by a photo of the neon-fronted Metropolis nightclub.

'There was another murder last night,' he went on breathlessly as she skimmed the text below the article. 'Some poor sod was strangled to death in the alleyway next to a nightclub.'

Alyssa rolled her eyes. She could already guess where he was going with this. 'Oh, come *on*. Are you seriously gonna pin every single murder in the Northern Hemisphere from now to the end of time on our friendly neighbourhood library killer? This one wasn't even in Thornhill or Craigslee. It was in the city centre. And look.' She jabbed a finger at the headline. 'Strangulation. Once again, different modus operandi.'

She saw Davy visibly deflating, a sullen scowl darkening his features. She felt her own shoulders sagging. Irritating as his insistence on leaping on every single tenuous 'lead' that came along was, she realised pricking his balloon no longer held the satisfaction it had once had for her.

'Look, I know you're desperate for some sort of breakthrough,' she said. 'Some smoking gun that proves McGuigan's innocence. But this clutching at straws isn't helping anyone – not McGuigan and certainly not you. Anyhow,' she went on, as he turned his chair around and began to wheel himself towards the desk, 'I've been doing some thinking, and I reckon I know a way we can put the matter of the killer's identity to bed.'

'Oh yeah?' said Davy, with little enthusiasm. 'Let's hear it.'

She fell into step with him. The idea had come to her in the wee hours of a long and largely sleepless night, and she'd made up her mind to put it to the test, to satisfy her own curiosity if nothing else.

'Let's assume, for talking's sake, that Ramage wasn't completely full of it and he really *did* see someone looking up how to get their hands on a gun. Right?'

'Right,' said Davy a tad cautiously as he manoeuvred himself into position behind the counter.

'And according to you, the only computers Ramage ever used were the two at the back of the reading room, nice and secluded and away from the prying eyes of the staff.'

'Right,' said Davy again, nodding slowly as he began to see where this was headed.

'Ergo, whichever one Ramage was using at the time, the killer must've been using the other. In which case, it's just a matter of figuring out who was sitting next to Ramage when he was logged in. It shouldn't be too difficult,' she went on, as the thrill of the hunt kindled in Davy's eyes once again. 'The booking system keeps a record of every login going back the last twelve months, right? And I'll tell you something else for nothing.'

'What?'

'If Ramage reeked half as much as everyone makes out, I'd bet my left butt-cheek the list of people willing to sit next to him's gonna be pretty short. We just need to find someone who's the right age, sex and whatnot.'

Davy grinned. 'Right enough. I can count the number of times I saw someone brave enough to breathe the same air as that manky bugger on one hand.'

They huddled around one of the computers at the desk, drawing repeated acidic looks from Marli, left manning the counter single-handed. The WebShare internet booking software used a dual-axis grid, the X-axis showing the time of day while the Y-axis listed the fourteen computers in the reading room. Each booking was represented by a coloured block which, when highlighted, listed the name and library card number of the user. Focusing on the two machines at the back of the room – numbers 13 and 14 – Alyssa and Davy wound back to the last day the library had been open prior to the murders – Saturday, February the twenty-seventh – and proceeded to work backwards, identifying all the times Ramage had been logged into one of the two machines and noting down the name and number of anyone who had an overlapping booking on the other.

As Alyssa had predicted, it was a fairly short list. Within twenty minutes they'd made it all the way back to the beginning of the year, which they both agreed was considerably further than they actually needed to go – and even then, the number of users who'd had Ramage for a neighbour at any point during that eight-week period was a measly twenty-one, despite him having logged on virtually every day. They discounted anyone with an obviously female name, which cut down the list by a third. Having noted the card numbers of the remaining fifteen users, they proceeded to enter each one into the cataloguing software, calling up the associated account, which contained various details, including name, address, contact number and date of birth.

They were able to rule out several accounts right off the bat. Of these, seven were well over the age of sixty and therefore unlikely to be physically fit enough to be the killer. Davy was able to identify a further five, eliminating them on the grounds of weight, height or disability. That left just three potential suspects who, over the course of the next fifteen minutes, they were also able to score out. One, a call to the phone number listed in his account details revealed, had been in hospital since the end of February, waiting for a heart-lung transplant, while another had been booked onto a computer in Summerhill Library on the other side of the city at the time of the shootings.

The third and final name initially showed promise. He was thirty-eight and, according to the relevant dropdown menu, not entitled to any concessions, which suggested he was fully able-bodied. Furthermore, he and Ramage had enjoyed a few brief minutes of crossover three days before the incident, and since then, he hadn't logged onto a computer at Thornhill or indeed any other North Kelvin library. In the end, though, he too had to be crossed off the list, when Davy belatedly remembered who he was, and that he had a false arm, which – they were forced to conclude – almost certainly precluded him from pointing a gun at anyone, let alone pulling the trigger.

'Ach, never mind,' he said, as Alyssa tossed the mouse on the countertop with a frustrated sigh. 'It was always a bit of a long shot. We're not licked yet.'

But if Davy had any ideas as to where they were supposed to proceed from here, he didn't share them.

As he wheeled himself away, Alyssa remained seated in front of the screen, slumped forward on the countertop. She hadn't expect-ed to feel quite so disappointed. A part of her had been hoping their search would throw up Paul McGuigan as one of the users – which would surely have been enough to force even Davy to concede that the police really had got their man after all. But then again, *would* it have? She'd once read that a position based on logic or at least sincere belief could be dismantled methodically by stronger counter-logic, whereas a position based on nothing but a desire for it to be true was unassailable. He'd probably just claim McGuigan's presence at the computer next to Ramage's was yet further evidence of a fit-up.

In any event, far from getting answers, let alone closure, their so-called investigation had come to yet another screeching halt. It was impossible not to feel at least a tad foolish for allowing herself to get her hopes up.

Alyssa took her lunch early that day. She needed to talk to the bank about getting another increase on her overdraft and figured going into the nearest branch in person would be more likely to yield positive results than trying to plead her case with some call centre drone over the phone. The cash settlement she'd been promised had finally materialised in her account a couple of days prior – a paltry sum which seriously stretched the meaning of the word 'generous' and clearly wasn't going to have the transformative effect on her finances that she'd hoped for. She concluded that if it really was intended to demonstrate the value the company placed in its staff, then that value was sorely lacking.

She got back to the library to find Pat and Marli waiting for her at the counter. One look at their faces was enough to tell her that something was afoot.

'Just so you know,' said Marli, before she could get a word out, 'Nikki Wyatt's here.'

'Aye, and she's brought some pals with her,' said Pat.

'Pals?' Alyssa frowned.

'Aye – that creepy bloke fae Legal with the halitosis and two others I havnae seen before. One's got a camera. The other's a reporter, I think. Ewan someone? Said they're with the *Tribune*.'

'They're in the break room now,' said Marli.

'In that case,' said Alyssa, 'I'm turning round and walking straight back out that door. They can dock my wages if they like. I'm not baring my soul to some hack so he can sell column inches.'

'Ah, c'mon, don't be so overdramatic,' said Pat, stepping out from behind the desk to block her path to the exit. 'Sure it'll not be that bad.'

'Oh yeah? Then why don't *you* go in there and cry your eyes out for them?'

'Love to, pet – only I doubt they're gonnae be interested in anything little old me has to say. Wasnae me who had the near-death experience.'

'Well, where's Davy, then?' She looked around. 'Get him to do it. I'm sure he'd love the attention.'

'Physio appointment,' said Marli. 'He left while you were out.'

'That's convenient,' Alyssa cracked. She couldn't imagine Davy turning down the opportunity for a shot in the spotlight and had no doubt he'd have been chomping at the bit to have his own per-sonal kiss-and-tell article in the *Tribune* if it had been on offer. Still, a physio appointment sounded by far the more appealing of the two scenarios, and she'd have given anything to swap places with him right about now.

'Put it this way,' said Pat, placing a fatherly hand on his shoulder, 'ye've got a captive audience waiting for ye in there, and odds are they'll print anything ye say. Could be a chance to tell a few home truths about how this service is run, hmm?' He raised an eyebrow encouragingly.

'*Yeah.*' Marli's voice dripped enthusiasm. 'You could tell them how they haven't stepped up security for us since it happened. How they refuse to actually perma-ban anyone, even the ones we get dog's abuse from.'

'Aye – they wannae know what it's really like working in a public library? Well, tell 'em about the lack of CCTV, the lack of support fae higher up, how we're all just one psycho away fae another massacre.'

Alyssa hated to admit it, but she was warming to the idea – not least because the thought of Nikki Wyatt squirming as she dished the dirt on the company seemed the perfect revenge for engineering this ambush. *Want me to talk to the press, Nikki? Well, how's THIS for talking?*

A moment later, she was heading towards the break room, spurred on her way by rapturous cheers and applause from her two colleagues.

Nikki was positively delighted to see her. She put her arm round Alyssa in a way that made her feel profoundly uncomfortable and showed her off to the two men from the *Tribune* as if she was an exhibit, introducing her as 'one of our most valued employees', before hastily assuring everyone present that all their employees were equally valued. The two men – one in an ill-fitting suit, the other in T-shirt and jeans and sporting a tiny camera with an absurdly long lens which left Alyssa wondering if he was compensating for something – just smirked at each other. Clearly, they had the measure of her.

They got underway, Caulfield – the one in the suit – asking the questions while Nikki and the grey man from Legal sat a little off to one side, the latter with his laptop open on his knees – transcribing the conversation, Alyssa assumed. He started off with a bunch of trite background questions about what had brought Alyssa over here originally and how she'd ended up working in libraries. Accordingly, she had some fun with him, making up a bunch of crap about how she'd originally studied bioengineering, but had decided her talents were wasted in STEM and jacked it all in for a job stamping books and helping net-clueless people reset their email passwords. Nikki interjected with a nervous little laugh each time Alyssa said something caustic or in vaguely bad taste, but she didn't start to get *really* hot under the collar until talk turned to the shootings. Had she been afraid she was going to die, Caulfield asked? Well, Alyssa said, that would be the standard response when standing face-to-face with a man who'd just gunned down four of her colleagues. How did she feel she was coping? All right, she supposed. She'd never survived a massacre before, so she wasn't sure if she was performing to expectations. Still, she must feel a certain sense of relief now, mustn't she, knowing the police had charged someone and he was safely behind bars?

Alyssa folded one leg over the other and gave a deep sigh, then fixed Caulfield with her most earnest look. 'Well, to be honest, Ewan, not really. See, we're all of us just a little on edge, on account of how, nearly six months after it happened, our working conditions are exactly the same as they were then, with absolutely nothing being put in place to ensure something like that never happens again.'

Nikki shot forward in her seat with an intake of breath, an objection on the tip of her tongue, but Alyssa beat her to it. 'I mean, don't get me wrong,' she said, holding up a hand to forestall her, 'I think it's absolutely swell, the job you do. Throwing prize-giving ceremonies to tell us how valued we are really puts our minds at ease when there's people out there who're more than happy to waste us with a fricking Glock. But then, I guess booking out the function room at the Excelsior once a year is more cost-effective than, oh, I dunno, some working CCTV cameras or a security guard.'

'I think what Alyssa means,' said Nikki hastily, sounding for all the world like she was clenching an ice cube between her butt-cheeks, 'is that what happened back in March has been a shock to us all. We all know what she's been through and—'

Alyssa turned to face her. 'No, that's just it – you don't. You say all the right words, make all the right facial expressions, but you have no idea what life's actually like on the front lines. How could you? You only grace us with your presence when there's either a crisis or a photo op. Meanwhile, we're sitting ducks out there, just waiting for the next shooting spree.'

She was genuinely enjoying this, and not just because of the constipated looks on Nikki and the legal beagle's faces. It was a new experience for her – her keenly honed contempt for authority dovetailing so neatly with a sense of solidarity for her colleagues. In her mind, being a loyal employee had always meant genuflecting to the bosses, burying your own thoughts and opinions, your own personality, to toe the company line. But here she was, getting to stick it to the man while standing shoulder to shoulder with her fellow foot soldiers. It was a bit like having your cake and eating it.

'But surely,' said Caulfield, as Nikki once again spluttered and struggled to formulate a coherent response, 'the odds of something like this ever happening again are one in a million? Gun violence is mercifully rare in this part of the world, and if the culprit is behind bars . . . ' He gave an encouraging little shrug. 'Surely you see what I'm getting at?'

'Sure I do,' said Alyssa. 'That's assuming, of course, he actually did it.'

Caulfield frowned. 'Is there any reason to doubt that?'

Alyssa opened her mouth to respond, then stopped. Did she really want to get into this? Did she even believe, in her heart of hearts, that there was even the slimmest possibility Davy was right? Again, she found herself wishing he was the one sitting here in the hot seat.

'It's a simple enough question,' said Caulfield. 'Are you saying you have reason to believe Paul McGuigan is innocent?'

Alyssa scrambled to come up with an answer that wouldn't result in her sounding like a prize jackass. 'Well,' she said weakly, 'the cops were very quick to make an arrest, and from what I gather, the evidence against him is entirely circumstantial. And he says he didn't do it, and, y'know,' she shrugged helplessly, 'innocent until proved guilty, I guess?'

She almost added *and I think he was stitched up by Claire Metcalfe, acting on the orders of the Secretary of State for Justice*, but decided not to push her luck.

The interview continued for a little longer, but the air had very much gone out of the balloon. Nikki succeeded in regaining control of the process, swooping in with her own corporate-approved boilerplate in response to any questions that could prove contentious before Alyssa had a chance to get a word out. They drew things to a close with a photography session, Alyssa affecting an arms-folded, standoffish scowl as the cameraman snapped her from various angles, flashbulb bouncing off the walls of the cramped little room.

She got out of there pretty sharpish after things wrapped up and headed out to the desk, concluding that there was something to be said for strength in numbers and that Nikki Wyatt was unlikely to give her a roasting in full view of the public. As the counter came into view, she realised some sort of dispute was in progress. The scruffy homeless guy – the one who seemed to spend his entire life sitting outside the newsagent across the road, come rain or shine – was on one side of the counter. On the other, Bindi was berating him in the tone of a prissy schoolmarm.

'No, no, no!' she was saying, at the sort of volume normally reserved for speaking to someone profoundly deaf. 'You can't do that in here. It's not allowed. Clear out! Or I'll have no choice but to contact the authorities.'

Alyssa stole a glance at the surrounding area. Several customers were dotted around the ground floor. One or two were making no secret of the fact that they were watching – and probably enjoying – the entire show, but even the ones with their noses buried in books were, she suspected, listening to every word. At the counter, Marli and Stevie stared resolutely at their computer screens.

'Don't you take that tone with me!' Bindi snapped, in response to something the homeless guy said that Alyssa hadn't been able to catch. 'I'll not stand for it. This is a respectable establishment and your continued presence is bringing it into disrepute. See?' She gesticulated with her entire arm as an elderly couple made a sharp retreat towards the exit. 'People are leaving. You're making them uncomfortable.'

Alyssa suspected their speedy departure had considerably more to do with Bindi's histrionics than the harmless presence of a man who probably didn't have anywhere better to go. She wondered if she was going to have the balls to intervene herself or simply act like Marli and Stevie and pretend it had nothing to do with her.

In the end, it was a choice she didn't have to make. Admitting defeat, the homeless guy turned and made his slow, shuffling way towards the exit, while Bindi watched with a look of undisguised satisfaction.

'That's right!' she called after him, again considerably louder than necessary. 'And don't even think about coming back. We've put up with your sort for far too long.'

'What the hell was that all about?' said Alyssa, drawing along-side the counter as the door swung shut behind the departing vagabond.

'Oh, *that*?' said Bindi, wrinkling her nose scornfully. 'Just one of life's undesirables doing his best to lower the tone.' She produced a small perfume bottle and proceeded to spray the air around the desk.

'Why – what did he do?'

Bindi sprayed a final blast for good measure. 'I caught him going around asking the other users for spare change.' She gave Alyssa a wide-eyed, beseeching look, as if to say *can you believe it?* 'Soon put a stop to *that*.'

Alyssa stared at Bindi, at a loss for words. She was no bleeding heart herself, but Bindi's naked lack of compassion for a fellow human being took callousness to a whole new level.

'He's probably hungry,' she eventually said.

'Yeah, well, I can't help his life choices.'

For a moment, Alyssa regarded Bindi with a look of utter disgust. Then, without a word, she turned on her heel and made for the exit herself, hot on the man's heels.

'And just where do you think you're going?' Bindi called after her. 'My shift finishes in five minutes and I'm not hanging around if you're not back by then.'

Alyssa crossed the road, headed into the newsagent and bought a sandwich. Cheese ploughman's. You couldn't go wrong with cheese ploughman's. Besides, she was still riding high on the wave of collectivist solidarity that had carried her through the interview and felt like spreading some of that newfound compassion for her fellow human beings. By the time she emerged, the homeless guy was back in his usual spot by the door, his grimy rucksack serving as a cushion. Alyssa bent down, holding out the sandwich.

'Here. Gotcha this.'

The man looked at it for a moment as if it was some sort of alien artefact. Then he lifted his head and gazed up at Alyssa with a smile that looked vaguely condescending.

'It's kind of you to offer, wee pet, but I've got about half a dozen identical ones in here.' He patted his rucksack with a grubby hand.

Alyssa just stared at him for several uncomfortable seconds, still holding the sandwich in her outstretched hand.

'Not that I don't appreciate the thought,' he went on, as she reluctantly lowered her arm, 'but I'd just as soon you'd taken the money you used to pay for that and given it me directly. Though a lot of folk don't like doing that,' he went on philosophically. 'They prefer physical goods cos, whatever they tell themselves, they like the control it gives them. With money, they don't have that power. For all they know, we might spend it on drink or drugs, or something else not on the "approved" list.'

Alyssa raised an eyebrow. 'And would you?'

'See what I mean?' He gave a little shrug. 'Fact is, for a lot of us NFA types, it's one mind-altering substance or another that gets us through those long winter nights when there's only a shop doorway 'twixt us and the elements. Sight more effective than a Boots ready-meal, I'll tell you that.'

She saw his point. A handout was a handout. If it came with strings attached, with stipulations about how it should be spent, then it really wasn't charity at all.

She held the sandwich out to him again. 'Add it to your collection anyway. Never know when it might come in useful.'

'Well, if it puts a smile on your face . . . ' He took the sandwich from her and slipped it inside his rucksack.

Drawing alongside him, she leant against the wall and gazed across the road at the library, following his line of vision. It was on some level a show of support, she supposed – showing him that however much of a bitch Bindi might be, *she* at least had some compassion in her. Not that compassion amounted to a hill of beans if you weren't prepared to actually stand up and assert it. She wondered, if she'd arrived on the scene a few minutes earlier, whether she'd have said anything or if, like Marli and Stevie, she'd just have stared at her computer screen and let Bindi carry on belittling and dehumanising the guy in front of a captive audience.

'What's your name?' she asked.

The man looked up at her with genuine wonderment. 'You know, that's the first time anyone's asked me that in as long as I can remember.'

'Well, what *is* it, then?' she shrugged expectantly.

He chuckled softly. 'It's Benny.'

'I'm Alyssa.'

'A pleasure to make your acquaintance, Alyssa.'

He extended his hand up towards her. She hesitated for a moment, the little voice at the back of her head telling her she didn't know where it had been, then threw caution to the wind and shook it. Nonetheless, she still took care to surreptitiously wipe her own on the back of her leggings once he released it.

They gazed out at the view before them in silence for a while. Benny fished inside his cagoule and produced some rolling paper and a tin of tobacco.

'Thing is, though,' he said, as he began to roll a cigarette, 'folk like me have this cloak of invisibility about us. The good people of this city only notice us when we inconvenience them – your colleague with the bangles and designer leggings being a case in point. Most of the time, they're so preoccupied with their own problems, they rarely stop to think about those of other people.'

Alyssa arched her shoulders defensively. She didn't like to admit it, but his words had struck a chord with her. How many times had she just walked past him, thinking of him – when she thought about him at all – as nothing more than a minor nuisance to be sidestepped?

'Yeah, well,' she said stiffly, 'we've all got problems.'

Benny laughed. 'Ain't that the truth.'

She gazed out at the view before her: the busy Chancery Street with its near-constant flow of traffic and, beyond it, the stone gates and the crumbling old library, standing there like some ancient monument to a bygone century.

'You must see a lot of sights, sitting out here all day.'

Benny nodded soberly. 'I do that, aye. Saw the ambulancemen bringing you out that day.'

'Yeah? You and half the known world, bruh.' Those photographs, she suspected, were going to haunt her till the day she died.

'Saw the immediate aftermath too. All those folk coming streaming out, running around like headless chickens. And the moments leading up to it as well. I saw the fragrant Mr Ramage coming out, effing and blinding, and setting off up the street. Then, not five minutes later, I witnessed our man in black striding up the pavement and into the building, bold as brass, and then . . . ' He left the rest unsaid.

'You didn't happen to see him without his ski-mask on, did you?' said Alyssa. She knew it was a long shot, but she had to ask.

Benny shook his head. 'Alas, no. That would have been most fortuitous, would it not? Though I can tell you that, among the community I inhabit, the overwhelming consensus is that the charming Mr McGuigan was a patsy.'

'Really?' It was the first time Alyssa had heard anyone other than Davy expressing a conviction as to McGuigan's innocence, and the effect was oddly disconcerting.

Benny nodded. 'Those of us with a, shall we say, *ambivalent* relationship with polite society tend to move in similar circles, whether our crimes include larceny and the procurement of illegal narcotics or merely cluttering up these nice clean streets. McGuigan was well known to the NFA crowd. Not to put too fine a point on it, but the man had neither the bottle nor the gumption to pull off anything so audacious.'

'Don't suppose you happened to share these observations with the police?'

Benny shrugged. 'The authorities interviewed all sorts that day. Local businessmen, library users, even your common-or-garden passersby on the street. But no one thought to talk to little old Benny. Mind you, immaterial now, isn't it? The police have their man, the streets are safe again for you and me, and DCI Metcalfe is no doubt looking at a juicy promotion. Everyone's happy.' He continued to work on perfecting his roll-up.

'And Ramage,' she said, 'you wouldn't happen to have seen him around, would you? Since the . . . event, I mean. Say at, I dunno, a soup kitchen or a homeless shelter or whatever.'

'Why? He owe you for some late returns?' Benny chuckled.

'No, I'm just trying to track him down,' she said, rather tersely. 'Have you seen him or not?'

Benny regarded her for a long moment – making her wait for it, she thought, punishing her for her ill-temperedness. 'I can't say I've had the pleasure. Not since the incident which dare not speak its name, in fact. But I'll keep these old peepers peeled,' he went on, before Alyssa could say anything else. 'And, should they happen to alight on anything, you'll be the first to know.'

It was as good an offer as she was going to get and, under the circumstances, probably better than she could have hoped for. And now, if she wanted to still have a job to come back to, she really needed to make tracks.

'Thanks, Benny,' she said, surreptitiously slipping a fiver into one of the many pockets of his rucksack.

Benny tipped two fingers to his head, Cub Scouts-style. 'Any time, wee pet.'

20

Alyssa's thumb slid across her phone's screen, raising the volume of the YouTube video above that of the hubbub in the coffee shop. It consisted of blocky, poorly focused footage of a wild-haired, bearded man delivering a full-blown sermon to his audience of twenty-six followers. The channel's title was 'THOUGHTS OF TONY BARBAROSSA', the chosen topic of this particular video 'THE RIGHT TO BARE' – sic – 'ARMS'. It had been uploaded a little over four weeks ago and had already garnered a princely eighteen views, including Alyssa's.

Over the last couple of days, she'd spent much of her downtime acquainting herself with the mad, mad world of the selfsame Tony Barbarossa. Davy might not have been enamoured by the idea of a deep dive into the comings and goings of his ex-colleague, but what he didn't know couldn't hurt him. And the dive had certainly been deep. Of the twenty-two videos on his channel, she'd watched eight so far. None ran for less than half an hour, and all were character- ised by a rambling stream-of-consciousness approach to his chosen topic, coupled with a delivery that was never anything less than self-assured. There was one, for example, about how the govern- ment was secretly putting lithium in the tap-water to keep the population docile, and another on his belief that the advent of penicillin had created a weak, supine populace that would be unable to survive the coming apocalypse. The latest had clearly been spearheaded by The Event and, more pressingly, the ensuing calls to toughen up Scotland's already heavily restrictive gun ownership laws. As far as Barbarossa was concerned, this was an outrage that would eventually lead to every citizen in the land rising up to reclaim their right to arm themselves to the teeth – for which the inevitable consequence of the occasional bloody massacre was a small price to pay. While common sense told her that someone who'd just committed armed murder against his ex-colleagues was hardly likely to incriminate himself with a video extolling the virtues of firearms ownership, there could be little doubt that Tony Barbarossa's mind worked very differently to that of a normal person.

'Here you go.'

Alyssa looked up, lowering her phone, as a steaming cup of coffee was set before her on the tabletop. It was a rich, deep-scented cappuccino with a swirly pattern of cream on top. The sandy-haired man who'd brought it over from the counter, and who now slipped into the seat opposite her, watched her intently from behind the lenses of his wide-rimmed glasses.

'Thanks.'

'Don't mention it. So.' He took a sip from his own cup, pausing to wipe stray froth from his upper lip. 'Library assistant, eh? That's a bit of a turn-up for the books, if you'll excuse the pun.'

He smiled encouragingly, cueing her to laugh, but she didn't bite. There was a time when she'd found his awful puns amusing, endearing even, but that was long past. For the umpteenth time, she wondered whether she'd done the right thing in agreeing to this meeting. She reminded herself she was here for a reason. Well, two reasons, really. Firstly, to try to draw a line in the sand. Secondly, to silence the voice at the back of her head that had been growing ever more incessant over the last few days. The voice that kept telling her that surely it was more than mere coincidence that, following a lengthy spell of all being quiet on the Western Front, the man seated opposite her had re-appeared right at the same time someone had tried to put a bullet in her.

She looked at him now, sitting there sipping his cappuccino, and tried to imagine him striding into a public library armed with a nine-millimetre handgun and blowing her colleagues away one by one before finally turning his weapon on her. It seemed so utterly far-fetched as to be almost laughable – the sort of thing that only happened in movies. And yet surely the idea of *anyone* walking into a library and shooting the place up was far-fetched, whoever they happened to be? Nonetheless, it had indeed happened, and the question at the forefront of her mind was not whether it was probable but whether it was *possible* – possible that he resented her *that* much. If he did, he was putting on a damn good act, drinking artisan coffee and making idle chit-chat like everything was perfectly normal.

'How are your folks? Both in good health?'

His voice snapped her back to the here and now. She took a sip, stalling for time as she tried to recalibrate her brain into conversation mode.

'They're . . . same as always, I guess. No major calamities to report.'

'That's good. My mum was asking after you. Wanted to know if I'd seen you recently.'

'And what did you tell her?'

'The truth?' He made it sound like a question. 'That the last time I spoke to you was over a year ago, at which point you made it only too clear you didn't want anything further to do with me.'

Took long enough for it to sink in, though, she almost said, but managed to stop herself.

'By the way,' he went on, 'I meant to say, I've still got a whole bunch of your stuff sitting in boxes at my place.'

'What sort of stuff?' She tried to sound uninterested.

'Clothes and DVDs and the like. I'd thought about giving it all to a charity shop, but I figured you might still want some of it.'

'I dunno. Maybe.'

In truth, she had at least a vague idea of what was in those boxes. She was pretty sure they included her *Breaking Bad* boxsets, and she knew she'd also left behind at least a couple of outfits she had half a mind to put on again someday – though she stopped short of actually admitting it. Better for him not to think he had any leverage over her.

'You could come over sometime and take a look?' His voice rose a hopeful octave. 'Whenever's convenient for you.'

Alyssa stared into her cup, saying nothing.

'Or I could bring them round to yours if you like?' Again that hopeful little inflection to his voice. 'Makes sense, seeing as I'm the one with the wheels.'

She shook her head. 'Not a good idea. This,' she gestured vaguely to their surroundings, 'is better.'

'Neutral territory, you mean?'

'If you like.'

'Fair enough.'

His disappointment was palpable, but he didn't attempt to press it. He was silent for a few moments, fingers tapping out a quiet rhythm on the tabletop, before leaning in towards her, trying a different tack.

'I heard about what happened. Back in March. The, um . . . the incident?' He dropped his voice to a whisper, as if even such an utterly innocuous euphemism was unsuitable for polite company. 'I saw you on the news, being brought out by the paramedics. I couldn't believe it. I was like, "That's my Alyssa!"'

It took all her willpower not to react to the implicit possessiveness in his choice of words.

'I was going to get in touch,' he went on, 'but . . . well, I wasn't sure how warmly my concern would be received.'

You thought right, buster. 'It wasn't you who sent the card, then? The one with the solitary iris and no note?' She managed to keep her tone casual, like she was merely expressing idle curiosity.

She saw a flicker of something in his eyes – apprehension, perhaps tinged with a hint of irritation.

'I mean,' she went on, 'I can only think of one person on this earth who'd send me an *iris.*'

'Well, it was always our flower, wasn't it?' He sounded huffy, defensive, resentful at having to justify his actions. 'I thought it would be a nice gesture – you know, to show I cared.'

'Fricking creepy is what it was. I mean, a single flower and an unsigned card? Who even *does* that? But then,' she went on before he had a chance to formulate an excuse, 'it's hardly the only weird, borderline stalkerish thing you've done in the last few months, is it? Or are you gonna tell me you haven't been hanging around on street corners, watching me, following me?'

For a brief moment, she thought he might be about to cry. He stared at her with wide, wounded eyes – as if, by calling out his behaviour, she was the one who was being unreasonable.

'I just wanted to see you,' he said, in a wounded tone. 'Only I didn't know how.'

'Most people just pick up the phone, Rory. Only I forgot – you've been doing that too, haven't you?' Something else occurred to her. She leaned towards him, staring daggers at him. 'Did you try and get into my flat the other night?'

He was so shocked, so affronted, that he actually shot back in his seat. 'Of course not! I couldn't. I *wouldn't!*'

She continued to glare at him, debating whether to believe him. It was the only one of the charges levelled against him he'd actively denied – but then, it was also the only one she couldn't directly pin on him. He could hardly claim not to have sent her the iris, and she'd seen him watching her that night, clear as day. Even the silent phone calls were part of a pattern of behaviour she recognised from before. Back when they'd first split up, he'd rung her incessantly, usually saying nothing – just listening in silence to her increasingly exasperated hellos until she slammed the phone down. He'd always withheld his number, but she'd known it was him. Eventually, she'd changed hers and the calls had stopped.

'Is there something you actually want, Rory?' she said. 'Something I can help you with? Or did you just bring me here to waste my time?'

Rory lowered his eyes into his lap, shoulders sagging despondently. 'I thought I was over you,' he said at last. 'Or at least, that's what I tried to make myself believe. I told myself I hated you, that you'd hurt me more than I could bear, that I never wanted to see you again. But then I saw you on the news, and all the old feelings I had for you came flooding back.'

She felt her heart sinking. Vindictiveness she could just about deal with, but she wasn't equipped to handle him pining for her. Particularly when it was something she had absolutely no intention of reciprocating.

'Right,' she said. 'And what d'you expect *me* to do about that?'

He lifted his head, looking across the table at her in exasperation. 'I'm trying to tell you I forgive you, all right? That I'm willing to let bygones be bygones, to put all the hurt and betrayal and . . . and *lies* behind me and move past it.' He gazed at her imploringly. 'We had something truly special, and I'm damned if I'm going to throw all of that into the dustbin of history just because we both said and did some things we regret.'

She stared at him in disbelief, then let out a sharp, derisory laugh. 'You *forgive* me? Are you for real? And I suppose I'm, what, supposed to fall to my knees in gratitude? Is that how you thought this would play out?'

Rory just stared back at her, jaw set, lips pinched together. The muscle below his right eye was twitching slightly, the way it always did when he was in danger of losing it.

'You think our time together was some sort of fricking golden age – a greatest-hits reel of true love? Let me tell you what it was like for me. You *suffocated* me with your controlling, with your neediness, with your attempts to tie me down. You even started talking about marriage – *marriage*, for fuck's sake! Is it any wonder I ran a mile in the opposite direction? It got so bad I couldn't even leave the flat without you demanding to know where I was going and who with, you were that untrusting.'

'And is it any wonder?' he shot back, his indignant tone matching her own. 'Turns out I had good reason. Or have you forgotten about the other men? Were they that unmemorable?'

She rolled her eyes, leaning back in her seat and beckoning to herself with both hands, inviting him to throw everything he had at her. 'Oh yeah, it's all coming out now, isn't it? Yeah, I admit it. I fucked other guys while we were together. And you know what? I'd do it all again. Because – get ready for the bombshell of the century – I am not your fricking property. I don't need or want your forgiveness, and I'm certainly not gonna throw myself back into your arms and beg you to take care of me. Cos that's what this is all about, isn't it? It's about you swooping in while I'm all fragile and vulnerable – my knight in shining armour.'

She was aware that at least half the other diners had ceased their conversations and were watching her and Rory, but she didn't care. Let them get a good long look. If their own lives were that boring, they were welcome to enjoy the show.

'Go fuck yourself, Rory,' she said. 'Take your forgiveness and shove it up your tightly wound butthole. And if I get any more weird deliveries or phone calls, or I catch you sniffing around outside my workplace again, I'm gonna take your creepy, obsessive behaviour straight to the cops and let them deal with you.'

Rory regarded her for a long, hard moment, his expression unchanging. 'And if you do that,' he said, his tone surprisingly calm, 'I'll see to it that everyone, and I mean *everyone*, finds out about your little secret.'

In the silence that followed, the mouthful of saliva Alyssa swallowed felt like a rock landing in her stomach.

'What?' Rory's voice remained calm and level – impassive, almost. 'You thought I'd forgotten? Oh, no. I remember every word whispered to me under the duvet that dark, wet night, after you'd had a little too much to drink and decided to . . . unburden your conscience.'

She said nothing. She sat there frozen, transfixed, her surroundings slowly melting away until it was just her and her pounding heartbeat while Rory, seemingly possessed of a newfound poise and self-assurance, drained the remains of his cappuccino and got to his feet.

'You just remember,' he went on, as he collected his jacket from the back of his chair, 'I know all about what you did. And, if you want it to stay that way – if you want me to remain the only one who knows – you'll drop any thought of involving the police in our private affairs.'

With that, he made for the door, patting her on the shoulder as he passed her.

For a long time after he was gone, she remained where she was, staring into the distance, thoughts racing around inside her head like sharks circling their prey. What had possessed her to tell him – *him* of all people – the secret she'd kept to herself for so long, breathing not so much as a hint of it to another living soul? How could she have been so careless, so naïve?

21

The rest of the weekend passed without incident, though the encounter with Rory continued to cast a lengthy shadow over everything, and try as she might, Alyssa couldn't stop thinking about it. On Saturday night she got a text from Jenny, asking if she wanted to meet up with her and the others, but she cried off, saying she had other plans. She hadn't seen them since the wobbly she'd thrown in Gobby's flat the previous week and didn't feel ready to face them just yet – especially not while she was in this mood. So she stayed in and contented herself with watching reruns of *The Simpsons*, but she found she couldn't get into it and none of the jokes seemed funny anymore.

She wasn't on shift for the next couple of days. The rota had been changed at the last minute, though on balance she wasn't all that fussed. At least it meant not having to face Davy or any of the more annoying customers. On Wednesday, she headed in at four-thirty for her evening shift. As she stepped into the break room, she was confronted by a cut-out newspaper article pinned to the notice-board, taking pride of place among the flyers from various trade unions and a handwritten poster pleading for volunteers to join the library pub quiz team. She advanced towards it, staring in disbelief.

'LIBRARY KILLER IS INNOCENT, CLAIMS SURVIVOR' screamed the headline. The article – by Ewan Caulfield, chief reporter for the *Tribune* – told of one Alyssa Marie Clark, a delicate damsel struggling to cope in the aftermath of an experience that had shattered her sense of self and her faith in humanity. The photo they'd taken of her in that very room was inset next to the text. She looked scared and defensive, her standoffish pose less that of someone broadcasting her contempt for the whole enterprise than someone trying and failing to convey that she'd been unaffected by her ordeal.

She read on, soaking up each and every untruth and embellishment. Apparently she was only able to get by thanks to the support of the libraries' upper management, whose care and compassion she'd been at pains to emphasise. '*However, five months after her ordeal, Alyssa's faith in the judicial process remains strained,*' it said. '*In a moment of candour, she tells me of her fear that the true killer is still at large and that the police, in failing to apprehend him, have left the door wide open for further attacks on library staff – including herself.*'

'*Alyssa Clark puts on a brave face for the world,*' read the final paragraph. '*Truly, she is the embodiment of a survivor: unbowed, unbeaten and unbroken. Yet, for all her courage, it's possible to glimpse the vulnerable young woman behind her steely-eyed façade.*'

She stood seething with rage. Rage at the newspaper and the treacherous Caulfield, but also at the person who'd pinned it up there, turning her into a public exhibit for everyone to gawp at. She was sure it had been Davy. He'd probably put it up to deliberately goad her. She tore it down, ripped it into pieces and flushed them down the toilet for good measure, then sat alone in the break room, not trusting herself to face the public in her current mood.

As she waited for her blood to come off the boil, her phone rang. It was DCI Metcalfe, and her mood was hardly any less black than Alyssa's. She too, it seemed, had read the article.

'It would have been nice to have had some advance warning before you came out with all that crap!' she snarled, so vehemently Alyssa could almost feel the spittle on her cheek. 'I suppose you think it's bloody clever, shooting your mouth off to the press, potentially jeopardising an ongoing investigation?'

Alyssa replied that, where she came from, there was such a thing as freedom of speech, which didn't seem to impress Metcalfe at all.

'Is that right?' she sneered. 'Maybe it's different over there in the States, but in this country we can and do hold people to account for the things they say.'

'Oh yeah? Well, instead of harassing innocent citizens, you might wanna actually, oh, I dunno, look into those other murders in Craigslee and the one outside Metropolis?' She was using her Valley Girl intonation again, hoping it would have the same effect on Metcalfe as it invariably did on her mother. 'Cos, way I see it, it's really not a great look to have a man banged up for these murders protesting his innocence while someone else is still running around butchering folks.'

'That,' said Metcalfe tersely, 'is believed to be a gangland dispute – nothing at all to do with what happened to you. If you have information pertaining to the identities of the perpetrators, I suggest you take it up with the Violence Reduction Unit, whose remit it is.'

And with that, she put the phone down, just as Alyssa belatedly realised that, among all the threats and spittle-flecked outrage, yet another pinhead had referred to her as a fricking American.

After that, there was nothing for it but to knuckle down to three hours on evening duty with Davy and Stevie, North Kelvin Libraries' most uninspiring odd couple. Davy was in an inexplicably buoyant mood, bustling about in his wheelchair, getting in her way at every opportunity. The evening dragged by, the good people of Thornhill seemingly even more averse to giving the library their custom than usual – to the extent that, when Mrs Ambrose and her grandson arrived at quarter past six with a tin of homemade chocolate brownies for the staff, Davy all but invited the old woman behind the counter to take the weight off her feet.

'You all do such a wonderful job,' she told them over and over, while Davy nodded sagely as if this was the most insightful thing he'd heard all week, before dispatching the gormless Stevie to make her a cup of tea. No one ever asked Alyssa to make cups of tea. She'd probably refuse if they did, but all the same she resented the fact she always got passed over. She wondered if it was because the rest of them had concluded she didn't have a nurturing bone in her body. If so, they were probably right. She looked at the grandson, standing nearby guarding the trolley dolly, and felt an odd sense of kinship with him – both of them somewhere they'd rather not be, both surplus to requirements.

'You ever get a day off from this?' she asked him, sidling over.

He glanced at her briefly, gave a slight smile and lowered his eyes to the floor. 'Heh, not really.'

'Well, take it from me, bub – all work and no play makes Jack a dull boy.'

He smiled again and said nothing. She got the distinct impression he probably didn't have much experience talking to girls – not ones under the age of eighty anyway.

He and his grandmother left shortly afterwards. Then at five to seven, the Lovebirds arrived. Alyssa heard them long before she saw them, their uncontrollable giggling wafting through from the foyer. It took them almost a full minute to find their way in, and when they finally staggered up to the desk and prostrated themselves over the countertop, their pupils were dilated to the size of saucers. Clearly they were under the influence – though of what, Alyssa didn't like to guess.

Courtney, the female specimen and seemingly the designated spokesperson, took a deep breath as if she was about to say something profound, then lost her train of thought and spent the next fifteen seconds looking confused and more than slightly annoyed.

'Hhhhhi,' she said. It came out as a drawling, breathy gasp.

'Hello,' said Alyssa, regarding her coolly.

'What's your name?'

Alyssa pointed wordlessly to her nametag.

Courtney leaned further over the desk, running her finger along each letter as she tried to read it. 'A–L–A . . . no, A–L–B . . . A–B–R . . . Abracadabra!' She waved her hands in the air like a magician, and she and Craig exploded into fresh giggles which lasted way past the point of being cute.

'Yeah, that's right,' snapped Alyssa. 'And now, if you don't mind, some of us have work to do.'

'Is your name *really* Abracadabra?' said Courtney, frowning and blinking slowly, her eyelids out of sync.

'Yeah, my parents hated me and decided to subject me to a lifetime of shame and ridicule.'

'I'm Courtney,' said the girl, placing a hand on her chest in solemn greeting. 'And this is Smelly-bum.' She waved vaguely at Craig – who looked altogether too pleased with himself for someone who'd just been referred to by his girlfriend as 'Smelly-bum'.

'I'm happy for you,' said Alyssa. 'Now please leave.'

Courtney straightened up enough to look Alyssa square in the eyes. She stared at her for a long moment with an expression that reminded Alyssa vaguely of a bull lining up to charge. In the end, though, she merely snorted, hauled herself off the counter and stomped off toward the bookshelves.

'Where's your books on love poetry?' said Smelly-bum, not moving to follow her.

'Love poetry?' said Alyssa. 'What do *you* want with love poetry?'

Smelly-bum shrugged, as if it was obvious. 'To read.'

Without moving any other part of her body, Alyssa extended her index finger towards the ceiling. 'Top floor. Shelf marked "Poetry". Dewey number 821.'

Smelly-bum didn't move. She wondered if he'd actually heard her. Then, without warning, he pushed himself backwards off the desk, propelling himself upright. He tottered briefly, and for an awful moment Alyssa feared he'd used too much force and was going to continue backwards and crack his skull on the floor. But a moment later he righted himself, turned and, with a loud cry of 'Wait for meeeeee!', went charging after Courtney.

An air of calm descended on the library. Stevie had gone through to the kitchen to make yet more tea. Davy was methodically explaining the finer points of the library's eBook service to a woman who looked to be of an age where the printing press was a new-fangled concept. Elsewhere, a middle-aged man was sitting in one of the armchairs near the Romance section reading a battered Mills & Boon, pausing to lick his fingers each time he turned a page.

The serenity was broken by a gale of raucous laughter above their heads.

'For the love of God, what *now*?' Alyssa got down from her stool and went to see what was up.

Craig had managed to get himself halfway up the spiral staircase but had gotten stuck and was now no longer in a position to go either up or down. He clung to the iron handrail, his entire body wrapped around it, cackling uncontrollably. Courtney appeared to have been attempting to come to his aid but had only made it up the first half-dozen or so steps before she too had succumbed to vertigo.

Alyssa had had enough. The business with Rory, the lies printed about her in the paper, the verbal abuse from Metcalfe – all of it had conspired to put her nerves on a hair-trigger. And now she'd hit breaking point.

'Pack it in, the pair of you!' she roared, so loudly the man in the armchair dropped his copy of *The Turkish Virgin Bride's Illegitimate Christmas Baby*. Alyssa, meanwhile, stood, hands on hips, glaring up at the Lovebirds as they stared down at her, their glazed expressions registering amusement, confusion and fear all at once.

'I've had it to here with you two,' she continued, oblivious to the various pairs of eyes staring at her from different corners of the room. 'You get yourselves down from there right now and you march straight out that door, and I don't wanna see either of you again till you've both sobered the hell up.'

She was actually doing quite a good impression of the stern-faced, riding-crop-toting librarians she'd always imagined stalked the corridors of public libraries, and it felt oddly cathartic – even if she was left with the sneaking suspicion that these two clowns were too out of it to understand half of what she was saying.

'Ach, they're not causing any trouble.' Davy wheeled himself over to her side. 'We're only young the once, after all. And they're so very much in love . . . '

But Alyssa wasn't having it. She continued breathing down the Lovebirds' necks till they'd managed to get themselves and each other down from the stairs, then frogmarched them out to the foyer.

'If it's not one thing with you two it's another,' she said. 'I've seen better-behaved monkeys in the zoo. At least the worst they do is shriek and throw faeces at each other.'

'Aw, please, miss.' Courtney, the more lucid of the two, turned to her with beseeching eyes. Perhaps it was the cool air seeping into the foyer from the gap under the door, or the dawning realisation that they really were in deep trouble, but she already seemed to have sobered up considerably. 'We willnae dae it again. If you just let us back in, we'll be good as gold from now on – honest.'

Craig, evidently deciding it was best to let Courtney do the talking, nodded vigorously.

'Uh-uh.' Alyssa shook her head. 'You've just blown your very last chance. I'm gonna talk to Denise tomorrow to get her to bar the both of you indefinitely.'

'Aw, *please*.' Courtney's hands were practically clasped in prayer. 'Don't tell Eva Braun on us. She's had it in for us fae day one. They all have.' She looked beseechingly from Alyssa to Davy, who by now had joined them in the foyer. 'But yous two, yous are all right. That's how come we always try and take it that bit further when it's yous. Cos we know yous aren't *nasty*.'

Alyssa raised an eyebrow. 'You're saying I'm a soft touch – that it?'

'Aye, but in a *good* way,' said Courtney, to yet more vigorous nodding from Craig. 'Yous're like . . . I dunno, it's almost like yous've got more . . . ' She turned to Craig. 'What was that word again? That thing – the thing I said they had. What was it?'

'Perspexitive,' said Craig proudly.

'Aye, that's it.' She turned to Alyssa again. 'Yous've got more perspexitive than the rest of 'em on account of yous getting shot.'

Alyssa's expression hardened. This was the final straw. Ignoring Davy's protestations, she grabbed each of them by the collar and marched them towards the door, ready to physically throw them out into the street if need be.

'We seen that bloke yous're lookin' for!' Craig suddenly blurted.

'Shut up!' Courtney kicked him hard in the shin, making him yelp.

'What d'you do that for?' he cried, looking at her, aggrieved.

'*Cos!*' she hissed.

'It bloody hurts!'

'I'll do more'n hurt you in a minute—'

'Would you just shut up for a second?' said Alyssa. 'What bloke we're looking for?'

'The smelly one with the bad skin,' said Craig, as Courtney glared at him in exasperation. 'We seen him!'

'Where? When?'

'I'm not s'posed to tell,' said Craig sullenly, lowering his eyes to the floor.

'What are you, five?' Courtney sneered. 'The café at the end of Beeston Street,' she explained, addressing Alyssa. 'They got internet computers there, and we seen him sitting on one earlier, before we came here.'

Alyssa turned to look at Davy. Their eyes met, both seeking an answer to the same question.

'Go,' said Davy. 'I'll cover for you.'

Leaving Davy and Stevie – who looked positively sick with horror at the breach of company protocol occurring before his very eyes – to hold the fort, Alyssa gathered her things and set off down the road to Beeston Street, marching the Lovebirds in front of her. It was about a ten-minute walk, taking them out of Thornhill and into Craigslee – land of the eternal police siren.

The Friendly Café looked anything but. It was a dingy, run-down affair – one of those places that did kebabs, pizzas *and* burgers, and where you could practically see the cockroaches scurrying across the floor. The internet access they provided was clearly a sideline: a couple of aged Packard Bell PCs in the corner, with a handwritten sign saying it was £1.50 for an hour, but free if you bought any of their specialty coffees. Alyssa wondered if the specialty was phlegm fresh from the mouth of the proprietor, who seemed to be in the habit of hocking it up every few seconds.

Ramage wasn't there – not that Alyssa had ever really expected to find him just waiting for her. Both computers lay empty, the only customer on the premises a corpulent man in overalls perched at a window-seat, chowing down on an extra-large kebab.

'We're no making it up, I swear!' said Courtney, nostrils flaring indignantly as Alyssa turned to the pair accusingly.

She looked at them long and hard, trying to decide whether she believed them. 'Right,' she said eventually, 'here's how it's going to work. From now on, the two of you are going to watch this place every second it's open, and report to me the second Captain Ugly rears his head.'

Courtney stared at her in disbelief. 'Every *second*?'

'We've got school and that,' said Craig helplessly.

'Pull the other one. I doubt the pair of you have seen the inside of a classroom since you started growing hair on your naughty bits. Do it together, do it in shifts – I don't care. But if you want to hang onto your library privileges, you're going to do exactly as I say. Now, have we got a deal?'

22

The Lovebirds hummed and hawed for some time but ultimately fell into line, the threat to deprive them of internet access ultimately too horrifying to countenance. Alyssa exchanged numbers with them and left after giving another stern warning not to even think about trying to pull the wool over her eyes.

By this time, there seemed no point going back to the library for what little was left of the shift, so she headed home for a long, hot soak in the bath. She didn't notice the blinking Facebook notification on her phone until she'd finished blow-drying her hair and settled on the sofa, microwave dinner at the ready.

You have a new private message request from **Frank Serpico**.

As a rule, she didn't respond to unsolicited communiqués, especially ones where the sender was using such an obvious *nom de plume*. Odds were he just wanted her to add him so he could inundate her with dick pics or something.

Her finger hovered over the 'Block' button, ready to consign him to oblivion, but something stopped her. There was, she concluded, some satisfaction to be derived from stringing him – and it was *always* a him – along for a bit, only to burst his balloon in the most humiliating way possible when the inevitable blurry close-up of his grotesque-looking genitalia arrived. If nothing else, it would provide her with a much-needed laugh.

She clicked Accept.

His message was short and to the point.

FRANK SERPICO
Hi

That was it? No 'show us ur tits'? No 'I want 2 cum on ur face'? Just 'Hi'? Seriously? She shot back her own, equally terse response:

ALYSSA CLARK
Who's this?

FRANK SERPICO
A friend.

She rolled her eyes. To be a girl with an active presence on the internet – particularly one who encroached into what a particular subset of its denizens perceived as 'their' territories, such as games and tech channels – was to leave yourself wide open to 'attention' of this sort. The only choice, she'd found, was to either develop a steel plate layer of armour or retreat and give them the satisfaction of having driven you off the web. And she wasn't prepared to do that, especially not when the tormentors were invariably scrawny, pasty-faced teenagers whose last direct experience of intimacy with the opposite sex had been when their mothers had had the misfortune to squeeze them out. This guy, she was sure, was one of the aforementioned. All that was missing was an avatar of Tyler Durden in *Fight Club* or Pepe the Frog or any of the other figureheads idolised by the wannabe hard men of the internet.

ALYSSA CLARK

I've got enough friends

FRANK SERPICO

What if I was offering information?

ALYSSA CLARK

What if I'm not interested?

FRANK SERPICO

What if I'm not going to take no for an answer?

She was running out of patience. Normally by now, most of the troglodytes she was used to toying with would have lost it and fired off a salvo of dick pics, or called her a fucking femoid cunt whore, or both. But this particular specimen seemed to have more staying power. Evidently he wasn't going to be goaded into prematurely blowing his entire load – either literally or figuratively.

ALYSSA CLARK

What do you want?

FRANK SERPICO

To chat.

ALYSSA CLARK

And why would I want to chat with you?

FRANK SERPICO

Because I think you'll be interested in what I have to say.

ALYSSA CLARK
Unlikely

FRANK SERPICO
Don't be like that.
There are things I can tell you that will blow your mind.

ALYSSA CLARK
If it's that white stuff comes out of your peepee when you stroke it, then hate to break it to you my dude, but that's not news

She was quite pleased with that, and even allowed herself a little victory smirk. She was sure he was going to lose the plot now and devolve into a string of angry, misogynistic obscenities, so she was surprised and a little disappointed when, a few seconds later, his response came through.

FRANK SERPICO
That's not what I meant.

ALYSSA CLARK
What then?

FRANK SERPICO
I mean I know what you're looking for.

She didn't want to give him the satisfaction of asking him what 'what' was. And yet, as the seconds ticked by and no follow-up message appeared, the weight of anticipation grew increasingly unbearable. She could feel her skin prickling. Her hands growing clammy. Succumbing, she tapped out another message.

ALYSSA CLARK

I'm waiting

For several long, agonising seconds, no response appeared. As Alyssa sat there, eyes glued to the screen, her microwave dinner forgotten, she realised she was holding her breath. She let it out slowly, kidding on that this was all just a bit of fun for her. That she didn't actually care what this guy had to say.

Eventually the little icon appeared to indicate that he was typing a response, and then . . .

FRANK SERPICO

However, four and a half months after her ordeal, Alyssa's faith in the judicial process remains strained. In a moment of candour, she tells me of her fear that the "real" killer is still at large and that the police, in failing to apprehend him, have left the door wide open for further attacks on library staff – including herself.

A bolt of ice shot up her spine. For several moments, she stared at the block of text, unable to successfully formulate a response. As that initial, brief spike of fear subsided, anger swiftly swooped in to replace it. Who the hell did this little shit think he was, baiting her, playing games with her, trying to put the wind up her? He was nothing – just a limp-dicked keyboard warrior hiding behind the anonymity afforded to him by a stupid nickname. He wouldn't be half as cocky if he was sitting in the same room as her. And she was damned if she was going to let someone like that have his way with her.

ALYSSA CLARK

Bored now

She switched off her phone and tossed it onto the table. It skittered across the surface and landed a few feet away on the floor, where she let it lie. Picking up her dinner, she strode through to the kitchen and scraped it into the bin, too consumed by anger to eat.

Anger, and a gnawing sense of foreboding that began in her belly and slowly clawed its way up to the back of her throat, like a suffocating, all-consuming tide.

23

Next morning, after yet another largely sleepless night, Alyssa arrived at work to find a stroppy-looking Denise waiting for her.

'I gather you left mid-shift yesterday evening,' she said stiffly, placing herself between Alyssa and the door to the staff area.

Stevie probably grassed her up, the little scrote. Just wait till she got her hands on the toadying creep.

'That's right,' she said, trying and failing to get by. 'I had a, uh, family emergency.'

Denise gave Alyssa an acrid look. 'Sorry to hear that,' she said, in a tone that implied she didn't believe a word and wasn't sorry at all. 'But you should have notified me or another manager before leaving your post.'

'Yeah, well,' said Alyssa, 'you can always use your handcuffs to chain me to the desk in future,' and took off before Denise had a chance to recover from her shock.

She found Davy waiting for her in the break room.

'Well?' he demanded. 'How'd it go last night? I was waiting for you to call.'

As succinctly as possible, she summarised the developments, or lack thereof, at the Friendly Café. There had been no messages from either of her teenage flunkies when she'd switched her phone back on that morning – and none from Serpico either, for that matter.

'Ah, he'll show up again,' said Davy, sounding curiously upbeat for someone who'd just been told his precious investigation had hit the buffers yet again. 'He's got to. Least we know for sure he's back in Glasgow.'

She considered pointing out that they didn't know *anything* for sure and that the Lovebirds were hardly the world's most reliable witnesses, but she hadn't the energy for a fight. So instead she let it lie and concentrated on getting on with the job, doing her best to be an attentive, courteous public servant.

Midway through the morning, Benny came in to peruse the latest edition of the *Tribune* – something he did nearly every day, though Alyssa couldn't think why he bothered. She imagined he had his ear considerably closer to the ground than the out-of-touch hacks who filled its column inches. Fortunately Bindi wasn't on that day, so he was able to do his reading without being assailed by a barrage of abuse, and Alyssa was able to once again avoid actually having to take a stand to defend his honour.

'There you go, wee pet,' he said, handing the paper back to her once he was finished. 'Much obliged.'

As he turned to go, she thought of something. 'Hey, Benny . . . '

He stopped in his tracks and turned. 'You called?'

'I, um . . . ' She chose her words carefully. 'I heard a rumour Gordon Ramage might have been seen around the Craigslee area.'

'That right?' Benny stroked his beard thoughtfully. 'Well, you don't want to go spending too much time listening to rumours. You never know what's a genuine tip and what's a load of old bunkum.'

Ain't that the truth. 'Be that as it may, I was wondering if you might be able to do me a favour.'

'That would depend, as always, on the favour.'

'It's nothing big. Just, I know there's a few hostels and soup kitchens and the like out that way. I was wondering, would you maybe be able to ask around, see if any of your fellow . . . '

'Down-and-outs?' Benny suggested helpfully.

'Whether any of them's happened to run into him,' she finished.

Benny pursed his lips and thought about it. 'I can try,' he said eventually, 'but no promises, mind? The thing you have to realise about these sorts of places is that the folk who frequent them are often keen to disappear, so there tends to be something of a mutual respect for privacy.'

It was the best she could hope for. She hesitated, not sure how best to phrase her next question. 'And, er, how will you get in touch? I mean, do you have a, well . . . '

'A what?' Benny's beady eyes drilled into her.

She let her shoulders slump. 'A phone. Do you have a phone?'

It didn't seem an unreasonable question, given that the guy didn't even have a roof to call his own. How much use would a phone actually *be* to someone in his position?

Benny scoffed, affronted. 'Of course I've got a phone! What d'you take me for? Some sort of philistine?'

She knew better than to attempt to answer that.

She exchanged numbers with Benny, half-wondering if she should get a second line for the veritable army of eyes and ears she seemed to be amassing. When her shift ended at one and she headed through to the break room to collect her things, she found Davy sequestered in a corner, his own phone to his ear. Realising he had company, he glanced up sharply, a look in his eyes that seemed almost guilty.

'Trouble in love?' she inquired.

'Hmph, something like that.'

'I'm all ears.'

Davy sighed and lowered his phone. 'I'm just off the blower from Barlinnie. I've been trying to arrange another visit to Paul McGuigan. I'm convinced if we could just have another go with him, we'd be able to get something useful out of him. Like, I dunno, the name of whoever he was holding onto that gun for. But they tell me he's refusing any further visits.'

Alyssa shrugged. 'Maybe he's lost his taste for Mint Creams.'

She'd considered cheering Davy up by telling him she had another potential lead on the Ramage front in the form of Benny and his contacts in the homeless community, but the look he gave her was so vulgar she decided to let him stew. She grabbed her jacket and bag and slammed out.

She headed straight to the Friendly Café. There was, of course, no sign of Ramage, but a decidedly bored-looking Craig was perched on a stool at the window, creating origami from paper napkins. He sat up in alarm as Alyssa came striding in, looking around nervously for someplace to hide. Finding none, he got to his feet and stood his ground with trembling knees. Without Courtney to skulk behind, he was reduced to an amoeba-like, quivering wreck.

'Don't look so alarmed,' she sighed. 'I just thought I'd come and check in. Where's your partner-in-crime?' Courtney, she'd concluded, was the brains of the operation, and she'd far rather talk to the organ-grinder than the monkey.

'Her dad made her go to school. Drove her to the gates and watched till she went in. She sent me to keep watch,' he added, drawing himself up tall, seemingly genuinely proud to have been entrusted with such great responsibility.

'Yeah, well, you should be there too. Might improve your chances of moving on to a positive destination.' She shooed him away with her hand. 'You're relieved. Go on, get lost.'

Craig was only too happy to do her bidding. With a final apprehensive glance over his shoulder, he skipped out of the café and hurried off up the street, rucksack bouncing on his shoulders.

*　*　*

Alyssa stayed in the café for most of the afternoon, drinking cup after cup of foul-tasting coffee and waiting for Ramage to show. Of course, he never did. Not that she'd been expecting him to. Even if the Lovebirds had been telling the truth, the likelihood of him coming waltzing in while she was sitting there felt vanishingly remote. Chances were that, if Ramage really wanted to keep a low profile, he'd know that hanging around the same place indefinitely was profoundly unwise.

As evening drew in, her will to live steadily diminished. She was on the verge of cutting her losses and heading for home when her phone pinged a notification.

FRANK SERPICO
Sup?

She knew what she ought to do. The same thing every article ever written advised you to do with online trolls. *Block and move on.* Every second she spent on this creep was simply playing into his hands, giving him the attention he craved. Once again, her thumb hovered over the 'Block' button. But then, just as had been the case last night, she found she couldn't go through with it. Call it curiosity, or a gluttony for punishment, but she couldn't just walk away.

ALYSSA CLARK
So what's your game then?
You looked up my name and thought hey I'll have some fun with her?

FRANK SERPICO
Recognised your profile pic.

It was the price you paid for living in an online, interconnected world. Once your likeness was out there, any halfwit with a basic knowledge of how a search engine worked could track you down. She cursed herself for letting the goon from the *Tribune* take her picture. It wasn't as if she'd been caught unawares, like with the infamous snap of her being spirited out of the library by the paramedics. This time she'd been a willing participant – no one to blame but herself.

ALYSSA CLARK

So what is it you actually want, other than to creep me out

Newsflash buddy, you don't scare me

Even before she'd sent the second line, she could see that Serpico was already formulating a response.

FRANK SERPICO

I'm not trying to creep you out.

But I have to be careful.

I could get in a lot of trouble just by talking to you.

ALYSSA CLARK

Oh yeah? How come?

Does your mom not let you talk to girls?

For a moment, nothing. Then . . .

FRANK SERPICO

No, because I'm in a position to know certain things about the shooting.

And about the shooter.

She froze. For several seconds, she clutched the phone with trembling hands. She told herself not to take anything he said at face value – that the chances were sky high that he was nothing but a bored fantasist out to get a rise out of her. And yet, that little nagging voice at the back of her head was worming its way into her consciousness, whispering to her.

Give him a chance. Hear what he has to say.

ALYSSA CLARK
Say I believe you
Say you're for real
Why talk to me?
Why not the cops?

FRANK SERPICO
It's complicated.
I could get in a lot of trouble if this got back to the people I work for.
Besides, my information is ABOUT the police.

ALYSSA CLARK
You mean corruption?

FRANK SERPICO
I'm not sure I should say.
I have to be careful.
This could be a trap.

This was like getting blood from a stone.

ALYSSA CLARK
Cut the crap
You've either got info or you haven't
Tell me or not
It's your choice

A lengthy pause. Then . . .

FRANK SERPICO
OK.
I work in the Procurator Fiscal's office.
Know what that is?

She didn't, not strictly speaking, but she had a vague notion they had something to do with deciding whether or not a case went to court.

ALYSSA CLARK
Yes
I'm not a moron

FRANK SERPICO
Of course you're not.
I'm low level, not a fiscal or a fiscal depute or anything.
But I see and hear things.
And I've seen and heard things about this case that would make your hair stand on end.

ALYSSA CLARK
Like what

FRANK SERPICO
Like the man they've got locked up didn't do it.

Alyssa felt her mouth going dry. She ought to know, after everything else that had happened, not to be so credulous. Not to pin her hopes on wild leaps of logic and conspiracy theories. And yet she couldn't help herself. There was something about the thrill of the hunt that made anything that might take her closer to a solution too alluring to ignore.

ALYSSA CLARK
OK then. Who did?

For a long time, Serpico didn't respond, and she began to fear she'd gone in too hard and scared him off for good. Then, finally, he began to type again.

FRANK SERPICO
I'll tell you everything I know. But there's a condition.
We have to meet in person.

She couldn't help herself – she actually laughed out loud, earning her a few quizzical looks from the few other patrons still in the café. The idea that she was dumb enough to fall for that was too idiotic for words.

ALYSSA CLARK
You can fuck right off

His response came through as a series of short, rapidly typed lines, each accompanied by a loud bling, like a series of emphatic exclamation points.

FRANK SERPICO
In that case, you get nothing from me.
I have to know you're sincere.
That you won't just go straight to the police.
I could get in a lot of trouble talking to you like this.
But if you agree to meet me, I'll know I can trust you.
You name the time and place.

She stared at the wall of text, not knowing how to respond. Again, the words *block and move on* screamed inside her head. And yet she couldn't. If there was the slightest chance this guy was the genuine article . . .

ALYSSA CLARK
The Blowfly. Renfield St
Tomorrow afternoon at 4.15
If you're not there after 10 minutes, I walk

She waited, again consumed by the nagging fear that she'd pushed too hard and frightened him off. Maybe she shouldn't have agreed so quickly. Should she have equivocated for a bit? Proposed some alternative arrangement that didn't require them meeting face-to-face?

Finally, his response appeared. It was only one word, but only one was needed.

FRANK SERPICO
Deal.

24

U dont know me but I know u. I know it wos u who shot up
the libary & kild those peple. I know ur name and whot u look
like and wear u live. What I want 2 know is how much is my
silens worth to u?

I know u r a resonabl man and will not do any thing fulish liek
take this 2 the police, after all u have far more to loose then
me. I am propposing we do a deal. 5000 pounds cash. A
small price 2 pay in xchange for my silens.

Bring the monney 2 the subway station at Ibrox at 9 oclock
on Friday nite. Thats 24 hours to come up with the goods
which is moar than enuf.

I dont care how u get it. Bring the monney and u will never
see or here from me again. Otherwise . . .

Tick tock.

Your's
A friend

25

The Blowfly was a dive bar located in a basement at the top of Renfield Street, within spitting distance – appropriately enough, as far as Alyssa was concerned – of the *Tribune*'s offices. It had been the first thing that had come into her head when Serpico had asked her to choose a meeting place, and it seemed as good a location as any. There was, after all, something to be said for a crowded venue. If Serpico turned out to be a crank, he was unlikely to be crazy enough to pull a knife on her or whatever while surrounded by a bunch of witnesses. The place wasn't exactly hopping – it rarely was on weekday afternoons – but there were about a dozen other people there, including two very loud, very gregarious guys and a girl with the most impressive assortment of facial piercings Alyssa had ever seen, holding court at a nearby pool table. If she got into trouble, she could always scream her head off and trust them to come running, armed with their cues.

She checked her phone, nestled in her left hand as instructed. The signal down there was dismal, but it still told the time just fine, and she could see it was now nearly 4.20. If he hadn't shown by now, chances were he probably wouldn't at all. The odds, she figured, remained exceedingly high that he was just some bored, spotty-faced kid in his mom's basement, no doubt rubbing himself raw at this very moment over the thought of her sitting there waiting for him.

The hell with him. She was going to wait out the ten-minute grace period, then walk. She signalled to a passing waitress and ordered another Bloody Mary – her second of the day. If she was going to be made to look like a twat, she might as well get well and truly blitzed doing it.

As the waitress moved away to fulfil Alyssa's order, she caught movement out of the corner of her eye. She turned to see a man making his way down the stairs at the other end of the building, moving with the sort of arrogant swagger that said that, as far as he was concerned, he was the most important person in the room. Broad, muscular shoulders; tight-fitting T-shirt; hair scraped back into a bun . . . she didn't recognise Tony Barbarossa until he was just a stone's throw from her table.

She instantly sat up straighter, the aftertaste of her first Bloody Mary turning to ash in her throat. Was *he* Serpico? Could this all be part of some convoluted ruse to pay her back for taking his job from him? All these thoughts and more shot through her head in the space of a few seconds. It scarcely seemed credible. And yet here he was, bold as brass, arriving within minutes of the appointed time.

Barbarossa glanced briefly in her direction and she shrank back, grateful for the dimness of her surroundings. Seeming to give her barely a second thought, he swaggered over to the bar, slamming a meaty palm on the counter to get the bartender's attention. After placing his order, he turned and rested his elbows on the surface behind him, lord of all he surveyed. His eyes fell once again on Alyssa, and again her blood ran cold. This time, his eyes remained on her for considerably longer, and she forced down a mouthful of dry saliva. Several seconds passed. Then Barbarossa straightened up and began to make his way towards her.

She found herself paralysed, unable to even think straight. She could only sit there and watch as he drew nearer and nearer. His piercing eyes didn't leave her, and no lie she told herself could convince her this could possibly end well.

Then, when Barbarossa was almost within touching distance of her, a figure suddenly collapsed into the seat opposite her.

'Hi,' he said a tad breathlessly.

Instantly, Tony Barbarossa melted away into the shadows.

For a moment, Alyssa remained more preoccupied by Barbarossa than with the new arrival, and she had to actually force herself to shift her attention to him. He was in his early thirties and over-weight, verging on obese, wearing an ill-fitting open-collared shirt and a cagoule. A sheen of sweat glistened on his forehead.

'Serpico?' she said, half-incredulously.

'Alyssa.'

She nodded distractedly, looking past his shoulder, eyes scanning the room for Barbarossa. There was no sign of him.

She forced herself to focus on the new arrival. She could tell he was nervous. Aside from the perspiration, he kept shifting his weight as if he was sitting on a bed of nails.

He couldn't be Serpico. No way.

'I thought you weren't going to show,' she said. 'I was about to leave.'

He shrugged. 'Well, here I am.'

'What's your name?'

A pained look came over him.

She rolled her eyes. 'Bruh, I'm not gonna pretend I really think your parents called you Frank Serpico.'

He shrugged. 'Call me Andrew, then.'

She wondered whether that was his real name. Probably not, unless he'd suddenly decided to be far less circumspect with her than he had until now.

'All right, Andrew-then, you said—'

She was cut off midstream by the arrival of the waitress, placing her Bloody Mary on the table. She nodded distractedly and waited for the girl to get out of earshot. The interruption had knocked her off her stride, and it took her a moment to find her train of thought again.

'You said you had information – information you'd only share if I met you in person. Well, here we both are. So what have you got to say? Come on,' she went on, as he shifted his weight again and looked right and left agitatedly, 'you dragged me all the way out here on the promise of something juicy. If you're gonna get cold feet now, I'm billing you for time wasted.'

Andrew was silent for a moment longer, then sighed, as if she was the one placing unreasonable demands on *him*.

'OK, look. I might have been *slightly* economical with the truth last night.'

She knew it. Had known it all along, deep down. He was nothing but a grade-A bullshitter. She looked around, half-expecting to find a gaggle of his pals clustered nearby, videoing the whole thing on their phones. But there was no one there.

She folded her arms and fixed him with her steeliest glare. 'You've got ten seconds to give me a good reason not to just get up and leave.'

Andrew leaned forward, beckoning to her to do likewise. She did so reluctantly, feeling mighty stupid sitting there with her nose just inches from his. If he thought this made them look inconspicuous, he was sorely mistaken.

'All right, so it's not me who works in the Fiscal's office. It's my mate. But what I said last night about them having put away the wrong guy – that's all true. My mate told me everything.'

Her expression didn't change. 'I'm listening.'

'Let's just say his face fit and it was made clear to those whose responsibility it was to secure a conviction that they weren't to look too hard elsewhere.'

'You mean pressure was put on the cops to get a result?'

'On the cops, on the Fiscal – on everyone with skin in the game.' Andrew was going a mile a minute now, his voice so low she struggled to make out every word, even though their heads were inches apart. 'My mate was there the day the head-kickers came in and laid down the law. The team working on the investigation were told to stop what they were doing and hand over all their files. The shredding that followed made the last days of Saigon look like an orderly and amicable transfer of power. But it goes deeper than that. This wasn't just about expediency. They didn't just want a quick arrest because it would look good in the papers. It's because they know who the real shooter is.'

Alyssa couldn't even pretend to hide her incredulity. 'They *know* who he is? Then why the hell are they wasting their time with that dickwipe McGuigan?'

Andrew gave her a withering look. 'You're not listening to me. *It's because of who he is.*' He enunciated the words slowly, placing the same heavy emphasis on each one.

'And who is he, then?'

Andrew straightened up, moving so suddenly that for a moment Alyssa thought he was going to hit her or something. He spread his arms wide. 'No idea! My mate wouldn't say. Said for my own safety it was best I knew as little as possible. But he's prepared to tell you. He sent me here to fetch you and bring you to him.' He gave a little shrug. 'We can go now . . . unless you want to finish your drink.'

As she followed Andrew up the stairs towards the exit, the voice at the back of Alyssa's mind told her that what she was doing was seriously foolhardy. That the whole point of meeting in a public space was to avoid ending up alone with a strange man whose motives she couldn't guess. But that voice was now only a whisper.

The street outside was teeming, the final stretch before the end of the working week serving as its own mini rush hour as those in a position to do so hurried to vacate the city centre before five o'clock hit and the whole place became gridlocked. Andrew weaved his way through the crowds, moving surprisingly fast for someone of his girth and only looking back occasionally to check Alyssa was still with him. She hurried after him, heart hammering jungle drums against her ribcage, focused square on the belief that, having got this far, to chicken out now would be as good as admitting defeat.

They continued to head east, the city centre with its shops and restaurants giving way to tenements and high-rises. She didn't know this part of Glasgow at all, and with each further step she took into unfamiliar territory, her sense of foreboding grew. And yet still she continued to follow him.

Andrew finally came to a halt outside the door to a block of flats and turned to wait for her. It looked abandoned, its walls covered with graffiti, many of its windows boarded up. It seemed like the sort of place you'd take someone if you were planning on having your wicked way with them.

'What are we doing here?' she demanded.

'This is it.'

'This is what?'

'This is where my mate wanted us to meet. Come on, it's just through here.'

He held the door ajar for her.

She stepped over the threshold, the drop in temperature as she entered the dank stairwell instantly palpable. The place was in semi-darkness, the electricity supply having presumably been cut off years ago. The tang of stale urine filled the air, along with something else Alyssa couldn't place. It wasn't until Andrew let the door slam shut behind him, plunging them into even greater darkness, that she realised it was her own fear.

She turned to face him. 'So,' she began, her voice echoing against their concrete surroundings, 'this mate of yours – how long's he worked for the Fiscal?'

'Couple of years.'

'And does he always share case details with you?'

'Sometimes. When he thinks I'll be interested.'

There was an amused note in his voice, as if he knew she was blabbing to hide her nervousness and was indulging her, stringing her along.

'And what's the penalty for getting caught divulging this sort of information to a third party?'

His face seemed to darken. 'You don't half ask a lot of questions. Save your breath. You'll need it.'

She swallowed heavily. 'For what?'

For a moment, he said nothing – just gazed at her with a look that plainly said *you know what I'm talking about.* Then he suddenly smiled. 'For the climb.' He gestured to the narrow stone staircase with its wrought iron bannister. 'Up that way. Turn left at the second landing.'

There was no backing out now. She'd left it too late. And perversely, she couldn't bring herself to actually turn to him and say *You know what? I've changed my mind.* It would sound ridiculous, like a long-distance runner suddenly claiming she wasn't actually bothered about crossing the finish line. It was crazy that her fear of losing face was a more powerful motivator than fear for her own safety – but there it was.

She gamely put one foot in front of the other, all the while conscious of Andrew's presence – a great lumbering shape behind her, his breath heavy in her ears, his sweat filling her nostrils, making her want to gag. She passed the first landing and continued towards the second, each successive step seeming steeper than the last until she reached the top of the stairs and paused to catch her breath. Andrew stepped onto the floor behind her, his bulk blocking the way back down. He gestured towards a heavily graffitied and partially kicked-in door.

'It's through to your left. Go on – he's waiting for you.'

Heart pounding, Alyssa pushed the door open and headed into a narrow, almost pitch-black corridor. With one hand trailing the wall and the other outstretched in front of her, she shuffled forward, feeling her way until she came to a dead end. She stopped, clutching around frantically for a handle or an open doorway, but there was nothing.

She heard the creak of floorboards behind her and spun around. In the half-light seeping in from the landing she could just make out Andrew, his frame filling the doorway, blocking her only escape route.

'What . . . what are you . . . ' Her voice sounded faint and shrill, like that of a young child.

'Oh, Alyssa.' Andrew's tone was amused and mildly chiding. 'You should have listened to your gut.' He began to advance down the corridor.

In the moments before he reached her, several thoughts raced through Alyssa's mind, but the overriding one was *This is it. I'm going to die here.* It was as if, ever since the shooting, she'd been living on borrowed time, and now the death she'd dodged on that day had finally caught up with her.

He was almost upon her when there was a rush of footsteps behind him, and then . . .

'C'MERE, YOU FAT FUCK!'

All of a sudden, there was a third person in the narrow corridor with them, grabbing Andrew, hauling him back. She heard sounds of grunting and scuffling and, as she lowered the arms she belatedly realised she'd been using to cover her eyes, saw two shapes struggling as they reversed towards the landing. She realised, too, that she was on the floor, knees drawn up to her chin.

Tony Barbarossa had Andrew in a headlock. He was bending him over the bannister, face-first, one arm wrapped round his neck, the other clutching the waistband of his baggy slacks, ready to hoist him over the railing and hurl him into the abyss. Andrew was whimpering and snivelling, but he didn't struggle. His survival depended on it.

'WHAT THE FUCK?' Barbarossa roared, his deep booming voice echoing off the walls. 'WHAT THE FUCK WERE YOU PLAY-ING AT? ANSWER ME!' He tightened his hold on Andrew's neck.

'Please!' Andrew wailed as Barbarossa yanked him up higher, forcing him to stand on tiptoe. 'Please, I wasn't going to hurt her, I swear. I was only meant to scare her.'

'WHY? WHAT'S THE LASSIE EVER DONE TAE YOU?'

'N–nothing!' Andrew squeaked, his pudgy fingers scrabbling at the muscular arm wrapped round his neck. 'I've never seen her before in my life. It wasn't my idea, honest! I was told to do it.'

Barbarossa glanced over his shoulder as Alyssa emerged shakily from the corridor, holding the wall to steady herself, then turned his attention back to Andrew. 'Speak,' he growled, lowering his voice marginally, though his tone became no less threatening. 'Who told you to do it?'

'My . . . my workmate,' Andrew stammered, 'Rory – Rory Blain. We work together at Laird's Estate Agents. He said . . . he said this girl'd treated him like crap. Cheated on him, broke up with him, wouldn't talk to him. He just wanted to teach her a lesson.'

'And you decided just to play along? For what? Shits and giggles?'

'No – for money. He paid me. Four hundred pounds cash. I'm in arrears with my rent and I needed the money and I— Please, I can't breathe!'

'Oh, ye cannae breathe, can ye? Well, cry me a fucking river! I'd cut off your balls with a rusty hook and make you eat 'em if I thought you had any.' Barbarossa snorted contemptuously. 'I'll give you fucking scared!'

He hoisted Andrew clean off the ground, raising him to waist level, holding him almost horizontal. Andrew squealed and squirmed, his legs flapping madly as if he was trying to fly.

'No, don't!' Alyssa, finding her voice at last, cried out, lurching forward with her arm outstretched.

Barbarossa glanced back at her again briefly. There was a look of disgust on his face, though she couldn't tell whether she or Andrew was its intended recipient. A moment passed, then he pulled Andrew back over the bannister and deposited him in a quivering heap at his feet.

'Ach, you're no worth it, ya pathetic dung beetle,' he sneered, poking the blubbering man with his toe. 'I could wring your neck as easily as a chicken's – and it's nae less than you deserve. But then *I'd* be the one called to account for myself, and where's the justice in that? Pah!' He spat contemptuously on the floor, then turned to Alyssa and sniffed. 'You planning on spending the night here?'

Alyssa didn't need asking twice. As Barbarossa began to head down the stairs, she hurried after him, dodging past the trembling bundle of Andrew and the pool of urine expanding beneath him. She tripped down the stairs behind Barbarossa and followed him outside, the fresh air and daylight hitting her like a shot of pure adrenaline.

As she stood there, gulping in lungfuls of air, her eyes watering in the light – watering, *not* crying, dammit – Barbarossa moved alongside her and gave her a quizzical look.

'Just what the fuck was that all about?'

Alyssa turned to face him. She got as far as 'I—' before her legs gave way and she dropped to her knees, then promptly emptied the contents of her stomach in a glorious projectile arc, the bulk of which landed on Tony Barbarossa's boots.

26

'Get this down ye. It'll do ye good.'

Alyssa managed to stop trembling long enough to eye the tall glass of whisky Barbarossa had placed on the bar in front of her. She glanced up at him warily, still not fully convinced this wasn't a case of 'out of the frying pan, into the fire', then picked up the glass, gripping it in both hands to keep it steady, and knocked back a mouthful.

'Good?'

She grimaced. 'Not exactly my beverage of choice.'

Barbarossa gave a little snort. She wasn't sure whether he was mocking her or if contempt for others was just a constant feature with him.

'Ready to tell me what all that was about?' he said, after she'd forced down another mouthful and set the glass down. 'I smelt a rat soon as I saw ye leaving wi' that shifty fucker. Figured it was only a matter of time before ye were needing rescued. Turns out I was right on the money.'

Alyssa took a deep breath and sighed. She felt monumentally foolish. She realised now that, like everyone else, Rory had probably read her interview in the *Tribune* and, based on it, had been inspired to exact his own special brand of revenge. And he'd have known exactly how to reel her in. He knew her better than practically anyone. Knew what sort of bait she'd be susceptible too. And she'd fallen for it like the pathetic, gullible fool she was. She was as big a sucker as Davy with his wild conspiracy theories. Bigger, in fact. At least he hadn't allowed himself to be lured to an abandoned building on the promise of a meeting with a non-existent Fiscal's assistant to learn all about an elaborate conspiracy at the heart of the Scottish legal establishment.

'Well?' Barbarossa's beady eyes bored into her.

So she told him, more or less. She explained how she and Davy had been investigating the murders, about the visits to Barlinnie and Abbotscraig, about Frank Serpico, and about Benny and the Lovebirds and their supposed encounter with Gordon Ramage. And the more she talked, the more idiotic she felt. It didn't help that Barbarossa sat there with a shit-eating grin throughout much of her account – a grin which only grew wider when she told him she'd even had suspicions about him, before giving way to gales of laughter.

'Dunno whether I should feel offended or honoured,' he said, once he'd recovered sufficiently to form words. 'Clearly my reputation precedes me. And so, after subjecting me to a thorough and scrupulous investigation, you concluded I wouldnae so much as hurt a fly.'

'Not exactly,' she said carefully.

He frowned. 'Do tell.'

She looked him as square in the eye as she dared.

'I've heard stories about you.'

'Aye?' He seemed unconcerned. 'And who, pray, are your sources?'

'I've got a few.'

'Mibby so,' he said, pausing to pick at something between his teeth, 'but I'm willing tae bet they all got it fae that wee shite Grogan.'

'They said you got fired for brawling with a customer.'

Barbarossa sneered. 'That's the story *he* tells. What he always manages tae miss out is that said customer took a swing at *me* first. I was only acting outta self-defence. But naw, they all believed *his* version of events. Gilded the lily something fearsome, so he did. Went tattling behind my back, accused me of a bunch of other shite I didnae do. I was oot on my ear before I knew it. Been fighting for compensation ever since.'

'But people said—'

'Aye, well, when it came doon tae my word against his, it was aye gonnae go one way.' He began to speak in a lisping, singsong voice. 'That wee Davy, he's just wonderful. He's the bee's knees, and so, *so* good with the punters. Bollocks!' he spat, so suddenly and with such venom Alyssa nearly jumped off her barstool. 'He's a sleekit wee shit-stirrer is what he is. Goes around whispering in folk's ears, spreading his lies and falsifications. He lives for the drama, that one – got so little going on in his own life the only amusement he gets is fae riding a coach and horses through other people's. It's aye been the same with him – sooks up tae ye, pretends tae be yer best pal. Then, the second your back's turned – BAM! Knife right between the shoulder-blades.'

Alyssa stared at him, struggling to make sense of this. 'Seriously?'

'You better believe it. One of his favourite party tricks was he'd encourage someone else tae break the rules, then dob the poor sucker in. He'd be like, "Och, no, it's fine. Take an extra thirty minutes for lunch. Anyone asks, I'll say you're with a customer." Or, "Quiet the night. You just toddle on home, leave me to lock up. Be our little secret." But then, soon as they took him up on the offer, guess who'd be on the phone to management, telling them you'll never believe what so-and-so's just done, stoking the fire then stepping back tae watch it burn.' His features contorted into a disgusted scowl. 'I'm telling you – pure snake in the grass.'

Alyssa sipped her whisky. All of a sudden, she found herself rapidly reassessing every interaction she and Davy had ever had. She thought back to the other night, when she'd left to go to the Friendly Café, looking for Ramage. She'd been convinced it'd been Stevie who'd grassed her up to Denise, but she was now confronted with the distinct possibility that Davy, having actively encouraged her to go, had been the one responsible.

'Mind, I cannae blame ye for being taken in,' Barbarossa went on, his tone increasingly philosophical. 'He's gie convincing, that one. Got a whole cavalcade of admirers wrapped round his little finger, all thinking butter wouldnae melt.'

'But not you.'

Barbarossa smiled thinly. 'Me, I watch and I listen. I dinnae take things at face value. And if there's one thing I've learned, it's that it's the goody-goody two-shoes you need to watch out for – the ones that are nicer than nice. If a person seems too good to be true, it's probably cos they *are*.'

She lifted her head, meeting his eyes. 'And what does that make you, then?'

He grinned suddenly, flashing two rows of sharp little teeth. The effect was profoundly unnerving 'Me? Just think of me as your guardian angel.'

She pondered this, wondering just how much she liked the idea of having someone like Tony Barbarossa as a guardian angel. 'Let me ask you this, then. Who do *you* think killed Jason and the rest?'

Barbarossa gave the question due consideration. 'Well, I'll tell ye one thing – it wasnae yer boy toy Rory.'

'What makes you so sure?'

'Simply this: if he's so much of a yellowbelly he has tae pay his fat friend tae do his dirty work, he's hardly gonnae march intae a library and shoot a bunch of innocent folk dead at point blank range. Odds are he'd shit his pants as soon as look at a firearm.'

Alyssa said nothing for several moments. Deep down, she'd

known all along that it was true – that the Rory she knew might be petty and vindictive, with a seriously obsessive streak to him, but that there was no way he was capable of cold-blooded murder.

'I thought . . . ' she began. 'I mean, I'd started to think maybe I was the target.'

She met Barbarossa's eye, giving a sheepish little smile. He didn't return it. He exhaled heavily, shaking his head soberly.

'That's a mighty big responsibility for anyone to bear – 'specially a wee lassie like yourself. My advice? Don't think about it that way. Whoever it was, whoever he was after and whatever they'd done in his eyes tae deserve it, he's the one who pulled the trigger. Naeb'dy else. So stop looking to blame yerself, or anyone else.'

Alyssa gazed down into the dregs of her glass, deep in thought. Until now, she hadn't realised just how heavily the thought of having been the cause of The Event, whether by any fault of her own or otherwise, had been weighing on her. She wasn't sure Barbarossa's words had done anything to lessen the leadenness of that weight, but there was a wisdom to them, not to mention a kindness, that she nonetheless appreciated.

'I'll have a word with him if you want,' said Barbarossa. 'This Rory. You just let me know whereabouts he stays. I'll see to it he never gies ye hassle again.'

She imagined Barbarossa going storming round to Rory's place, making him bow and scrape for mercy like he did Andrew, and for a moment was almost tempted to say yes. Then she realised that in doing so, in sending a violent thug to put the fear of God into him, she'd be making herself no better than him. Far better to keep her head down and hope that, content with having put the fear of God into her, he'd now cut his losses and get on with his life. A forlorn hope, perhaps, but one she was going to have to cling onto. At the very least, today's events surely indicated he'd given up any thought that she'd ever take him back.

'No,' she said, with a heavy heart. 'Thanks, but no.'

'Fair enough. Offer stands if ye ever change yer mind, but.'

She got to her feet. 'Thanks for the drink,' she said, meaning it. 'And thanks for rescuing me.'

Barbarossa flashed his carnivorous teeth again. 'Any time.'

27

Alyssa stumbled through the city centre, still half in a daze. Her legs felt like jello and the evening sun shone in her eyes, making it difficult to see where she was going. In retrospect she wondered if she should have waited a while longer before setting out again, but the thought of whiling away several hours in the company of Tony Barbarossa had put paid to that, guardian angel or not.

As she came to a stop at a set of traffic lights, waiting for the little man to turn green, she became aware of her phone ringing in her pocket. She fumbled with it with clammy hands. The caller ID said . . .

'Benny?'

'That you, wee pet?'

'Who the hell else would it be?'

'Quite so.' If Benny was at all taken aback by her tone, he didn't sound it. 'My apologies for the late hour of this call, but I thought it might interest you to know that I've just been conversing with an old associate of mine, and he informed me that a man matching our mutual friend Mr Ramage's description has been seen kipping in a hostel on Faraday Road the last few nights. You *did* say you were looking to track him down, and to alert you if I heard anything . . .'

'You're right, Benny,' she said, fighting to inject a bit of gratitude into her tone, 'I did. Thank you. Uh . . . whereabouts did you say . . . ?'

'Faraday Road, Craigslee. Head down Chancery Street from the library for about a mile, then take a right turn onto Poplar Drive, and it's first on your left. Don't say I'm not good to you.'

She made the journey in just over forty minutes, catching a bus to the end of Chancery Street and running the rest of the way. The Faraday Road Hostel was an anonymous-looking concrete brick building with a tiny concierge desk in the foyer. The thickset bearded man behind the grating looked up as Alyssa tumbled in, gulping down air.

'Sorry, missy, it's men only.'

'What?' She blinked back confusion. 'No, I'm not looking for a bed. I'm trying to track someone down. I was told he was staying here.'

She fished out her phone, called up the photo of Ramage at the Linview Inn and held it up to the grating. The man regarded it for a moment, before lowering his eyes with a shake of his head.

'Can't give out that kind of information, I'm afraid.'

'But—'

'No buts. Our clients have a right to their privacy. Can't help ye – sorry.'

She opened her mouth to protest again. Then, realising it was futile, she lowered her shoulders, turned and tramped back down to the street. She stood on the pavement, gazing up at the building and wondering if there was another way in, before concluding she was on a hiding to nothing. Even if she managed to get inside, what was she going to do? Search every room till she found Ramage? And what then?

She sniffed the air. It was a nice night – warm but not unpleasantly so, a gentle breeze in the air. She could stand to stay out for a while longer. It wasn't like she had anything better to do.

She took herself over to the other side of the road and leant against a tree that was sprouting out of the pavement like a giant overgrown weed, the entrance to the hostel firmly within her sights. She wished she had a cigarette on her – or, for that matter, that she smoked. A person standing alone on a street corner inevitably looked shifty, but put a lit cigarette in their hand and all of a sudden they looked like they had all the reason in the world to be there. Desperate to give her hands something to do, she got out her phone and alternated between scrolling through her messages and glancing up at the hostel. Frank Serpico, she noticed, had deactivated his Facebook account. Surprise, surprise – not. She wondered who had been responsible for the messages – Rory himself or the fat friend he'd sent to meet her in his place. She supposed she'd never know.

Over the course of the next hour and a half, about a dozen people came and went from the Faraday Road Hostel – all of them men and all looking decidedly sorry for themselves. She wondered, from their point of view, what was worse: the blow to their self-esteem or the uncertainty of not knowing from one night to the next whether they'd have a roof over their heads. She was grateful she was unlikely to ever have to find out.

On the periphery of her vision, she saw the door opening and a figure emerging. Her eyes shot up from her phone, her gaze sweeping over the man standing on the top step, struggling to keep hold of a laden shopping bag as he fumbled with the zipper on his tracksuit top. Then she did a double take. Surely . . .

Holy shitballs, it *was* Gordon Ramage.

He looked awful, his clothes stained and crumpled, and she wouldn't have been at all surprised if he'd spent at least a few nights on park benches and in shop doorways since being turfed out of the Linview Inn. His hair was longer and greasier than ever, though much of it was concealed under the same navy-blue beanie with the Scotland flag he'd worn on the day of The Event. She watched as, having finally zipped up his tracksuit top, he looked left, then right, then made his way down the steps and set off. She gave him a moment, then headed after him.

He reached Chancery Street and headed east, moving with the briskness of a man on a mission. She matched his pace, keeping him in her sights but not getting too close. She thought about calling or texting Davy, letting him know what was happening, then decided against it. She could already hear the I-told-you-sos in her head. For now, she was going to find out where Ramage was headed, then figure out her next move from there.

When she'd been following him for half a mile or so, he turned into the nearby subway station. She watched from the entrance as he bought a ticket from the machine before heading through the turnstile and down the stairs beyond it. She gave him time to get out of sight, then hurried inside and scrabbled to find change for the machine.

A minute later she alighted on the long subterranean platform, flanked on either side by the tracks of the inner and outer circles of Glasgow's paltry underground rail network. There were about a dozen passengers on the platform – including Ramage, standing at the far end with his back to her. She remained where she was, keeping him in her sights and hoping he wouldn't turn in her direction. She wished she'd had the presence of mind to bring her jacket with her, or that she had some other way of covering up her tattoos. If he caught sight of her and recognised her from the day of The Event, a million to one it'd be them that gave her away.

The familiar metallic screech of aged wheels on even more aged rails reached her ears. The LED ticker above her head informed her that a train was approaching on the outer circle. The screeching grew to near ear-splitting levels. The squat little train came into view, its distinctive orange livery – from which it had earned its nickname, the Clockwork Orange – emerging out of the blackness of the tunnel. It came to a standstill. The doors opened. Ramage and the other passengers began to embark. Alyssa waited till he was inside before boarding the adjacent carriage.

As the train set off, she stood gripping the overhead handrail and kept her eyes firmly on Ramage, visible through the window in the door separating the two carriages, hunched in a seat at the far end. At each station they came to, the pattern was the same: the doors opened, a bunch of passengers got off, a bunch more got on, but Ramage remained seated. Kelvinhall, Hillhead, Kelvinbridge – he didn't move. St George's Cross, Cowcaddens, Buchanan Street – same story. She began to wonder if he planned on passing the entire evening going round and round the circuit. He might even be hoping to get away with spending the night here. It was probably a sight more salubrious than the Faraday Road Hostel.

Bridge Street, West Street, Shields Road – they were south of the river now, more than halfway round the circuit – and Ramage still didn't move. She was half-toying with the idea of simply marching up to him and attempting to affect a citizen's arrest when, as the train began to slow ahead of its approach to Ibrox, he got to his feet and, gripping the handrail, made his way over to the doors. The train came to a halt. The doors opened, he disembarked and she hurried out after him.

The narrow platform was heaving with passengers waiting for the train on the other line, many of the largely male crowd sporting football scarves in the same team colours. Of course – the stadium was just up the road. There must have been a match on tonight. Judging by their ebullient mood, it had gone in their favour.

The train pulled away, the screech of its wheels growing quieter before being submerged altogether beneath the hubbub of conversation. She stood on tiptoe, craning her neck past the throng, trying to keep Ramage in her sights. She could just make out the top of his beanie about ten feet away from her, facing the inner circle line.

If he was going to get on the next train and go back the way he'd just come, she was going to throttle him.

The screeching began again. The next train on the inner circle was arriving. The waiting passengers began to move forward en masse. Ramage disappeared from view.

The train pulled into the station, its noise mingling with, then overwhelming, the general chatter. A quartet of teenage boys in football scarves jostled one another, one pushing in front of the others, anxious to get first dibs on seats. A woman standing next to Alyssa turned to her companion with a disapproving tut and shake of her head.

Then, even as Alyssa watched, a shape fell from the platform onto the track in front of the oncoming train, as if propelled by unseen hands. A scream. A shout. Metal screeching on metal as the driver desperately tried to bring the train to a stop. The sound of what followed was, perhaps mercifully, drowned out by the various competing noises, but there could be little doubt as to what had happened. The train continued on for several more feet, past the point at which the shape had landed on the tracks, before finally coming to a standstill.

When Alyssa became aware of her surroundings again, she was on her knees, her breath coming out in ragged little gasps. The noise surrounding her was an incoherent cacophony as people milled around, colliding with her, brushing against her, not paying her the slightest attention as they pressed forward – some no doubt to provide whatever help they could, others just eager to catch a glimpse of the grisly spectacle.

As she knelt there, trying desperately to fill her lungs with enough air to carry on breathing, she glimpsed movement out of the corner of her eye. She turned in its direction. A gap briefly appeared in the multiple sets of legs moving to and fro in front of her and she saw a solitary figure hurrying up the stairs. She only saw him briefly, but of one thing she was absolutely sure: in spite of it being the height of summer, he – it was definitely a he – was wearing a heavy black duffle coat.

Her eyes returned to the platform as, a few feet away, she caught a glimpse of something else – a small, forlorn bundle, trampled by a dozen pairs of feet. She knew instantly what it was even though, like the departing figure, she only saw it for an instant.

A navy-blue beanie with a Scotland flag.

28

Somehow, she forced herself to move. It was the approaching sirens that did it for her, cutting through the fog and reminding her that this was actually happening. The cops would want to know what she was doing here, how she'd just happened to be present at the time of the incident – and that was a conversation she didn't want to have right now. Amid all the chaos and confusion, no one seemed to notice her slipping through the crowd and up the stairs. As she power-walked up the pavement, keeping her head down, an ambulance and multiple police cars went hurtling by in the opposite direction, sirens wailing. No prizes for guessing where *they* were headed.

Despite the very real horror of what she'd just witnessed, a strange euphoria increasingly took hold the more distance she put between herself and the subway. Davy had been right all along. McGuigan really was innocent, the real shooter was still on the loose, and she'd just seen him killing Ramage with her own eyes. And she knew exactly where she needed to go now.

Two buses and another brisk walk later, she arrived outside the Grogans' house in Scotstounhill. She'd tried calling Davy multiple times on the way there, but for some reason he wasn't answering his mobile. Most of the house was in darkness, but the light in his bedroom window suggested he was in.

The front door was unlocked. Alyssa let herself in and hurried up the stairs. She opened the door to Davy's room to find him sitting with his back to her, eyes glued to the TV. It was tuned to a twenty-four-hour news channel and showed rolling footage of what she immediately recognised as the exterior of Ibrox Subway Station.

The floorboards creaked beneath her feet as she stepped into the room. He turned and looked up at her.

She nodded at the TV. 'So you've heard the news.'

He stared at her blankly. 'News?'

'The death at the subway station. It was Ramage. I followed him there and saw him fall onto the tracks.' She paused to let it sink in. 'Davy, he was pushed. I'm sure of it. By a guy in a black duffle coat.'

For several moments, Davy simply gazed up at her, as if what she'd just said had no bearing on anything whatsoever. 'Oh,' he eventually said.

She stared at him in disbelief. 'That's it? That's all you've got to say? I tell you I've just seen Gordon fricking Ramage get creamed by a guy wearing the same outfit as the killer and all I get is "Oh"?'

Davy held her gaze for a moment longer, then slowly lowered his head. 'Like it matters anymore.'

'What the hell's gotten into you?'

As if in response to her question, the image on the TV screen changed to the familiar mugshot of Paul McGuigan's face that had appeared alongside countless articles and TV bulletins in the last several weeks. 'LIBRARY KILLER CONFESSES' screamed the text at the bottom of the screen.

Alyssa grabbed the remote from Davy's lap and dialled up the volume.

' . . . the news came through in the late afternoon, that Paul McGuigan, held on remand since the twelfth of May, had signed a full confession, admitting to the murders of Eva Baldini, Laura Craddock and Jason Stockridge, and the attempted murders of the two surviving victims. DCI Claire Metcalfe, heading the investigation, gave a brief statement.'

The report cut to Metcalfe, looking tired but triumphant, standing on the steps of the police's city centre headquarters as she addressed an assembled throng.

'Since the beginning of this investigation,' she said, 'my colleagues and I have worked tirelessly to see justice done. I am therefore pleased that Paul McGuigan has finally accepted responsibility for his actions and hope that his confession will provide some measure of peace to the families of the deceased, and to the survivors.'

Alyssa switched off the TV and stared at the blank screen in silence. She felt oddly lightheaded, as if she was drunk or tripping or something, and wondered briefly if it was possible that this, and the rest of the evening's events, were all part of an extended hallucination.

'I don't get it. Why would he do it?'

'Isn't it obvious?' Davy's voice was a dejected monotone. 'He knew his only hope for a more lenient sentence was to give in and sign whatever they put in front of him. Let's face it – he probably figured a few years in the slammer compared pretty favourably to anything he had to look forward to on the outside.'

'But we've got proof he's not the killer. If he's sitting locked up in a cell at Barlinnie, who pushed Gordon Ramage onto the tracks?'

'Actually *saw* him get pushed, did you? They had a bunch of eyewitnesses on the news earlier. They all seemed pretty convinced he fell.'

'Yeah, well,' she retorted, 'what would *they* know?'

But even as she spoke, doubt began to creep in. What *had* she seen? Not the actual act of pushing itself – just the result. But what about the figure in the duffle coat going up the stairs? She'd seen *him*, hadn't she?

Well, so what if she had? Plenty of men wore black duffle coats, though admittedly not in the middle of summer. And anyway, she'd only caught sight of him for an instant, behind a sea of milling legs. Was it possible her mind had simply seen what it wanted to?

She advanced toward Davy, forcing such thoughts from her head. 'We have to go to Metcalfe with this. Surely it'll at least throw doubt on the confession.' She tugged at his arm. 'Come on – it'll sound better coming from both of us.'

Davy jerked his arm away. 'Why? If he wants to rot in jail, let him.'

'What happened to not wanting to see an innocent man go down?' She tried an encouraging smile. 'Come on – you were the one who turned me on to this whole "miscarriage of justice" business in the first place.'

'Yeah, well, shows what a fool I was.'

She was taken aback by his vehemence. As she stared down at him, something dawned on her that she now realised, deep down, she'd known all along: that Davy had some personal stake in this – one that went beyond the desire to prove a man's innocence.

She crouched in front of him, forcing him to look at her. 'Just who is Paul McGuigan? What's your deal with him? He's not just some random waste-of-space skaghead, is he?' A thought occurred to her. 'Did you and him have some sort of a thing going on?'

Davy's eyes flared angrily. 'Of course not!'

'Then what? Tell me. I'm the one that's been risking my neck here. I deserve to know why.'

Davy stared back at her defiantly for a moment longer, then slowly lowered his eyes.

'He's my cousin.'

'Your *what*?'

She wondered if this was some sort of joke. If it was, she certainly couldn't see the funny side of it.

'Well, not *cousin* cousin. More like "close friend of the family". His folks and mine were tight. We grew up a few doors down from each other. Used to play at each other's houses.'

The more she thought about it, the more it made sense. There was the trip to Barlinnie for a start. At the time, she'd thought it remarkably convenient that he'd managed to secure visitation rights to someone he only knew through work. And then there was the way they'd been with each other – the easy repartee, the sense of familiarity.

'Why the hell didn't you tell me?'

Davy shrugged irritably. 'Cos.'

'Cos what?'

'Cos I was worried you'd think my judgement was compromised.'

'Oh gee whiz, you *think*?'

'I had to get you onside,' said Davy in a wounded tone. 'I knew I'd have a hard enough time persuading you to give him a fair hearing, even without the family connection. I thought if I could get you to take him at face value, you'd see there was no way he could have done it. But now . . . ' He trailed off, head bowed.

'I see,' Alyssa said coldly. 'And is there anything else you've forgotten to mention? Any more revelations to come crawling out of the woodwork?'

She expected a vehement denial from him, but instead, the expression on his face when he lifted his head to look up at her was one of shame.

'What? What is it you're not telling me?'

Davy let out a sigh of deep despair. 'Last year, one night back in November, there was a hold-up at a cash-and-carry in Thornhill. Two men in masks stormed in and told the shopkeeper to empty his till. One of them had a gun. There was a struggle, the gun went off and the two robbers fled the scene. No one was hurt, but it was headline news for days. The cops hunted high and low, but they never found them.'

Alyssa arched her shoulders belligerently. 'So?'

'Same night as the hold-up, Paul McGuigan showed up here out of the blue – out of breath, sweating bullets, looked like he'd just seen a ghost. He said could he come in and use the loo? Little-known fact about Paul: he's a nervous shitter. Anyway, I thought it was mighty strange – he wasn't normally one for social calls. He had a rucksack with him. Left it in the hallway while he ran to answer the call of nature. While he was gone, I took a quick peek, and – well, you can guess what was in there.'

She could indeed. 'The gun.'

Davy nodded. 'I never said anything at the time, and he never brought it up. Ten minutes later, he was on his way. Next day, when I found out about the hit on the cash-and-carry, I put two and two together. I never for a minute thought the gun was his,' he added, a hint of defensiveness in his voice as Alyssa opened her mouth to speak, 'and I couldn't imagine him pulling the trigger. Best I could figure, his pal was the instigator and gave him the gun to hang onto in case the cops came a-knocking at his door. And Paul, big schmuck that he is, went along with it. He always was more of a follower than a doer.

'But what I saw that night kept gnawing away at me. And then, when the shootings happened, first thought that entered my mind after I came round was that Paul had got himself mixed up in something and the library got caught in the crossfire.' He gazed up beseechingly at Alyssa. 'But you understand why I couldn't tell the police? They were already convinced he was guilty. If I'd told them about the gun I'd've been as good as tying the noose around his neck.'

'Oh, I understand perfectly.' She practically spat the words out. 'Tony Barbarossa was right about you. You're just a liar.'

'Tony Barbarossa?' Davy's voice quavered with disbelief. 'You spoke to Tony Barbarossa . . . about *me*?'

'Yeah, and boy did he have you sussed.'

She'd begun to pace the room, unable to keep still, desperate to find an outlet for the rage bubbling up inside her lest she take it out on him physically.

'Have you any idea what I've been through in the last few hours? I've had some psycho lure me to an abandoned building to rape me or kill me or whatever else he fancied doing with me. I've watched a guy get mangled by a train. I've been to Hell and back for this shitty investigation of yours, and all the while you've been sitting on your fat ass making up *stories*.'

'Well, poor you!' Davy threw up his hands in mock-anguish. 'Poor, long-suffering Alyssa. She's so hard-done-by.' The look in his eyes was one of pure venom. 'You think you've suffered? Jason's dead, Laura's dead, Eva's dead, Paul's in jail, I'm stuck in this . . . this . . . this *thing*. But you – you get to walk away from it all like nothing ever happened.'

On some level she knew this was the truth. Right at that moment, though, she had no intention of conceding any ground.

She rolled her eyes. 'Oh, come on. You love it really.'

'What exactly is it you think I love?'

'You know what I mean. The hugs. The sympathy. The attention. It suits you to a T to have everyone clucking around you, telling you how brave you are, how proud they are of you. You think I haven't noticed the way you lap it up?'

Davy stared at her, unable to believe what he was hearing. 'Is that seriously what you think?' He let out a sharp, barking, hysterical laugh. 'You talk about Hell? Well, I'm *living* it. Every second of every day, I'm in pain. I know I'll never climb Ben Nevis or walk down the aisle or take a piss standing up or do any of the other things able-bodied people take for granted. But I don't complain. I don't sit there wallowing in some self-pitying, "woe is me" victim-hood fantasy. Why? Because I know making other folk feel worse won't make me feel better.'

She couldn't think of anything to say – or at least nothing that wouldn't sound utterly empty. She'd assumed, in spite of all logic to the contrary, that he really was just a big dopey, happy sap, perfectly content with his lot despite having been condemned to a life not of his choosing.

'But like I said,' he went on, his tone less strident but no less angry, 'you don't have to live with the consequences, so what do you care? After all, it wouldn't be the first time you got to walk away unharmed while someone else lost their life, would it?'

She saw red. How fucking dare he make this about *that*?

Her jaw tightened. She didn't have to listen to this. No way.

'Eat my entire ass,' she spat, then turned on her heel and stormed out.

29

Neither the walk to the bus stop nor the bumpy ride back into town that followed did anything to cool the anger that burned inside Alyssa's chest. She wasn't even sure who she was angry with really – Davy, herself, McGuigan, or someone else entirely. All she knew was that she had a red-hot urge to seriously fuck someone up.

She couldn't face going home – not in this state, and not till she could be sure it was safe. Irrational though it was, each time she shut her eyes, she pictured sinister, duffle coat-wearing figures lying in wait for her, ready to pounce as soon as she was alone. No, she needed to be somewhere public – somewhere where there was strength in numbers; where she could disappear into the crowd.

Not far from the city centre was a bar – the appropriately named Escape – that served drinks strong enough to obliterate one's senses and played the sort of overpowering, brain-mushing music that seemed just the ticket for someone who wanted nothing more than to clear her head of all thought and lose herself to the pursuit of getting very, *very* wasted. She headed inside, laid claim to a seat at the bar, ordered a vodka shot and told the bartender to keep 'em coming.

As she sat there, knocking back shot after shot, doubt began to creep into her mind as to what she'd witnessed at the subway station. The more times the official version of events was repeated on the rolling news coverage on the plasma TV above the bar, the less convinced she was by her own recollection. Perhaps everyone else was right. Perhaps it *was* just an unfortunate accident, and the person responsible for the murders of her colleagues was indeed who everyone else – including himself – said it was. But it still didn't feel right.

She was staring into the dregs of her glass, contemplating all the inventive ways there were of committing ritual suicide, when she became aware of a presence by her side. She turned to find a man in his twenties, with a shiny face and one button too many undone on his flared shirt, standing facing her, a wide shit-eating grin plastered across his rosy features.

'Help ya?' she said, decidedly nonplussed.

'I know you,' he said, pointing at her with a finger that looked uncannily like overstuffed bratwurst.

'I doubt that,' she said, and turned back towards the bar.

'No, no, no, I *do*,' he insisted. 'You're . . . ' He waggled his finger in her direction, eyes clenched shut as if he was fighting constipation. 'Got it!' He snapped his fingers. 'You're that lassie from the papers. The one who took a bullet in that library shooting. I knew it!' He looked around, grinning, as if expecting the entire bar to break into spontaneous applause.

'Well, good for you, bub.' Alyssa signalled to the bartender with her empty glass.

'Here.' The red-faced man placed a thick hand on her shoulder, causing every muscle in her body to stiffen. 'Don't suppose you'd stretch to a selfie? Something I can show my mates.' He waggled his phone suggestively.

She tilted her gaze up to him, keeping her expression neutral. 'If you don't take your fucking hand off me right now, I'm gonna snap it off and force-feed it to you.'

Slowly, the man withdrew his hand, all the while staring at her, a bemused half-smile on his face. 'Yeah, all right, doll. Just tryna be friendly. A smile costs nothing, y'know.'

'Hey, suck my dick.'

He scoffed, shaking his head. 'Whatever.' He turned to go, muttering under his breath, 'Tight-arsed Yank bitch.'

She was on her feet before she even knew what she was doing. Grabbing a handful of thickly gelled hair, she slammed his face into the bar, the element of surprise ably compensating for the fact that he was considerably larger and heavier than her. As he reeled round to face her, leaning against the countertop with blood running from his nostrils, she flew at him again, fists swinging, so blinded by her rage she had no idea which of her blows – if any – were actually landing on their target.

She was still swinging when the on-site security guys hauled her off him.

Alyssa sat on an upturned drinks crate in the storeroom at the back of the bar with her knees drawn up to her chin. They'd locked her in here while they waited for the police to arrive – presumably in case she either scarpered or attacked any of the other clientele. But now the cops had been here for nearly half an hour, in the form of two stony-faced constables, standing guard either side of her instead of carting her off to spend the weekend cooling her heels in the cells.

'Don't say much, do you?' she sneered at the pair of them. 'Howsabout a round of "Never Have I Ever" to pass the time?'

At that moment, the door swung open and Claire Metcalfe strode in, touting her familiar beige handbag and sporting a decidedly rumpled suit. She acknowledged the two officers with a flick of her head.

'Leave us.'

Mystified, Alyssa watched as they trooped out, the last to leave shutting the door behind them. Metcalfe stood before her, gazing down at her, hands on hips.

'Well,' she said, in a tone that reminded Alyssa uncomfortably of her own mother, 'fancy running into you here.'

'Yeah, small world.' Alyssa drew her arms tighter about her legs, wondering what all this was in aid of.

'I gather you've been creating a bit of a scene.'

'Come to gloat, have you? I'd've thought you'd be out tonight celebrating your big win with your piggy pals.'

'My big win?'

'Yeah, you got what you wanted – Paul McGuigan, guilty as charged.' Alyssa curled her lip in a parody of a smile. 'Fixed him up good, didn't you?'

Metcalfe's eyes narrowed. 'If you're suggesting what I think you are, you can stop right there. That's a pile of flaming horse-shit.'

Alyssa affected a conciliatory shrug. 'Maybe. Gotta admit, though, it's not a great look. Right from the word go, you lot are fully fuck-ing erect for him being guilty. He protests his innocence for months, then tonight he suddenly changes his mind, just hours before a guy who claims to have known who the real killer is gets creamed by a train. A guy you folks weren't exactly busting your asses to find.'

Metcalfe said nothing. She just glowered down at Alyssa with a face like pickled tripe.

'All's I'm saying,' Alyssa went on, 'is, if I was in the business of making hay, I'd have enough to fill a barn. You gonna tell me you weren't leant on to get a result? Come on, just between us girls.'

'No more than any detective on any high-profile investigation. Of course there was pressure. There always is. But not in the way you seem to think. I don't know what sort of fanciful notions you've been getting into your head, but there's no grandiose conspiracy. Believe me, everyone wants the man who murdered your colleagues to answer for his crimes, from the lowliest constable right up to the Justice Secretary.'

The Justice Secretary. 'Funny you should mention him. I saw the two of you at the prize-giving. Looked awful cosy, so you did.'

Metcalfe gave a dry smile. 'So you saw the two of us together and you thought, "There he is, buttering her up. Promising her a cushy promotion if she closes the case by the end of the week".'

'Something like that, yeah.'

'Well, if you'd actually *heard* what was being said instead of witnessing an isolated moment and jumping to conclusions, you'd know that what was actually happening was that he was trying to persuade me to accompany him up to his hotel room once the ceremony was over. And I was very firmly telling him to get knotted.'

'He . . . he was propositioning you?'

Suddenly it all seemed so utterly, depressingly banal.

'I have it on good authority he ended up copping off with your Director of Library Services instead. I'm still not quite sure how I should feel about that.'

Alyssa gave a wry smile. 'Sorry for him, probably. He can't have known what he was letting himself in for.'

Metcalfe gave a faint smile of her own.

'So what's your story, then?' Alyssa asked. 'What's someone with an accent like yours doing here in bonnie Scotland?'

Metcalfe looked almost sheepish. 'Fell in love with a Scotsman, didn't I? Anyway, I could ask you the same question. Doesn't take a detective to figure out that's not a rich Glaswegian brogue I'm hearing.'

Alyssa shrugged. 'No great tale to tell. Grew up in a tiny town where everyone was someone's cousin. Decided I didn't wanna grow up to be a clone of my parents. Found out about the whole ancestry visa thing, figured Scotland was far enough and different enough to suit my needs, jumped on the next flight . . . and here I am. True story.'

'But with more than a few gaps in it, I'll warrant,' said Metcalfe. 'So you came over here all on your lonesome, leaving behind your entire family – everyone you'd ever known. That's got to take some guts. Least my lot are just a hop across the border.'

'Yeah, well,' said Alyssa quietly, 'I had my reasons.'

'Not wanting to become your parents. You said.'

Alyssa was silent.

Metcalfe raised an eyebrow. 'Oh, so there's more?'

'Does there need to be?'

'You tell me.'

'Never mind. Forget I said anything.'

She thought Metcalfe was going to push the matter, but after a few seconds, when no follow-up question emerged, she relaxed somewhat. It seemed Metcalfe had got the message.

Or perhaps she was just playing the long game.

Metcalfe clicked her tongue, as if calling a dog to heel. 'Come on. Let's get you out of here.'

Reluctantly, Alyssa dragged herself to her feet and followed Metcalfe out of the storeroom. The place was eerily quiet, though Alyssa wasn't sure if that was because her antics had cleared the bar or because it was after closing time. She looked around for the two constables, but there was no sign of them.

Metcalfe led her out into the street. 'We'll take my car.'

Mystified, Alyssa followed her over to the ageing VW Golf parked a little way up the pavement. Metcalfe opened the passenger door for her and she got in. As she waited for Metcalfe to circle round to the driver's seat, she wondered how an assault charge was going to affect her visa status. Not in anything approaching a positive way – of that she could be certain.

She noticed they weren't moving. Next to her, Metcalfe hadn't even buckled her seatbelt.

'We just gonna sit here all night?'

Metcalfe didn't seem to have heard her. For several moments she sat there, arms folded, seemingly deep in thought.

'For what it's worth,' she said eventually, 'I get the whole "not wanting to become your parents" bit. My dad worked nine to five in an office from sixteen to sixty – marketing frozen peas, of all things. My mum was what was referred to back in the day as a housewife. Even as a tiddlywink I knew I wasn't going to follow in either of their footsteps. I needed to feel like I was making a difference.'

Alyssa turned to face her. 'That why you became a cop, then? To make a difference?'

'Well, it wasn't for the pay, or the holiday entitlement, or the adulation of the public, I'll tell you that much.' Metcalfe grimaced. 'I dunno. *Some* days it feels like what I'm doing matters.'

'And today's one of those, right?'

Metcalfe glanced in Alyssa's direction, gave a very slight smile by way of response. 'Truthfully,' she said after a moment, 'these days, I'm finding more and more that my sense of fulfilment doesn't come from the job but from arriving home at night to a warm house and hugs from my husband and my girls. I guess you could say I've mellowed. But then, I suppose motherhood will do that to you.'

Alyssa made a gagging noise at the back of her throat.

'Hey.' Metcalfe shot her a reproachful look. 'Don't knock it till you've tried it.'

'I'll pass, thanks.'

'You've never wanted kids?'

Alyssa almost laughed in exasperation. 'Yeah, cos they're the solution to every problem! No, I've never wanted kids, thank you very much. It's not a crime.'

'Never said it was. But you might feel differently one day. I know when I was your age it wasn't something I was ready to contemplate. But then I met my husband, and we had our first daughter, and . . . ' She shrugged. 'Everything changed.'

'Well, bully for you. Way I see it, the world's overpopulated enough as it is without me adding to the problem.'

'Not in Scotland,' said Metcalfe. 'We've got an ageing population.'

'Well, there ya go. There's another thing I got wrong. 'Sides, I'm not responsible enough to look after a sprog.'

'I'm sure that's not true.'

'No, it is. Believe me.'

'How can you be so sure?'

Alyssa opened her mouth, then shut it again. She considered saying nothing more, but she had a sneaking suspicion Metcalfe, whose job it was to ferret out information, wasn't going to be thwarted by the silent treatment. And besides, this wasn't just about satisfying an inquisitive Detective Chief Inspector. She wanted to talk about it.

No, she *needed* to talk about it.

'You love your girls, right?'

'Right,' said Metcalfe, puzzled.

'And you'd do anything for them.'

'Of course.'

'And if anything happened to them, you'd never forgive yourself.'

'I'm sorry, but I don't see where this is—'

Alyssa slammed her hand on the dashboard, cutting Metcalfe off midstream.

'Responsibility. What I'm talking about is responsibility.'

Metcalfe said nothing, seeming to recognise that further inter-jections on her part were unlikely to help. But she continued to eye Alyssa intently, watching, waiting.

'I had a little sister,' Alyssa said shortly. 'And she drowned. And it was my fault.' She stared straight ahead, feeling Metcalfe's eyes burning into her.

'I'm sorry,' Metcalfe eventually said, filling the silence. 'That's awful. Terrible. And I'm sure it must be a horrendous weight to bear. But you really can't hold yourself responsible for—'

Alyssa swung around to face her, eyes burning with righteous anger. 'Aren't you listening? I said it was *my* fault. *I* was the one whose idea it was to go out on the lake. She only came with me because *I* was going. *I* was the big sister. *I* was responsible. Me.'

She punctuated each short, sharp sentence by whacking the dashboard with an open palm, all the while glaring daggers at Metcalfe, daring her to disagree.

'And your parents,' Metcalfe began, 'did they—'

'They never blamed me,' said Alyssa immediately. 'I don't know if they thought it was too much to lay on my shoulders, or if they figured they'd already lost one daughter and couldn't face a lifetime resenting the one they had left.' She gazed back at Metcalfe, steely-eyed, her voice dropping to a tight whisper. 'But *I* blamed me. And every time they're nice to me, every time they show me concern or compassion or love, it's like she's dying all over again, because . . .' She stopped, realising where she was headed.

Metcalfe's gaze didn't leave her. 'Because . . . ?'

Alyssa opened her mouth to speak, then once again stopped. She knew, if she went any further, that she'd be crossing the point of no return; that she was about to tell Metcalfe the same secret that, of all the people in all the world, she'd previously only shared with Rory. And look how *that* had turned out.

But she no longer cared. After over twelve years, she was done with hiding behind half-truths and evasions. It was time to come clean.

'As . . . as I was swimming up to the surface, I felt something grabbing my leg. Five little fingers wrapping around my ankle. And I didn't think. I just lashed out, kicking, trying to break free. And

I felt my foot colliding with something – with a head. And then the fingers let go and I was on my way. That's when I knew what I'd done.'

She waited for Metcalfe's response, for her judgement. But none came. Metcalfe simply met her gaze without speaking, her expression inscrutable, waiting for Alyssa to continue. So she did.

'I reached the surface and managed to get the boat upright and drag myself aboard. I know I could have gone back in. Looked for her. It might not have been too late. But I couldn't bring myself to go back down into the dark.'

She suppressed a shudder, the cold piercing her bones as keenly as if she was back there now, lying in a bedraggled heap on the floor of the little rowboat, retching up water.

'I could have saved her, but I was too selfish, too self-absorbed, too wrapped up in saving my own skin for that. And I think . . . deep down, I think a part of me knew I wouldn't be able to face her after what I'd done. A part of me was glad she wouldn't be around to tell anyone. And ever since, I've made sure I never ended up in a situation where I've been responsible for another person's life. Because I can't cope with that level of trust. I don't *deserve* that level of trust.'

'You were a child yourself,' said Metcalfe, her voice soft and husky. 'It was an accident. You can't . . . ' she trailed off, before trying again. 'It's tragic, but you can't spend your whole life beating yourself up over something that happened when you were a child. You can't let that put you off having children of your own.'

Alyssa shook her head vehemently, staring fixedly ahead once again. 'You shouldn't bring a life into this world unless you're prepared to be responsible for it. And I'm not responsible.'

She felt the anger ebbing away, replaced by the same aching sense of loss and desperation that, as surely as night comes after day, inevitably followed.

For a long time, neither of them spoke. They sat there in silence, each lost in their own thoughts.

'Have you ever thought about talking about this to someone?' said Metcalfe eventually.

'Talking to you, aren't I?'

'No, I mean like a professional.'

'So they can tell me I need to make peace with my childhood so I can progress to being a fully functioning adult?' Alyssa pulled a face. 'No thanks. I've got enough people telling me I need to become a responsible grown-up-type-person in the real world without paying for the privilege of some glorified witchdoctor telling me the same. Besides, I'm kinda happy with my zero-responsibility existence.'

She wasn't sure whether she was trying to convince Metcalfe or herself. Metcalfe certainly looked deeply sceptical, sitting there, regarding her with pursed brows.

'I'm not sure it's true, you know,' Metcalfe said eventually. 'That you can have a zero-responsibility existence, I mean. I'm not sure *anyone* does – not in this day and age. Responsibility comes in all shapes and sizes. It's not something you choose; something you opt into or out of – whether it's my responsibility as an officer of the law or the responsibility to brake when you're driving and someone steps into the road in front of you. And what you do in the library, that's . . . well, it's not nothing.'

Alyssa pulled a sardonic face. 'Yeah, it's really up there with curing leukaemia or putting men on the moon.'

Metcalfe ground her teeth in frustration. 'That's what I'm trying to explain. I'm not saying all responsibility is equal. There are varying degrees. But everyone has it, whether they realise it or not. Have you ever stopped for a moment to think how many people's lives would be changed for the worse if that library of yours wasn't there? Or if one day you and your colleagues were all replaced by machines? Honestly, on any given day, I'd hazard a guess you make a meaningful difference to more people's lives than my colleagues and I ever do.'

'Seriously?'

'Think about it: on an average day, you'll have . . . what, three hundred, four hundred people through your doors? Each and every one of them an individual with their own unique set of needs. You print off that boarding pass so they can make their flight that leaves in an hour's time. You help them sort out their benefits claim so they won't have to face going hungry. You track down that rare book they've hunted high and low for. But most importantly, you give people who've nowhere else to go a place where they can sit and put their feet up, where no one's going to ask them why they're there or expects them to buy something. And who knows? Maybe the sum total of your interaction with them is smiling at them and wishing them a nice day. That might still be the single most meaningful social interaction they'll experience all day, and the fact you don't realise how important that is . . . well, I don't know where to start.'

Alyssa had no words. She'd never thought about it like that before, and there was something oddly humbling about being told she mattered that touched even her blackened, cynical heart.

'Plus, you keep the act of reading alive. Take my two, for instance.'

Metcalfe rummaged inside her handbag and produced one of those little pocket photo frames – the sort that opens like a book. Inside was a picture of two girls on the cusp of school age, both grinning as they jockeyed for pole position in front of the camera.

'Melanie's four; Riley's six. For the longest time, I couldn't get either of them interested in reading for love nor money. If it didn't have a flashing screen or make a noise, they didn't want to know. Then about a year ago, Riley's school took her class on a visit to their local library, and honestly, the girl who showed them round was nothing short of amazing. Ever since, she's been mad about reading. It used to be the iPad you had to prise out of her hands before bed. Now it's Roald Dahl.'

'Yeah?' Alyssa did her best to sound impressed, even though the literary pursuits of someone else's kid hardly figured high in her interest stakes.

'She even managed to pass the reading bug on to me,' said Metcalfe, a tad sheepishly. 'Though in my case, it's audiobooks. Losing myself in someone else's world for half an hour makes the morning commute just a bit more bearable. God only knows what I'd do if you lot ever shut up shop.'

Alyssa smiled blandly, hoping Metcalfe wasn't going to ask for her recommendations from the current bestsellers chart.

'Of course – and I probably shouldn't be telling you this, you being a librarian and all – but I still haven't gotten round to signing up for a ticket of my own. Mostly I just take stuff out on one of my kids'. But hey – an issue's an issue, right?'

'Yeah, that's *kinda* against the rules,' Alyssa said – aware, as she spoke, that something about Metcalfe's confession had set off a faint alarm bell somewhere deep inside her. 'I mean, people do it all the time, but you really shouldn't. Technically it's identity theft. Drop by sometime with proof of your address and I'll set you up with your own.' *Provided I still have a job there after tonight.*

'I might just do that. Not the best example to be setting, me being an officer of the law and all.' Metcalfe chuckled, the tired lines on her face momentarily transforming into laughter lines. 'Suppose we ought to shake a leg. Buckle up.'

Wordlessly, Alyssa reached for her seatbelt and snapped it into place as Metcalfe turned the key in the ignition and pulled away from the kerb.

* * *

She must have fallen asleep for a while, lulled by the rhythm of the car. When she next came to, they were drawing to a halt once more. Alyssa blinked heavily and turned to look out of the window, expecting to see the imposing façade of a police station. To her surprise, she found that they were parked across the road from her own flat.

She turned to Metcalfe in confusion. 'What are we doing here?'

'This is where you live, isn't it?' Metcalfe shrugged.

'Yes, but . . . but . . . ' Alyssa spluttered helplessly, unable to find the words she was looking for. 'Aren't I going to be charged?' she eventually said helplessly.

'I don't see what good that would do anyone. The bloke in question already said he's not interested in pressing charges.' She gave one of her lopsided little lip curls. 'I reckon his ego's more bruised than any other part of his anatomy. Besides, I've at least three witnesses willing to state on the record that you had serious provocation.'

Alyssa couldn't think what to say. She just stared at Metcalfe in silence, wondering how she could ever repay this debt.

Metcalfe flicked her head. 'Go on, shake a leg. You look like you need your bed, and . . . well, I *know* I need mine.'

Alyssa unbuckled her seatbelt and scrambled out, a part of her still fearing Metcalfe would change her mind and cart her off to the cells. As she slammed the passenger door shut and turned to go, Metcalfe wound down the window.

'Think about what I said about talking to someone,' she said. 'It doesn't help anyone to bottle up your feelings, least of all yourself.'

Alyssa said nothing, but she gave the smallest of nods – an indication that she would at least consider it.

Metcalfe started the engine and pulled out into the road. Alyssa remained where she was, watching until the Golf's taillights disappeared from view. With the fresh air on her face once again, her mind was beginning to turn, replaying their conversation from earlier. Through the haze that clouded her thoughts, brought about by drink and lack of sleep, she kept returning to a single utterance.

People do it all the time, but you really shouldn't.

And then it came to her – her 'eureka' moment. She saw it now, as clear as day. She and Davy had been on the right track all along, trying to identify the person Ramage had seen researching guns based on who had been logged into the computer next to his. But they'd managed to overlook one small but vital detail.

You could log in with any card. It didn't have to be your own.

PART THREE

30

Next morning, Alyssa was standing on the library doorstep bright and early, waiting to be let in along with the punters. She wasn't due on shift, but what she needed to do could only be done from a library computer.

It was Pat who opened the doors. His expression, when he saw Alyssa at the head of the queue, was one of surprise, laced with suspicion.

'Didn't think we were getting *you* today.'

'My internet's on the fritz at home. I need to do some internet banking.'

Pat, she knew, suffered from a deep-rooted distrust of all modern technology. She doubted he had a firm grasp of what internet banking actually *was*, and was therefore unlikely to pry too deeply.

She entered the main library to find Marli and Stevie getting set up for the day, switching on computers and changing date-stamps. They looked at her with the same puzzlement as Pat.

'Davy not in?' she asked. She wasn't entirely surprised. Probably still licking his wounds after last night.

'He's got a physio session first thing,' said Pat. 'He'll be along later. Why? Want him for something?'

She told him it was fine and took herself up to the office, where she fired up Denise's computer and got to work.

Opening up WebShare, she wound the timeline back to the

beginning of the year and began the same process she and Davy had embarked on some days earlier to identify people who'd used either of the computers at the back of the reading room at the same time as Ramage. This time, however, she didn't discount anyone based on age, gender or physicality. They could be a one-legged three-year-old girl in a vegetative state for all she cared. If the killer had been fraudulently using their card to access the internet, their own identity was irrelevant. If you were planning on shooting up a library, you'd want to cover your tracks – and what better way to do that than to use someone else's credentials? She was amazed she hadn't thought of it before.

With the list of twenty-one names and card numbers copied into a Word document, she then proceeded to call up each account in the cataloguing system, harvesting their contact details. Of the twenty-one, sixteen had provided the library with a phone number. Eleven had given an email address, which left all but one of those who'd declined to give their phone number accounted for. All twenty-one had provided a postal address – though she knew from experience that, of all three possible contact methods, these were the least likely to be up to date.

With the list of sixteen names and phone numbers in front of her, she worked her way down the list, calling each in turn, with the same pitch each time.

'Good morning, sorry to trouble you. I work for North Kelvin District Libraries and was wondering if you could spare a few moments of your time? We've experienced a significant increase in people attempting to access our services using stolen library cards recently and wanted to check whether by any chance you'd been a victim of theft? You haven't? Are you sure? Would you mind confirming whether you actually have your card to hand at the moment – just for your own peace of mind?'

Few of the people she phoned were thrilled at being disturbed early on a Saturday morning for such a seemingly trivial reason. She couldn't blame them for being crotchety. If she'd been in their shoes, she'd have been giving herself both barrels.

Of the sixteen names, ten took her call. All were able to confirm that they did indeed have their cards within their sight, though she supposed it was possible some of them might just be saying that to get rid of her so they could go back to their lie-in. She left answerphone messages for the six who hadn't picked up, entreating them to ring her back at their earliest convenience and hoping they wouldn't notice that the number she gave them was for a mobile phone – her own. Then, having put the phone down for the last time, she drafted an email to the four who'd provided an email address but no phone number, delivering much the same spiel in written form, and once more asking them to get in touch.

The person who hadn't given either a phone number *or* an email address was going to be trickier to get hold of. The name 'Netta Ambrose' didn't ring a bell, but Alyssa noticed she'd given a flat in Craigslee as her home address. It was only about a ten-minute walk. Might as well pay her a visit. Nothing ventured, nothing gained. She transferred the Word doc to her phone and prepared to make tracks.

'Get all your messages taken care of?' Pat said as she hurried back through the main library.

'Almost. When Davy finally puts in an appearance, tell him we weren't just pissing in the wind.'

'Aye, I'll be sure and tell him that,' said Pat, sounding decidedly nonplussed.

Netta Ambrose's residence was a ground-floor flat at number forty-four Bletchley Street – a hideous eyesore of a concrete slab at the top of a steep hill. It was a bright, sunny day – one of those rare days in Glasgow that genuinely felt like summer, causing the residents to emerge blinking and disoriented from their homes to marvel at the strange, light-emitting globe above their heads – and Alyssa's vest top was clinging to her back by the time she reached the summit. She was also gagging for a pee and wishing she'd gone at the library.

She stood to catch her breath, soaking up the various sounds of everyday life around her: the periodic rumble of passing cars; the occasional shouts of children from the nearby playpark; the monotonous drone of an ice cream van playing 'Lili Marlene'. It seemed almost quaint, like a snapshot of a bygone age, but she didn't let outward appearances deceive her. She knew this was a seriously rough area, and the less time she spent there the better. She headed up the path to the block of flats and rang the buzzer next to Mrs Ambrose's name.

'Yes?' The voice that came crackling through the intercom was frail and reedy, almost a caricature of an elderly Glaswegian granny.

'Hello . . . Mrs Ambrose?' Alyssa spoke into the mouthpiece, enunciating loudly and clearly on the assumption that the woman's hearing probably wasn't great. 'My name's Alyssa Clark. I work in Thornhill Library. I was wondering—'

'Hold on, dear. Can't make out a word you're saying.'

The intercom went silent. A moment later the door emitted a loud buzzing sound. Alyssa tried it and found that it opened for her.

She stepped into the communal hallway and found herself faced with several identical doors. The one at the far end of the hallway was ajar; a thin, wizened face poked out. The woman to whom it belonged regarded Alyssa for a moment from behind a pair of bottle-cap glasses, then smiled.

'Oh, it's you, dearie. I thought it might be burglars.'

Alyssa recognised her almost instantly. Of course, Mrs *Ambrose* – the dotty old lady who had the same conversation with you every time you saw her, and who was forever bringing in biscuits and chocolate. She smiled sheepishly and headed over.

'Nope,' she said. 'No burglars today, I'm afraid. Just me.'

'Come in, come in.'

With surprising forcefulness for someone of her age and frailty, Mrs Ambrose took Alyssa by the arm and hauled her over the threshold.

'I don't often get visitors, you know. But then, that's the way of it these days, isn't it? Everyone's so busy, leading their own lives, and—'

'Well, I won't take up too much of your time,' said Alyssa, trying without success to extricate her arm from the woman's grip. 'I just came to ask a couple of quick questions.'

'Oh.' Mrs Ambrose seemed momentarily disappointed, before her face brightened. 'Well, come through this way and you can ask your questions somewhere comfortable.'

Reluctantly, Alyssa followed her through to a small, compact area doubling up as a living room and dining room. In one corner, a small flickering TV showed footage of a bunch of people in kilts prancing about in a field, the lack of audio adding to the comedic effect. At the far end, the table had been laid for two.

'What's happening here, then?' said Alyssa. 'I thought you said you don't get visitors.'

For a moment, Mrs Ambrose looked confused, then her face lit up in understanding. 'Oh, it's just my grandson Calvin. He always has his lunch here on a Saturday. He comes to see me when he can. But of course, he's grown up now and doesn't get much time to—'

'If I could just ask you these questions, please.' Alyssa smiled encouragingly, hoping she hadn't been too abrupt.

'Of course.' It was clear from Mrs Ambrose's tone that she was a little put out. Nonetheless, she gestured to the sofa. 'Have a seat, dearie, and ask away.'

'Thank you.' Alyssa sat down, though she had the distinct feeling she'd be unable to get free again once the sofa's folds had claimed her. 'It's just one question, really. A number of borrowers have reported having had their library cards stolen recently, and—'

'Oh, that's just awful.' Mrs Ambrose sat facing her in an armchair, her face a picture of genteel shock. 'Who would do a thing like that? And to think, it doesn't cost a penny to get one of your own—'

'Exactly. Bad people. Takes all sorts. But what I came to ask is, have you lost yours recently?'

'Oh, no.' Mrs Ambrose was emphatic. 'Certainly not.'

'You're sure?'

'Sure as sugar. I use it to take out books almost every week. Don't know where I'd be without it. Of course, I'm not always able to make it down there myself – dodgy hip, you see? But my grandson's ever so good about seeing to my returns and choosing new books for me. He knows exactly the sort I like. We go together when we can. Did I mention him before? He—'

'—has his lunch here every Saturday, yes,' said Alyssa. 'Mrs Ambrose, I really don't want to take up any more of your time than necessary, and I certainly don't want to interrupt your preparations for lunch. If you could just let me see your card so I can confirm you've got it, I'll be on my way.'

'Of course.' Mrs Ambrose beamed, eager to help. 'It's just here on the side . . . ' She turned to the table, then frowned as she realised it lay empty. 'Or did I leave it on the bedside cabinet? Or perhaps the kitchen worktop . . . '

Alyssa suspected she'd be here all day if Mrs Ambrose had anything to do with it. At this rate, she'd still be cooling her heels when the dutiful grandson showed up for lunch, and then there'd be all sorts of awkward questions about just what she was doing making house calls about something as trivial as a stolen library card that might not even have actually been stolen.

'Actually,' she said, launching herself to her feet, 'I could do with using the little girls' room. If you'd just point me in the right direction, then you can go look for your card.'

Mrs Ambrose frowned, clearly not understanding the euphemism. Then it all clicked and her mouth widened into a big, beaming smile.

'Of course! Down the hall, last on your left.'

Alyssa found the bathroom without much difficulty – there weren't exactly many options in the small, cramped flat. While she was taking care of business, the tinny, distorted strains of what she'd been reliably informed was known locally as 'teuchter music' began to emanate from the living room. Even through the closed door, the volume was piercing. The old dear must be as deaf as a post.

Alyssa stepped out of the bathroom and was about to head back down the corridor when she noticed the next door down lying slightly ajar. She pushed it open a fraction more. Inside, she could make out the shapes of a bed and a dresser. She paused, unable to hear anything but the music coming from the living room. Might as well take a quick peek. If she found the card in there, she could knock this whole thing on the head and get out of here before Mrs Ambrose talked her into a coma.

She stepped inside, shutting the door behind her. The curtains were drawn, the room swathed in semi-darkness. Like the living room, it was tiny, most of the floorspace taken up by the bed and a double wardrobe. She stepped gingerly around the bed, casting her eyes over the carpet and bedside cabinet. No sign of the card.

She approached the dresser by the window. Several framed photographs were arranged in front of a large circular mirror, with considerable attention having been paid to the overall composition. Mrs Ambrose featured in a couple of them, as did a middle-aged couple whom Alyssa assumed were the old woman's son and daughter-in-law, or vice versa. The man was dressed in some sort of military uniform and had one of those humourless, unsmiling faces. The woman looked somewhat more personable, but there was something cowed and submissive about her, existing in the shadow of her husband, his arm draped protectively – or was it possessively? – around her.

The largest photograph, slap-bang in the middle and blessed with an expensive-looking gold-embossed frame, was of Mrs Ambrose's long-suffering grandson. Alyssa picked up the frame to take a better look. He was standing with his hands in his pockets, facing the camera with the hint of a nervous – or possibly sheepish – smile at the corner of his lips. She didn't envy him, trailing around after the dotty old woman on her trips to the library *and* having to spend lunch with her every Saturday.

She was about to put the picture back when something made her stop. Something so unremarkable her eyes hadn't even processed it – though her unconscious mind certainly had, and was now sending warning signals shooting to her brain, desperately trying to alert her to what she hadn't spotted. She stared at the picture, trying to figure out what was wrong with it. Then she saw it.

Toggles.

Toggles on a black duffle coat, knee-length, done up at the front.

Slowly, she lowered the picture, placing it back on the dresser, her suddenly clammy hands leaving prints on the glass. She stood stock still and listened. The music from the living room continued to play, the jaunty fiddles a mocking parody of the gravity of the situation she now found herself in.

Run, Alyssa. Get out of here and run like hell.

She crept to the door and carefully slid it open, grateful to the music for drowning out its creaking hinges. She looked out into the corridor. The coast was clear, the front door at its far end practically calling her with open arms.

She set off, moving as quickly as she could without making any noise. She cleared the distance in a few seconds, her hand reaching into her pocket for her phone. She'd call Metcalfe as soon as she got out of there. Metcalfe would listen. She'd have to.

As she placed her hand on the door handle, something cold and hard touched her ear, gently skimming the bottom of the lobe. She froze, her breath in her throat.

Slowly, heart pounding, she turned. Mrs Ambrose's grandson stood facing her, his arm extended in front of him in a straight line, pointing the same Glock 17 9mm at her as he had on the morning of Monday the first of March.

'I wouldn't do that if I were you,' he said softly.

31

With the barrel of the gun pressed between her shoulder-blades, Alyssa walked slowly back down the hallway and into the living room. In her absence, the curtains had been closed, though the TV continued to flicker and blare its Highland dance music. Mrs Ambrose sat in the deep armchair facing the doorway, her expression one of neither surprise nor fear. Rather, it was . . . resignation, almost – as if she'd made her peace with the situation.

'Move.'

Alyssa heard Calvin Ambrose's voice in her ear, felt his hand on her shoulder, found herself being shoved forward. She stumbled across the room, colliding with the sofa.

'Sit.'

She did as she was told, eyes not leaving the stern-faced young man for an instant.

Still training the gun on her, he crossed over to the TV and switched it off, finally silencing the oppressive din. He advanced towards her, holding out his free hand.

'Phone.'

She handed it over, wondering if he was planning on communicating entirely in one-word, monosyllabic barks. He glanced disinterestedly at the screen before pocketing it.

Alyssa chanced a look in Mrs Ambrose's direction, weighing up the odds of the elderly woman intervening on her behalf. It seemed unlikely on the face of it, and yet she couldn't picture this nice old lady, who'd brought the library staff so many goodies and was forever telling them what a wonderful job they all did, watching as her grandson—

As he what? What was he planning on doing?

She tried not to think about it. Tried not to panic, even as she felt the terror welling up inside of her, like a hard lump in her belly that was expanding with every breath.

'It's all right, Nana,' said Calvin, without looking at her. 'It'll be all over soon.'

That didn't sound good.

Alyssa tried to focus, to think logically – as much to quell the terror threatening to overwhelm her as anything. What was clear in her mind was that the man now pointing a gun at her had shot her once before and murdered three of her colleagues in front of her. She couldn't count on him having any qualms about killing again.

She looked across at Mrs Ambrose, who hadn't moved from the armchair. She appeared tense and apprehensive, but not scared.

'You warned him I was here, didn't you?'

Mrs Ambrose nodded tightly. 'While you were in the little girls' room.'

'She smelled a rat as soon as you got here,' said Calvin. He scoffed. 'A house call about a missing library card? That would have taken going beyond the call of duty to a whole other level. And we know you lot aren't big on doing that.'

You lot. There was something spiteful about the way he said those words, like he was spitting out something foul-tasting. She wondered what he was getting at.

Something else occurred to her. For Mrs Ambrose to have warned her grandson, that could only mean . . .

'You *knew*,' she breathed, staring at the old woman in disbelief. 'You knew what he'd done.'

Mrs Ambrose said nothing.

'Of course she knew,' Calvin retorted, answering on her behalf. 'Where else was I going to keep this?' He flicked the gun slightly, without taking Alyssa out of its sights. 'This was the last place anyone would ever think to look. It's been in a shoebox in the hall cupboard ever since.' He swallowed, his Adam's apple bobbing like a cork. 'I was going to turn myself in. But I couldn't. She wouldn't let me.'

Alyssa stared at Mrs Ambrose in disbelief. 'So you harboured a murderer?'

'Of course.' Calvin's response was firm and unwavering. 'We're family.'

At that moment, there was a sound of tyres and the purr of an engine as a car pulled up outside. In a flash, Calvin darted over to the window. Alyssa watched as he pulled the curtain back and peered through the crack.

'It's the cripple,' he said.

Alyssa's heart leapt into her throat. *Davy?* What the hell?

Calvin shot an accusing look at her. 'Did you tell him you were coming here?'

'No!' She felt oddly affronted. 'I didn't tell anyone.'

Calvin pointed a finger at her, like a teacher about to upbraid a child, then seemed to change his mind and balled his hand into a fist. 'That's good,' he said, nodding vigorously. 'That's very good.'

The phone on the side table next to Mrs Ambrose's armchair emitted a buzzing noise. Instinctively, the old woman reached for the receiver.

'Leave it,' Calvin barked.

She withdrew her hand instantly.

All six eyes in the room stared at the phone with a kind of morbid fascination as it continued to trill for a few seconds before eventually ringing out. Calvin glanced out through the gap in the curtains again.

'What's he doing?' Alyssa found her voice at last.

Calvin scoffed. 'Trying every buzzer till someone lets him in.'

They sat for another minute or so, all on tenterhooks. No one spoke. Outside, the ice cream van began playing 'Lili Marlene' for the umpteenth time. Then, through the thin single-glazed window, Alyssa heard Davy's voice.

'Uh, yeah, hi, um – I said I'd drop some odds and ends off with my granny, but it looks like she's popped out. I've got a key to her flat, but I can't remember the code for the main door. Don't suppose you could be a lifesaver and buzz me through?'

Don't, Alyssa thought. *Please don't let him in.*

But a moment later, she heard Davy's voice again – 'You're a star; an absolute, gold-plated star' – followed by a loud, droning buzz, indicating that the main door was now unlocked. Soon after, there was a knock on the door to the flat.

Calvin turned to Alyssa, a warning finger raised. 'Don't move a muscle. And don't even think about trying to warn him. If you do, I'll . . . I'll . . . I'll make it hurt.'

Stowing the gun in the waistband at the back of his slacks, he strode out of the room. Alyssa listened as his footsteps receded down the corridor.

Frantically, she turned to Mrs Ambrose. 'Do something,' she hissed. 'Talk to him. Don't let him do this.'

'I . . . I can't.' Mrs Ambrose refused to meet her eye.

'He's your grandson. He'll listen to you.'

Mrs Ambrose shook her head. 'I can't,' she said simply, and turned away, fixing her eyes on the far wall.

Alyssa heard footsteps and the squeak of wheels in the corridor. She turned as Davy and his wheelchair appeared in the doorway, Calvin behind him with the gun pressed to the back of his head. Davy's eyes fell on Alyssa, who stared back at him, tongue-tied.

'What—' he began.

Calvin dunted the back of his head with the muzzle of the gun. 'Not one word, fatty.'

Davy's hands shot up in a gesture of surrender.

'Over there.' Calvin pointed the gun at the sofa.

Wordlessly, Davy wheeled himself over, reversing himself into the space by Alyssa's side.

'What are you doing here?' she hissed.

'Yes, I could ask the same,' said Calvin.

Davy shrugged. 'Find Friends,' he said simply.

'What?' Calvin sounded incredulous.

''Scuse me?' said Alyssa.

'When I got into work, they said you'd been and gone,' explained Davy, addressing Alyssa as if Calvin and his gun weren't there. 'Said you'd gone up to the office to do "internet banking", but when they went up they found a file open on the PC with a bunch of names and addresses. Pat said you'd told him "we're not just pissing in the wind" or something. I figured you'd found some new evidence, looked you up on Find Friends, saw you'd been at this address for the last fifteen minutes, thought I'd better come and find you, case you'd got yourself in trouble and needed bailing out.'

You moron. You absolute, weapons-grade moron.

Calvin, meanwhile, was still curtain-twitching at the window. He glanced in Davy's direction. 'How did you get here?'

'Taxi,' said Davy sullenly.

'And you told it to wait, I expect?'

Davy nodded.

'Then we'll wait too.'

They sat in silence, all four of them, like guests at a particularly uncomfortable family gathering. Calvin remained by the window, one buttock perched on the sill, watching through the curtains, all the while keeping the gun trained on Alyssa. Alyssa imagined the driver parked at the kerb, meter running, fingers drumming the wheel, checking his watch.

'So then,' said Davy, breaking the silence with forced bonhomie, 'how's everyone's day been so far?'

Calvin shot him a withering look and adjusted the angle of the gun from Alyssa to him. Davy mimed zipping his mouth shut.

They continued to wait. And wait. Finally, Calvin stirred.

'Here he comes.'

They listened as footsteps tramped up the path. A moment later, the phone by Mrs Ambrose's side buzzed. She looked to Calvin.

'Answer it,' he said. 'Tell him your grandson's here.'

Mrs Ambrose fumbled with the receiver, all thumbs. 'H–hello?' she croaked. Listened. 'Yes, he's arrived safely.'

Another pause. All eyes on the room were fixed on her.

'Er . . . just a minute.' She lowered the receiver, covering the mouthpiece, and looked to Calvin. 'He says he's owed eight pounds ninety.'

Calvin thought for a minute, tapping the barrel of the gun against his forehead, then made his decision.

'Buzz him through. Tell him to come to the door.'

Mrs Ambrose put the phone to her ear again. As she explained to the driver what was going to happen, Calvin strode over to the sofa and grabbed Alyssa by the back of her vest, hauling her upright with the gun's muzzle pressed behind her ear.

'You, with me,' he said. 'I don't trust you.' He turned to Davy. 'Any funny business from you, and I'll shoot her in the kneecaps. Got it?'

Davy nodded, eyes wide.

With Calvin steering her, Alyssa exited the living room and headed down the corridor toward the front door. There, they came to a halt, while Calvin, keeping the gun trained on her all the while, took out his wallet and extracted a £20 note. He handed it to Alyssa and gestured to the door with the gun. Taking the hint, Alyssa bent down and slid it under the door. There was silence for a moment. Then . . .

'This is a twenty,' said the muffled and bemused voice beyond the door.

'Keep it,' Calvin snapped.

Another pause. 'Aye, fair play tae ye, pal,' said the driver. 'You have a grand day now.'

As his footsteps receded, Calvin grabbed Alyssa by the back of her top again and propelled her back through to the living room. He deposited her in her seat with a rough shove and moved over to the window, resuming his observational position. A moment later, they heard a revving engine, followed by tyres treading asphalt as the cab took off.

As silence descended once more, Calvin turned to face his prisoners. 'Well,' he said, with an almost singsong cadence, 'what *am* I going to do with the two of you?'

Alyssa didn't respond. As far as she was concerned, saying anything at this point was tantamount to asking for a bullet.

'You don't have to do *anything* with us,' piped up Davy, who either didn't share Alyssa's thirst for self-preservation or still hadn't twigged just how precarious their position was. 'You could just let us go.'

'I could, couldn't I?' Calvin mused, as if the idea held genuine appeal. 'I could just open the door and let you walk out. Or roll out, in your case. And what d'you suppose would happen then?' His expression hardened. 'I'll tell you. Every police officer in Glasgow would have this place surrounded in ten minutes flat.'

'It doesn't have to be that way,' Davy protested. 'We won't say anything. Or . . . or we could give you a head start. You know, time to get away.'

'Who says I *want* a head start?' said Calvin, as if it had just been suggested he enjoyed carnal relations with barnyard animals. 'You think I'd run away? Leave my nana?' He was beginning to pace now, gesticulating wildly with the gun, punctuating each sentence with a fresh jab at the air. 'I didn't ask you to come here. I didn't ask you to poke your noses where they weren't wanted. If you'd just minded your own business, we wouldn't be in this mess. This is your fault.'

'And if you hadn't killed my friends in cold blood,' Davy said, his voice suddenly icy, 'then we wouldn't have poked our noses in.'

It occurred to Alyssa that getting out of here in one piece might not actually be Davy's primary concern. On some level, he seemed to be actually relishing this – the opportunity to look the man who'd killed his pals and put him in a wheelchair in the eye and have some sort of reckoning with him.

'Why?' he continued, spitting the word out like a poison dart. 'Why did you do it? What did they ever do to you?'

Calvin looked at Davy, his pupils twin smouldering orbs. 'Not to me,' he said quietly.

Alyssa followed Calvin's gaze. Her eyes settled on Mrs Ambrose, who sat, hands folded in her lap, looking like she wished the floor would open up and swallow her whole.

'Your . . . your nana? But what . . . '

Calvin's mouth was a thin, taut line. 'Because of how you treated her.'

Alyssa stared at him in stupefied silence. 'I'm sorry,' she said eventually, as firmly and matter-of-factly as she dared given her present situation, 'but I don't have a clue what the fuck you're talking about.'

'Five pounds. That's what this is about. FIVE POUNDS!' He roared the last two words at the top of his voice, causing everyone in the room to flinch involuntarily. 'A few days late returning some crummy books. Any reasonable person would have let it slide.

They'd have taken one look at her, seen that she was a frail old woman who can't get about too easily and just waived it. But no – you had to belittle her, humiliate her in front of everyone, make her feel like some sort of criminal. And why? What had she ever done to you? She's just a harmless old lady who brings you chocolates and who's paid her taxes all her life, and you made her feel *this* small.'

'I . . . I didn't,' Alyssa stammered, bristling at the very suggestion that she could have been responsible for what Calvin was describing.

'You did.'

'I swear. I didn't even *work* there till fifteen minutes before you came in and blew us all to kingdom come.'

'You're not LISTENING!'

Alyssa slammed her mouth shut instantly. She sat there, every muscle in her body taut, clenching her teeth to stop them chattering.

Calvin gave a dismissive snort. 'You, him' – he waved the gun in Davy's direction – 'someone else, what difference does it make?' He gave a mirthless little laugh. 'You think this is just about the late fees? It's *everything*.' He began to ream off on his fingers, 'It's your complacency. Your disinterest. Your snobbery. What, you . . . you think we don't have ears? I *hear* you!' he yelled, so forcefully a fleck of spittle flew across the room from his mouth and landed on Alyssa's knee. 'Every time I walk through these doors, I see you, all of you, clustered around that desk, gossiping, complaining, passing judgement.'

Alyssa chanced a glance at Davy, trying to gauge whether he had any idea what Calvin was talking about. Davy stared straight ahead, jaw set, his expression inscrutable.

'You moan about your customers right in front of them. "Oh, here comes so-and-so again. You'd think someone'd buy him some deodorant for his Christmas." Or "Dozy old bat, doesn't she know that's the sixth time she'd had that book out?" 'Oh yes,' he nodded, as a flicker of something approaching recognition registered on Davy's face, 'you think we don't hear you, but we do. We hear it all. Every pithy putdown, every "funny" nickname you come up with for us, every complaint about how you don't get enough tea-breaks or how your employers have added some trivial duty to your responsibilities . . . all the while ignoring the people with *real* problems. *Real* hardships. But you don't care. None of you do. You all just look the other way.' His lip curled as he shook his head in disgust. 'You see us, but you don't *see* us.'

He fell silent and bowed his head, as if the effort expended on his outburst had sapped him of all his energy. The room felt eerily still.

'We see you now,' said Davy gently. 'We're listening. You've made your point perfectly clear.'

But Calvin didn't seem to hear him. 'I've killed others, you know,' he went on, seemingly to himself. 'Others who hurt us. Disrespected us. They won't be doing *that* again.'

'You mean Gordon Ramage?' The words were out of Alyssa's mouth before she had a chance to consider that adding fuel to this man's fire probably wasn't the wisest of moves. 'That *was* you, wasn't it?'

Calvin swung around with a dismissive snort. 'He tried to blackmail me. I knew he wouldn't be satisfied, no matter how much I gave him. But I'm not talking about him.'

Davy nodded. 'The two boys in Craigslee.'

'They've terrorised this estate for years. Made the residents' lives a misery. But the police did nothing, even though everyone round here knows what they're like. What they're capable of.'

'And the man outside Metropolis?'

Calvin gave something approaching a smile, as if buoyed by the memory. 'That was more of a spur-of-the-moment thing. I saw him giving this woman grief, refusing to take no for an answer. I watched her rebuffing him again and again, and I just thought, "How can this man have got through life without anyone teaching him basic manners or respect?" This world is full of people who refuse to take responsibility for their actions.'

'You . . . you never told me.'

All three of them – Alyssa, Davy and Calvin – turned in Mrs Ambrose's direction. She hadn't moved from her armchair, but she was staring at Calvin, confusion and disbelief etched into her wizened features.

Calvin hurried over to her, dropping down onto one knee and laying his hand on top of hers. 'I couldn't, Nana,' he said. 'I couldn't involve you. Because I knew if I did, you'd feel you had to protect me, to lie for me. I didn't want to incriminate you further. I've already asked so much of you.'

It was then that Alyssa made her move. She'd been biding her time for a while now, sizing up her chances of either overpowering Calvin or making a run for it. Now, with his back to her, she leapt to her feet and made for the door.

But Calvin was too quick. In a trice, he crossed the room, barring her way. Alyssa came up short, the gun's muzzle pressing into her forehead. She stood there, trying her damnedest to hold her bladder, as Calvin's eyes burned into her flesh, his nostrils flaring with each breath.

'Back,' he snarled. 'Back in your seat.'

Slowly, she backed up, lowering herself onto the sofa. She could feel the imprint the gun had left on her forehead. Could feel, too, the sense of impotent rage bubbling up inside her at the utter helplessness of her situation.

Calvin regarded her, tilting his head. 'Have you got a death wish?'

She shook her head.

'You act like you do.'

'No,' she whispered.

'Because if that's the case, I'll happily oblige. See, if I'm going to make that getaway, I'm going to need one of you with me as insurance. I can't take both of you, can I?' He scoffed at the very absurdity of the idea. 'You'd slow me down too much. So which is it to be? You . . . ' He moved the gun from Alyssa to Davy. ' . . . or Fat-boy?'

Alyssa felt a tear trickling down her cheek. 'Please,' she whispered. 'Don't make me choose.'

'You already did,' said Calvin.

For a second, no one moved or spoke. Then, without warning, Calvin pulled the trigger.

Davy jack-knifed like he'd just been electrocuted. He slumped sideways and fell out of his chair, hitting the floor. Mrs Ambrose shrieked and covered her eyes.

Alyssa was off the sofa in a trice, dropping to her knees next to Davy. With considerable effort, she rolled him onto his back. He was breathing heavily, both hands pressed to his chest, blood oozing between his fingers.

'Look at me!' she said, forcing the words out through clenched teeth. 'Davy, look at me. Just keep looking at me and focus on breathing.'

Davy stared up at her, his wide eyes locked with hers. She saw the terror in them and forced herself to ignore her own rising panic.

'It's OK,' she said. 'Everything's going to be OK.'

She was aware of Mrs Ambrose whimpering softly. Calvin circled the pair of them, saying nothing. Alyssa lifted her head and stared up at him as he stood before them, scratching the back of his neck with the barrel of the gun and gazing down at them.

'Call an ambulance,' she whispered. 'Please.'

Calvin stared back at her, unmoved. 'Why?'

He seemed remarkably unperturbed by what he'd just done. It was as if the act of pulling the trigger had served as a crossing of the Rubicon, a point of no return. He couldn't wind back the clock, so there was nothing for it but to follow through.

Alyssa watched him warily, following his arm from shoulder to fingertip, eyes settling on the gun. If she lunged at him now, could she get it off him before he had a chance to take aim and shoot her?

Once again, he seemed to read her mind. 'Don't even think about it. I spared you once, but I won't make that mistake again.'

Alyssa stared at him uncomprehendingly. 'You *spared* me?'

'What, you thought I was just a lousy marksman? That I managed to kill three of your colleagues with a single shot each, but just happened to miss any of your vital organs, even though you were standing right in front of me?' He shook his head. 'I let you off lightly.'

'Why?' She hissed the word through clenched teeth.

He shrugged. 'Because you smiled at me.'

She couldn't believe what she was hearing. 'I *smiled* at you?'

'You mean you don't remember? On the bus. When we both got off at Chancery Street, fifteen minutes before . . . ' He trailed off. 'I stood back to let you go first, and you smiled at me.' He blinked several times, confusion etched into his furrowed brows. 'You really don't remember?'

'No. And even if I did, it didn't mean anything. It was just a smile. It's just something normal people do.'

Calvin's expression soured. The effect was akin to the faintly glowing embers of a fire being doused.

Davy let out a deep, agonised breath. Instantly, Alyssa's attention was on him.

'It's OK,' she whispered, clutching his bloodied hand with her own. 'Don't worry.'

'I . . . don't feel so good,' he muttered, the words escaping from his mouth with each gasping breath.

'Yeah? Well, I've got your bodily fluids all over my banging new top. How d'you think I feel?'

He managed a faint smile. 'Always about you, eh? Don't ever change.'

She forced a strained smile of her own. 'That's right. Little Miss Selfish, me. You just hang in there and insult me some more. Help'll be here soon.'

'Liar,' he said, and closed his eyes.

Alyssa slapped his cheeks frantically. 'Don't you go to sleep on me. Don't even think about it. See?' she laughed manically as, with considerable effort, Davy forced his eyes open again. 'You're gonna be fine, you know that? You've gotta be, cos you and me, we're buddies, yeah? And in case you hadn't noticed, I haven't got a whole lot of those. Not real ones anyway. So I can't exactly afford to lose you.'

As she knelt there, squeezing Davy's hand for all she was worth, trying to keep him awake, she became aware of a change in Calvin's demeanour. Where previously he'd projected an air of self-assurance, he now seemed tense and uncertain. He stood rigid, eyes flicking this way and that, brows knitted together in a pensive frown.

'It's quiet,' he said.

Alyssa listened, doing her best to filter out Davy's rasping breaths. Calvin was right – it *was* quiet. Like, *really* quiet. Now she thought about it, she couldn't remember the last time she'd heard 'Lili Marlene'. All the other everyday noises from outside – sounds so commonplace you didn't even normally register them – had stopped too, replaced by an eerie stillness that made her scalp itch and her gums prickle; made her want to yell, scream, stamp her feet, do anything to break the smothering stillness.

Calvin moved to the window, pushed back the curtain with the end of his gun and peered out. He pressed himself right up against the wall, craning his neck to a painful-looking angle to increase his field of vision. He drew a sharp intake of breath and sprang away, dropping low.

'What is it?' Alyssa demanded.

'*Police.*' His voice was a tight whisper, his eyes wide with icy panic. 'With guns. They've sealed off the whole street.'

A little flame of hope sprang up inside Alyssa, quickly tempered by the realisation that Calvin was more likely to kill them now than ever. She watched as he looked around wildly, his fringe plastered to his forehead by a film of sweat.

His eyes alighted on her. He reached out and grabbed her by the arm. 'Was it you?' he demanded, squeezing her bicep in a pincer-like grip. 'Did you call them?'

'Of course not! How could I? You took my phone.'

Calvin relinquished his grip on her and set his sights on Davy. 'Did you?'

Davy, clammy and grey-faced, shook his head.

Calvin bit his bottom lip, the cogs of his mind churning. Slowly, he lifted his head, staring across the room to the armchair where his grandmother sat, dwarfed by the heavy upholstery and seemingly shrunken to a fraction of her original size. She wilted under his gaze, avoiding his eyes and appearing to become smaller still.

In a sudden movement, Calvin bounded over to her. She still wouldn't look at him. 'Show me, Nana,' he ordered her.

She withdrew herself even more, drawing her arms up to protect herself.

With a sudden roughness that shocked Alyssa, he grabbed hold of the old woman. There was a brief struggle and then she relented, going limp in his arms as he extracted something from the folds of the armchair beneath her. He stood holding a small Nokia phone, staring at it in disbelief. As Mrs Ambrose cowered, whimpering, he backed off, put it to his ear and listened for a moment. Then, slowly, he lowered it and turned to stare at his grandmother.

She gazed back at him, eyes moist with fresh tears. 'I'm sorry, Calvin,' she said softly.

The look on Calvin's face was that of a man whose entire world had just collapsed, like a believer who'd just been shown irrefutable proof that there was no higher power.

'Calvin? Calvin Ambrose?'

The disembodied voice – a woman's – was crackly and distorted by a megaphone, but Alyssa recognised it at once.

'This is DCI Metcalfe of the Major Investigations Team. We know you're in there, and that you're armed. We don't want to hurt you, Calvin. We just want to talk.'

Calvin stood there, staring in the direction of the voice. The phone, falling from his limp hand, landed on the carpet. Alyssa chanced a glance at it. The last call made, to 999, was still active.

'Calvin, are you listening?' Metcalfe again, her voice firm and unwavering. *'Give me a sign that you can hear me.'*

Calvin seemed to reach a decision. Whirling to face Alyssa, he grabbed her arm. 'You're coming with me.'

'What?' She dug her heels in, refusing to budge. 'Where?'

'I don't know. Somewhere. They'll not shoot me as long as I've got you. Now move.'

He tried to haul her to her feet. Again, she resisted, clinging tight to Davy. Their combined weight was too much for Calvin to dislodge.

'No! I'm not leaving him.'

'Fine, then you can die together,' said Calvin matter-of-factly, raising the gun to her.

Alyssa stared back at him, jaw set, steely-eyed. She'd moved beyond the point of fear. If he was going to kill her in cold blood, he was damn well going to have to do it while looking her in the eyes.

At that moment, with an anguished wail, Mrs Ambrose launched herself out of the armchair and threw herself upon Calvin, grappling with him for the gun. For a few moments, they lurched this way and that, grunting, panting, scrabbling, pushing, until—

BANG.

For a brief moment, it was as if time had been suspended. The two were frozen in one another's arms, like a stone carving of two warriors locked in combat. Then Mrs Ambrose's head lolled, her eyes rolled back in their sockets. A thin trickle of blood escaped from the corner of her mouth. She lay in Calvin's arms, limp as a ragdoll.

'Nana,' he whispered. Then more plaintively, in a voice more like a child's than that of a grown man, 'Nana?'

She slid out of his arms, landed in a crumpled heap on the floor, and lay still.

Calvin dropped to his knees, the gun falling from his hand. As he shook her shoulder, repeating the word 'Nana' over and over, each utterance more frantic than the last, Alyssa was aware of hurried movement outside. She heard the pound of heavy, racing footsteps. Saw, through the thin lace curtains, the shapes of multiple figures passing by the window. Heard a loud thud coming from the direction of the front door, followed by another, and another. Calvin, meanwhile, draped himself over the lifeless body of his nana, a long, low keening sound escaping from somewhere deep inside him.

BANG. Another blow to the door. BANG. Another.

Alyssa watched as Calvin slowly straightened up. His eyes zeroed in on her. 'You,' he said, his voice a shrill, accusatory whisper. 'Look what you've done.'

'*You* did this,' she snarled. 'Own it.'

For a moment, he just stared at her. Then a look of cold determination came into his eyes. She realised what he was going to do moments before it happened. She wanted to cry out, tell him to stop, but no sound came out. She watched, helpless, as he picked up the gun, placed the barrel in his mouth, shut his eyes and pulled the trigger.

BANG. The back of Calvin's head exploded in a shower of blood, bone and other things Alyssa couldn't bring herself to think about. A Rorschach pattern of red splatter hit the curtains behind him. For a second or so remained on his knees but still upright, before falling backward, the shattered remnants of his parietal bone hitting the floor with dull thud.

BANG. The door finally caved in. Multiple pairs of booted feet raced up the corridor.

Alyssa turned to Davy, ready to reassure him that help was on the way, only to find him lying wide-eyed, mouth hanging slightly open, head lolled to one side. One arm was twitching slightly by his side, but otherwise he was completely still. No rasping breaths. No rise and fall of his chest.

For a brief moment, she was back in the icy waters of Wollaston Lake, scrabbling frantically, trying to free herself from the inky depths that had claimed Emily. And then she was back with Davy. She'd seen this before, in a video they'd shown her during her emergency first aid training.

Cardiac arrest.

He's gone into cardiac arrest.

And you know what to do.

Rising to her knees, she placed the heel of her left hand on the centre of Davy's chest, her right hand on top, locked her fingers together and began to perform cardiac massage.

'One-two-three-four-five. *One*-two-three-four-five . . . '

She heard herself counting out loud, the words piggybacking

onto each breath of air expelled from her lungs. Her Wayfarers, already hanging precariously from one ear, fell off, dislodged by the force of the compressions.

She was dimly aware of the room filling with bodies – blurry figures in black, brandishing assault rifles; of the chatter of radios; of a man's voice firing questions at her; of another barking rapid-fire instructions – but still she kept pounding on Davy's chest. She wasn't going to stop until he started breathing again. Or until someone pronounced him dead.

'Ma'am, you'd better take a look,' she heard one of the officers saying into his radio. 'It's a total bloodbath in here . . . '

32

The afternoon following the incident at 44 Bletchley Street, Paul McGuigan was released from prison, all charges against him dropped with immediate effect. He emerged blinking to a crowd of cameras and microphones. Grinning dopily and clearly relishing his role as the media's newfound *cause célèbre*, he listened to the avalanche of questions put to him with neither the inclination nor the wit to respond. What had been his first thought when he heard the news? How did it feel to be completely exonerated? What was he going to do now he was free?

'Well,' he said, when the chatter of voices finally died down and a sea of faces stared at him in expectant silence, 'I huvnae had a fix the twelve weeks I've been in there, so first thing I'm gonnae dae is attend tae ma vital needs.'

In the days that followed, the press raked over the case with their usual mixture of flawed reasoning, wild conjecture and self-righteous braggadocio, pondering how such a grave miscarriage of justice could have occurred. Almost immediately, the blame fell squarely upon the shoulders of the senior investigating officer, DCI Claire Metcalfe, with a number of failings cited in her approach. Corners had been cut, it seemed, and speculation was rife that, with her eye on a cushy promotion, she had sought to make a quick arrest and failed to exercise due diligence – a theory which her superiors, and their public relations machine, were in no great hurry to repudiate. Rumours mounted that Metcalfe was not long for her position in the Major Investigations Team, and the tabloid scribblers began to question just how much the nation's taxpayers would be expected to cough up for the inevitable golden handshake. Meanwhile, a Dr Anna Scavolini, senior lecturer in criminology at the University of Glasgow, wrote an excoriating article for the *Glasgow Tribune*, upbraiding the police for scapegoating an individual who, she asserted, had clearly been targeted because of his underprivileged upbringing. Assumptions had been leapt to, she said, with the police once again demonstrating an over-eagerness to equate low social status with criminality.

Speculation, too, was rife as to just what could have caused Calvin Ambrose to do what he did. His employers refused to speak to the press, while those of his former colleagues who were prepared to do so – anonymously, of course – would only say that he'd been a quiet individual who kept to himself. 'To be honest, I really didn't know that much about him,' one source told the *Daily Chronicle*. 'You couldn't imagine he was capable of doing something like that. But then, it's always the quiet ones, isn't it?'

Four months later

The cemetery was a simple and modest affair, located on the city's Southside, a mile or so west of Bellahouston Park. Alyssa entered through the south gate and followed the footpath up a gentle slope, periodically stopping to check the scrap of paper with its scribbled instructions, or to adjust her grip on the bouquet of flowers she'd picked up at the supermarket. She wasn't sure if she was supposed to bring a vase to put them in, or if they were the right kind, or if there even *was* a right kind. She just knew you were meant to bring flowers when you visited someone's grave. And she figured he'd have appreciated it, in a way. The traditional touch.

They'd finally finished engraving the tombstone the previous week, hence her decision to visit now. She'd thought about just giving the whole thing a miss, of course. But when it came down to it, she'd realised she had no choice. If she didn't, if she passed up the opportunity to pay her respects, it would only continue to gnaw away at her. And besides, the counsellor she was seeing had said it would do her good. He hadn't actually used the word 'closure', but that was what she took him to mean.

Eventually, she found what she was looking for. The winter sun shone high in the sky behind her, causing her to cast a long shadow over the tombstone. Still clutching the flowers, she stood facing it, reading the inscription.

'Brought you these,' she said, waving the bouquet awkwardly. 'Cos, y'know, it's what ya do.'

Ugh. She'd promised herself she wouldn't do the whole 'talking to a dead person' thing. It was corny, it was mawkish, and it was always something she'd had a sneaking suspicion only people in movies did. Or people who'd seen people in movies doing it and figured it was what you were supposed to do. Or something.

'I hope you're at peace now. Both of you.'

She tossed the flowers, still in their plastic wrapping, onto the grass at the foot of the slab, and bowed her head in silent contemplation.

'You know,' said a voice behind her, 'talking to yourself is often the first sign of madness.'

'For Chrissakes,' said Alyssa, turning in exasperation, 'you really know how to kill the mood.'

'At least I'm not the one blaspheming on consecrated ground,' said Davy cheerily, wheeling himself to a halt beside her.

'You got my message, then.'

'That I did. Characteristically cryptic though it was, I success-fully decoded it as a plea for emotional support and figured I couldn't leave you to face the Devil on your lonesome. 'Sides, I figure I've kinda got unfinished business with this yoke myself.'

Alyssa turned to face the tombstone again. 'How long d'you give it before someone vandalises it?'

Davy pondered the matter. 'I reckon about a week.'

'Ridiculous as it sounds, I kinda feel sorry for him.'

'I get that. Troubled soul and all that.'

They were silent for a minute or so, both preoccupied by their own thoughts.

It was Davy who finally broke the silence. 'I don't blame you, by the way.'

Alyssa stirred. 'Sorry?'

'The whole "him shooting me" thing. I don't hold it against you for not instantly leaping to your feet and offering yourself up as the sacrificial lamb. Odds are he'd already made his choice, what with my coming with this cumbersome apparatus as part of the deal.' He patted the armrest of his chair.

'I know that,' said Alyssa.

And, on some level, she *did*. It would have been the easiest thing in the world to drive herself to distraction telling herself it was all her fault – that she had Davy's blood on her hands. Indeed, the old self-absorbed, tunnel-visioned her probably *would* have done that, heaping blame and guilt on herself; her own personal cross to bear. Of late, though, she'd been taking a lot of comfort in Tony Barba-rossa's words:

Whoever it was, whoever he was after and whatever they'd done in his eyes tae deserve it, he's the one who pulled the trigger. Naeb'dy else. So stop looking to blame yerself, or anyone else.

She hadn't seen him since that evening in the bar. She wondered occasionally what he was up to. Striding across windswept mountains and into glens and gullies, no doubt, a deer carcass draped across his shoulders. She'd realised, in retrospect, that he'd been doing the whole 'no commitments, no ties' lifestyle thing a whole lot more effectively than she ever had. He'd successfully divested himself of all society's trappings and responsibilities and made himself truly self-sufficient, while she'd done everything she could to deny her responsibilities as a member of society while still inhabiting it, reaping the advantages it conferred. You couldn't have it both ways. Purely by existing within the system, contributing to it with your taxes and your purchases and your labour, you benefited from it, and it from you. It was a complex, symbiotic relationship, but one you couldn't escape. You either cut yourself off from it completely, or not at all.

'Besides,' Davy's voice cut into her thoughts again, 'it's thanks to you I'm still standing.'

Alyssa managed a small, awkward smile, but she couldn't look him in the eye. Gratitude and praise made her uncomfortable at the best of times, and this was several orders of magnitude greater than anything she'd ever experienced before. She didn't know how to respond. *Ah, it was nothing* didn't exactly cut it when you'd successfully brought someone back from cardiac arrest.

'Well, obviously not *standing*,' said Davy, 'but you get the picture.'

And, just like that, all the awkwardness evaporated, and Alyssa felt the weight lifting from her shoulders. There were going to be no great outpourings of you-saved-my-lifes, no tearful embraces. It wasn't in either of their natures. Far better to make do with the implicit understanding that what they'd gone through together had forged a bond between them that could never be undone.

They were silent for several more moments, side by side as they contemplated the tombstone.

At length, Alyssa stirred. 'You done here?'

Davy breathed an exaggerated sigh of relief. 'Thought you were never gonna ask.'

'Then let's blow this popsicle stand.'

They turned to go, Alyssa letting Davy take the lead. As they made their way down the hill, she paused momentarily, glancing back towards the tombstone. For a moment, she imagined she wasn't on the Southside of Glasgow but in another cemetery altogether, of similar size but several thousand miles away, outside a small town in rural Saskatchewan. They never had recovered Emily's body, but her parents had paid for a small plot of land and a tombstone, so they had something tangible with which to mark her memory. Something concrete. She'd never visited it herself – couldn't face it. And now she knew she never would. Because she didn't need to. Her sister's memory didn't reside in a hole in the ground or on a slab of granite, but somewhere far closer to home.

'Goodbye,' she whispered, then turned and hurried to catch up with Davy.

Behind her, the heavy stone slab stood tall, stained by the passage of time and constant exposure to the elements, the words carved into its stone surface as indelibly as the events of the previous spring and summer on those who'd survived.

THOMAS AMBROSE

❖

HIS WIFE
NETTA, NÉE MacLEÒID

❖

THEIR DAUGHTER
HOPE

❖

HER SON
CALVIN

* * *

Alyssa caught the bus back to Thornhill for her afternoon shift. Officially, Davy was still on sick leave. Unofficially, she knew he wouldn't be back. The last couple of times she'd seen him, he'd been making noises about it being time for a change. She couldn't exactly blame him. When you'd been shot not once but twice in the line of duty, it was probably time to accept that someone somewhere was trying to tell you something. She knew she was going to miss him – even if, over the last few months, she'd already got used to the library without his annoyingly cheerful presence.

As the bus wound its way onto Chancery Street, she fired off a quick text to her dad, wishing him a happy birthday and promising to Skype him later. She was making an effort to talk to her parents at least once a week these days – yet another initiative suggested by her counsellor. She still hadn't gotten round to having A Conversation with them about Wollaston Lake, but of late she'd been dropping the odd hint and she got the sense her mom might, slowly but surely, be edging her way towards a bit of soul-baring of her own. Either way, she was content to give it time – for them all to reach the place they needed to at their own pace. And she realised that, over the past several weeks, she'd made a degree of peace with the events out on the icy waters twelve years ago. She hadn't fully absolved herself of blame, but she had come around to accepting that it wasn't all her fault. Responsibility was considerably easier to bear when you weren't shouldering it alone.

The sessions were helping, she supposed. At least, they weren't having a negative effect. It wasn't something that came naturally to her – talking about herself, expressing her feelings. She suspected it never would, but she had to admit that, since starting them, she hadn't experienced any further flashbacks or panic attacks. Perhaps talking about her problems to the same person in the same place at the same time every week allowed her to compartmentalise – to get rid of all her anxieties in a single, concentrated expulsion. Like a deep cleanse. Or an enema. It was probably too early to call this concrete evidence of cause and effect, but she was unquestionably sleeping better, and she no longer lived with the constant fear that some random loud noise would cause her to black out and crap herself in public or whatever.

Which, she had to conclude, was a positive development.

She hadn't seen much of her friends since that night at Gobby's flat when she'd thrown a wobbly. Partly it was because, after avoiding them for so long, it would have been difficult to reinsert herself into the group without it coming off as awkward, but partly as well it was because they'd naturally drifted apart. In a lot of respects, she'd always been the tagalong of the group – older than the others by a few years and late to the party by virtue of them having already known each other for years before she arrived on the scene. However, the rumblings she was hearing were that even the original three were no longer bound together quite as firmly as they'd once been. She'd met up with Jenny for coffee a couple of times, and gathered from her that Gobby had got a job stacking shelves in Asda, which wasn't the most glamorous job in the world, but it was a start. Spud had got himself into college and was studying engineering, with an eye to going on to uni in a year or so. Jenny herself was working in Next and was going to put herself forward for the position of assistant manager once the current incumbent went on mat leave in the new year. A few months ago, the dissolution of the gang would have left a massive hole in Alyssa's life, but things had changed. She'd been spending a lot more time with her library colleagues, and had even been to a few of their infamous pub quizzes – though, as yet, no one had got her in front of a microphone on karaoke night. These days, Stevie seemed a whole lot less exasperating than he once had. Even Bindi seemed to be making an effort to be more considerate of others, though Alyssa suspected it had less to do with a genuine change of heart and more to do with a growing realisation that no one liked her much.

Rory hadn't made any further contact with her since the business with Andrew, and a part of Alyssa wanted to let herself believe she really had seen the last of him. Perhaps he'd found some other poor girl to obsess over and treat as his personal property. If so, good luck to her. She supposed she could have gone to the police about him – his threat to tell everyone about her secret having lost much of its power over her thanks to recent events – but for now at least, she concluded that she'd have a more stress-free existence if she didn't rock the boat. Another part of her, though, suspected that he was merely lulling her into a false sense of security and that it was only a matter of time before he made his presence felt again. Well, if and when he did, she'd deal with him. Until it happened, she was content to watch and wait, one eye permanently looking over her shoulder.

She entered the break room to find a small frizzy-haired girl facing the mirror hanging on the wall, her lips fluttering as she repeated some silent mantra to herself. As Alyssa shut the door, she spun around with the look of someone who'd been caught doing something shameful.

'Oh,' she squeaked. 'Sorry. I was just . . . '

'It's all right,' said Alyssa, wondering whether the new recruits were getting younger or she was just getting older. 'You must be Jade.'

'That's right, yeah.' The girl nodded, her eagerness to please seeping out of every pore.

'I'm Alyssa. First shift, huh?'

Jade gave a shy little smile and fingered the pendant hanging around her neck.

'Don't look so nervous. Had all my shots – promise.'

'It's not that,' said Jade, a tad sheepishly. 'It's just . . . have you worked here long?'

'A while,' said Alyssa, both surprised and pleased to meet someone who appeared not to know the whole saga of her twin brushes with death.

'Are the stories true? Only, this place . . . well, it's kind of got a reputation.'

Alyssa smiled. 'You'll be fine. We've got our share of eccentrics, but they're pussycats, really. 'Sides, the world would be a whole lot less interesting without all the weirdos. Anyone shown you around?'

Jade shook her head.

Alyssa thought about it. 'Well,' she said, 'I could give you the grand tour, tell you the history of each and every asbestos fibre, but I reckon that'd be a waste of both our times. Best way to learn, I figure, is to get your hands dirty. What d'you say?'

Jade considered this for a moment, then nodded. She was clearly bricking it, but nonetheless willing to jump in at the deep end, and Alyssa had to respect that.

'All right, then. Stick with me and you'll be fine.'

As she headed out into the main library, Jade trailing behind her like her loyal shadow, Alyssa saw that a queue had begun to form at the main desk. The two others on duty were trying valiantly to deal with everyone, but it was a losing battle. They were going to need an extra pair of hands.

Quickening her pace, she headed behind the counter and commandeered the empty computer terminal, before fixing the next person in line with her most obliging smile.

'How can I help?'

Postscript

The so-called Library Murders had a wide-reaching impact both on North Kelvin District Libraries and other local authorities throughout Scotland. Within a year, functioning security cameras were standard in all libraries and other council-operated buildings. All staff were given mandatory training in self-defence and de-escalation techniques, and all counters were fitted with panic buttons. Many privately grumbled that these measures were a low-cost, low-effort sop to placate staff concerns and that, should a similar incident occur in future, they would be as much use as a chocolate fireguard. Others took a more philosophical stance, pointing out that no one could have predicted the events of the first of March and that no solution could be, to coin a phrase, bullet-proof.

Eight months after the murders, a scandal rocked both North Kelvin District Libraries and the Scottish Government when photographs were published on the front page of the *Chronicle* purportedly showing Justice Secretary Kip Formby and Nikki Wyatt, Director of Library Services, booking into a prestigious hotel together. Both parties refused to comment. Formby's indiscretions cost him both his marriage and his position on the frontbench, while Wyatt weathered the storm but accepted a transfer to a less public-facing position within the extended council family – a move which her employers were at pains to stress was in no way connected to the aforementioned scandal.

Footfall at Thornhill Public Library continued to dwindle until, just over a year after the incident, it was closed in favour of a brand-new, purpose-built complex on the other side of Thornhill. The original venue was put on the market but, at the time of writing, has failed to attract a buyer.

Author's Note

It's inevitable, whenever an author writes a novel set in a profession in which they've worked themselves, that questions will arise regarding the authenticity of the events portrayed. The most diplomatic answer I can give is that the parts which seem real are probably made up, and the parts which seem made up are probably real.

While it's impossible not to be influenced by the many weird and wonderful experiences accumulated over the course of more than a decade on the front line, I feel obliged to stress that the organisation depicted in the novel, North Kelvin District Libraries, is a wholly fictitious one and bears next to no resemblance to the one I actually worked for. There is nowhere in Glasgow called Thornhill, and no Craigslee either, and none of the libraries mentioned actually exist. Furthermore, none of the characters featured in *The Library Murders* are based on any of my real-life colleagues, past or present, or any member of the public. So if you're trying to figure out whether a certain character is supposed to be you, you can stop right now. The denizens of Thornhill Public Library are considerably more dysfunctional than the ones I've had the pleasure of working with, though it's safe to say we all have our share of war stories about . . . let's just say *challenging situations*, the details of which would easily fill several more books. Library staff provide a vital service, and the challenges they face are often grossly underappreciated. As such, they have nothing but my respect.

My thanks once again to my editor, the redoubtable David B. Lyons, for wrestling with my manuscript and helping fashion it into something coherent. This is my third book now with David, and each time he succeeds in helping me to see the wood for the trees. Thanks also to Jacqui Baird for giving me the inspiration for the cheese ploughman's incident with Benny, and to my late granny for the 'I saw a hand . . . ' birthday party story – two events that I can definitively confirm happened in real life.

Finally, the usual suspects deserve their moment in the spotlight for looking over the various drafts and for offering invaluable advice: Suze Clarke-Morris, Sarah Kelley, Catherine Mackenzie, Daniel Sardella, Anne Simpson and Caroline Whitson. Whether it was typo-spotting, guidance on hospital protocol or simply steering me away from anything that might have been a little too on-the-nose, you helped make this novel what it is.

PS. Support your local library. Go on, you know you want to.

PPS. The Daniel O'Donnell fan club magazine is a thing. Look it up.

FREE TIE-IN NOVELLA

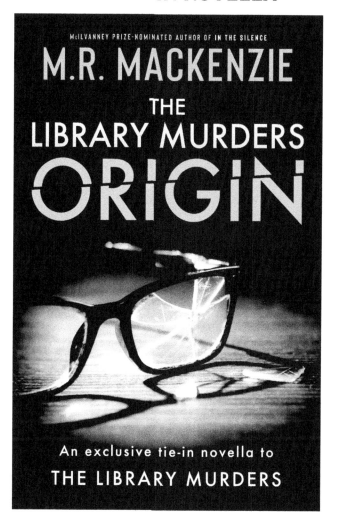

Explore the point of view of *The Library Murders*'
killer in this FREE novella, available at
mrmackenzieauthor.com/libraryorigin

Printed in Great Britain
by Amazon